Also by Adrian Goldsworthy

Hadrian's Wall

The Vindolanda Series

Vindolanda
The Encircling Sea
Brigantia

THE ENCIRCLING SEA

ADRIAN GOLDSWORTHY studied at
Oxford and became an acclaimed historian
of Ancient Rome. He is the author of
several books, including *Anthony and
Cleopatra*, *Caesar*, and *The Fall of the West*.
Vindolanda, his first novel about Flavius
Ferox, is also published by Head of Zeus.
Visit adriangoldsworthy.com

THE ENCIRCLING SEA

VINDOLANDA II

✠

ADRIAN GOLDSWORTHY

HEAD
of ZEUS

First published in the UK in 2018 by Head of Zeus Ltd
This paperback edition first published in the UK in 2018 by Head of Zeus Ltd

975312468

A catalogue record for this book is available from
the British Library.

ISBN (PB): 9781784978181
ISBN (E): 9781788541879

Typeset by Adrian McLaughlin

Printed and bound in Great Britain by
CPI Group (UK) Ltd, Croydon CR0 4YY

Head of Zeus Ltd
First Floor East
5–8 Hardwick Street
London EC1R 4RG

WWW.HEADOFZEUS.COM

For Kevin, with many thanks

BRITANNIA AT THE START OF THE EMPEROR TRAJAN'S REIGN

1 Vindolanda
2 Coria (Corbridge)
3 Bremesio (Piercebridge)
4 Alauna
5 Bremenium (High Rochester)
6 Cappuck*
7 Trimontium (Newstead)
8 Magna (Carvoran)
9 Luguvallium (Carlisle)
10 Kirkbride*
11 Broomholm*
12 Milton*
13 Dalswinton*
14 Glenlochar*
15 Alauna (Maryport)
16 Aballava (Burgh-by-Sands)
17 Maia (Bowness-on-Solway)

*Roman forts probably occupied
at the time the story takes place,
but whose Latin name remains
unknown.

0   20   40   60   800 km

N

CALEDONII

VACOMAGI

Oceanus
Germanicus
(North Sea)

VENICONES

EPIDII

SELGOVAE

VOTADINI

7

6   4

5

12   11

13   TEXTOVERDI

NOVANTAE

14

17   9   8   1

16 10   LOPOCARES

HIBERNIA

15

CARVETII

Oceanus Hibernicus
(Irish Sea)

BRIGANTES

BRITANNIA

Eboracum
(York)

PLACE NAMES

Alauna: Maryport in Cumbria
Aballava: Burgh by Sands
Baiae: now underwater in the Bay of Naples
Bremenium: High Rochester
Bremesio: Piercebridge
Coria: Corbridge
Corinium: Cirencester
Deva: Chester
Eboracum: York
Gades: Cádiz in Spain
Londinium: London
Lugdunum: Lyon in France
Luguvallium: Carlisle
Maia: Bowness-on-Solway
Magna: Carvoran
Mona: Anglesey
Thule: A mysterious island in the far north, whose identity is uncertain. The Romans may have applied it to one of the Shetland Islands, or even Iceland or Norway.
Tomi: Constanta in Romania
Trimontium: Newstead
Uxellum: Ward Law, although the identification is uncertain

PROLOGUE

S HE HAD GIVEN very precise instructions about her grave. Those last days were wracked with pain, and the lines on her face grew so sharp that she looked twice her thirty-nine years. Yet always she was lucid and precise, and when the end came he had done as he had been told, even though he did not understand why this stunted tree and this headland were so important.

It had often been like that in all their years together. She told him what to do and he obeyed, for his trust was complete. She saw things and knew things hidden from other mortals. That was simply the way of it and it was her power and wisdom that had kept them alive and allowed them to thrive in this place so far from their home. The others had not listened and had died or become slaves again. Only his men had survived and found a new place to live, where their neighbours feared them and brought tribute. None had dared to attack them for more than ten years, and that was her doing, for word of her magic had spread, and people feared her even more than they feared the savagery and steel of his warriors.

She looked very small now, and such was her power that he had often forgotten that her body was so tiny. They had dug the grave as a square, a spear's length on either side and as deep. It had been hard, for the ground was stony, and sparks flew as the blades of the pick-axes struck against the rocks. He had begun the work, but all of the brothers from those first days, the men of the oath, had taken a hand and before the sun rose the next day it was done. They carried her, wrapped tight in white linen they had taken from a merchant ship. Her face was uncovered, and her hair coiled up on either side of her head. Perhaps it was the pale light of the new morning, but he could no longer see the streaks of grey. She seemed young again, and at peace, her white skin smooth like a child's. It was over, the agony as her innards had rotted away was done. She had held on for months through sheer will, not expecting to win the fight, but waiting for a sign. He would never forget the smile spreading across her face when the news reached them. She had told him what he must do and then her spirit had left, leaving only the clay of her body.

They covered her with a blanket before they began to shovel earth over her remains. He stood, black shield in one hand and spear in the other. When they finished he remained. It was hard to judge time, but whenever he thought an hour had passed he would walk seven times around the low mound. Sometimes others came and shared the vigil, but never for long, and when the sun set he was alone.

At dawn they came back, three warriors in mail with swords at their belts, leading the master of the merchantman they had taken.

'You know why you are here?'

The man nodded. He was a Briton from the far south, one who had adapted to the ways of Rome and eked out a living carrying goods along the coast. A storm had blown him off course, and they had found him.

It was not chance. They had taken their ship out to sea for the first time, testing it after repairs that had taken many years

2

to complete, because it was hard to find good timber here in the wilds. A year ago their boats had rowed out to take a becalmed trading vessel that happened to be carrying a cargo of oak.

Since then everything had slotted as neatly into place as if each piece was the work of a great craftsman.

'Your son knows what he must do?' The merchant's son was to be released and to keep their little ship and the rest of the crew, but only after he had sworn to help arrange matters.

'Yes, lord.'

'Kneel.'

The man obeyed. He had auburn hair, thinning on top, and one of the warriors grabbed the long pigtail at the back and lifted it out of the way.

The sword hissed through the air, and the finely-honed edge cut through flesh, muscle and bone. With a *thump* the severed head dropped onto the earth, and a jet of blood sprayed across the grave, the soil sucking it away in a moment.

'Is everything ready?'

'Yes.' The tallest of the warriors, a man with long blond hair and a thick beard, answered.

'Then do not wait a moment,' he said. He could feel her power surrounding him. Their tale was not over. New strength would be brought to him to guide him in the years to come. For all the sorrow of this loss he felt renewed, almost young again. He had warriors, he had a fine ship, and soon he would see new power at work, leading them all on. It was a time for blood and a time for vengeance.

The others left and he returned to his vigil. Then he smiled, because he knew her spirit had come to him. 'Not long, now,' it seemed to whisper in his ear.

I

FLAVIUS FEROX PATTED Frost fondly on the neck, took off her bridle and let the grey horse wander free. Snow, another mare so like the first that they might have been twins, was already cropping the grass, and he trusted the animals not to run away. Neither of them looked tired, even though he had driven them hard during the night, riding up high where the patches of grubby snow became an unbroken field of white. Some of the time he had led them, taking a steep and rugged path to come down into this valley beside the dark lake, relieved to find that his memory was good. The stream was where he remembered, rushing down the slope, chattering noisily and swollen with melted snow, so that there was only one safe place to cross on this side of the loch. He had come to this place only once before, some five years ago, but the brooding presence of the lake had stuck in his mind as if he had known that one day he would return.

This was his last chance. If they had not turned north then they would have to come this way and he would meet them here and perhaps he would die or perhaps not. If they got past him, then by tonight they would reach their own lands and be safe among their tower-building kin. Ferox did not know these lands and its chieftains well enough to think that any would aid him, and with the nearest Roman outpost more than two hundred miles away they were unlikely to fear the empire. For the moment, the power of the emperor and Rome came down to one centurion. Ferox doubted either the emperor or Rome would ever know what happened here or care if he turned around and rode away, letting the raiders escape. No one would blame him, and he had taken no oath to the poor family who scratched a living on their little farmstead. All he had done was promise to do his best to find their little girl and bring her home, and that was enough to make him chase the raiders for seventeen days and had brought him to this place. It was also enough to keep him here. By noon or soon after he would know whether or not he had guessed right and the raiders were coming this way.

Ferox took some of his dry kindling from a bag, gathered as many sticks as he could find and lit a small fire on the high bank above the ford. The burn provided water, and he used a flat stone and the pommel of his dagger to grind up some army biscuits, tipping the crumbs into a bronze pan, before adding slices of onion and the last of his salted bacon. He laid it down beside the fire and decided to wash and shave before he cooked.

The mist was thinning, burning away in the early morning sun, so that the shepherd and his boy saw him before they were close. He was a big man, dark of hair and grim of face, wearing just trousers and boots, his broad chest bare as he crouched beside the stream, scraping at his chin and upper lip with a razor.

The shepherd was old, his hair and beard long, white and filthy, suggesting that neither water nor razors had figured much in his experience. Yet it was the size of the lone man, the scars on his chest and the scabbarded sword lying within reach that made him wary. Together with the horses and the mail shirt draped over a pile of bags, they made it clear that this stranger was a warrior.

6

Ferox waved a hand and went back to his task without paying them any more attention. After a while, the shepherd whistled and came forward, a shaggy dog beside him, while the boy chivvied the half-dozen sheep they had with them. The warrior nicked himself and cursed, making the dog growl and keep growling, even when the tall man shrugged and rubbed his face with a rag.

'Good morning, father,' he said, touching a hand to his brow. That was the custom in these parts, but his accent was strange.

'Roman?' the shepherd said after a while. He knew little of the iron race from the south, for they had never come in great numbers to these high glens.

'Aye,' the tall man said. He was standing now, and made no move to pick up his sword. 'My name is Ferox and I mean you no harm. I've a broth boiling, if you and the lad have a mind to join me.'

The old man looked uncertain, at least as far as it was possible to tell behind the wild hair and dirt. No doubt he feared to give offence while wanting to get away from the warrior as fast as he could. The dog growled again, and the shepherd prodded the animal with his foot to silence it.

'Thank you, lord, but we are in haste.' He stared for a moment. 'Will you give us the way?' His voice was nervous.

Ferox made a sweeping gesture. 'These are your lands, father, not mine.' He stepped back away from the sword to show that he meant them no harm. Even so the old man was nervous as he hurried through the ford, the dog barking to urge the sheep through the rushing water. Two were heavily pregnant ewes, and another a lamb from the first to arrive a few weeks ago. The boy was more curious than frightened, staring at the stranger with wide eyes. Only the grey horses unnerved him.

'Kelpies,' he squealed as one of the mares trotted over. The shepherd cuffed the boy and forced him on. A strange warrior and a Roman was more to be feared than the spirits from the lakes said to take the form of pale horses.

Ferox smiled. Since the snow had cleared few people had left tracks near the ford, and most of them were shepherds like these. There was no sign of any horse passing this way, for this was poor country. No one lived closer than ten miles, and even then only a few huts and farms were dotted around. There were not many people until you got lower, heading towards the coast.

Ferox bent down and splashed more of the icy water onto his face. There was a pouch left beside his sword and he fetched it, reaching inside. He pulled out a caltrop, four iron spikes welded together so that whichever way it fell one of the sharp, two-inch points stood straight up. Stepping into the stream, he dropped this and a dozen more in a couple of rows running across the ford. They vanished, lost in the bubbling water, and he had to hope that they would do their job and not simply be pushed deep into the mud. The last one went in, and once again he reached down and cupped a handful of water to splash across his face. Feeling refreshed, he picked up his sword, walked back to the fire and dressed in his tunic, padded jerkin and shirt of mail. They would not get here for a couple of hours at least, so he sat down cross-legged by the fire and started to cook.

The sun rose and the last of the mist cleared. An eagle circled high overhead, a tiny shape even though Ferox knew that it was a big bird searching the hillsides for newborn lambs. This was a good time for predators and he hoped that good fortune would stretch to cover him. He wondered whether the hunting bird with its sharp eyes could see his prey coming. That is if they were coming, for he might be wrong, even though he was sure that he was not. There were only two ways they could go, and this was the harder route, but it led more quickly to the lands of the Creones and he no longer doubted that that was their destination. Vindex was not convinced, so he and the two other Brigantian scouts had headed north, trusting to the better going to catch up with their quarry. In the meantime, Ferox had taken the high pass so that he could get ahead of them, if they went the other way. There were five or six men – the tracks left by one of the horses were odd and left him unsure whether the rider was a warrior or captive – so that the odds were not good if he was right.

'Take one of the lads with you,' Vindex had said. 'Give you more of a chance if you do meet them.'

'No.' Ferox had not needed to look at them to be sure. One of the scouts was too young, too unpredictable, the other reliable enough, but not a killer. 'Keep them with you. You'll need them both if I'm wrong.'

The Brigantian had stared at him for a while, the evening shadows making his long face more skull-like than usual. 'Trying to be the hero again,' he said at last. 'They always die at the end of their story.'

'Don't we all.'

Vindex sighed. 'Aye, we do. No sense in rushing though, especially for you these days.' The tall Brigantian did not say any more and just shrugged. After a moment he had grabbed the horns of his saddle and vaulted up onto his horse. 'If the trail goes cold once it is daylight we'll come to you. Least I can do for a friend is burn his corpse. That's if I can find all the pieces.'

'Liar, you just want to steal anything they leave behind.'

'That too. Those are nice boots.'

Ferox grinned. 'Clear off. Maybe you are right and they are going north. In that case I'll come and pinch your boots.'

He tapped the side of his scabbard, a gesture of Vindex's people. 'Ride to good fortune.'

'We'll do our best.'

Ferox spat on the grass. 'Oh well,' he said, 'if you're not even going to try.'

The Brigantians cantered off. 'Good luck,' Vindex called back just before he went over the brow of the hill.

That was yesterday, and now Ferox wondered whether the scouts had seen the trail left by the fugitives turn just as he had said it would, heading west towards the coast. Vindex and his men should be coming this way by now, but they would have to ride a good way to reach the pass and then loop around the loch to get here. Unless their horses sprouted wings, they would not arrive in time to make a difference.

Ferox looked up again, blinking as he followed the hovering eagle, for the sun was bright and warm with the promise of spring. Movement caught his eye and he saw another bird some way off, but only after pulling down the wide brim of his hat and squinting did he see that this one was a raven. He was right then, for the Morrigan's bird never came by chance. The goddess knew that a fight was coming and warriors would shed their life blood in this place.

'Well then,' Ferox said out loud and at once despised himself. As a boy he had been taught the value of silence and calm. The Silures were the wolf people, hunters of animals and men alike, predators who knew that the slightest movement or sound could betray an ambush, so they schooled their boys to make stillness the greatest pleasure and idle talk the worst vice. Ferox had spent too many years among Romans who chattered away, weeping or laughing freely, seeming to need noise to reassure themselves that they were still alive. Yet he had left his people long ago, sent as one of the hostages when the chieftains of the Silures had surrendered to the Roman Empire. In truth, he had been Titus Flavius Ferox, centurion, oath sworn to serve Rome and its emperor, for longer than he had been anything else, but in his soul he was still of the Silures, grandson of the Lord of the Hills, the man who had fought the Romans longer and harder than anyone else before making peace.

The wind picked up, hissing through the grass. As a child, he had been told that the winds sometimes carried the voices of those who had gone on to the Otherworld and now walked in shadow. He listened hard, for a moment longing for his grandfather to speak to him, but if there were words he could not catch them or the message was for someone else. Perhaps he was now too Roman to understand, for his people also said that running water carried the echoes of old magic and old tears, the words of gods and spirits reaching back to the start of all things, and yet all he could hear was the soft roar of the stream. He was a long way from his homeland, and a long way too from the army. Ferox was *regionarius*, a centurion charged with keeping Rome's peace in the region near the fort of Vindolanda, but he and the scouts had come far from his territory.

The eagle dived, swooping down fast, and Ferox followed it until it vanished behind the hills above him. The raven was still there, flying in lazy circles, and he imagined its cold black eyes watching him. Well, the bird must wait and so must he, for there was nothing else to do. Opening a pouch, he checked that the leather thong of the sling was still supple and hefted the two lead shot, wondering once again why they were cast in the shape of acorns. For a moment he considered practising with it, but he had just the two lead shot and did not trust pebbles to fly as true so did not want to risk losing them. He tried to remember when he had last used a sling and could not, which

11

meant that it was long ago and he wondered whether he had lost the knack. He thought of this and other things he wished that he had done or not done. Otherwise he just waited, trying to think as little as possible.

If Vindex was right and he was playing at being a hero then waiting at the crossing of a stream was fitting. In the stories, heroes like the Hound were always guarding fords against invading armies, challenging each warrior to face them one at a time, killing them and taking their heads. Sometimes they died and the place was named after them. It was hard to imagine anyone in this part of the world caring about him let alone remembering his name or what would soon happen. That shepherd would not bother and his boy was more likely to remember the ghostly grey horses.

The raven gave its harsh call just as the horsemen appeared, riding out from one of the shallow gullies into the valley almost a mile away. They came steadily towards him, trotting their horses once they reached the flatter land. Ferox did not need to stand up to see them and so stayed by the fire and spooned up some of the broth, revelling in the smell as he blew on it to cool it.

There were seven horses, one of them a big chestnut and the rest small shaggy ponies. They were closer now, heading straight towards him. The ponies were ridden by men in hooded cloaks, four of them carrying spears. Two smaller figures were perched on the tall horse. The one in front had long hair, blowing wildly in the wind, and even though it looked dark he knew that this was only the dirt and damp of the journey and that it was the vivid red of the girl's whole family.

Half a mile away they stopped and he guessed that they had noticed him. A couple of the horsemen clustered together to talk. Ferox sipped the broth, grimaced at the taste, which failed to live up to the promise of its scent, but knew that this was the least of his problems. Let them hesitate, let them delay, he thought, and Vindex would come a little closer so that he might arrive in time to find a corpse that was still warm.

They started forward again, one riding out on either side of the main group, looking to see if he was alone. Their hoods were thrown back and he saw that the warriors all had the hair shaved on the crown of their heads and plaited into a long pigtail at the back. These raiders were northerners, men from the farthest reaches of Britannia, which meant that the stories he had heard from frightened farmers were true. They were strange folk in the north, and some said that they were descended from the Old Folk, the workers of flint and makers of the great stone circles. They also said that they worshipped cruel gods, long since forgotten in other lands, but still powerful in their dark magic near the edge of the world.

They were closer now, within a long bowshot, although bows were rare in these parts and Ferox was glad to see that none of the warriors carried one. He could see that one of the men had his hands tied together in front of him, just like the two girls on the chestnut. He did not recognise him, but he looked fairly young and his hair was short like a Roman's. It explained the odd tracks he had found in the last weeks, of a horse ridden badly and sometimes being led. He had wondered whether the rider was a captive, but the heavy prints showed a pony well laden and raiders rarely took men as prisoners, because they needed to be watched more closely and would not bring as high a price as a slave, so he had guessed that the horseman was one of their own, but injured.

Who this prisoner was would be a mystery for later – if there was a later – and for the moment it meant that he had five enemies and not six. He could almost hear Vindex making some arch comment like 'Easy then' and tried not to smile at the thought. The warriors riding on each flank went back to join the others, sure that the man sitting by the fire was truly alone, for there was nowhere to hide in this gentle grassland. One of the others shouted at them and they galloped up to look down over the banks of the burn.

Ferox stood up. He had the sling held tight inside his right fist and the two bullets in the other hand. He did not hurry and stretched his back as if he was stiff before strolling towards the ford.

'Who are you, stranger?' one of the nearest warriors called out. Like the other he had a stout spear and small square shield, the boards unpainted, but dotted with iron studs.

Ferox ignored him. He reached the place where the bank on this side dipped down and became no more than a little slope a couple of feet high leading into the ford.

'Give us your name,' the warrior shouted again.

Ferox stopped. His broad-brimmed hat was the sort peasants wore in the lands around the Mediterranean, something rarely if ever seen in these parts. Back in his region everyone recognised it, but he doubted that these men had spent long enough there to hear of it or him. He smiled at the man and did not reply.

'Just kill him!' the second warrior to ride up to the burn screamed at his companion, hefting his own spear, but making no move to throw it.

The other warrior bared his teeth, hissing and waving shield and spear towards the Roman. Both men were in their early twenties, and Ferox doubted this was their first raid. They looked handy enough, but reminded him of Vindex's two scouts – dangerous only when they followed others.

'I want to talk,' he said at last as neither man came at him. 'But I don't talk to children.'

The warrior on his right twitched his spear at the insult. He still did not throw and after a moment spat towards the Roman.

Ferox said no more, and two more riders came forward to stand their horses between the other two. These were the ones that mattered and he could see the livid blemish covering cheek and chin of the smaller man. Along with the wildcat's tail woven into his pigtail, it marked him as the Red Cat, a stealer of horses and cows whose fame stretched far beyond his own people in the north. Ferox had never seen him before, but once or twice he had come across his track and that of the animals he had stolen. They said no one ever caught the Red Cat or even knew his right name. It meant the burlier man beside him was his older brother, Segovax. His eyes were so dark that they made Ferox think of Morrigan's raven and that was fitting for he was known as a killer without mercy for man, woman or child.

The fifth warrior was the youngest and stayed back with the captives.

'Speak, Roman.' Segovax had a rasping voice.

'You know who I am?' Ferox said.

'Should I care?'

'I am Flavius Ferox, *centurio regionarius*, and I have come to trade with you on behalf of our great lord and *princeps* Trajan, the ruler of the world.' Ferox was slightly surprised to find himself invoking the emperor, but decided that it could do no harm.

Segovax did not appear impressed. 'Again, should I care about you or your pox-ridden emperor? He does not rule here, and you are alone.'

'I would trade for your captives.' Out of the corner of his eye Ferox saw the raven circling, much lower down than before.

'No trade. Give us the path, Roman.'

'Help me!' The shout came from the young captive, who kicked his horse so that it ran away from the others towards the ford. 'Save me, I am a Roman and demand your protection!' he screamed. The young warrior followed him, and swung the shaft of his spear, slamming it against the captive's head and knocking him to the ground. The man fell heavily, but started to push himself up with his tied hands. Another blow, this time from the blunt butt of the spear, struck his head and he slumped back down.

Segovax had not even turned and neither he nor Ferox showed that they had noticed the escape attempt.

'I want your captives,' Ferox said. 'I offer much in return.'

For the first time, the Red Cat spoke. 'You have nothing we want.' He was the only one not carrying a spear, and Ferox saw the hilt of a long knife on his right hip.

'Nothing we cannot take if we want,' his brother added.

'What about your lives?'

Segovax spat, unimpressed. 'You are a long way from your Rome. Is one of the girls kin to you? We'll trade either of them for one of your horses.' His brother gave him a sidelong glance. The Red Cat was not used to buying any animal.

'I want them all.'

The Red Cat laughed.

Ferox flicked the sling so that it hung down, dropped one of the acorn-shaped bullets onto the leather patch, and brought it high, whirling.

'Bastard!' Segovax shouted and the four warriors urged their mounts forward. Ferox loosed, aiming for Segovax, but his horse was nervous of the rushing water and pulled away, its head up so that the heavy lead missile smashed into its teeth. The animal reared, screaming and slipping on the muddy slope.

Segovax was thrown forward and he screamed as the pony rolled over onto him and bones broke.

One of the warriors swerved away from the falling man and horse, but the other one and the Red Cat splashed into the ford. Ferox slipped the second bullet into the sling, raised it, swung and released the lead acorn with such force that it drove into the shaven forehead of man next to the famous thief, flinging his head back. The man dropped into the stream, water splashing high.

The Red Cat was nearly across, but then his horse reared, foot bloody from a caltrop, and Ferox wished he had picked up some suitable stones because he would have been able to get off at least one more shot. Instead he dropped the sling and grabbed the bone handgrip of his sword. It slid smoothly from the scabbard, the long, old-fashioned blade so perfectly balanced that it was a delight to feel it in his hand. The Red Cat was down, thrown from his horse as it bucked in agony, the man beside him was dead or dying, and the other warrior leaped from his horse to wade through the ford, sensing that there was some unseen danger. Ferox drew his *pugio* dagger in his left hand and went down the little bank to the edge of the ford.

'Come on, you mongrels,' he yelled.

The Red Cat was up, a long knife in one hand, and he paused to wrap his cloak around his left arm because he had lost his shield. The other warrior went to the right, wanting to take the Roman from two sides. He had his spear up, and Ferox trusted him not to throw it because he saw that he had only a little dagger at his belt, and like most of the warriors of the far north did not possess a sword.

The Red Cat swung his cloak, feinting, and then cut with the knife, just as the other man stamped forward, lunging. Ferox slipped in the mud, slashing with the *gladius* and feeling it bite on the thief's right arm. He tried to push the spear thrust aside with his left hand, but as he stumbled there was no force in the move and the spear head hit him on the side. He felt the heavy blow, knew that some of the mail rings had broken and that the tip had driven through the padded coat underneath.

Ferox staggered back, trying to regain balance, and hissing because his side hurt. The Red Cat swirled his cloak, flinging it at the Roman, but the wool was wet and heavy and it fell short. He switched his knife into his left hand because his right arm was bleeding. The warrior followed up, stamping forward to thrust again with the heavy spear, but then yelped. There was blood flowing in the water by his foot and Ferox guessed that he had found another of the caltrops. The man looked down, puzzled and angry, lifting his foot, the iron spike still stuck fast in his boot.

The warrior's guard had dropped and Ferox lunged with the gladius, going over the top of the man's little shield and driving into his throat. The Red Cat came at him, so as he twisted the blade to free it he punched with the fist holding his dagger, knocking the dying man into the thief.

A horseman was up on the far bank, driving his horse down into the stream, spear held high and yelling in high-pitched rage. It was the youth they had left with the prisoners, and he only saw Segovax under his still writhing horse at the last moment, but managed to urge his mount into a jump and sail over, landing with a great splash in the water. The animal stumbled, and the lad nearly lost his balance, but recovered and kept going.

'Run!' the Red Cat screamed at the boy.

Ferox tried to shuffle through the stony ford, wary of caltrops, and slashed at the thief, making him jump back.

'Run, boy!' the Red Cat shouted again, but the youth ignored him, riding straight at Ferox, who stepped aside and jabbed at the horse's head with his dagger. It reared and the young warrior fell into the stony water, his spear flying from his grip. Yet there was fight in the youth still, and he pushed up, trying to grab the Roman's legs.

The centurion slid back, keeping his balance, and prepared to jab down with his sword.

'No!' the Red Cat called and threw his knife down into the burn. 'We give in.' He stepped towards them, left hand clutching his wounded arm, and kicked the boy who was still struggling towards the Roman. 'It's over, child.' He looked up at Ferox. 'We give in, Roman. Spare his life.'

Ferox nodded, and up above the bird of Morrigan cried again.

The two warriors were dead, their blood washing away down the stream towards the loch. Segovax was unconscious, right leg and arm both broken and maybe other injuries as well. Ferox let the youth help the Red Cat by binding his wound and then tied them both at the wrist using the ropes from the captives. The male captive was still unconscious, but the girls sat in silence by the fire, eating hungrily.

'Did they hurt you?' he asked the red-haired girl as gently as he could. She shook her head, so that when he went to do his best for Segovax he did the job gently and with all the skill he could muster. He dragged the man up onto the bank, cut up one of the spear shafts to make splints, tying them tight. The man was awake, but silent, his eyes cold and full of hate.

The scream shattered the peace in the little valley, frightening the raven which had settled on one of the corpses. Ferox looked up and saw that the male captive had woken and taken a spear, walking up beside the Red Cat and the boy and driving the weapon into the boy's back. He fell forward, and the captive jabbed with the spear again and again, grunting with the effort.

Ferox ran over, drawing his sword. He expected a wild look in the captive's face, but instead there was just pleasure.

'Bastard!' The Red Cat spat the word, and then rolled out of the way because the spear was now aimed at him.

'He is mine!' the young man shouted in Latin, his tone expecting obedience, and Ferox reversed his sword and struck with the dome-shaped pommel against his forehead. The former captive dropped.

The Red Cat rolled and managed to push himself up on his elbows and then stand.

'You had better kill me,' he said in a flat tone. 'Because if you do not, then I swear by Sun and Moon that I will kill you one day.'

Ferox stared at him, but put his blade back in its scabbard. 'You'll have to wait your turn to try.'

Half an hour later he saw a pair of horsemen down by the loch. He did not recognise them and they kept their distance and watched. An hour after that, a dozen horsemen appeared from the other end of the valley, and the two watchers galloped away. The new group headed straight for him, and one of them cantered ahead.

'I found some friends,' Vindex said, pointing back at the approaching horsemen, all of them heavily armed. The leader, a huge, bearded man, waved in greeting.

'Didn't know you had any.'

'You have been busy, I see,' the Brigantian said, looking around at the debris of the fight.

'Yes.'

Vindex glanced at the centurion's side, seeing the rent in his armour. There had not been time to ease the mail shirt off and bind up the injury.

'Bad?' the scout asked.

'No.'

'Pity,' Vindex sighed. 'I really could do with a new pair of boots.'

II

'REMEMBER HIM?' Vindex asked, jerking his head up towards the top of the tower.

Ferox glanced up. They were approaching the main double gateway of Vindolanda, the top of the timber parapet some thirty feet high. A pair of sentries peered down. They were mail-clad Batavians with fur-like moss glued to the tops of their bronze helmets, but he knew that the scout was not speaking of them. There were three stakes mounted on the parapet, although at the moment only one was occupied. The head impaled on top of it was black, flesh long withered away and skin shrunken tightly around the skull.

'Aye, I remember.' Ferox had never learned the man's name, but his followers called him the Stallion, and he had claimed to be a druid or priest and worker of magic sent by the gods to purge the lands of the Romans. His message was one of hatred and blood and the year before last he had raised an army to make his vision come true. Ferox had warned his superiors of the impending storm and been ignored until it had broken, and then had helped them gamble and somehow smash the fanatics. A lot of people had died, some of them horribly, before they had won, and he still shuddered at the thought of what had happened and what might easily have followed. Ferox had wounded the Stallion in the battle, but the priest had escaped only to be sacrificed by his own allies a few days later. Ferox and Vindex had found his corpse swinging from a yew tree and brought the head back here as ordered.

'Still haven't heard much about Acco,' Vindex added, once he realised that his companion was not going to say any more. Acco was a true druid, one with the old knowledge, and he had supported the Stallion and then inflicted the triple death when the man was beaten.

'One day, we will.' Ferox worried that Acco had vanished for he feared what the man was doing. The Stallion had been a wild dog, unthinkingly angry, his beliefs a mishmash of old ideas and exotic rituals taken from half the religions of the empire. Acco was different, one of the last of the true druids, a man who had seen the groves at Mona before they were burned, and if his loathing of Rome was just as strong it was cold and calculating. It was he who had sacrificed the Stallion, giving him slow poison and then slicing at his flesh with a flint knife as the noose had slowly strangled the man. The triple death of a magician was meant to propitiate the gods for his failure, and brought immense power to one who performed it.

'Maybe he's died,' Vindex suggested without conviction. 'He must be getting on a bit.'

'Huh,' Ferox grunted. Acco was out there somewhere, waiting, plotting, and they must keep searching for any news of the man because otherwise it might be too late when he appeared.

'Yes.' Vindex decided that he would get no more from the centurion and instead turned his horse to leer at their captives. He pointed up at the two empty stakes on the tower. 'Look at that, boys, they must have known you were coming!'

Segovax and the Red Cat ignored him, but that was nothing new. In the two and a half weeks they had spent travelling back, the brothers had said almost nothing. Segovax did his best to hide his discomfort, and Ferox could not help admiring the man's strength and determination. Vindex had wanted to kill them both.

'Best for him,' he claimed. 'Poor bugger will be in pain all the way and there won't be anything nice waiting at the other end. And the other one swears that he'll kill you – and me as well – so why not sort him out now? Don't fancy sleeping with one eye open all the way home either.'

The Red Cat was fitted with shackles to the wrist and another pair for his legs whenever they dismounted. Vindex had brought them. 'Just in case,' he said, and wanted to do the same to Segovax.

'Reckon he'd can't do much with a leg and arm bust,' Ferox insisted.

Vindex was unconvinced. 'If that one had no legs and no arms he'd still try to bite you.'

They compromised on using a shackle to fasten the man's good arm to tree or log whenever they stopped for the night. Each time they fitted it, Segovax said nothing, just staring into their eyes. Almost the only time he spoke was to tell them that the boy stabbed to death by their captive was the Red Fox's son. Like his brother, he swore to kill Ferox as soon as he got the chance.

'You're good at making friends, aren't you?' Vindex said. 'Still sure you don't want me to finish them both?' Ferox did not answer.

It was easier in the first week when they were accompanied by the high king's men. These were the friends Vindex had encountered, a dozen big warriors led by a German exile called Gannascus. The first time they had met, the big man had almost killed Ferox, but since then respect had grown to friendship, at least as far as their different loyalties allowed.

'Give them to me,' the big warrior said. 'I'll take them back to Tincommius. The high king has been wanting their heads for years. The sly little one has taken too many of his best horses.'

'They are my prisoners, and I'm taking them back,' Ferox insisted.

'Huh. Twelve of us, four of you, and our home a lot closer.' Gannascus looked grim and even more massive than usual. 'We could take them if we wanted.' He held Ferox's gaze for a moment and then threw back his head to roar with laughter, something he did very often. He patted the Roman on the shoulders, laughing even more when Ferox winced because of the graze to his side.

While they rode with Gannascus and his men they were too formidable a band to attract the attention of casual attackers. It also meant that it was easier to guard their prisoners. Ferox was still surprised to have met the German so far to the west. Tincommius' influence was spreading wider than he had thought. The high king was a friend to the Romans, an ally, at least while it suited him, which merely meant that he treated the Romans just as they treated him. Yet his strength kept growing, while the garrison in Britannia was weak and likely to get weaker soon enough. Ferox had heard rumours that Trajan was planning for a big campaign on the Danube. At best that would mean few new drafts coming to keep units up to strength, and at worst it would mean more troops being posted away from Britannia. The tribes all knew that Rome was weaker than in the old days when the Romans had first came to the north. That sense of retreat was something the Stallion had used to inspire his supporters. Acco did the same and he was still out there. In the past, the druid and high king had been friends and they could easily join together again. It would be a dangerous combination because both men were as clever as they were ruthless. Ferox feared that one day he would face them and Gannascus in battle. Maybe that would be the end of his story.

For the moment he was glad to have the big man's company, and sorry when the German and his warriors left them to go east. That left four of them to share the watches. He ignored Vindex's fresh suggestion to kill the prisoners. 'Or at least let me slice up that vicious little bastard.' He meant the young Roman they had freed from captivity, who claimed to be called Marcus Claudius Genialis and swore that he was the son of a very rich and powerful man called Claudius Probus. Ferox had heard of neither of them, but the sixteen-year-old carried himself with an arrogance that suggested someone used to being obeyed in every whim.

'Don't seem very grateful for being rescued,' Vindex commented in the language of the tribes after watching the angry youth scream at Ferox and demand that he execute the two brothers. The centurion refused, never raising his voice, and after a while turned his back and walked away. Genialis then went to Gannascus, promising gold if he killed the men. The big German had only a little Latin, but seemed to understand. He smiled, bellowed his great laugh and then knocked the boy flat.

After that Genialis brooded in silence until the German and his men left them when he made a new attempt to make the centurion obey him. When Ferox refused, the sixteen-year-old told him that he would rue the day, before stalking off to sit on his own. Every now and again he glared at the prisoners, or at Ferox.

'Who'd miss him?' Vindex asked. 'I mean, put it this way, if you were his father would you really want him back? After all, no one knows we found him. Except Gannascus and no one will ask him. Those two certainly won't care.' He gestured at the two girls. Brigita was the snub-nosed redhead, thirteen years old and the one who really ran her family's farm, making sure that her sick father and vapid mother did nothing too foolish. The other girl was fifteen, but small for her age, a slave in the household of Aelius Brocchus, commander of the cavalry *ala* at Coria to the east, who was also the owner of the tall chestnut horse.

A couple of days ago Genialis had lured her away from their camp into some woodland. Ferox had heard the slave's screams and arrived to find her thrown down, her already ragged dress torn open. He had not been gentle with the youth. Genialis was still sporting a raw black eye along with some other bruises, and it had taken all his willpower for Ferox not to kill him then and there.

'It would be a pleasure,' Vindex pleaded. 'Who would ever know?'

'Just tie him up and keep him tied until he is off our hands. You never know, he might be a runaway pretending to be freeborn. Then they'll whip him or kill him. Perhaps both.'

'Well, let's hope,' the Brigantian said dubiously.

There had been more complaints, more promises of vengeance and dire punishment for them all, but when the scout raised his hand Genialis fell back into his sullen silence and did not break it for the remainder of their journey. He rode behind the two captives, one of the Brigantians beside him, watching all of them for any false move. Brigita and the slave girl, Aphrodite, with the other scout brought up the rear.

As they had ridden through the civilian settlement or *canabae* outside the fort, Ferox had felt the army's grip closing around him once more. There had not been time to stop off at his own little outpost, as he wanted the trip over and them all off his hands as soon as possible. He had toyed with the idea of taking Brigita back to her family, which would have meant a diversion of no more than five miles, but had decided against it. It would be too cruel to bring her home with two of her abductors still in tow.

Instead he drove them hard to reach Vindolanda quickly. It was hardest on Aphrodite, sitting uncomfortably astride the chestnut wearing a borrowed tunic far too big for her and an old and stained cloak. It was even harder on Segovax, although the man had such an iron will that he did his best not to show it. The two brothers kept their faces impassive after the manner of the northern tribes – and Ferox's own people. Their eyes stayed cold and full of hate.

'Halt!' The sentry outside the gateways bawled out the regulation challenge.

'Flavius Ferox, centurio regionarius, with three scouts, two prisoners and three others requests entrance to the fort.'

'Sir!' The Batavian stiffened to attention, spear straight on his shoulder and shield close into his body. Ferox was surprised at the precision, but as he led them all under the gateway he saw two ranks of soldiers paraded inside. He guessed that they were not waiting for him.

'Good morning, sir.' There was an *optio* in command of the detachment, and as Ferox searched in his memory for the man's name it came to him just in time.

'Good morning, Arcuttius,' he nodded. 'Expecting visitors?'

'Yes, sir. They're late, though.'

Ferox was tempted to ask, but he knew the optio as someone who applied regulations to the letter. Arcuttius was not given to chatter, especially not to someone outside *cohors VIIII Batavorum*. He would have to make it an order if he wanted to get an answer, and saw no reason to go that far. The Batavians were a clannish bunch, and even though he had fought alongside them quite a few times he remained an outsider.

'Is the Lord Cerialis in residence?' Ferox asked instead.

'Yes, sir.' Flavius Cerialis commanded the Batavians. He was young, eager and ambitious, and after a year and half in Britannia was getting the feel of the place. He and his wife were also close friends to Aelius Brocchus and his wife, which should make it easier to restore to them their horse and their slave. Aphrodite had said very little during the journey home, only to confirm that she had strayed from their house and met up with one of their grooms, also a slave, who was exercising the chestnut. Ferox guessed that it was not the first assignation, but this one turned sour when the northerners appeared, speared the groom, and stole her and the horse. The raiders had come across Brigita the day before, as she was walking towards Coria to sell a goat at the market and to buy an axe if she could find a decent one at a good price.

'Good,' Ferox said. 'Well, I had better stop dawdling and report to the *principia*.' He nudged Snow forward along the main road of the fort, the *via praetoria*, which ran straight towards the other main road of the fort, behind which stood the great buildings of the base – the principia where the administration went on, and the *praetorium* where Cerialis and his household lived. Both were big, with four ranges around a central courtyard, and their walls were rendered and painted white so from this distance they looked to made of stone and not timber. For sheer size they were dwarfed by the pair of granaries next to them, their roofs towering over the rest of the fort. Yet the barracks on either side of the road were big enough buildings.

'Like a nest of ants.' The Red Cat had broken his silence for the first time in days, and was staring around at the whitewashed buildings with their shingle and slate roofs. A party of soldiers marched past, not carrying spears or shields but in mail and wearing helmets and marching in step to orders bellowed at them by the old sweat in charge. The thief stared at them. He did not understand the words, but the tone was obvious.

'How can a man submit to that?' he asked his brother, his tone genuinely baffled. 'How can they live like this?'

Vindex snorted with laughter. Ferox knew that the scout's own views were similar. Vindolanda was a fair-sized fort, built to accommodate the large Batavian cohort and various other detachments as well as details passing through, and it must seem huge to a man used to lone houses, farmsteads or villages with no more than a couple of dozen huts at most. The base for a Roman legion was some ten times bigger, while the cities of the empire, let alone Rome itself, made any army outpost look tiny.

'Is this Rome?' Segovax asked.

'No, brother, they say that lies a week or more to the south. This must be the dun of one of their greatest chiefs.'

'Huh. Why live here, surrounded by so many? It's like an ant's nest.'

The Red Cat nodded. 'They are strange folk.'

Vindex rode up to join Ferox. 'Most they've said for weeks.'

'Yes. They may talk a bit more when they realise what they're facing.' Ferox had hoped to learn more on the journey home and had failed to get anywhere with the captive brothers. There had to be a reason why they had come so far from their own lands. The horse was a good one, but the Creones and other peoples of the north generally preferred the smaller native ponies because they were so hardy and sure-footed in the rugged country. It was true that Brigita and Aphrodite could be traded or kept as slaves, and yet they need not come so far to abduct a couple of young girls. Genialis seemed the key to unlocking the mystery, for as far as Ferox could tell the others had all been incidental captures. The northerners had come to take him – or maybe someone like him – and Ferox could not understand what they had hoped to gain. The sulking youth was no help. Perhaps he was telling the truth and his father was rich, so might pay a ransom. Yet what would men from the far north want with so much coin?

'Perhaps when they come face to face with their deaths they'll talk a bit more freely,' Ferox said, without conviction.

Vindex was not impressed. 'Why should they?'

'There are different ways to die.'

'You really think you're going to frighten that one?' Vindex nodded back at Segovax. 'Or the other one. I think that you should have let me kill them quick and clean.'

Ferox wondered whether he was right. He had to admit to grudging respect of the brothers, and did not much relish the thought of them ending up on crosses or in with the beasts in the arena.

'Too late now,' he said. They were almost at the junction of the two roads. 'You stay here and watch them while I go in and make the arrangements.' He jumped down and strode across towards the archway of the principia. The ground was hard packed, but spongy underfoot. It always seemed to be wet at Vindolanda. As he walked he tried to work out what day it was. Must be sometime after the Ides of April, he reckoned. While they were in the far reaches of Britannia it had not mattered. As they had headed north he had known that Beltane was weeks ago, the snows were melting, lambs being born, lengthening days and spring approaching. Now that he was back with the army, he was entering another world, which set everything down in writing. At least he knew which year it was. Our Lord

31

Trajan was consul for the third time with Sextus Julius Frontinus, also holding the office for the third time.

'A tough bastard, that one. Clever too.' His grandfather's description of Frontinus suddenly came into his mind and he guessed that he was grinning. The Lord of the Hills had fought the Romans for many years and held them off. Then Frontinus came as legate to govern Britannia, and made crushing the Silures his priority. He did it, too, taking heavy losses, but inflicting even more and overrunning more and more of their territory. After the surrender, by that strange custom of the Romans, he became their patron, arranging much of Ferox's education, securing him citizenship and a commission as centurion. If afterwards the young Silurian's career turned sour, that was his own fault, from his obsession with the truth and the freedom with which he spoke his mind. Frontinus had been a good patron and no Roman aristocrat ever forgot past services they had done for someone or his obligation to them.

Ferox returned the salute of the sentry and went through the arch into the courtyard. The main offices were ahead of him, just next to the shrine housing the cohort's standards. There was more than the usual bustle about the place, although that could simply be the season. In winter, most of a unit was often at its base, but as soon as the spring arrived a lot of large and small detachments would march away to train, work on some building project or for other tasks.

Cerialis was not there, so Ferox dealt with Rufus, the centurion on duty for the day, aided by the prefect's *cornicularius* who made notes of everything. As usual with the army it took longer than he expected or was truly necessary. Half a dozen Batavians were despatched to take the captives to where they would be held.

'May be a while before due process can be done and they'll be nailed up,' Rufus told him.

'In that case, get them to have a look at the bigger one's injuries.'

The Batavian centurion raised a bushy eyebrow at this mark of concern. 'No sense killing someone unhealthy, I suppose.' In the meantime, the cornicularius was writing a note on a wax tablet to Privatus, the freedman head of the prefect's staff, to send people to look after Aphrodite and stable the horse. Word was to be sent to Brocchus to inform him of their rescue. Genialis would also go to the legate's house, to be held in the servants' quarters until his identity was established.

'Tell them to watch him,' Ferox said. 'He might be a runaway.'

'Yes, a lot of them like to talk big. What about the other lass?' Rufus was as red-faced as his name suggested, although his hair was an undistinguished brown.

'I'll take her back to her people.'

'Not stopping with us? I am sure that the Lord Cerialis would wish to thank you on behalf of his friends.'

Ferox shook his head. 'I want to get her home. Her folk are good people.'

'As you wish.'

'I shall come back soon to have a word with the prisoners.'

Rufus grinned. 'I am sure we can assist in making them cooperate.'

As Ferox left he saw the captives already being led away. He glanced at the big two-storey praetorium, unable to stop himself, but apart from the messenger running to carry the note to Privatus there was no sign of anyone. As he turned away he thought he saw movement in one of the upper windows. There was no sign of anyone when he looked back.

He hauled himself up onto Snow's back. After so many weeks

33

travelling, being in the saddle felt almost more natural that walking. The fort oppressed him and he wanted to be away.

'Are you going south?' he asked Vindex.

'Aye. We'll ride after we've had a rest.' His chieftain had sent word for him to go back and recruit a new batch of warriors to serve their Roman allies as scouts. 'Should be back in ten days or so.' The gaunt-faced Brigantian leaned close and dropped his voice to a whisper. 'Did you see him?'

Ferox decided to interpret this as a question about Cerialis. 'The prefect is in his house preparing to greet visiting officers.'

'What about her?'

Ferox ignored the question. He gestured to Brigita, who rode on one of the ponies taken from the northerners. 'Come on, child. Let's get you home.'

A *cornu* trumpet blared as they were approaching the gate. Arcuttius and his men snapped to attention, slamming the butts of their spears into the ground, as a dozen horsemen came into the fort. The leader was a small man, and although in armour and wearing a deep green cloak he was bareheaded. His hair was white, and even before he turned and Ferox saw his face, he knew who it was and his heart sank. Crispinus, senior tribune of Legio II Augusta, was his superior officer and had a knack of turning up whenever trouble started.

The young aristocrat acknowledged the salute and then cantered his horse towards him.

'Flavius Ferox! This is a happy chance,' he called warmly.

'My lord.'

Crispinus offered his hand, surprising Ferox since the son of a senator had no need to be so welcoming.

'This is splendid. I sent a rider to Syracuse, but he returned to say that you were not at the *burgus* and had been gone for well over a month. They said you might be dead for all they knew, so it is definitely an improvement to see you alive and well and here. But are you leaving us?'

'Yes, my lord, I must return this girl to her family.'

'You ride well, my child,' the tribune said, revelling in Ferox's surprise at this knowledge of even a few words in the language of the tribes. The girl looked nervous, but managed a thin smile. 'So pretty, as well,' he added and made her blush.

'You are learning, my lord,' Ferox said in Latin.

'As I once told you, centurion, that is why I am here.' His escort clattered up to join him. 'I must go. See that you are back here tomorrow by noon. I need you. And that rogue of yours, Vindex, as well. Farewell, Flavius Ferox!' He sent his horse running down the road, surprising the troopers with him who took a moment to follow.

Ferox sighed as he rode out through the gateway, and did his best not to think about whatever it was the tribune had planned for him. Like it or not, he would have to do it, both because he was a soldier and must obey and because he had taken an oath to the tribune's father and was bound to his family. It was just that life tended to become a lot more complicated around Crispinus. The year before last he had wondered whether the man was part of a conspiracy against the emperor. The traitor turned out to be someone else – Ferox felt some pleasure at the memory of punching and kicking the young aristocrat as a ploy to lure the real conspirator out. It was hard to know whether Crispinus still held a grudge, but since then he had twice sent Ferox off to perform duties that had proved complicated and unpleasant. This one was unlikely to be any better.

'*Omnes ad stercus*,' he muttered.

'Sir?' the sentry outside the gates was puzzled.

'Nothing, lad, nothing,' he said, and rode off to take the girl to her family.

III

BRIGITA'S PARENTS WERE shocked when the two of them rode up to the little cluster of round huts with their tall conical roofs. Her father was patching up some of the thatch on one of the huts used for their cows, and he broke down, coughing hard amid his tears, and had to be helped off by two of his sons. Her mother prayed loudly, thanking Taranis and Vinotonus and Cocidius and any other god she could remember for answering her prayers. In a moment, half a dozen grubby and thin children, all with the same snub nose and bright red hair, were around them, wailing and yelling. The father begged him to stay and share their food, the others all howled the same thing and when Brigita joined them he agreed.

He had learned a lot from the girl on the ride here. Perhaps it was the realisation that she was about to go home or because there was no one else apart from him, she had started to talk and then kept on going, telling him every detail of what had happened. She seemed to need to speak as if that would consign it all to the past, so he had let her, not asking questions and simply listening.

At first she spoke about the farm, and how hard it was to feed them all when her parents did not let her run things properly. 'The old axe rusted and then snapped because father did not look after it. The goat no longer gave enough milk, so it was better to cook it or sell it and we needed something to buy the new axe – and a spade and some seed if I raised enough. You can get good deals in the market at Coria if you know where to look.' Her assurance was coming back, and Ferox was pleased to see it. He did not quite understand why it was that this one child seemed brighter and more organised than the rest of her family. Everything to her appeared as a problem needing a solution. If she had had been born in the empire to a family with even a little money, he suspected that she would have made ten times as much by the time she was fifteen and a hundred times as much before she was twenty.

The northerners had appeared from nowhere when she was heading for Coria. They were not gentle, but did not really hurt her – neither did they touch her that way. They did slit the goat's throat and carved off enough meat for several meals. That was not news to Ferox, for he had found the carcase and seen several of their camp fires after her family had sent word to him and he began the chase. They took Brigita one evening and then Aphrodite the next morning, finding her in a secluded glade a little nearer to the garrison town. 'She was humping with a man, when he should have been looking after that big horse.' Ferox was more surprised by her directness than her evident disapproval of someone avoiding work. 'They all laughed at him as he sprang up in terror and ran for the chestnut, leaving her to them. Didn't do him any good, for they rode him down and speared him before he could reach it. It was horrible, but they did not harm her. Not then, and just led us off to a patch of woodland where they camped. A man met them later. A thin man, but he kept his hood low and I never saw his face. They talked to him, and a little later the youngest one stayed with us, while the others went off with this man. The boy was kind with us, but kept us tied and said he would hurt us if we tried to escape. He tried very hard to look fierce, but I think he was afraid.

'After darkness fell the four of them came back with Genialis. I think the boy was really relieved to see them. The other man had gone. Genialis was bleeding from the lip and nose, and bound by the wrists. He cursed them and they were not gentle with him. I do not like him,' she added and Ferox smiled.

Most of the rest about their journey north confirmed what he had already guessed. They had kept away from people, even as they passed beyond the tribes allied to Rome, and kept away from the most frequented paths. Otherwise they drove the animals and their captives along. When one of the warriors wanted to rape the slave girl, Segovax told him to wait until they were safe. '"There is no time to waste. If we're not back by the next new moon then all of them will die,"' Brigita said, frowning as she tried to remember his exact words. '"If we get back by then I'll let you do whatever you want, but for now keep it to yourself." Again and again as the days passed he reminded them of how they must get home to save them, but once I overheard him speaking quietly to the one with the mottled face. He was worried that they would not make it in time. "The black men have no mercy. They are men of the night. They will kill and eat them all."' The girl looked terrified as she repeated the words. 'They say that there are demons and monsters in the far north that devour the flesh of men.'

'So they say,' Ferox answered, and for a while they spoke no more while he tried to work out what it all meant. There were plenty of strange things in the world, but as yet he had never seen a monster, still less one that could arrange for a man to meet the northerners and guide them to their quarry. It all confirmed his suspicion that they had come to take Genialis, and it sounded as if they had been made to come by threats. That permitted a little sympathy, if not enough to make him regret catching up with them. The new moon had risen thirteen days ago, so whoever was being held and threatened was most likely dead by now. Segovax was not an easy man to frighten and was unlikely to have been bluffed by someone who did not plan to live up to their threats.

Ferox sat cross-legged by the fire, surrounded by the boisterous noise of the children as they chattered away, but for all his efforts could not understand why anyone from so far away would be interested in Genialis. Neither Segovax nor his brother were easy men to push around, and yet someone had compelled them to raid so that they could snatch the youth. Something odd was happening, and all his senses told him that it was not over. He wondered whether Acco was involved, but could not see anything that the druid could gain. After a while the sheer joy of the family swept over him and he simply laughed with them, trying to judge how much he must eat not to give offence, while knowing that they were poor and not wanting to take too much meat for his share.

It was dark by the time he was able to make his farewells and leave. Nudged by Brigita, the father presented him with a pale blue stone threaded onto a slim leather thong.

'It is lucky,' the man assured him, his eyes a little glassy from the smoke of the fire and the beer he had drunk.

Ferox thanked him, and placed it around his neck. Then he left and rode into the night. It was gone midnight when he reached the burgus, the small square fortlet with its single gate where he spent most of his time when he was not riding out. It was now the closest thing he had to a home and it felt empty and lifeless after the crowded and smoky roundhouse filled with the excited and happy family. The guard in front of the entrance was a little late in challenging him, but otherwise all seemed well. Another man, a Thracian who was almost at the end of his twenty-five years in the army, nodded with the licence granted to old hands and then rang the bell to announce his arrival. Ferox went under the gate, but it was too dark to read either of the painted signs fixed over the entrance, the larger one informing the world that this burgus had been built by Legio II Adiutrix, and the one above with the name Syracuse. Years ago, he had read that the Emperor Augustus had a room in the palace where he would go when he did not want to be disturbed, and that sometimes he would stay there for days on end, speaking to no one, working on great legislation in privacy or just pottering about on little projects for his own amusement. For some reason, the story had stayed with him, and it had been his little joke to dub this unimportant little outpost with the name.

The guard turned out, just two men because there were only a couple of dozen *stationarii* there these days, less than half the original garrison. The rest were asleep, although no doubt a fair few had just been roused by the bell and were now cursing whichever fool had rung it. The Thracian rang it once and did not keep on, which meant that it was not an alarm, so no need to worry. There rarely was any need to worry up here, for things had been quiet for more than a year.

Ferox dismissed the guard, and as he rode to the far end of the courtyard where his own quarters lay he saw glimpses of lamplight from the cracks in the shutters. There were no petitioners waiting for him at Syracuse, which was not really surprising at this hour, although Crescens assured him that a lot of people had come over the last weeks.

'The usual things, sir. Cattle, sheep and other livestock allegedly stolen. A shepherd claims to have been attacked and robbed. No killings, though.' The *curator* had come to his quarters to report and now held up the writing tablet with a detailed list of the claims. Crescens was in charge of the day-to-day running of the little outpost and the most senior man there whenever the centurion was away. Slightly built and very neat in his appearance, even at this time of night, he was a fussy, unsympathetic cavalryman eager for promotion, but had mellowed in the last two years and now treated the men fairly instead of parading the power brought by his temporary appointment. 'Most people seemed to know you weren't here, so didn't come.'

'Any news?'

Crescens opened the writing tablet. Although he ran the place efficiently enough, no one was ever likely to accuse him of imagination.

Ferox waved him down. 'I do not mean the appeals. Is there anything else I should know about?'

The curator frowned. 'A couple of men were sick with ague at the end of last month. Repairs to the roof of the gate-tower are still awaiting a supply of wooden shingles, supposed to be on their way. Also, the two new men allocated as stationarii have not arrived, but word has come that they are at Vindolanda. One is in hospital and the other under arrest charged with drunkenness, abusive language to a superior officer, and urinating against the wall of the principia. The man in hospital may also be charged if he recovers.'

'Some high drama, no doubt,' Ferox said, 'or perhaps low farce?'

Crescens had read the words without emotion and did not appear to register the centurion's irony. 'Yes, sir,' he said, and went on to report other minor digressions or omissions of duty committed by men who were under his charge here at Syracuse.

Ferox let his mind wander. He had had little hope of learning anything useful from the curator. Crescens was not the sort of man to sniff the air and sense what the locals or even the soldiers under his command were feeling and thinking.

'Thank you, curator,' Ferox said when the man reached the end of his list. 'There does not seem to be anything urgent in that lot, so I shall bid you goodnight and apologise for having disturbed your rest.'

'Just doing my duty, sir,' Crescens assured him. 'Happy to do it.'

I'm sure you are, Ferox thought to himself as the man stamped out. The curator was very keen to please these days, hoping to be recommended for promotion and sent back to his unit.

Philo had been hovering in the background, and now swept in with a bowl of warm water and a towel and a cup of *posca*, the rough drink of soldiers and slaves. The little Jewish boy was seventeen and looked younger. If Crescens always strove to be the epitome of military smartness, the young slave far outstripped him in his uncanny neatness. As usual his tunic was spotless and bleached so well that the white wool appeared to shine.

'Thank you,' Ferox said to him. 'And now you can turn in as well. The morning will be soon enough for you to set about cleaning all these clothes.' He could sense the lad's disappointment, and after weeks out in the wilds both he and his clothes were a mess. 'Go to sleep,' he insisted before the boy attempted to persuade him. 'I need to think, and I need to be alone. But thank you again.' Ferox smiled to reinforce the words.

'I am glad you are back, lord,' Philo said and obeyed, going to the side room containing his cot and his few worldly possessions.

Ferox sighed once the boy had gone. Philo always made him feel that he was not really good enough to own such a slave, and even that he was so unutterably filthy and irregular in his habits that he was not really fit for human society. A philosopher might say that this was a good reminder that there was no justice in the world. A bone-weary centurion had not the energy to probe such ideas, so he washed, had some of the drink, and then sat on the stool and stared at the bare plaster walls. After a while he took the blue stone from around his neck and stared at that instead.

It was not worth much, at least not to a Roman who could buy plenty of cheap jewellery, most of it brighter and more colourful. For a family who barely scraped along, it was a treasure. Ferox was not sure whether this made any claims of good luck associated with the trinket unlikely. Maybe their life would have been a lot worse without it. In his experience, bad as things were, they could usually be worse. They were a happy bunch in their way, and if a few of their children had perished that was a sorrow experienced by many and it did not haunt them. They had young Brigita, who might well organise them all and bring plenty. He chuckled aloud at the thought of what might have happened if she had gone north and been sold as a slave. Pity the family who bought her, for she would soon be running the place for their own good – like Philo, only a good deal more determined. Or they would have beaten her until she submitted. The smile went. At least he could be pleased that she was home – a real home, with her own family. He felt very alone.

Ferox had loved once, a woman with a dark beauty, and for a few months he felt as if he had had a home. She had picked out Philo at a slave market and he had bought the small boy to please her. Back then he did anything he could to please her. Then she had left, in the middle of the grim business when he was tasked with investigating the officers involved in the failed coup led by Saturninus against the late and unlamented Emperor Domitian. He had done his job, even though he soon realised that the men under suspicion were dying, whether or not he discovered evidence of their guilt. He drank, and was surely gloomy and difficult, but he did not think that that was the only reason why she left. There was something else, something from the past that she had made him promise never to ask about. She had gone without word, without a clue, leaving only Philo behind, his pitch-black hair and dark eyes reminders of hers. It had broken him and he had drunk even more heavily, and in the end they transferred him to Britannia and sent him to this nowhere place in the far north because no one else wanted him. The Silures were peaceful, his grandfather already dead from fever, and he no longer mattered politically. He was made regionarius of one of the least important bits of land in the empire and left to rot if that was what he wanted.

Then two years ago, he met her. It was on a day when he was too hungover to care much whether he lived or died, and he and Vindex had ridden to warn a coach and party of cavalry about an ambush. They were too late, but managed to rescue the lady and her maid who were riding in the carriage. The lady was Sulpicia Lepidina, wife of Cerialis, and he had begun by mistaking her for the slave. Somehow, they had all survived, and later he learned that the attackers were the Stallion's men, wanting to take her and sacrifice her to make a great work of magic. Cerialis was from the royal line of the Batavians, which made her royal in their eyes, and so of greater value. He had saved her then, and then a second time when there was an attack in the fort itself. It was Samhain, the feast of the dead, when spirits from the Otherworld walked on the earth and the laws of life did not apply, and he had come to her then, found her, and they had made love.

On the Kalends of August the following year, the Lady Sulpicia Lepidina, *femina clarissima*, daughter of a former consul and wife to the prefect, gave birth to a son. Before she had whispered the news to him, he had known that the child was his. Publicly it did not matter, for Cerialis, who already had three children and so had met the laws set down by all the emperors since Augustus, had acknowledged the child as his, naming him Marcus Flavius Cerialis and accepting the substantial expense of paying for another son's education and career.

He had rarely seen the lady since then, and never been alone with her, but he hoped that she sensed his joy and knew that he would protect her and their secret forever. The law was unlikely to be generous to him, for adultery was an offence against the Republic as well as the individual, threatening the family life on which the state depended. If discovered he would be dismissed from the army, perhaps even sent into exile on some bleak rock – that is if they could find one more out of the way than here. He might even be executed, for it was rumoured that Trajan's views on such things were especially strict. None of that really mattered to him. Worse – far worse – was that she would be humiliated publicly, divorced and probably sent to a bleak rock of her own.

Ferox had a son he had glimpsed just twice, a boy he would never hold, probably never know, and certainly could never acknowledge or be acknowledged by and all the while he loved a woman who was married to another man and could never be his. For the moment his joy triumphed over his despair at the hopelessness of it all, but he worried that he was feeling the urge to start drinking again.

He clutched the blue stone tightly. Nine days after a boy was born Roman parents gave him the *bulla*, a gold charm worn around the neck until the boy became a man. The Silures did

45

something similar ten days after birth, and they gave the child a stone or bead on a thread, much like this one. Ferox felt the smooth surface with his fingers and clutched it tight.

When Philo found him the next morning he was still somehow perched on the stool, body slumped forward onto the table. The slave sniffed, but there was no scent of beer or wine, or indeed any of the old signs he had not seen for well over a year. His master was clutching something in his hand so tightly that his knuckles were white.

IV

'Hﾤow much do you know about Hibernians?' Crispinus asked him almost as soon as he came into the little room. Ferox had ridden to Vindolanda the next morning as instructed, arriving just before noon. He did not glimpse the prefect or his wife on his way through the fort, and felt the usual mix of relief and disappointment because he did not see her. A clerk at the principia sent him to one of the side chambers, where he found the tribune waiting.

'A little, my lord,' Ferox said. 'I have never been to their island, but have met a few over the years, coming to raid, coming to trade or just running away from enemies at home. You recall the ones we met at Tincommius' feast?'

Crispinus snapped his fingers. 'I had half forgotten. They wore long tunics, did they not, instead of trousers like the rest of the…' He trailed off.

'I believe barbarians was the word you were looking for, my lord.'

'I had also forgotten your refreshing impudence. And no, that is not what I was about to say. I was trying to remember whether or not I could describe the Venicones and Vacomagi as Caledonians, and indeed whether all might be termed Britons.'

'Many Romans would, my lord.'

'While others, including your good self, Titus Flavius Ferox, would know better and would not. Yet what would such a Roman say?'

'He would assume that his listener had the wit to understand that all the peoples of these islands were different, just as there is no such thing as a typical Hibernian. They have their tribes and clans, many of them very different even to close neighbours. Language unites them and us up to a point, although sometimes it is hard to follow the different dialects.' The tribune watched him in silence, so after a while he added a respectful, 'my lord.'

'It is not courtesy I am looking for, centurion, but enlightenment and understanding. You always remind me of an oracle, giving answers that are as precise as they are unhelpful, even misleading. And so, as with an oracle I suppose I must frame each question as precisely as a lawyer, but it would be nice if you trusted me.' From their first encounter the tribune had time and again asked for trust, which made Ferox all the more reluctant to give it.

'Perhaps it would be simpler if you explained what this is all about?' Ferox knew how much sheer delight the chance to launch into a great speech gave to a well-bred Roman. Crispinus loved asking question after question about each thing that caught his attention. Yet he seemed to listen to the answers and remember a lot of what he heard, even if he could not quite come to think like someone who was not Roman. He was well into his second year in the province as tribune of the legion, and had grown a lot in that time, if not in stature then in strength and confidence.

Crispinus gave his great bray of a laugh, still surprising in someone so small and normally so poised in every movement. He was dressed in a bright white military tunic and boots, with a bronze cuirass heavily decorated with embossed sea creatures and nymphs and girded with the thick purple band that marked his rank. 'Very well. And of course you are right, and I have plunged in without telling you of what will happen next month. Well, I should tell you that two kings are coming from Hibernia to visit us, one each from the Rhobogdioi and the Darinoi, although they claim to speak for other peoples as well. As far as we can tell they are seeking our friendship, presumably some form of recognition, and no doubt other things that shall become obvious. The noble Neratius Marcellus has placed me in charge of arranging this business, and has also decided that it should take place near the coast, at the time when much of the army in the north will be training and preparing for his inspection. The legate feels that a display of our might cannot do any harm. After all, Hibernians have sometimes come across the sea to raid us, have they not?' Neratius Marcellus was the governor of Britannia and a shrewd man, as was his nephew Crispinus, for all his facade of languid charm.

'Yes, my lord, sometimes. When I was a boy they came along our coast a couple of times – and we sent boats across to plunder them. I hear it is rare now, but a few years ago there were several landings up here on the west coast near Alauna and even Maia.'

'We have garrisons in both, do we not? In fact, thinking about it, didn't the cohort at Maia catch a couple of boatloads of raiders last summer? I was down south at the time, but I like to take an interest in what goes on in this part of the world and I remember reading of it in a report that came to the legate's office in Londinium. Claudius Super wrote that the men they caught and executed were Hibernians.'

'Yes, I know.' Ferox did not add that Claudius Super was a halfwit who could not tell a Hibernian from a turnip. The man was the senior regional centurion, supervising a handful of other *regionarii* here in the north, including Ferox.

'Then I take it from your tone that you do not agree.'

'They were Novantae, my lord, with a couple of stray Selgovae tagging along, not Hibernians. The Novantae have been coming across the bay in their little boats for generations. They stopped for a while when we garrisoned their lands heavily, but since most of the posts were abandoned, they are growing confident again. I am guessing that the report did not mention a couple of other raids that got away with captives and plunder a few weeks later.'

'It did not.'

'Thought not. We managed to catch one lot out of three, and to be honest were lucky to do that. They'll be back this summer and in much greater numbers.'

'Why?'

'Because they think they can get away with it.'

'Well, given that a lot of troops will be on manoeuvres in the area, I suspect the legate may want to do something about that. For the moment, let us put that aside. As I explained, I need to arrange the reception for these visiting kings, and I shall need you by my side to help in the negotiations. Neratius Marcellus will conclude any agreement, but the details will be left to us.'

'As I said, my lord, I only know a little about them.'

'Such modesty is unbecoming, and might even be mistaken for a reluctance to be in my company, were such a thing possible to conceive. It does not matter. You know more than anyone else to hand, and you are a junior officer who will do what he is told!'

'Sir.'

'That's better. As you have proved in the past, your suspicious and untrusting nature ideally suits you for diplomacy. Any ideas at the moment?'

'Women, my lord.'

50

'An admirable thought, and always welcome, yet I struggle to see the relevance.'

'A lot of the peoples of Hibernia are ruled by queens as well as kings, and all revere them. Did the governor's wife ever come to join him in Britannia?'

Crispinus gave a wry smile. 'I fear my aunt lacks a robust constitution and, with great reluctance, decided that three or four years apart from her husband would be for the best. From all I can tell, neither of them regrets that decision. Still, I see what you mean and will think on it, for we might be able to find some suitable ladies to help host our guests. After all, we have a senator's daughter here at Vindolanda. Have you seen the noble Sulpicia Lepidina lately? I know the two of you are good friends since our escapades back in the first tribunate of our lord and emperor.'

Ferox tried to spot any hint of irony, but saw nothing apart from the mischief and amusement that was the young aristocrat's normal expression. 'I have not, my lord.'

'Well, this might be a problem with which she can assist. I must say motherhood suits her, for she is in even finer bloom than before, and that is saying something.' The compliment was genuine and appeared innocuous. 'A truly remarkable woman.'

'It is not my place to judge such things, my lord,' Ferox said, and regretted it instantly. It would have been far better to have said nothing.

Crispinus ran a hand through his almost white hair. He was not yet twenty-three and the old man's hair was an odd contrast with a face still not formed into the rigid lines of adulthood. 'Your idea of your proper place continues to baffle me, centurion.' Ferox wondered whether the pause before the young aristocrat spoke had been unnaturally long, and tried to assure himself that he was imagining things.

'Well, no matter,' Crispinus resumed. 'I think that is enough for the moment. You will hear more at the *consilium* to be held in two hours' time. This is to be a busy summer, as you may already have guessed that there will be a lot for us all to do. Especially you, so all in all it is a relief to find that the rumours are not true and that you are not dead.'

Ferox could not think of anything witty to say, so contented himself with a simple 'Sir', which prompted another quizzical stare.

'The little farm girl is safely reunited with her folk, I trust?'

The sudden change of topic caught Ferox off guard. 'Yes, my lord.'

'Aelius Brocchus is due to attend the consilium this afternoon so he will be able to take back his own property. He is a fine man, and from what I hear the horse was expensive, while the girl is a favourite of his wife. The girl is not too damaged I take it?'

'Terrified, mauled about a bit. As far as I can tell they did not rape her, if that is what you are asking, my lord.'

'Ah, the old quick anger. I thought you Silures were supposed to keep a stony reserve, immune to provocation?' Ferox said nothing. 'And I also suppose that that is the answer I deserve,' the tribune added after a moment. 'It is hard to imagine the life of a slave, and yet one would think the absolute lack of control over your own life helps to make them immune from fear when abducted. After all they have no freedom to lose. Still, perhaps it is different for a slave with kind owners and a comfortable life. Losing that must bring a pang.'

'They butchered her lover in front of her,' Ferox said.

'Unpleasant, of course. Oh yes, I had forgotten one thing I wanted to ask. How did you hear about the taking of the horse and girl – Artemis, is that her name?'

Ferox guessed that the mistake was deliberate. 'Aphrodite, my lord.' Crispinus shrugged as if it was no matter, but Ferox knew that he had a very good memory for detail. 'We did not find out who they were until we got them back. There were tracks of a horse unlike one of the local ponies, and from the prints and others of feet we guessed at two girls as captives, but that was all we knew.'

There was another pause. 'The oracle speaks again, without really answering.'

'Does the tribune wish to know why we were hunting raiders when all they had done was steal a farmer's daughter?' Ferox spoke louder than he had meant, and was annoyed at the look of amusement on the tribune's face, but at least it calmed him. 'I went north,' he said, choosing his words with care, 'because the family live in my region and these men had come into my region to kill, steal people and property. I will never permit that if I can help it. Never. And I went because the family are good people, and could not spare one of the children, especially this one.' The anger was coming back and he fought it.

Crispinus was smiling broadly. 'I have missed your fire, Flavius Ferox. You truly are an unusual man. So unusual that you would fight one against five for the sake of a family of no importance, and a child whom you barely know. Ah, for once I surprise you!' the tribune added triumphantly. Ferox realised that he must have spoken to Vindex, which meant that he had probably known all about it in the first place. Crispinus was playing his usual games, working towards something else.

'Well, that is all very admirable, and it has had a fortunate outcome for Aelius Brocchus, who as I said is fine man. It is also a source of delight for Claudius Probus, who may not be a very fine man but is a rich one and, like all rich men, well connected. People whose names might surprise you – well, they surprised me – wrote letters on his behalf to me, let alone more important men like our legate.'

Ferox had a feeling he knew what was coming next and his face must have shown it. Crispinus must have seen something in his face. 'Yes, I share your view of young Genialis, and I have only met the lad once, and that briefly. To me he seemed as appealing company as a louse laying eggs in your tunic, so that I dread to think what weeks in his company will have been like. Still, miraculous as this may sound, his father dotes upon him, and Probus is a man worth indulging, for it is always better to have the rich as friends than as enemies.'

'Vindex wanted to kill him,' Ferox said.

'I know, he told me, and I for one do not blame him, but certain courtesies should apply.'

'We kept him tied up for most of the trip back.'

Crispinus waved his hand dismissively. 'I am sure it did him the world of good. But do not worry about a sulking child. The father is a practical man of business, and he will be grateful.'

'Sir.'

'Oh, we are back to that are we? Go away, Flavius Ferox, for you make me tired. Try to be more forthcoming whenever your opinion is required at the consilium.'

In the event he sat in silence for most of the council. Crispinus was the senior officer present, even though he was the youngest, although at times he deferred to Cerialis as their host. The commander of the Batavians looked full of vigour. He was a tall man, even taller than Ferox although less heavily built and more in the proportions a sculptor would give to a statue. His face was conventionally handsome, enhancing an expressiveness that was refined by long practice in oratory.

His hair was red gold, its thick growth lightly trimmed by his barber every few days. He was twenty-five, and with his good looks, expensive uniform and cuirass, and that sense of a man performing a role, it would be easy to mistake the man for a mere dandy, like many of those who served in the army as a stepping stone to prominence in society. Like some, but not all of those, Cerialis was a brave man, and also a more than decent soldier, while his Batavians were devoted to him, and not simply because he was from the house of their kings. In the brutal campaign two years ago he had proved himself to be a leader that his men could trust. Ferox could see no ill effects from the wounds he had suffered in the battle where they had defeated the Stallion's army.

The others were all men he knew, and most had served in that same brief and bitter conflict. Aelius Brocchus was of average build, slim and hawk nosed, his deep brown eyes keen and his statements always precise. He was a Baetican from Gades, his skin a rich brown hinting at as much Carthaginian as Iberian blood in his ancestry. Beside him was Rufinus, prefect in command of the cohort stationed to the west at Magna. He was an African, with the precise, slightly antiquated Latin of that province, and had a narrow, eager face and a short, well-groomed beard.

'I wondered whether it would make me look more martial,' he joked when the others asked him about it. All three men were equestrians, the class below the Senate, and were following the usual career. Cerialis and Rufinus were in their first command, each placed in charge of a cohort of auxiliary infantry, whereas Brocchus was at the third stage and, having already led a cohort and served as one of the five junior tribunes in a legion, was now in command of one of the prestigious *alae* of cavalry. He was thirty-three, which meant he had risen through the posts reasonably quickly, making him senior in years as well as rank to the others in spite of the fact that all were called prefect.

Crispinus was the son of a senator, and when he finished his term as the senior tribune in Legio II Augusta he would go back to Rome and soon be enrolled as a senator. A man with ambition would seek a range of civil and military posts, commanding a legion around the time he was thirty, a senatorial province without much of a garrison a few years later, and a military province with a fair-sized army in his forties. Ferox had no doubt that the young aristocrat had ambition, and probably the connections, perhaps even the money to rise so high. His birth and his likely future made him the most important man in the room, but none of the others gave any impression of deferring to the younger man, not least because of his courtesy and fondness for self-deprecation. This was the way the empire worked, and in this case the four men trusted each other.

Ferox was junior in rank and class and had never seen any point in resenting a world he could not change. He was relieved when Crispinus announced that Claudius Super was unable to join them, owing to illness.

'Nothing serious, I trust,' Cerialis said, showing a genuine concern that Ferox could not find it in his heart to share. The prefect and his wife often entertained the senior regionarius to dinner. Claudius Super was another equestrian and, unlike the other men, actually from Italy. Yet his family's wealth and influence had not been sufficient to secure him command of an auxiliary unit, so that instead he had been commissioned as a centurion in a legion, with lower pay, prestige, and in all likelihood a far less impressive career ahead of him. Claudius Super never missed an opportunity to remind others of his high birth. Ferox did not dislike the man for that, but he despised him for his crassness, stupidity and arrogance, which too often caused trouble and disturbances when none were necessary.

'I do not believe there is cause for worry,' Crispinus replied, 'and in his stead we can raise any appropriate matters with Ferox.'

They spent the first hour planning the assignment of troops from each garrison to join the spring and summer's training programme and exercises. None of the forts were to be wholly stripped of soldiers, for there was always work and administration to be done, and there was no harm in keeping just enough to mount the odd patrol and respond to any minor problems.

'Our noble legate is of the opinion that there is no prospect of serious uprisings in this area during the rest of this year. This judgement is based on all the reports he has received, including those of the regionarii. I take it there is no reason to change this assessment?' Crispinus and the others all looked at Ferox.

'No,' he said, still unsure what was meant by the abduction of Genialis, but unable to see in it hints of trouble on any great scale. 'There is no reason to alter it. After all, the distance is not so great. Within a few days all the troops could return to their garrisons.'

'Indeed – and come with plenty of company from the other detachments involved in the training. Good,' Crispinus concluded, and went back to the details of how and when to move each contingent and ensuring that it would be properly supplied wherever it went. Cerialis' cornicularius acted as the main recorder of their decisions, although there were several other military clerks with him to make copies where necessary.

Halfway through the second hour they turned to the census that was to begin around the time of the army exercises, in the region to the north. 'We may be called upon to provide some soldiers to assist in the process,' Cerialis informed them.

'And I seem to remember from history that the first census on a conquered people is sometimes resented, perhaps violently.'

'Would you like strangers coming around asking lots of questions about your family and your possessions, all the time knowing that the mongrels want to tax you?' The room went silent save for the surprised gasp of the cornicularius. Ferox had not realised that he had not just thought the words but spoken them out loud. After a moment Crispinus and the three prefects all burst into laughter, the soldiers following their lead.

'Fair enough,' the tribune said, 'the tax gatherer or the one who paves the way for him is bound to be an unwelcome guest. Reminds me of that little poem of Catullus about the worst wind blowing at a man's house being his mortgage.' There was more laughter. 'Finally, there is one more matter, in fact one directly from our most noble princeps, who instructed the outcome of a trial to be read out in every army base since it concerned military discipline as well as other matters.' Crispinus paused, deliberately overacting in feigned discomfort. 'I fear it is all a little sordid,' he went on.

'Well, that should brighten things up.' Rufinus was smirking and the other two prefects chuckled.

'Yet it is a sad tale, of betrayal and infidelity. I almost feel I should set it to verse!' That brought open laughter. Ferox clenched the fingers of his right hand as tightly closed as he could.

'There is – I am tempted to say *was* as it sounds like a story – a young aristocrat just come back from his time as tribune in a legion. Now where have I heard that before.' There was more laughter, and the prefects were enjoying it. The clerks looked bored and were still scratching away to finish their notes. Ferox decided a smile was appropriate.

'In this case the legion was in Syria. Hot climate, you know, eastern passions and dark appetites, so the setting will give you warning. Now our young tribune was married to a young lady called Gallitta. Well, there's no law against that, although the wise young tribune remains unattached so that he can devote all his strength and intelligence to serving as a soldier.'

'Of course,' Brocchus cut in, the words dripping with sarcasm. Most senior tribunes did as little work and spent as little time with their legion as possible.

'They were young and in love.' Crispinus almost sang the words as he ignored the interruption. 'And the thought of parting for months or years was too much to bear, so the dutiful wife packs up all her perfumes, her silks, her intimate things, and follows her husband to Antioch. Little more than a blushing bride, her innocence left her unprepared for life in that den of iniquity.' Ferox felt his heart sink at the obvious direction of the story.

'You've been there then,' Brocchus interrupted again.

'How could you think such a thing?' Crispinus smiled happily, then frowned as if pondering something. 'Ah yes,' he said at last. 'Gallitta, I recollect her now. No more than seventeen. Small girl, a little plump, but in the right places. Generous hearted, if I recall. That, I fear, is part of the tragedy.

'Alas, when he arrived our young hero did his best to be diligent, working hard, and accepting missions away whenever he was ordered by his superiors. That was the problem. Poor little Gallitta was left at his house in the legion's base, so close to Antioch, alone with her perfumes, her intimate things, and her silks. Fortunately, there were kind folk to console her. One was a centurion – well, we all know what they're like.' He pretended to notice Ferox sitting in the corner of the room for the first time. 'Of course, not all of them, dear Flavius Ferox.'

'Centurions are the pillars of the army,' Brocchus said flatly, while the others grinned.

'Well, the pillar in question was a bit crooked, but a mature man and vigorous in every way, while ardent in his determination to console the lonely wife.' Crispinus spread his hands apologetically. 'I am tempted to add consoling her several times a night and in the afternoons as well, but that would be to embellish too far the raw judgement and summary sent from Rome. Such lewdness is inappropriate, for I have no wish to shock the delicate mind of the cornicularius either.' The prefect's clerk had been giving the speech his rapt attention for some time now, his work forgotten.

'As comedy must teach us to beware, the husband came home earlier than expected, in time to see this pillar of the army scrambling out of the window. Once again, I shall refrain from adding details from my sordid imagination.'

'You can leave it to our sordid imaginations,' Rufinus said.

Cerialis grinned. 'Speak for yourself,' he said, patting the other man on the shoulder.

'The tribune went to the legate of the province to complain, and the governor wrote to the emperor to report this breach of discipline, which so undermined the hierarchy of the army – not to mention the sacrosanct and honoured institution of marriage. To cut a long story short…'

'Bit late for that,' Rufinus whispered loudly.

'As I say, to cut a long story short, the centurion is dishonourably discharged, and sent in exile in perpetuity, unless the emperor chooses to change his mind. He's gone to Tomi, so can no doubt console himself with following in the footsteps of Ovid.'

'One shagger after another, and good riddance to them both,' Rufinus said. For the first time Cerialis looked a little shocked, evidently at the word not the sentiment.

'What distressed the emperor was that the betrayed husband

now thought the matter solved. With his rival packed off to dwell among the barbarians, he settled back to domestic bliss – no doubt several times each night and so on... It was up to the Lord Trajan to remind him that adultery cannot be committed by one person on their own. Back in Rome the former tribune was ordered to make a formal accusation against the affectionate Gallitta, who was of course found guilty. As a blushing new divorced woman, she is now in exile – of course somewhere a long away from Tomi as well as from Italy.'

'Any chance it's Britannia?' Rufinus said, licking his thin lips underneath his beard and laughing with the others.

Crispinus hushed them and made his face serious. 'The point of all this is to emphasise the dangers to military discipline and the good of the empire that come from such gross misbehaviour. The centurion brought shame on his rank and the army. Not only has the emperor decreed that his offence and punishment be announced throughout the army, but he is also to be named, so that all shall know of his dishonour. And that name is...' He paused, shook his head and reached down for one the tablets on the table. 'Ah yes, it is Titus Flavius Ferox.'

Ferox jerked upright in his seat before he could stop himself and banged his knee against a table leg, hissing with the pain.

'Dear me no, that's the wrong note,' Crispinus said as the others roared with laughter. 'It is Caius Julius Similis. My apologies, friend Ferox, of course no one would ever imagine that you would behave in so shameful a manner. Will you forgive me?'

'Of course, my lord,' he said, laughing along with the others because it would have been odd if he had not joined in. Junior officers were obliged to share the humour of their superiors.

The consilium finished on this cheerful note. Ferox left, heart still pounding, and trying to convince himself that it was all just coincidence. Crispinus was a clever man, a politician to the bone, who loved intrigue. The year before last Ferox had wondered whether he was one of the men conspiring to replace Trajan with another emperor. The tribune's uncle, Neratius Marcellus, had been willing to consider the possibility, believing that his nephew was the sort of man to end up on the winning side, whichever side it might me. Ferox was still not sure that the young aristocrat was wholly innocent, and suspected the governor also harboured a few doubts. Could Crispinus know about his night with Sulpicia Lepidina? Was all this long oration meant as a hint, just like their earlier conversation? The tribune was a man to store knowledge, keeping it for when it might be useful.

Ferox left the principia, thinking that everything had been so much simpler when he was far off in the north away from Rome and Romans.

V

A VISIT TO the prisoners proved fruitless. There was a range of buildings behind the granaries, mostly used as workshops and for storing equipment, but at one end it was divided into a dozen cells, each fitted with heavily barred windows and a solid door. Most were empty at the moment for there was only a handful of soldiers confined for various delinquencies. The brothers were on their own, Segovax lying out on the straw and rush carpeting, muttering and twitching in a fevered sleep.

'*Medicus* says they'll know in a day or two whether or not he makes it, sir,' the guard told him, in a tone of utter indifference to the outcome.

The Red Cat sat on his haunches beside his brother, chanting too softly to catch the words. There was no window in their cell, and with just the light through the little opening in the door Ferox could see no more than his outline. He did not need to see it to sense the man's hatred and knew at once that there was no point asking any questions.

'Which one is posted to me?' he asked the guard.

'In the corner cell, sir. He's got twenty days, breaking and carrying rocks at the quarry starting from tomorrow. Do you want to see him, sir?'

'It can wait.' Men detached from their units as stationarii were

63

occasionally sound men, keen and eager. More often they were ones their units did not want, the drunks, the undisciplined, the incorrigible brawlers, the thieves, the queers and the lazy. He would have to wait and see what this one was like, and the other, if the man ever recovered consciousness.

Ferox wanted to be away from Vindolanda, so returned to the principia and asked for Frost to be brought to him. Tomorrow was the eighth day after the Ides of April and the birthday of the City of Rome, which meant the sacrifice of a pale, well-fattened cow and other ceremonies. It did not matter that there was scarcely anyone from Rome or Italy in the fort, and that apart from Cerialis and a few of the other officers, the Batavians were not Roman citizens, still they would parade and hear prayers and make offerings for the growth and harmony of the city. It was the way of the army, wherever it was based, but Ferox was eager not to be invited to stay, for Cerialis was bound to host a dinner and there was a risk that he would be invited.

The horse arrived quickly, and apart from a short conversation about nothing with one of the centurions of the cohort, he saw no one else he knew. It had rained overnight, so the main roads of the fort were even muddier than usual, and there was a fatigue party of soldiers out filling in runs left by carts and packing the earth down flat. He rode off, aware that his horse was leaving fresh prints in the mud. He noticed one of the workers rolling his eyes and gave the man a nod in response for he remembered fighting alongside him against the Stallion's men. The soldier recognised him and grinned. The party were all Tungrians, part of the small rump of cohors I Tungrorum left at Vindolanda, with the records of a much-depleted unit that was scattered in small detachments all around the province.

Riding out of the gate always brought a moment of relief for any soldier, at least when times were peaceful, but Ferox kept Frost at a brisk walk as he made his way through the narrow-fronted shops, bars and houses of the canabae. A fine rain started to fall, even though the sun was bright ahead of him, and it turned swiftly into a heavy shower. People scattered, running for shelter where they could find it. Ferox pulled his broad-brimmed hat down more tightly and checked that the brooch held his cloak securely. The rain did not last long, and by the time he was at the edge of the settlement it had stopped. One of the last buildings was unique because it was built partly from stone and had two storeys, and even more because it was the most expensive brothel for well over fifty miles in any direction. It was run by Flora, an old friend, but she did not like anyone to call on her without an appointment so he rode past. On his right was the temple of Silvanus, a tall square building surrounded by a veranda on each side. The entrance was a simple archway, and in front of it a four-wheeled *raeda* carriage waited.

Frost must have sensed her rider shift in the saddle for the mare stopped. The raeda was owned by Cerialis. It was the same one Sulpicia Lepidina had been travelling in when she had been ambushed on the road to Coria. Once before he had seen it in this place, when the lady visited the temple to make an offering and to spend time in its silence. On that occasion, she had appeared just as he and Vindex were passing, and he had spoken to her and as always felt himself struggling to keep his balance.

Ferox kicked the horse angrily in the sides. She snorted, shook her head, and lurched into an ungainly canter. He recovered, calming her, and brought her back to a brisk walk. Lingering here might seem suspicious, while hurrying past might appear equally odd as well as rude. He tried not to stare at the temple as he passed. The lady's maid waited in the shade and shelter of the veranda, just as she had done when they had met here the first time. The girl saw him, and bowed her head respectfully. It was good Vindex was not here, for he was bound to have leered or called out, or worse still wanted to wait. There was no sign of Sulpicia Lepidina. The horse walked on, leaving the temple behind. There were the usual beggars and vagrants clustered by the road, some even in the cemetery on the left. He scanned the hunched, filthy and crippled figures as he always did these days. Acco had travelled among them in years gone by, but he was not there.

As Ferox searched for any hint of the druid he saw the upright stone marking the grave of Titus Annius, the commander of the Tungrians who had died from wounds suffered back in that same grim autumn. He had been a good man and a fine soldier. The inscription proclaimed that his daughter had erected the monument to him. That was a fiction, since the centurion had no children, but he had left his money to benefit his soldiers and their widows and children. One lass of eight had lost her mother to fever weeks before the fight and became an orphan when her father was hacked down, standing protectively over the wounded Annius. By some legal trickery, it was arranged for the dead centurion to have adopted the girl. Cerialis and his wife were now supervising her education and she might enjoy a far better life than was usually open to a soldier's daughter. That is, if she was lucky.

Ferox sighed, wondering once again whether he had made the right choices in that straggling fight amid the burning heather and whether it was his fault that Annius had died. He rode on, for the past was the past and could not be undone. Ahead of him the road joined on to the main east to west route between Coria and Luguvallium, and for once he decided to follow it for a while before heading off for Syracuse. He glanced back once, just before the fort disappeared into a fold of the ground, and saw tiny figures by the carriage. He thought he glimpsed a flash of golden hair, but could not be sure. Ferox rode on, trying to leave his memories behind. The rain started again, growing heavier and heavier as the clouds closed in until it was hard to see far in any direction.

At Syracuse there was a man waiting to complain that a neighbour was stealing the best of his new lambs. He named the culprit, swearing that he was to blame. Ferox knew that more people would come in to make similar charges over the days to come. It was always the same at this time of year, as the weather grew warmer and animals were let out to pasture. The next day the accused turned up alleging intimidation and blows from the first man. Beside him waited a grey-haired woman who often came to Syracuse or to other Roman authorities. Her family had perished five years ago from a sickness that had swept through the lands at that time. Only a little boy survived, and he fell into a river and drowned a year later. Since then she travelled around the countryside searching for him. Often people gave her food and shelter for a night or two. Sometimes they drove her away because they were afraid that she brought bad luck.

'Lord, please find my lost boy,' she called as Ferox rode into Syracuse. 'He's tall for his age, lord, and good looking. He's all I have.'

'I'll try,' he said, forcing himself to pause for a moment. 'If I find him I will send word.'

'Thank you, lord, thank you. He's all I have left.'

Ferox went through the gateway. He saw Crescens and beckoned him to come over. 'See that she gets some food,' he told the curator. 'And treat her gently.' The old woman had visited so often that even the sympathetic found their patience and tempers fraying. Last time one of the milder soldiers had hit her because she clung to his leg begging him to help. 'Tell the men to treat her as if she was their own mother.'

There were other visitors, bringing petitions or complaints. Apart from thefts there were feuds and the arguments that often spilled over after the winter months when families and kin were cooped up together for much of the time. A husband had struck his wife after their latest row, but this time she fell and hit the iron guard around the fire, cracking her skull so that she died three days later. The headman from her old farmstead wanted the centurion to come with him so that the killer would grant a proper blood price to her family. Ferox was tired, but knew that if nothing was done quickly then more killing was likely, so he got a fresh horse and rode out with the man. There was not much for him to do, but his presence was a reminder that it was better to settle everything quietly rather than let the Romans intervene. The husband was in mourning, sleeping in the open away from the houses to cleanse himself of the deed, and agreed to the price of a cloak, two sheep and the best lamb born from his remaining flock in each of the next five years.

It took a day and a half to deal with it all, for the farms were on the very edge of his territory. By the time he returned to Syracuse a messenger from a chieftain was waiting with news of another death. This time it was no accident, for a wife who had been beaten again and again over the years had finally snapped and smothered her husband while he lay in a drunken stupor.

No one at the settlement blamed her, but blood was blood, and the dead man had family who were likely to seek vengeance. The chieftain wanted the woman taken away somewhere safe, so that she could start a new life and there would be no need for a feud.

'I'll come,' Ferox told the man, and gave orders for two of the cavalrymen among the stationarii to accompany him in case of trouble. 'If Vindex and any of the scouts arrive, tell them to join me,' he told Crescens. The Brigantian and his men were already a day late, and he wished that the gaunt warrior was with him, because he would have to ask his clan to take the woman and find a place for her somewhere.

It was another long ride, made worse because the rain was constant and blown into them by a strong, gusty wind. A council was held in the chieftain's hall, which was a roundhouse only a little larger than the others at the farmstead. It was an angry meeting, with supporters of the woman recounting all that she had suffered and asserting that the dead man received no more than long overdue justice. 'Who will miss him?' they claimed, while the woman said nothing, and appeared stunned by the whole business. Against her, the man's cousin repeated that a death called for vengeance and punishment.

'Cut her to show her shame,' he insisted, and the men with him bellowed their approval. 'We are Textoverdi,' he went on, 'and we do not kill our own without punishment. Mark her to show her disgrace!' He drew a thin dagger. The old custom was to slice a woman's nostrils and ears, and scar her cheeks as a permanent sign that she had been faithless to her husband.

The chieftain was a kind man but not a bold one and did not stand up. Ferox clapped his hands hard. It was not a gesture these people used, and the sound echoed around the house, bringing silence. He stood, and his hand went to the hilt of his dagger, for he knew this was sharp and he did not like the look of the man's knife.

'Let one who has no tie or kindred to either husband or wife settle this. Come, woman.' He beckoned to her. She came without hesitation, used to obedience. When she came closer he could see the fading marks of old bruises on her cheeks and arms. With one hand Ferox brushed her hair back to uncover her left ear. 'This is justice,' he said, not believing it, but wanting to make a show for her enemies. He pulled the lobe of her ear taut and sliced it off. The woman barely winced, showing that she was very familiar with pain. 'Let her be exiled from these lands.

'Do you have children, girl?' he whispered.

'A girl, lord.'

'Let her take her child and I will send her far away, so that the shame is gone from the people's eyes. That is justice.'

The chieftain raised his arms and yelled in acclamation of the judgement. The dead man's cousin looked sullen, but Ferox thought that he could sense the man's relief at avoiding a blood feud. The daughter, a babe in arms, was swaddled and passed to the mother and they left straightaway, even though there were only a few hours of dull light left, because he did not want to give the cousin time to think it all over. At least the rain had stopped, and the chief loaned them a pony for the girl, for he wanted her off his hands as soon as possible.

It was almost dark when one of the two troopers came up alongside Ferox. It was the Thracian, the man with only a few months left to serve in the army.

'We're being followed, sir,' the old soldier said.

'I know. One of them, over on the right, keeping pace, but a little ahead.' Ferox did not add that he was sure whoever it was had come from the south and not followed them from the farmstead.

'You've better eyesight than me, sir,' the Thracian said. His name was Sita, but no one ever used it. 'Want me to ride ahead and try to loop back?'

'Good idea. Don't make it too obvious and don't take any chances.'

The Thracian grinned. 'Not me, sir.' He trotted off, going straight ahead as if riding to find the path or look for a campsite. Ferox brought Snow to a halt and turned back to smile at the woman. 'We'll rest soon.'

Something whipped past just inches from his head. 'Stay with her,' he called to the other trooper. 'Keep her safe.'

Snow surged forward with only a gentle touch of his feet, and he steered the mare to the right, heading for the darkness under a patch of trees. He could see the even darker shape of a horseman. A second arrow came at him, and he ducked so that it flicked his shoulder and bounced off his mail armour. The Thracian was galloping, shield up and spear ready as he closed on the man. He was closer, but the third shaft was still aimed at Ferox. He swerved, sending Snow to the left, but a sudden hollow in the long grass caught both of them by surprise and the horse stumbled, flinging him against her neck, the saddle horns driving into his legs. The arrow scarred the grey horse's back and she tried to turn away from the pain.

The horseman turned, shooting another arrow as he fled into the trees. It thudded into the Thracian's shield.

'Bastard!' Sita yelled as he closed the distance on the man.

'I want him alive!' Ferox yelled. The man tried another shot, but the shaft went high and his own horse was going too slowly to escape his pursuer. The horseman dropped his bow and tried to drive his horse on.

The Thracian aimed his heavy spear with all the care and skill of a veteran, driving it into the square of the man's back with such force that it came out through his chest. The man did not cry, and all Ferox heard was a grunt as the breath was knocked out of him. He knew before he got there than their attacker was dead.

'Sorry, sir,' the Thracian said in the flat tone of an old sweat who was not remotely apologetic, but knew that he could not be punished for it.

'I wanted him alive.'

'Think he wanted you dead, sir.' A man with only a few months until discharge was not about to run the risk of trying to take someone alive. 'Reckon he's a deserter, sir?' The dead man was dressed like a Roman in tunic, trousers and cloak, and his hobnailed boots were the sort worn by soldiers, and quite a few other people. On top of that, Ferox had never heard of any horse archers in this part of the world, or anywhere in Britannia, unless they were trained by the army.

'Maybe.'

Ferox saw the Thracian looking warily behind them at the sound of approaching horses, but he had already seen the riders approaching and did not turn. Instead he examined the corpse. The man was of middle age, thicker set than most Britons – a Rhinelander perhaps?

A horse stopped a few yards away.

'You're late,' Ferox said without getting up or looking around.

'I got married,' Vindex said happily, and that did surprise him. When he turned the scout was grinning broadly. 'You trying to be a hero again?'

Ferox smiled. 'Not me,' he said. 'Someone just tried to kill me.'

'Nothing new then.'

VI

T HE WIND GREW stronger as the tide turned, plucking at Ferox's hat, so that he took it off and tucked it into his belt. His hair blew in front of his eyes and he realised that he ought to give in and let Philo trim it. He laughed, startling Vindex and the two scouts who rode with him for he had not spoken for a long time, and then he gave the mare her head and she bounded up the hill towards the tower, racing at a pace none of their ponies could match. They followed, flecks of water spraying from the animals' legs, and the two warriors exchanged glances because they were new men not yet used to the centurion's strange ways.

Ferox reached the top some way ahead of the others and reined the grey in. The watchtower was to his left on the highest point of the ridge, a hundred paces away from a cluster of roundhouses where a family lived and farmed. The tower's timbers were rendered so that they gleamed white even on this dull day. It had a black-painted wooden platform projecting so that men could walk out and see in all directions, and a shingle roof shaped like a low pyramid. Around it was a circular rampart and ditch. He could see a sentry outside the entrance, another pacing the walls and a third on the platform veranda. Such vigilance was admirable, although it did make him wonder whether the little garrison knew that there was a party of senior officers on the loose. This was Aballava, the last crossing of the great winding river before it opened into the sea, and he was here to meet with Crispinus, Cerialis and others to help them select a site for the camp they were to build.

Ahead of him the land fell away, fields turning into salt marshes and dunes and then the sea itself, more blue than grey even in this dim light. Ferox took a deep breath, drawing in the scent of salt and old seaweed. Seagulls circled overhead, seeming almost to hover as they floated on the currents of air. One swooped low, not far in front of him, and he watched it, marvelling at the elegance as it climbed again and soon was soaring away, screaming.

'Nasty creatures,' Vindex said. Earlier in the day one had dived down and snatched a piece of bread from his hand.

Ferox ignored him, lost in memories of long ago. The sea here was bluer, the hills across the water closer, but the scents on the wind and the gulls overhead were the same as the coast of his homeland.

'Bleak, isn't it,' Vindex added when his friend did not reply. His two warriors caught up, glanced at the view, and remained unimpressed. One walked his horse round and stared southwards.

'That's a pretty sight,' Vindex said. There was a herd of cattle in the distance, at least a hundred big brown cows and bullocks grazing in the fields, with herdsmen riding around and among them. There were a few farmsteads dotted across the plain, each with their own little collections of animals, five or six cows, a few pigs and goats, tended by each family.

'Must be a big chieftain of the Romans to have so much,' the other scout said admiringly.

'That lot belong to this Probus?' Vindex asked, and at last Ferox dragged himself away from the sea and joined them as they looked south.

'Reckon so. He's got the right to grazing all along this coast and for miles inland.' In the last weeks Ferox had learned that Genialis' father supplied the army with a lot of animals, from cattle for meat and hides, to mules and ponies for pack and draft, and remounts for the cavalry.

'Who gave him the right?' Vindex asked, his tone implying that he guessed. 'I'm guessing no one asked these folk here whether they minded.'

'There's enough grass for everyone,' Ferox said, hoping that it was true. Probus had gone to someone working for the procurator who had gone to someone working for the legate, who had gone to someone higher up and so on. A lot of gifts would have been given, a lot of favours promised, and then suddenly a great swathe of land was opened to a big investor. Probus had a dozen or more herds like this one, apart from all his other animals, and that was just his stock up here. From what he heard the man owned more herds near Eboracum and Deva, helping to feed the demands of the big legionary bases, and sold to the towns and villages as well. He also owned ships and traded back and forth between the Germanies and Britannia, especially up the east coast. Here in the west there were fewer ports, at least this far north.

'He's an ambitious man,' Crispinus had told him back at Vindolanda. 'Knows how to make his money work for him.' That much was certain, but an air of mystery clung around him. 'He's supposed to have been a soldier, and certainly still looks like one,' the tribune had explained, 'but no one is quite sure when and where he served. Cannot have served the full term so must have been discharged, presumably honourably, and a decade or so ago he pops up in Londinium with a lot of money. Claimed to be a Nervian, and did not get the franchise until later, when a rich freedman adopted him and made him his principal heir. The freedman died soon afterwards,' the tribune said, arching an eyebrow. 'Just coincidence apparently.' His tone suggested that he did not believe a word of it. 'Ever since then he's kept on growing. I will say this, though, the animals he supplies are pretty good, so he's better than a lot of contractors.'

'Are these folk Carvetii?' Ferox asked, knowing the answer but preferring not to discuss the injustices of imperial administration with the Brigantian.

'They are and they aren't,' the scout said. 'They're kin of ours, of course, and often they join with us at the great gatherings and stand beside us in battle.' He paused. 'That was in the old days, before we were good allies of Rome.'

'Of course.' The Carvetii were one of the big clans, like the Textoverdi, and both were and were not Brigantes, depending on what was going on, and in the past had fought with and against each other. 'In the old days,' he repeated. 'Well, let's not waste time staring at wealth we'll never have, and have a word with them at the tower.' He set off, fishing out his vine cane from the rolled blanket behind his saddle. As he came closer he twitched his cloak back so that the sentries would see his mail and the rest of his uniform. With the cane of office it ought to show them that he was a Roman and a centurion.

The soldier brought his oval shield up and raised his spear in challenge. He was wearing a black tunic, which marked him out as one of the Vardulli from Magna on detached service at the tower.

'Halt!' he called. 'Announce yourself.'

'Flavius Ferox, centurio regionarius, with three scouts.'

'Sir!' The spear came upright as the auxiliary stamped to attention. 'Advance, friend.'

A legionary was in charge of the seven men currently stationed there, and came out from behind the tower as they rode into the little outpost. As was usual, the door to the tower was on the opposite side from the main entrance, so that no one could rush straight in. There was no gate, but beside the rampart there were a couple of wooden beams mounting sharpened stakes that could be lifted and set down to block the entrance.

'Have you come from Luguvallium, sir?' the legionary asked him. He was a stocky man, and his segmented cuirass made him look even broader and more powerful. Yet Ferox could sense that he was nervous and was not someone who liked to make decisions.

He shook his head. 'No, we came from the north. Trouble?' he asked.

'Might be, sir. One of the tribesmen came in this morning, saying that he had seen boats on a beach a couple of miles away. Three or four of them. I sent a man out to look – one of my best. But he hasn't come back.'

'Gone long?'

'Long enough, sir. He took the only horse we have,' he added gloomily. There was no beacon outside the tower, nothing to light and give warning to the countryside or bring help from the troops four or five miles away at Luguvallium. 'I was about to send one of the lads on foot with a report.' He held up a tablet sealed with wax.

Ferox told one of the scouts to carry the message. 'Go to the fort and tell them to send out at least forty men.' With a dozen or so warriors in each boat, there could be a significant band of raiders nearby, so better to be prepared. 'If you meet anyone on the way warn them of the danger.' He sent the other man with him. 'Ride together, but your job is to find the Lords Crispinus and Cerialis and make sure they know of the danger. Suggest they come here if this is the closest shelter.'

'Have you got any dry kindling, anything that will burn?' He turned to the legionary.

'Sir?'

'I'm going to look for these boats, and if I find them, then I will see if I can burn them, so I want to be able to start a fire.'

The man understood, and rushed off, shouting to his men.

'So, we're going to set light to some boats?' Vindex asked.

'That's the idea.'

'And you think their owners might not be keen on the idea.'

'Probably not.' Ferox patted him on the shoulder. 'You don't have to come. After all, I have to keep you safe now that you're a responsible married man.'

'Piss off.'

'Ah, good man.' This was to the outpost commander who had returned with a sack of straw and twigs and two torches, the heads soaked in tar.

'We use them to light up the top of the tower at night,' he explained. 'Is that enough? We have got a couple more.'

'That will do splendidly. I'd be grateful for the loan of a *lancea* if you have one.' The legionary beckoned to one of his men, who handed his slim spear to the centurion. Ferox hefted it and felt the balance. 'Thank you.'

'Look!' The shout came from the man at the top of the tower. He was leaning on the rail of the balcony, pointing, but the rampart blocked their view. 'Farm on fire!'

'There's a beacon anyway,' Ferox said to the legionary as they slung the sack over his blanket roll. He took one of the torches and gave the other to Vindex. 'Time for us to go.'

'Good luck, sir!'

'And to you.' Raiders willing to burn a house were not worried about hiding, and it probably meant that they had come to take heads. A few dead villagers might satisfy young warriors hungry to prove themselves, but they might try to win even greater fame by killing the little garrison here – or better yet a tribune, a prefect and the half-dozen troopers escorting them if they happened to stray across them. Ferox was not sure whether he was riding away from or into danger, but he did know that the raiders would need their boats to get home, or face a very long walk through country where it would be easy for the Romans to find them.

'How many do you reckon?' Vindex asked.

'I'd guess at least one for each boat. Either youngsters or older men who aren't as nimble as they used to be. Doesn't sound as if there are many patrols along the coast, so they probably would not leave more and weaken the band.' The Silures used to sail and row across the Channel to raid the northern Durotriges and even the Dumnonii further west, until the Romans stopped them by putting little outposts near some of the best landing places. When he was seven he had hidden under some sacks and sailed on one expedition, and still remembered the terror when he was discovered and the crew joked about throwing him overboard. Instead they left him with the older boys and an old boat wright to look after the boats. It seemed weeks before the men returned with two captive women and began the voyage home. He doubted that the Novantae did things that differently. They would be sensitive about their boats, but would also want all their best men with the main raiding force.

Vindex thought about it for a while. 'So we need to kill three or four, maybe more?'

'Or just drive them away.'

'Oh yes, of course, easy as that. What if the rest of them turn up while we're there? They've hit that farm, might be enough for them to think of going home to boast.'

'That's fine, I have it all planned out. In that case we run away, very, very fast.'

Vindex laughed. 'Just wanted to hear you say it.'

They kept inland. The man had claimed to see the boats further along, a least a couple of miles away, and Ferox led them along the slope of the low hills so that they could see some way inland. There was no more sign of the raiders, apart from the column of dirty smoke rising from the burning farm.

'That's where I'd land,' Ferox said, pointing ahead, and he led them up the slope. Near the crest he stopped the mare and jumped down, creeping forward until he could peer over to scan the beach. The tide was coming in, covering the pale sand, and at first he saw nothing. 'There.' A lone figure stood flicking pebbles into the water, having to walk quite a way to find each one because there were few on the beach. A little way behind him was a high bank covered in scrub and a few stunted trees. In front of the bank were dark shapes, covered in brush. He counted three, but suspected another was out of sight behind the bank. He showed Vindex their quarry, and then the two men headed back behind the crest and rode along the hillside. They came to a defile, leading towards the beach. It meandered down, so that for a while they wondered whether it would take them away from the hidden boats, and then suddenly the beach was in front of them, the lad flicking another stone into the waves.

'Come on,' Ferox said quietly. There was no sense in stealth so speed was their only choice. The grey mare responded instantly, as if she was as fresh as the dawn, and shot down the gentle slope, feet quiet on the sand. Vindex followed.

The lad turned, bent to pick up a stone and then straightened up, staring in horror. Closer, another young tribesman loomed up from behind one of the bushes, a javelin in his hand. Ferox threw first, the lancea quivering in flight and striking lower than he had aimed, driving into the lad's stomach. He folded over, screaming in agony. The boy who had been searching for stones reached for a dagger at his belt, then though better of it and turned to run. Ferox had drawn his gladius by now, and when he drew level was about to cut, then changed his mind and jabbed down with the pommel. The youth dropped like a sack of old clothes.

Frost kept going, and it was a moment before he could wheel her round to face the boats. The youth was still down and not moving. An older man and a very young boy were with the boats. Each had a spear, although in the boy's case this was no more than a sharpened stick. Suddenly he ran straight at Ferox, and the older man cursed and came after him. The boy was fast, sprinting across the sand, his crude spear held low. Vindex was faster, cantering down behind the two Novantae. He hurled his spear, a heavier shafted weapon than the light lancea, and it was starting to drop from sheer weight when it hit the old man in the thigh.

'Drop it, boy!' Ferox yelled, swerving his mare out of the way. Vindex was on the other side, and the boy stopped, turning to each of them, jabbing with his spear even though they were out of reach. The old man was sitting on the sand, spear still in his leg. He was groaning loudly as the blood pooled around him, and suddenly the boy noticed him and screamed words they did not catch. He let the sharpened stick fall to the ground, dodged when Vindex tried to grab him, and ran to the old man.

Ferox dismounted. 'Let me look,' he ordered. The wound was bad, the old man's leathery face already paling from loss of blood. 'Find me rope or cord, boy. Quickly.' The lad nodded and ran off to the nearest boat. 'Give me a hand,' he called to

Vindex. There was a dagger in the man's belt and Ferox drew it and tossed it away.

'This is going to hurt, father,' Ferox said as softly as he could. He nodded to the Brigantian. 'Now.' Ferox held the old man as tightly as he could while Vindex yanked the spearhead out of the man's leg, bringing another great gush of blood.

'Bollocks,' Vindex hissed as the blood soaked his trousers. The boy had brought rope and Ferox tied it hard above the wound. 'Get moss, or anything to stuff in there,' he said to the lad.

'Thank you,' the old man said, but his eyes were hard and suspicious. 'Brigantian?'

'He is,' Ferox told him. 'I am a Silure.'

'Never heard of them.' The old man's breath was coming in gasps. He might live long enough for his friends to find him or he might not. It was doubtful that they would be able to move him.

'Tell me, father,' Ferox asked him as gently as he could, 'what do you know of the men of the night, the black men?' He could see Vindex frowning, but ignored him.

For the first time, the old man was terrified. 'Do not speak their name! Please, not now, not now.' He struggled, and the rope loosened, sending a gout of blood soaking into the sand. The old man flung himself to the side, reaching for his dagger. Vindex drew back his bloodied spear to thrust, but the man collapsed, shook twice and then died.

'What was that all about?' he asked the centurion. Ferox was not paying any attention, for the boy had returned and was staring at the dead man. His eyes were glassy, his mouth hung open, but the child made no sound.

'Come on,' Ferox said, 'let's go and light some fires.' In the event it was easy, for the Novantae had lit a fire in the shelter of the dunes and the embers were still warm and easily coaxed back to life. Ferox used some of the kindling to get it going again. In the meantime, Vindex piled anything that would burn into the nearest boat. It was long and slim, designed to be rowed, and made from wood planks, as was the boat beside it, and he spread some of the flammable material onto that one as well, smashing a couple of the oars to add to the pyre. The other two boats had wooden frames covered in stretched hides. 'What are we going to do with those?' he asked.

'Cut one up as well as we can,' Ferox said, wishing now that he had asked for an axe at the tower. For some reason he had just assumed that they would come in wooden boats. 'Slash any cord you can find and make holes in the hide. Use this,' he handed over his pugio, for the heavy blade could be punched with some force.

'Why not the other one as well?' Vindex asked.

'Leave it. That way some of them can get away, but most cannot. Should help the harmony of their merry band.'

Vindex shook his head. 'You really are a vicious bastard, aren't you?'

'I'm a Silure.'

'And a Roman.' Vindex kissed the wheel of Taranis he wore around his neck. 'At least you're on my side.'

Ferox held one of the torches in the fire, turning it slowly as the tarred head caught alight. 'Here...' he passed it to the Brigantian '... take this.' He picked up the second torch and repeated the process. It took a while for the fires in the boats to light. The wind was blowing hard off the sea and they had to crouch over the kindling to shelter it. Eventually the flames caught and grew.

'Good enough,' Ferox said. Even if the Novantae came back soon and managed to put them out they would not be able to use either boat, especially if the wind remained strong and stirred up the waves.

The boy was still with the old man, sitting next to him and holding his cold hand. Over on the sand, the lad Ferox had knocked out lay still, but they could see that he was still breathing

'Leave them,' Ferox said in answer to the unspoken question. 'Let their own folk look after them. Unless you want a slave for your new wife?'

Vindex ignored the suggestion. 'Poor kid,' he said. Ferox was not listening. There was a horseman up on the path they had followed down to the beach. He was a tribesman, his hair washed in lime and combed up in a spiked fringe, his face striped with blue paint. He wore a pale yellow and green checked tunic and dark trousers, and carried a little round shield and a spear. His horse was a warm brown with black legs, mane and tail, and like so many army horses its saddle and harness decorated with round silvered *phalerae*.

'Looks like they did get the trooper,' Ferox said. The man stared at them and at the smoke rising from the boats, before turning and galloping off. That meant his friends were not with him, but did not tell them how far behind they were.

'We'd better go,' Vindex said, swinging up into the saddle.

Ferox led his mare over to the boy. 'Good luck, son,' he said. 'The others will come back to get you soon.' The lad stared up at him, his cheeks wet with tears and stung by the wind. 'Boy, have you heard of the men of the night?' He was not really expecting an answer, but found himself asking the question anyway and did not know why. A gull was on the sand, probably drawn by the smell of blood, but contenting itself for the moment with pecking at an old shell. It stopped, its beak a vivid yellow and its wicked eyes staring into his.

'They say they came long ago as a curse on the lands.' The words were whispered, so that Ferox had to strain to hear them. 'They came from the sea to kill men and eat their flesh. Now they sleep under waves, until a storm rouses them to feed again.' At last the boy looked up, challenging him. 'They say that it is bad luck even to mention them.' There was a belligerence in his tone, as if he was willing the curse on the Roman.

'Good luck, son,' Ferox said again, and hauled himself onto Frost's back. The seagull still watched him, and he wondered what god or spirit possessed it.

They rode along the beach, not risking going back the way they had come in case the rest of the Novantae were close. The tide was still coming in, and at times they had to go through the foamy surf, spray flying up from the feet of their horses before they reached another patch of firm sand.

Cloud came in off the sea, bringing a fine drizzle and blotting from sight the far shore. It also meant that they did not see the pillar of smoke until they were closer. The hills blocked their view, but both men knew that it came from the direction of the tower.

'We're humped,' Vindex said as they rode on.

VII

THE HOUSES WERE burning, the smoke whipped by the wind towards the tower. They risked riding up onto the ridge because the only Novantae they could see were on foot. Most of the warriors were clustered in the ditch or on the slope of the earth rampart surrounding the watchtower. With so few men, it was too large a circuit for the garrison to defend against the thirty or so tribesmen attacking it. He could not see any dead or injured warriors, but at least one of the Romans was dead, lying outside the gate where he must have been surprised by the attack. There really ought to have been time for him to flee through the entrance, so Ferox wondered whether the man had frozen and been caught. That would leave just five men to hold the place, so the legionary had wisely drawn back into the tower. The warriors would have to expose themselves to javelins and other missiles if they tried to break in, but the Romans were trapped, and if the attackers could use the fire from the burning houses to set light to the tower itself, then they would be left with the choice of choking, burning, or running out to be cut down.

'Is this where we run away, very fast?' Vindex asked.

It was the wise thing. They had one spear between them, for the lancea's shaft had snapped when he had tried to free it from the dead warrior. With more missiles and the speed of their horses, they might have been able to nip at the band of tribesmen, bringing one or two of them down while keeping out of harm's way. Two of them could not hope to do much more than die with the garrison if they charged in.

'Hello,' the Brigantian added, a moment later, 'he's made good time.' The warrior riding the captured horse came streaking across the hilltop, heading for the men clustered around the rampart of the tower. 'This'll make 'em angry.'

Ferox grinned. 'You mean they weren't already? They're Novantae, they were born angry.'

'Time to go, then?'

A trumpet blared and a lone horseman came up over the lip of the hill, his deep green cloak billowing behind him as the tall black horse pounded across the turf towards the fort. The high red crest of his glittering helmet rippled as he sped towards the tower, sword raised high. A moment later another man came, riding a dark bay horse, wearing a yellow-brown cloak and with a spear held underarm like a hunter. Then there were six or seven more, all galloping, and one was the *tubicen*, still sounding the charge, the notes on his thin bronze trumpet ragged as they surged forward. He and most of the others had green shields and the tops of their helmets were dark.

'Heroes,' Vindex said wearily. The leader was Crispinus, with Cerialis and his Batavians close behind. 'I'm guessing we can't run away any more.' Ferox set Snow into a canter and was off. 'No,' the Brigantian added, 'I guess not,' and followed.

Snow was tired, and Ferox had to reach back and slap her to force the mare into a gallop. A few of the Novantae saw them and turned, but most were looking at the main charge. For a moment Ferox hoped that they were just the leaders, and that behind the tribune and prefect was a *turma* or two sent from Luguvallium. There was not, and there were only the officers

87

and their escort. He noticed Claudius Super with the leading Batavians, the high transverse crest of his helmet marking him out as a centurion. It would have been better if the horsemen had kept their distance, using their javelins, but it was too much to expect prudence and good sense when three officers were together.

Crispinus was several lengths ahead of the others. A spear was thrown at him and passed harmlessly overhead. The tribune headed straight for the entrance to the circular rampart, hacking at a warrior as he passed, but the man flung himself to the ground before the blow struck and the young aristocrat kept going. Then Ferox saw him drop his sword and grab hold of his horse's mane. The animal tensed and jumped and he realised that the garrison must have drawn the spiked timber barricades across the gap in the rampart. Crispinus' black stallion seemed to sail through the air, and then vanished into the little outpost. Behind him, Cerialis had seen the danger. He leaned to the side to drive his spear into the back of the warrior on the ground, pinning him to the earth, and then put his bay at the barricade. Warriors were rushing towards him. His horse stuttered in its rhythm, and then Ferox wondered whether he had jumped too soon, before it flew up and over.

Claudius Super was not so well mounted, or as fine a horseman, or perhaps it was just that his gelding was disconcerted by the warriors swarming around him. The animal stopped, rearing as a spear was thrust into its chest, and the centurion was flung down. One of the Batavians threw his javelin and spitted the man who had wounded the animal, but he and the other troopers had all halted, milling around outside the ramparts. Another horse was struck, another rider down in the grass, and two warriors were on him in a moment, slashing with their long, blunt-tipped swords.

Ferox saw that the mounted warrior was coming for him. He nudged Snow so that the mare shifted a little to bring him up on the man's left side. They were closing fast, but the captured horse was tired or did not trust its rider and began to swerve away. Snow barged against its rear, nearly unseating the warrior, and Ferox slashed with his gladius, opening the man's throat.

He rode on, straight at the confused mêlée outside the entrance. The tubicen was leaning against the neck of his horse, his scale armour punctured by a spear that had driven deep into his belly. Hands reached up and pulled him down. Another Batavian's face was a mass of blood from the blow of a sling stone. Claudius Super was on his feet, helmet gone, his back against the sloping rampart and sword flicking from one opponent to the next.

A man flung himself down in front of Ferox, spear held ready to thrust up into the horse or ram between its legs to trip it. Snow was galloping too fast to stop or avoid him, so he copied the other officers and gripped the mare's mane, urging her into the jump. He felt that wonderful power as the horse leaped, heard a dull thump as one of her feet struck something and then she was over, running on, uninjured as far as he could tell, and there was a scream as Vindex came on slowly and speared the man as he lay stunned.

The three uninjured Batavians had all sprung down from their horses, which ran away from the noise and the fighting. They stood protectively round the blinded man, keeping the warriors at bay for the moment, until one wearing mail and a bronze helmet jumped forward, pushed a spear aside with his shield and thrust with his sword into a trooper's face. Other warriors were scrambling up the rampart and climbing over the parapet. Someone was shouting, the words lost amid the chaos of men and horses.

Two warriors were in Ferox's path, their stout spears levelled, and Frost would not face them but skidded to a stop. Vindex arrived, making the men flinch, and Ferox was able to urge the mare past the tip of one man's spear and cut down hard, missing his head but biting into the warrior's bare shoulder. The warrior cursed and thrust at him one-handed, the spearhead hitting him in the side without breaking through his mail. He slashed down again, the blade slicing across the man's face, so that his nose and a flap of skin from his cheek hung down. The warrior swung his spear like a staff, hitting the Roman across the belly, and Frost was startled, pulling away, so that Ferox lost his balance and fell, slamming hard into the ground.

For a moment, the horse was between them, but the grey leaped away and the warrior came at him, his face a ruin, shoulder bleeding, and spear held firmly in both hands. Ferox rolled, the spearhead sinking into the turf where he had lain, and then rolled again, as the man yanked it free and stabbed again. The centurion was on his front and somehow he still held the bone grip of his gladius so he flailed with the sword, hitting the man above the ankle, shearing through muscle and bone to cut through the leg. Vindex was leaning down from the saddle, reaching to help haul Ferox to his feet, his own opponent lying sobbing on his back, clutching at the great gash in his stomach.

Ferox saw that Snow was too far away to catch and ran alongside the Brigantian's horse as he headed for the tower. Most of the warriors were still clustered around the Batavians. One threw a spear at Vindex, hitting his horse on the shoulder, and the animal quivered, sinking down on its front knees. The scout jumped down, but the warrior fled as Ferox charged towards him.

Outside the entrance another Batavian was down, jabbed in the belly by the mail-clad warrior. The legionary in command of the outpost appeared, which meant that they had pushed the spiked barricade open to create a gap. The man punched a warrior with the boss of his heavy shield, making him rock back, so that a thrust took him in the throat. The gladius stuck, and a moment later the tribesman in mail cut with all his strength, slicing through the legionary's wrist so that his hand was left clutching the blade as the stump pumped blood across the warrior.

The last of the Batavians hustled his wounded comrades in through the entrance, Claudius Super shouting that he would protect them. The senior regional centurion went for the mail-clad warrior, jabbing low and making the man jump back. Ferox saw that Vindex was with him and pushed forward, grabbing the shaft of a spear to push it aside and rolling his wrist to thrust over a warrior's little shield into his chest. The wound was not deep, but the man gave back, gasping for breath and letting go of his spear.

Claudius Super tried to grab the mail-clad leader's arm with his left hand and punch at his face with his sword, but the Novantian was too strong and fast for him. He slammed his small round shield into the Roman's face, breaking his nose, and then brought it down and then up under his chin. The centurion fell, and the warrior steadied himself and then raised his sword to jab down.

Ferox charged at the man, screaming, and the noise made the leader turn before he struck. The Roman cut down, because there was not time for a properly aimed thrust and he felt his arm jar as the blade hit the man's shield. Vindex was beside him, facing another man with a long sword and a heavy silver torc around his neck.

The man in mail stepped back, so that the stunned Claudius Super was just behind him, and levelled his shield. His sword was an army issue *spatha*, the long blades used mainly by the cavalry, and he knew how to use it. Ferox knew that it was only a matter of moments before other warriors closed around him and it would be hard to beat a man with the longer reach, so he jumped, hurling himself at the tribesman just as his mare had cleared the warrior on the ground. It took the man by surprise and he cut down too late because Ferox was already past the main force of the blow, his whole weight slamming into the Novantian's body. His feet were against the downed Claudius Super, and the man was pitched over, Ferox on top of him, pounding at his head with the pommel of his gladius.

Distracted for a moment, Vindex's opponent gave him an opening and the Brigantian cut down, his sword ringing where it hit the man's torc, but knocking him down with the sheer force of the blow.

'Come on!' Crispinus had appeared, a long spear in his hands. Ferox hit the warrior in the face once more and pushed himself up. The downed man was not moving, and the centurion grabbed the shoulder doubling of Claudius Super's mail cuirass and started dragging him into the shelter of the rampart. Vindex faced the other warriors, who for the moment were hanging back and he taunted them, begging them to come and be killed. None of them did.

'Come on, you fool!' Ferox screamed at his friend and pulled the unconscious Super through the slim gap into the enclosure. There were two dead Novantae inside, and another bleeding out his life from cuts to the body and legs, as well as the tribune's black horse lying on its side, a broken spear deep in its belly. Cerialis stood, wild-eyed, his cuirass and face stained red and the blade of his sword dirty. For the moment, the other warriors had retreated to the far side of the parapet. A stone rattled against the side of the tower next to the prefect and he jeered at the man who had thrown it. The legionary was being helped inside the tower itself.

'Stop pissing about!' Ferox yelled. 'Get inside, you pillock!'

Vindex spat and then strolled through the entrance. Ferox watched to see that no one came at him from behind, but for the moment the enemy seemed cowed. He guessed that the man in mail was the main leader, and saw that another man was kneeling beside him, helping him to sit up.

A stone struck his side, at the same spot where he had been grazed the previous month and Ferox knew that it would be sore tomorrow. He helped the last of the wounded men into the tower. Vindex followed, and they dropped the heavy bar to hold it shut and followed the others up the ladder to the next storey, the fit struggling to lift the injured. Once they were there the room was crowded, but they managed to pull the ladder up after them.

'That should hold them,' Crispinus said, his attempt to sound calm ruined when his voice cracked into a squeak. 'I mean that should hold them,' he said in a deep bass and smiled.

Ferox pushed through the crowd to the other ladder, which led up to the top. There was an auxiliary up there, lurking in the doorway so that he could see out but was not exposed on the veranda.

'What have you got to throw?'

'Just that, sir,' the man replied, judging from his tone that the newcomer was someone senior. He gestured at a basket half-full of stones from the beach. They were rounded, chosen to fit into the palm of a man's hand, and from this height they could give a nasty blow, and even crack a skull or break a bone if they hit just right.

Vindex's cadaverous face appeared through the trapdoor. He was grinning, filled with that strange exhilaration that came sometimes in battle. Ferox knew the mood well, although he did not feel it today. It made a man feel that he could do anything.

'Help me,' he said, grabbing one of the handles on the basket. The Brigantian took the other and they dragged it over to the doorway. Ferox took one stone, hefting it, but before he could do anything else, Vindex plucked up a stone in each hand and strode out onto the balcony. He raised his right arm and threw in one motion, and Ferox heard a cry from down below. By the time the Brigantian shifted the other stone into his right hand and flung it down, Ferox was outside and saw the missile strike a warrior full in the face, snapping his head back. The man dropped behind the parapet. Ferox looked for a target, saw a man bob up over the rampart, whirl a sling, and ducked. The stone clipped against the fence rail on the edge of the platform and pinged harmlessly up. He rose, threw his own stone, but the man had vanished and it hit the parapet a good few feet away from where he had aimed.

'Mongrels!' Vindex yelled, and seemed to be enjoying himself. Ferox wondered about trying to wrestle him back inside the room and decided against it. It would be a hard struggle considering the mood the Brigantian was in, and for the moment the danger was not so very great. Instead he handed him a couple of stones.

Crispinus appeared, pulling himself up through the trapdoor and then drawing breath. 'That's a steep climb,' he said, grinning.

'Worse for the man coming next,' Ferox said before he could help himself. The tribune frowned, and the next man up was Cerialis. 'Old joke in the legions,' Ferox explained. 'Back from the days before they wore breeches. A man's climbing up the ladders in an assault tower and says, "Phew, this is hard work."

The man coming after replies, "Maybe, but it's better than staring at your arse.'"

Crispinus was about to say something when a sling stone banged loudly against the wall. Vindex had ducked just in time. He sprang up. 'Bastards!' he yelled, and hurled both the stones in his hand. 'Serves you right!'

Crispinus had flinched and did his best to appear relaxed. 'Everything in hand, centurion?'

'For the moment, my lord.'

'Good, good.' The tribune decided that he must go out onto the veranda, which meant that Cerialis was obliged to follow. The taller man hunched slightly as he came through the door, and stayed like that, no doubt keenly aware that he presented a much bigger target than the short aristocrat. Ferox followed, offering each man a stone.

'We shouldn't bunch up, my lords,' he said.

'Of course.' Crispinus did not move. He was tossing the stone from hand to hand, searching for a target. 'We should have no trouble holding them off until help comes from Luguvallium.'

'If they don't smoke us out, my lord,' Ferox said. He had seen that a couple of the warriors were carrying torches lit from the burning farm. 'We need to keep them back, but we are running out of missiles.'

'I see.' Crispinus tossed the stone he was holding back into the basket. 'Better not waste this then. Do you think they will keep attacking?'

'They've lost a lot of men,' Ferox explained. 'Down!' he yelled, for a couple of warriors had popped up above the parapet. A sling stone gave a dull clang as it hit the top of Crispinus' helmet, yanking it sideways so that one of the cheek pieces drove into his skin and drew blood. A javelin sank into the fence around the platform and stuck there.

Vindex had not ducked and flung a stone, hitting one of the warriors on the shoulder before he vanished behind cover. Cerialis told the auxiliary to help Crispinus back inside. The tribune's eyes were glassy, but Ferox doubted that the blow was serious.

'Will they try to burn us out?' Cerialis asked, crouching behind the fence with Ferox.

'Depends on their pride,' he said. 'It might be we've stung them and they feel they must kill us in vengeance. Be another hour at least before anyone comes from Luguvallium, so they've got time.'

If the prefect was nervous he did not show it. He glanced down at the stone in his hand.

'Then again, they've lost a lot of men.' He saw the question in the prefect's eyes. 'Oh, I know they've still got plenty, but seven or eight of them are down, and that's a lot of people to lose on a raid. We've burned their boats, so most will have to find another way home.' Cerialis looked surprised, and Ferox realised that he had not had a chance to report what he and Vindex had done. 'So what they really need now is horses to get away. They've picked up some from us. Yours and mine, my lord, I'm sorry to say, as well as the ones from the troopers.' Cerialis' horse had vanished from the enclosure while they were climbing the tower, so a warrior must have sneaked inside and led it out.

Ferox stood up. Vindex was prowling up and down the platform, stone in hand, waiting for the next warrior to appear, but he did not look at him. The centurion pointed, and the prefect stood up beside him so that he could see properly. Five warriors were riding up past the burning farm, leading another half-dozen horses.

'I thought that might happen,' Ferox said. 'There didn't seem to be quite as many of them as there should have been.' He stared past the riders out onto the plains. The neat herd of a few hours ago was scattered, the little shapes of brown cows spread over the fields in ones, twos and small clusters.

'You will have to explain, centurion.'

'There was a herd of cattle out there, belonging to Probus, I'm guessing. Cows are not much good to these lads – how would you get one in a boat? – but the herdsmen had horses.' Now that they were closer Ferox could see the severed heads dangling from the spears of the riders.

'Poor devils,' Cerialis whispered, half to himself.

'Aye. Still, I'll not pretend I'd rather it were us than them,' Ferox said. 'They may have given that bunch a chance to get home and us a chance to live.'

A warrior swung over the top of the parapet and dropped onto the walkway of the rampart. He had a burning torch in each hand, and had waited until the restless Vindex was on the opposite side of the platform. Ferox shouted a warning, snatched the stone from the prefect and ran to the fence, but by the time he reached the spot the warrior had run underneath them and was out of sight. Another man bobbed up, spear ready, so the centurion flung his stone. The man ducked back.

'Come on out and fight in the open!' Vindex was even wilder than before, and for an instant Ferox was afraid that he would swing his legs over the fence and try to jump down from the top of the tower. The warrior appeared again, sprinting for the entrance this time. 'Got you!' the Brigantian yelled. His first stone went high, the second was flung in a rage and hit the barricade instead. The warrior ran out and vanished.

'Brave man,' Cerialis said. Ferox was trying to lean out and look down towards the door of the tower. He could not see smoke, and the smell of burning might be no more than the torches. Suddenly he was dragged back just as a sling stone bounced off the rail where he had been. Cerialis had him around the waist.

'Apologies, centurion, but it seemed necessary.'

The door did not burn, and once the Novantae realised this they began to leave. Ten loped off towards the boats. The rest waited for a short while and rode off towards the ford. Two rode double, supporting wounded comrades, and two more had captive women slung across the necks of their horses, and Ferox felt flat as he saw them because he knew that for the moment there was nothing he could do. They must have come from the farm or another settlement. With their other trophies, the heads, the horses, and weapons including Crispinus' fine sword, there might be enough marks of victory for the leader to claim that their losses were worth it.

Ferox watched them as they went down the slope, saw them wading into the ford, but then the rain came, heavier than before, and the cloud was so low that he could not see them anymore. The scent of salt was even stronger, and the circling gulls were joined by carrion birds.

The patrol from Luguvallium arrived half an hour later. There were just fifteen of them, and Ferox wondered what fool had sent so few. Crispinus insisted on taking the horse from one of the troopers and leading the rest in pursuit, berating the decurion in charge who insisted that he had been sent to reconnoitre and not to chase barbarians. The appearance of Cerialis left the man overwhelmed with forceful senior officers, and he gave in. Ferox doubted that they would catch up, and hoped that the two officers would have the sense not to fight unless the Novantae were careless and vulnerable.

'What about us?' Vindex asked him. He had calmed down once the enemy left, and was surprised not to be going with the cavalry.

'I'm going back to the boats.' Ferox did not explain, and the scout may have sensed that he did not really know why he wanted to go.

It was getting dark by the time they had walked to the beach. On the way, they found the headless corpse of the cavalryman sent out from the tower. The dead man looked very pale in his nakedness. There were slashes across his thighs, arms, and chest, as well as the deep wound to the stomach that had brought him down. That was the way of the Novantae, the injuries meant to weaken the man so that he would not become a danger to his killers in the Otherworld.

They cut off a couple of branches from a tree, sharpened the ends and drove one into the ground on either side of the dead man so that it would be easier for the burial party to find him.

When they got to the beach the fires had long since died down, and the carcases of the three boats looked black in the fading light. The good boat had gone, but on the beach lay the two corpses, and the little boy sitting beside the old man. He was staring out to sea, clutching the dead man's cold hand. The older lad, the one the centurion had knocked out, was nowhere to be seen.

'Why did you not go with them?' Ferox asked.

'They did not want me,' the lad said in a flat tone. He squeezed the corpse's hand even more tightly. 'My uncle was the last who cared. The others are gone.'

'How old are you, boy?'

'They say I have nine summers or maybe ten.' He was small for his age, but up close Ferox thought that to be about right.

Ferox sat down on the sand beside him. 'If you wish, we will set you on your way, give you food, and you may walk home.'

The boy said nothing, still gazing out to sea.

'Or, if you give me your word, I will take you into my service for seven years. Then you may go wherever you will.'

'I hear the Romans take boys as if they were women.'

'Some fools do,' Ferox said, 'but I do not. No one will do that with you.'

'Good,' the boy said. 'When I am a few years older I want a wife with pale skin and long black hair that she can wrap around me to tie us together for all time.'

Ferox wondered whether the child was even older, and thought again how the words of poets settled in the mind even of the young. 'It will be up to you to find her.'

'I will do it.' At last the boy turned to face him. 'What will you want as service? I can fight if you give me a sword.'

'In time,' Ferox said, managing not to smile. 'For the moment you will look after the horses. Do you know much about horses?'

'Not as much as I know about boats.' It was a boast, but Ferox sensed real knowledge behind it. He ignored Vindex's muttered 'Well, can you use a shovel?'

Ferox stood up. 'Will you swear to serve me for seven years, swear by the gods your tribe swears by and by moon and stars and the cold wind?' He thought that was the way the Novantae took an oath.

The boy got up. 'I swear.'

'Good. Then what is your name, child of the sea?'

'Some call me Bran.'

It did not sound like any name he had heard, but if the boy wanted to hide his real name then that was up to him. 'Then come with us, Bran, unless you have more to do for your uncle.'

'It is done. The sea and the birds will take him and the others.' The boy's eyes were glassy, but he did not break down.

'Come, Bran.' Ferox held out his hand and the boy took it. They walked off the beach. Vindex waited for a moment, and kissed his wheel of Taranis before he followed, wondering about the future.

VIII

N ERATIUS MARCELLUS, *legatus augusti pro praetore*
of the province of Britannia, sat on a folding chair
on the raised platform and waited for the blaring
trumpets to cease. There were a dozen *cornicines* on either side
of the dais, eight from each of the three legions represented at
this parade, and as they repeated the rising scale the blare was
enormous, drowning the warbling sound of the high Hibernian
horns, shaped liked the letter S. One of the chieftains covered
his ears.

The last hanging note of the fanfare ceased, and there was
silence, apart from the gentle rippling of flags and cloaks in
the breeze. Three officers stood behind the legate, and next to
them was the *aquilifer* of II Augusta, holding aloft the precious
standard of the legion, the gilded bird with wings upraised and
clutching a thunderbolt in its claws. The eagle did not normally
leave a legion's base unless most of the unit took the field, but
the legate had wanted one of Rome's eagles to witness the
scene, so had given specific orders. To guard it II Augusta had
sent their first cohort, twice the size of the other nine cohorts in
the legion, and drawn from the biggest and most experienced
soldiers, who stood in eight ranks behind the podium. The
other two legions stationed in Britannia had each sent two
cohorts, with VIIII Hispana parading on the right of the legate

102

and XX Valeria Victrix on the left. Altogether there were almost two and a half thousand legionaries, and over three thousand auxiliaries, a third of them cavalrymen, standing at an angle to the legionaries to form three sides of a square. The standards of all the units, more than seventy of them, were divided into two parties formed beside the trumpeters. This was the field force that the legate had assembled for the summer's manoeuvres, but it was also a grand show of strength for receiving the Hibernian rulers.

Ferox stood in front of the platform to act as interpreter. It took a while for the ringing in his ears to stop after the fanfares. The chieftain who had covered his ears shook his head a few times after the noise stopped. Otherwise, neither the kings nor their nobles and escorting warriors showed any reaction at all. They would see an army parading, shields uncovered to show their elaborate insignia, metal of armour, weapons, and fittings polished to a high sheen, leather brushed and wooden shafts oiled. Ferox would make sure that in the days to come the visitors were told that this was but a fraction of the army of the province, and that Britannia's garrison was an even smaller part of the mighty army of the emperor. It was possible that they would believe him.

Neratius Marcellus began his oration, and Ferox was relieved that the legate spoke in short, direct sentences, giving him plenty of time to translate. The Hibernians had brought a man with them who whispered an explanation to the kings, but there was no harm in making the meaning clear to all. It was bland enough stuff. Neratius Marcellus welcomed them in the name of Trajan, spoke of the great majesty, power and kindness of the emperor who ruled the world, and of his desire for friendship with all those who showed suitable respect.

Epotsorovidus, king of the Darinoi, made answer on behalf

of them all, speaking of the great fame of the emperor and their desire to be good friends and allies of Rome. The king was happy for Ferox to convey his words to the legate. He spoke of the fame of his own people, their courage and faithfulness to friends, and their great desire for peace. The king was tall and very thin, his neck long with a protruding Adam's apple, and he slurred his words as he spoke. He must have been forty and looked far older, his moustache and long pigtails dyed red, but even so showing flecks of grey. His right hand waved in the air whenever he spoke, looking weak rather than emphatic, and his voice lacked spirit. He wore armour of gilded scale, a long sword on his right hip and carried a high pointed bronze helmet under his left arm. His tunic reached to just below the knees, and beneath it his legs were thin and bony.

His queen was half his age, and just as tall, and with her raven-black hair bound in a long tress and coiled on top of her head like a tower she loomed over him. Her dress was a bright scarlet, and must have been new, for no dye would last in so bright a shade for very long, but she had covered it in a checked cloak so that only a little showed through. It was also enough to reveal the hilt of a sword, much like the one her husband wore. Her face was slim, her eyes as grey as his yet filled with a force that her husband utterly lacked. There was a hardness there, a cruelty even, at least if she felt it necessary, that almost took the edge off her beauty. Ferox had struggled not to smile when he was told that her name was Brigita. The chase to the north and rescue of the little girl seemed an age ago now, and he hoped that she was getting over the terror of capture, and going back to terrorising her family into looking after their animals and crops properly.

King Brennus of the Rhobogdioi was far shorter, with a great round belly, made all the bigger by the loose-fitting mail that hung around him like a tent lifted in the wind. He had a thick beard, and if he had a wife or wives he had not brought them along. There was cunning in his eyes, the cleverness of a child who thought only of himself and how to get what he wanted. He said nothing, content to let others speak on his behalf, and his gaze flicked around. Often he stared at the queen, and his desire was obvious, and no doubt shared by most of the soldiers who could see this tall woman.

Afterwards, the legate withdrew, and Crispinus led the Hibernians to a meal prepared for them in a large tent, big enough to accommodate a hundred people. An officer was detailed to accompany each of the chiefs and other leaders, while soldiers from the legate's *singulares*, a bodyguard picked from all the auxiliary units in the province, matched the number of their warriors. There was no woman to accompany the queen, for this was a day for the army and the rules of the camp applied. Brigita did not appear to mind, but she said nothing, letting the men do all the talking. It was not a great feast, but slaves brought in delicacies and the first gifts of many. There were Roman swords and finely engraved helmets for the kings, a yellow silk dress for the queen, who barely looked at it, and made Ferox wonder whether a sword might have been a better choice.

By this time, the parade had reformed and each unit was ready to march past in all their finery. Crispinus bade his guests walk out and stand in front of the pavilion. Legio II Augusta led, eagle at its head. The Hibernians said nothing, and simply watched the soldiers marching past. Ferox noticed one or two of the warriors thought it funny to see so many men in neat rows, marching in step. The other legions followed, then the auxiliary infantry. Several of their prefects were with the guests and he sensed each man become more alert as his own unit approached, nerves and pride mingling, since they did not want the slightest blemish to appear among their own soldiers.

'They must be marching round in a circle,' Brennus said before the parade was even half way through.

The cavalry brought up the rear, always a wise precaution on a day like this, for they left behind them a field dotted with piles of manure. Ferox thought of Bran, who was in the army's tented camp under Philo's supervision and tasked with caring for Frost and the new horse he had bought to replace the stolen Snow.

'No chariots,' Brennus muttered when the last horsemen had passed. His tone suggested a degree of pity for the Romans as well as satisfaction in his own might.

An escort took the guests to some roundhouses hastily constructed for them in an annex of the main camp, and Ferox breathed a sigh of relief that his task was over for the day. Tomorrow, Crispinus would take the Hibernians to a farm near Alauna. It was owned by Probus, and said to be large and comfortable, and would house the visitors during the negotiations to come. The merchant had offered it to the legate and tribune, presumably in the hope of general or specific favours. Cerialis and Sulpicia Lepidina were to join them, as was Aelius Brocchus and his wife.

Ferox walked away from the camp to be alone and to think. Neratius Marcellus had his main force in a low ramparted marching camp near the foot of the hill of Aballava, and after a while Ferox turned to look back at the smoke of cooking rising from the tent-lines. A more permanent fort was to be built a little further away, to house a reinforced cohort, but work had not yet begun on its construction. Up on the hill, the silhouette of the watchtower was dark against the skyline. The legate also planned to demolish the outpost and replace it with a proper fort. During the coming months, the army would train and build, and build and train, as the army always seemed to do whenever senior officers were worried that the soldiers might become idle. In the meantime, he was bound to meet Sulpicia Lepidina, and he did not know what to say to her, or what he should not say.

A horseman trotted towards him. It was Claudius Super, still bandaged around the arm and head but riding well, and in these open plains Ferox could not vanish or pretend that he had not seen the man.

'Ferox, my dear fellow, I have been looking for you.'

'Just stretching my legs, sir.'

'Don't blame you.' The senior regionarius jumped down, wincing a little when he struck the ground. 'Being here, and seeing that tower, does take me back to our battle.'

It had scarcely been a battle, which did not mean that those who fell were any less dead than the men at Cannae or Arausio.

'I am glad to see that you are recovering,' Ferox said, because it was what he ought to say. In truth, since the skirmish Claudius Super had been openly grateful, praising his courage and skill. It was a change from the contempt he had so often shown in the past.

'For that I owe you my thanks. In fact, that is why I have sought you out. You saved my life.'

'There were others there.'

'There were, and your modesty becomes you, but it does not change the truth. If you and your scout had not come when you did then I doubt that I would have made it into the tower.' He had a bag hanging from one of the horns of his saddle and reached into it. 'I'm not much of a craftsman, but it is my duty to give you this, as one citizen to another.' It was a wreath of oak leaves, woven clumsily, so that a lot of twine was needed to hold it together. 'The legate is agreeable, and the report will go to the emperor and a proper crown be made when it is awarded formally.'

'You do not need to do this, sir.' The *corona civica* was one of the oldest awards, given for saving the life of a fellow citizen.

'Oh, I do. Traditions are important, don't you think? They are what makes us Romans.' The tradition was that the saved man make a wreath and give it to his rescuer, although it was a rare custom these days. Claudius Super took the old ways seriously, perhaps because he was so desperately proud of his family name and worried by their lack of great wealth.

'If the noble Crispinus had not come out through the gap in the barricade then I am not sure any of us would have made it. Grateful though I am for you acclaim, is it not fitter that you give this to him? I am sure the legate would acknowledge his claim to the award. He is a brave young man in his first post.' Ferox did not bother to add that this meant he was likely to rise high, that the corona civica would do his career no end of good, and that such a man was likely to prove a more useful friend in the future than a mere centurion. He could see the other man coming to the same conclusion, a little slowly, for his was not a quick mind.

'I still believe you should have this.' To his credit, Claudius Super was reluctant to give up his first idea.

'Many years ago, another citizen presented me with a crown. He was killed sixth months later. I would rather not wish such ill fortune on you.'

'Would you not?' Claudius Super grinned. 'I have scarcely been a friend to you in the last few years. If it is any consolation, I apologise for my behaviour. You are a fine officer and a good Roman, and I should probably have listened to your advice more often in the past.'

'Then take it now. Give the wreath to the tribune. It will mean so much to him and he is a brave man, worthy of honour.'

'Very well.' Claudius Super offered his hand and Ferox shook it. 'At least you have taken that from me. Good fortune as you help the tribune with these Hibernian rascals. Dare say they want gold and weapons from us and will only give us a couple of glass beads. That queen looks a bit of an amazon, though. Did you see her sword? Pretty enough, but not sure I'd fancy meeting her on a dark night. Oh, I don't know, though.' He leered at Ferox.

'Good luck, sir,' Ferox called as Claudius Super rode off, still thinking that he had rarely met a bigger fool.

IX

THE HOUSE WAS large and L-shaped, the smaller wing containing a bath. A line of rowan trees grew beyond it on the side facing the sea, and in years to come they might become tall and thick and help to take the bite out of the strong westerly winds, but for the moment they were young and small. The house itself was new, the red-brown tiles still clean with scarcely any patches of moss and dirt to dull the brightness of the baked clay. Its rendered walls gleamed in the sunlight, finished only at the end of the previous summer. One day, it seemed that additional wings would be built to form a square, and a garden was already taking shape in what would become the middle. It had a pond in the centre, although the fountain did not yet work. A short distance away was a barn and stable, as well as a couple of squat, plainer buildings to house the slaves and freedmen who worked here. Two others, a workshop and a big storeroom, remained half-finished, but work on them was suspended in deference to the visitors.

Ferox got the impression that the Hibernians would have preferred something more familiar, preferably thatched and round, but the distinguished guests accepted rooms in the main house. A few of their servants and warriors stayed with them, while the rest went to the slaves' quarters. Crispinus was full of praise for the house, which their host modestly declined, saying that the tribune was too generous. It was all a charade and both men knew it, but played their part as civilised men. Compared to many of the villas in southern Britannia, let alone those in Gaul, this was a modest establishment, the inside still heavy with the scent of limewash and new wood. By the standards of the estates in Italy and Spain it was tiny and crude, and it was one of three owned by Probus, the only one up in the north. The other two he had bought rather than built, and his hints implied that they were a good deal grander.

Probus was a man of medium height who seemed a lot taller until you stood beside him. Both the king and queen of the Darinoi topped him by several inches, but it seemed that they had met him before and he greeted them warmly. As Crispinus had said, Probus still had the air of a soldier, his movements neat and controlled, his long tunic hitched up high by a decorated belt, and his hair kept short. There was an old scar above his right eye, and others on his shins and arms. He spoke clear and precise Latin, the sort learned from a tutor, with only the odd word hinting at a Rhineland accent. His face was round, his frame big, like a lot of men with some Germanic blood. For all his careful manners and courtesy, it was when he had come in from the estate, smelling of damp wool and sweat, that he seemed most natural and, even when still, there was a sense of restless energy and sheer force about him.

Ferox did not trust him, and was not sure why. Genialis was with his father, urged into a lifeless speech of thanks to the centurion for saving him. It was enough to content the father, but the youth was always on the edge of things, looking sullen and resentful, except when he saw the queen, when his expression changed to one of blatant desire. On the second day, Ferox went to the stables to check on Bran and the horses. As he was coming through the door, he heard a shriek of pain. In one of the boxes, Genialis lay on the ground, with the Novantian boy on top of him, bending one of his arms back so that the youth shrieked again. Bran noticed him, twisted the arm once more, and then sprang up. Genialis, who was almost twice his size, pushed himself up, darted a look of hatred and then ran away, not saying a word. Bran nodded, leaned over to pick up a brush, and went back to cleaning Frost.

That afternoon, Ferox took the boy and his two horses over to the fort. It lay on the rise above the beach, an old temporary camp that had over time been kept in use, even though it was laid out for a mixed force a little smaller than a cohort. Detachments from various cohorts spent a year or six months here, and sometimes even legionaries came to the base, but a few months ago all of them had been posted back to their parent units to take part in the legate's planned manoeuvres. Apart from a small number of clerks and men to perform essential fatigues, the fort had lain empty until a week ago, when Aelius Brocchus brought five *turmae* of his ala Petriana to act as escort to the Hibernians. There were also twenty Batavian horsemen to accompany Cerialis, and the two prefects had declined Probus' hospitality. Instead, they and their families occupied the praetorium. It was a good deal smaller than the one at Vindolanda, and when a slave led him out into the central garden it was filled with excited noise.

Young Aelius was eight, thin and gangling, and seemed to be the leader, although Flavius was just a few months younger and did his best to keep up. The boy had flame-red hair, far more vivid in colour than his father, but otherwise the face was a smaller version of the prefect. Both boys were crouching over the central pond, using nets to fish out the leaves floating in the water, and because of this Ferox might not have noticed the slight crook in Flavius' back unless he had been looking for it.

Two smaller children, a girl and another boy, kept trying to push their way through and help, but were resisted with much splashing and merriment. The younger boy had a squeal that echoed around the courtyard. Two nurses were doing their best to stop the children from getting soaked. One of them bounded forward, when she thought the little boy was too close to the edge, but her foot slipped on the stones edging the sunken pond and she fell headlong into it with a great slash. The two oldest boys laughed so much that they had to lie down.

'Welcome, Flavius Ferox.' Sulpicia Lepidina had been sitting on a bench, reading a letter, but rose to greet her guest. 'It is good to see you.' She was in pale blue, one of her favourite colours, without a cloak for the afternoon was warm. Her golden hair was pinned back in a bun, the simplicity of the style only adding to the delicate beauty of her face. As she stood, the bright light of the afternoon sun fell on her, shining so brightly that neither dress nor under-tunic could hide the darker lines of her limbs and body.

'Indeed, yes, it is good to see an old friend.' Aelius' mother Claudia Severa sat, rocking a baby in her arms. She had not looked up, and was making faces and little noises as she calmed the child. Ferox had not noticed her. 'He really has your eyes.' Claudia Severa always had a pleasant, gentle expression on her round face, its open kindness making her an attractive woman. Now she smiled up at her friend with great fondness.

'They may go dark,' Sulpicia Lepidina said. 'Are you well, Ferox?'

'Quite well, thank you, my lady. I trust that you are both well, along with your families.'

'We are indeed. This is scarcely Baiae, but it is nice to be close to the sea.'

'Pity the water is so cold,' Claudia Severa lifted the baby to her shoulder and patted his back. 'Come on,' she said encouragingly and was rewarded with a remarkably loud belch.

Sulpicia Lepidina wrinkled her nose in shock distaste. 'I am tempted to say that you can tell that he is a man, if I did not know that little girls can be quite as vulgar in their emissions.' She noticed that Ferox was staring at the child and his head of thick black hair. She smiled.

'I think he's ready to nap,' Claudia Severa said. 'Do you want him inside or out?'

'Inside, I think. It will start getting colder soon and we don't want him getting a chill.'

Claudia Severa stood up. 'You keep an eye on these other rogues. And possibly our guest as well! I shall make sure the girl settles him properly.' She carried the baby away, his head resting on her shoulder. His eyes were closed by the time she walked past Ferox.

'Now, what can I do for you, centurion?' Sulpicia Lepidina's blue eyes sparkled.

'I come to ask a favour, lady.'

She smiled again, raising an eyebrow. 'Indeed?' The sun glinted on one of the brooches fastening her dress. Ferox stared at it, and the smooth pale skin of her shoulder and neck. The lady coughed politely. Behind him there was another shriek and the sound of more splashing.

'I was wondering whether the Lord Cerialis would let a servant boy and a pair of horses join your household in the fort?'

'Certainly.' Cerialis appeared at one of the entrances to the garden. 'That will be no burden at all, and they are welcome.' He grinned, coming forward. 'It is good to see you, Ferox. For all that we owe you this is a slight thing.'

'Yes,' his wife agreed. 'Although I was about to reprove the centurion for neglect. It is more than a year since he last saved me from ambush or murder. He is slipping.'

Cerialis laughed. 'Well, do not worry, my dear, he saved me a couple of weeks ago, so he is keeping in training.'

'If I remember rightly, my lord, you were doing pretty well before I turned up. I saw you jump that barricade.'

The prefect was pleased at the compliment. 'Well, we were all there. Pity we couldn't catch them.' The chase had found no more than a couple of warriors who must have died of their wounds and been left behind. 'I fear that the Novantae will be back and Brocchus agreed. We will mount regular patrols along the coastline for as long as we are here.'

'That is wise, my lord.'

'We thought so.'

'May I ask why you wish us to take your man and your horses?' Sulpicia Lepidina asked. 'Is the stabling not good at the villa?'

'It is fine, my lady, but the company is less conducive.'

She gave a slight nod. 'Genialis?'

'That little shit!' Cerialis hissed the words. 'My apologies.' He looked at the children still playing around the pool. 'I do not think they heard.'

'He stayed in our house at Vindolanda for two days,' the lady explained. 'It was two days more than he was welcome. He has an unfortunate manner, and an even more unfortunate tongue.'

'It wasn't his tongue that bothered me,' Cerialis cut in, anger flaring again. 'That little...' He paused, controlling himself. 'That lad treated our slaves as if they were his, and if he treats his own that way, then it is only a wonder that he has not been murdered. If it were not for his father I would have...' He glanced at his wife, whose expression suggested that she had already heard this and much more. 'I assume he has taken a dislike to your slave.'

'He is not a slave, but a freeborn boy in my service. But, yes, and my boy gave him a beating in return.'

Cerialis brightened. 'Then he is truly welcome.' He chuckled happily. 'Wonderful news. Still, I am sure you are right and the little tick will return with some of his own slaves to repay the compliment.' A soldier appeared, stopping at the entrance and saluting. 'I must go, I am afraid. Flavius,' he called. 'Try not to drown everyone!'

'He dotes on the children,' Sulpicia Lepidina said after her husband had gone. 'All of them.' The same maid slipped again and ended up back in the water.

The lady came close, for there was no else in the little garden. 'I hope you like the look of the child? He has your hair, I think, although I assure everyone that he takes after my father. He has been grey for twenty years, so I doubt anyone here would remember that his hair was more brown than black.'

Ferox did not know what to say. She was close, and he longed to reach out and hold her closer still, just as he feared that anyone seeing them now would be sure to suspect something.

'My husband does not have the slightest idea that he is not the father.' She was whispering, and her eyes flicked around to make sure that there was no one paying attention, before they stared up into his. 'He came to me one night, just a few days after that Samhain. It was the first time for many months and he has not come back since then. In truth he was drunk, but so drunk that he does not know that he did not really perform. Since then he has gone back to the slaves or his whores. Genialis angered him because he struck one of his favourites.'

Sulpicia Lepidina gave a thin smile at his surprise to hear her speak so bluntly. Then she sighed. 'He already had three children, enough to satisfy the law, and did not want the cost of raising another one, but when I told him of my condition he was pleased. I think it flattered his vanity that he was so potent. Men are…' She did not finish the thought. Her eyes stared into his, imploringly. 'I have missed you.' They did not touch, but the words were like a caress and his skin seemed to tingle.

Ferox felt a fool, and wondered whether she believed him to be uncaring, deliberately avoiding her. 'He is the most wonderful thing I have ever seen,' he said, and saw relief in her eyes. 'I have stayed away because it is dangerous, and I could not bear the thought that I brought harm to you or to young Marcus.'

'And to you.'

'That does not matter. It has not mattered for many years.'

Something tugged at his tunic. He looked down, to see the smallest boy clutching at him. The other three children hung back, clearly believing that the licence granted to the smallest would not extend to them. One of the maids stood with the main group. The other was in the pond, skirts lifted high as she squeezed the wool to wring out the water.

'Please, sir, would you help us lift the bucket?' They had filled a bronze pail with water and it now stood in the pond.

'Of course, young man.' Ferox did as he was bidden. Claudia Severa reappeared and laughed to see the centurion playing with the children. He was soon very wet.

'I had better go,' he said, when the mothers declared that it was time to dry off and get ready for their food. Both ladies wished him well. Privatus, the head of the slave household, had already sent someone to lead Bran and the horses away, so he strolled back the quarter-mile to the villa. There was a ship in harbour, unloading supplies to be carried by wagon up to the legate's main force. Gulls swarmed in the sky above the vessel, which made him think they were carrying food of some sort. A warship was further out to sea, riding under sail with its oars drawn in. The sail was dyed a blue-grey, and the hull painted in the same colour. Ferox wondered whether they could arrange for the Hibernians to take a look at the ship, for he doubted that they ever been on board a trireme.

Crispinus liked the idea. 'I shall write to the legate. Three triremes from the *classis* are due to arrive next week, so there ought to be an opportunity.'

'There was one off-shore today.'

The tribune frowned. 'Really. I did not know any ships were around. Oh well, these sailors do dislike telling anyone else what they are doing – and use words no one else understands even when they do! Sometimes I feel they do not think that they are part of the army like the rest of us.'

There was supposed to be a dinner that evening in honour of their royal guests, but Epotsorovidus was ill and the Hibernians remained in their rooms. Crispinus was impatient, although there was nothing that could be done. The next morning the king was recovered, and the guests were taken to the parade ground outside the fort. Brocchus had prepared a *Hippaka Gymnasia*, the display of horsemanship and weapons handling that was the speciality of the cavalry alae. One turma performed first, in polished armour and helmets. They began by throwing light training javelins at posts set up on different sides of the square. Then the best men did the same drills with full-weight spears.

The next turma arrived in a cavalcade of colour and noise. The men wore brightly coloured tunics, decorated armour, and silvered helmets with masks covering their faces and shaped like characters from the mimes. Long yellow crests rippled in the wind, and two men carried *dracones*, standards fashioned like the open mouths of dragons, which whistled as they galloped, sucking in air and making the striped fabric tubes attached to them shake and hiss. The horses wore chamfroms of leather, bright with studs and with bulbous domes dotted with holes over the eyes, making them look like the helmets of gladiators. Everything was done fast and with precision, the riders split into two teams who weaved across the whole parade ground, taking turns to lob blunt-headed javelins against the other team's shields.

The Hibernians sat cross-legged to watch and openly showed their delight.

'Pity we haven't a water organ,' Brocchus said. 'It's even better to music.'

'Never mind, they'll hear all that when we take them to the games.' Neratius Marcellus was staging a festival at Luguvallium, partly for the entertainment of the Hibernians but mainly as some relief from work and training for his soldiers. There would be beast fights, gladiators and executions. The Red Cat and his brother, who had survived his fever, were among the prisoners to be killed as a warning to others. Ferox was determined to try to speak to the brothers one more time.

'It will be a grand show, my lords,' Probus assured them. He was supplying the gladiators for the fights, for it appeared that he owned a school in Londinium. 'None of your rural rubbish. We're bringing up some prime men – Falx among them.'

'The Dacian?' Crispinus said. 'Fights as a Samnite? Yes, I saw him last summer. Could hardly believe the speed in such a big man. Surprising enough when a Samnite wins at all, but he is lethal.'

'I cannot remember when I last saw a really good fight.'

Brocchus sounded wistful, and soon the three men were deep in a conversation about fighters past and present. Ferox had little interest in the subject. He could admire skill with a sword, but there was a pointlessness about gladiatorial fights that depressed him. On the other hand, he enjoyed the display of the ala Petriana, even if it was rather theatrical, for at least these men would fight real enemies, and when Epotsorovidus asked a question about the draco standards, he was happy to answer, even though it brought back memories of Dacians and Sarmatians hunting his men as they tried to escape from the great disaster under Fuscus. They went on for a long time, before Probus announced that he must leave to help with the arrangements for the games.

That night the dinner was held, and he had spent time explaining to their guests how the Romans dined reclining on couches. Neither of the kings were enthusiastic, but they were guests and obeyed. Brigita wore the dress she had been given, striding into the dining room like a tiger with a pink ribbon around its neck. The kings lay on either side of her on the couch, both awkward and uncomfortable, switching from one elbow to the other as they twisted and turned. She lay flat, pushing up on both arms whenever she wanted, so that the front of her dress hung very low. Three warriors stood behind them, although in deference to their hosts none carried weapons.

'An under-tunic might have been wise,' Sulpicia Lepidina whispered to her husband. Ferox was on the couch with them, looking straight at the Hibernians – and sometimes trying not to look straight at the queen.

Crispinus, Brocchus and Claudia Severa occupied the central couch, and the tribune gave a little speech of welcome, which Ferox translated, doing his best to fix on the eyes of the

Hibernians and not let his gaze drop. The kings made noises of gratitude, while the queen just glared at him, head cocked to one side. All the while the yellow silk sagged down, exposing much of her breasts. Her skin was pale, yet clearly saw a lot of the sun for it was covered in freckles. Between her bosoms was a tiny scar, straight and neat as if it came from a blade and was deliberate.

The Romans spoke during the meal, and when Crispinus gestured or he felt it appropriate, Ferox put the thoughts into the language of the tribes, speaking slowly because the Hibernian dialect differed in many ways.

'Silure?' The queen's voice was high-pitched and soft, surprising him for he had expected her to sound deeper, even manly.

'Yes, although now I am a Roman.'

'Huh!' The noise could have meant anything. She lay down, resting her chin on her hands and considered him. It was easier to look back now that she was more covered. 'I hear the Silures fight dirty,' she said.

'We fight to win.'

'Huh.'

Ferox was glad that the queen did not point out that his people had not won when they had fought the Romans. She appeared to have lost interest, and said no more during the entire evening. Now and again she would shift as she lay, sometimes revealing a good deal. Once, the queen turned faster than the silk dress could move so that her right breast came free of it altogether. Cerialis was drinking wine and almost choked in surprise, but nothing was said. Ferox felt Sulpicia Lepidina quivering beside him, so that he could feel the cushions move. He tried not to think about her closeness and failed. Brigita was not making it any easier, and the sweet torment of lying

121

next to a woman he loved and desired, but could not touch, went on and on.

For a while, the queen rested on her elbow, seemingly uncaring, for she could surely have not been oblivious that one whole breast was on view. Ferox wondered whether it was deliberate. As the evening went on Epotsorovidus and Brennus began to speak a little more freely.

'This summer is the time for the tribes of Hibernia to choose a high king over all the high and lesser kings,' he explained to Crispinus. 'They say all the tribes, but I'm guessing it is their own peoples and perhaps some of the others in the north. The choice has not been made, but the noble Epotsorovidus...' he nodded a head to honour the man since he would surely hear his name mention '... is favoured by many.'

'And they think a message of support from us would help swing it all in his favour.' The young aristocrat spoke slowly, toying with the ideas as they came to him. 'Or do they want gold to help make friends? I should think both of those are possible, if they will act in a friendly way in return.'

Ferox spoke to the kings for a while. The men smiled when he spoke of gifts and friendship. After a while he turned back to the tribune.

'They want that, my lord. They also want something more.'

The tribune waited. He glanced at their guests, smiling. The queen shifted again, and yanked the edge of her dress up so that she was properly covered. It made Crispinus flinch, as if fearing that it was his gaze that had made her aware of her revealing pose. 'What else do they want from us?'

Ferox asked the kings again, just to be sure. One of Sulpicia Lepidina's arms rested just beside him, a slim bracelet on her wrist. She had delicate fingers, the nails immaculately trimmed, and a ring on only one finger. Just once, earlier in the meal, he had brushed against her skin. That light touch, and the subtle scent she wore, kept him on edge and he longed for the meal to be over.

'My lord,' he began, 'I think they want a legion.'

X

I T TOOK SIX slaves to drag the bear away, while more were scattering fresh sand to cover up its blood, and the blood and entrails of the *venator* who had misjudged his attack on the animal and come too close. The other hunters would have soon have finished the beast off, but the crowd of soldiers and civilians from Luguvallium had cheered when a lithe Hibernian warrior had jumped down into the arena and grabbed the dying man's spear. They cheered even more when he dodged the bear's attacks, wounding it time and again, gradually weakening it. Even the *venatores* had urged him on, instead of resenting his intrusion, and joined in the great roar of triumph when he vaulted into the air and stabbed down, using his own weight to drive the heavy spear deep into the animal, pinning it to the ground.

In the great Flavian amphitheatre at Rome they sprayed perfume into the air to smother the reek of blood and death. Here in northern Britannia, in a temporary arena where the tiers of seats were raised so that all could see over the seven-foot-high timber wall down onto the sand, there were few such refinements. Over the course of the morning, the venatores had killed four bulls, five bears, a dozen wolves, two lions and four panthers, so that the place stank like a slaughterhouse.

Most of the time the Hibernians kept a polite silence, and he suspected that they were bored. It had always struck him that these beast fights took away all the excitement of hunting and kept only the final butchery. The Hibernians had shown a lot of curiosity when they saw the big cats, asking a lot of questions about where they came from and whether or not they hunted people. Ferox answered as best he could. The queen was not there, for the Roman ladies had decided that the blood of the arena was not fitting for ladies to attend, and had stayed at Alauna with her, planning an excursion of their own. Brigita's absence took a good deal of the spirit out of the kings, so that little of importance was said. Her husband seemed rudderless when she was not by his side, even if the queen spoke so rarely.

Ferox suspected that she might have enjoyed the gladiatorial fights to be staged in the afternoon, and was a little surprised that they had all not come along. In his experience women – some supposed to be fine ladies – were usually among the most enthusiastic members of the audience, baying for blood, aroused almost to frenzy by the muscle-bound men hacking each other to pieces. In some strange way, on the days women were excluded, it somehow all seemed less violent to him, but he wondered whether this was simply his imagination.

There was little for him to do as the kings on their own were not inclined to talk of great matters. The day after the dinner further conversations had made their request clearer. They asked for an army. He had translated the word as legion because it was often used in that way, and he thought it more likely to get the attention of Crispinus and the others. 'They say army,' he explained later, 'but I think they just mean a force of soldiers. Fifty or sixty, maybe even a hundred.'

'A token of support?'

'Something like that,' Ferox said. 'Big enough to look impressive and led by someone important.'

Crispinus rubbed his chin. 'You mean me.'

'I'm only a centurion, my lord, I don't mean anything at all. You brought me here to translate.'

'And give advice.' The tribune made up his mind. 'I believe the legate will agree to this. There is no harm in winning the loyalty of neighbours, so that they respect our power. Could stop any more raids on the coast.'

Ferox said nothing.

'You do not agree? And please do not give me any more nonsense about knowing your place and not having an opinion. Would you agree to these terms?'

'Hibernian raids are rare, my lord. Whatever we agree here will not stop the Novantae, or the tribes like the Creones from further north.'

'But it will do no harm, surely?'

Ferox sensed that the tribune liked the idea of leading an expedition to the mysterious isle of Hibernia, where he could claim that the locals had submitted to the majesty of Rome and the emperor – in the person of a young aristocrat. Along with the recommendation to receive the corona civica, which he would most likely be awarded in due course, it would conclude a spectacular term as tribune with the legions.

'Tell me why you are worried,' Crispinus demanded.

Ferox was not sure what to tell him. When he was growing up his people always said that Hibernia was an unlucky place, ill-omened and full of ancient terrors. Perhaps that helped to make him suspicious, but he was sure it was something else.

'They are hiding something,' he said at last.

'Isn't everyone?' Crispinus laughed. 'Tell me you do not believe the stories of cannibals and monsters. That is what I read about Hibernia – of course all written by people who have never seen the place.'

'I just do not trust them, my lord. She is...' He hesitated, but he knew that it was the silent, beautiful queen who worried him the most. 'She is up to something.'

'I should be greatly surprised if she was not. She's a woman after all – and a queen at that – and every Roman knows that you cannot trust royalty. Look at Cleopatra. But I often find it is easier to deal with people you do not trust. It's just a question of working out what they really want, and then making sure that it does not get in the way of you getting what you want. Untrustworthy people tend to be selfish, which makes them simple to understand.'

Ferox gave up, for it was obvious that the tribune had made up his mind. 'You are always asking me to trust you, my lord.'

'Indeed I am, and I wish you would. But you are a truly unusual man, so the rule does not apply. Do not worry, it will all work out well, and we shall come back safely.'

'We?'

'You do not think I could do without your sage advice, centurion.'

'Sir.'

'Your enthusiasm is as inspiring as ever.'

'Yes, sir.'

Neratius Marcellus had opened the games earlier that morning, but left after an hour and was not to return until the afternoon when the gladiatorial bouts were due to begin. Crispinus left with him, and no doubt was waiting for his chance to convince the legate to send him and a suitable force to Hibernia.

Now that the beast fights were over for the day, there would be a pause for two hours before the games resumed. Ferox took the Hibernians to a feast arranged for them by Probus, who spoke the language of the tribes quite well, and was happy to rely on his own knowledge and the interpreter they had brought with them.

'You deserve a rest, centurion,' he said. 'Plenty to do in Luguvallium.'

Ferox went to the field behind the makeshift arena where they kept the stores and the cages. A tiger growled as he passed one long iron cage. It had been a while since he had seen one of these beasts and he had forgotten just how big they were. There were two, a sign that the legate was spending a good deal of his own money, unless this was more of Probus' work, for he was supplying animals as well as gladiators.

The brothers were at one end of a smaller cage, sitting on their own. The other five men in the cage looked cowed, and Ferox wondered whether they were as frightened of the two northerners as of what was about to happen. He recognised two of them as cattle rustlers, and another as a man who had murdered a drunken soldier. The other two were strangers, but he knew that several robbers and bandits were here to die in the arena.

'Come to gloat?' Segovax's voice was flat, but it was a change from his usual silence. They were both filthy, their hair straggling and wild and beards long. They were not due to play their brief role in the games until tomorrow, so the slaves had not yet come to clean them up.

'No,' Ferox said. 'I would like to talk.'

'Why?' The Red Cat did not look up.

'To learn.'

Segovax moved fast, springing to his feet and grabbing at the bars, and roaring like a beast, in spite of the chains around his ankles and wrists. Somehow, Ferox stopped himself from flinching.

'Come in here, Roman, and I will teach you.'

'My brother killed a man yesterday.' The Red Cat was still sitting cross legged and head bowed. 'The man wanted some of our ration of swill. My brother ripped his throat out with his teeth.'

Segovax grinned. Two of his front teeth were broken and the rest badly stained, although it was hard to tell whether this was from blood.

'You can try that trick on the beasts over there.' Ferox pointed at the caged tigers.

'Is that how we die?' Segovax spoke like a true warrior, without emotion.

'Have they not told you?'

'The scum guarding us say little and even less is worth hearing,' the Red Cat said. 'One says we are to burn, another that they will cut off our pricks and choke us with them, another that we will drown. They are like birds chirping and saying nothing.'

'None would dare face me without these bars,' Segovax bellowed, shaking his chains.

'I did,' Ferox said.

'And you should have killed us both. A better death than this.'

'Who are the men of the night?' Ferox asked. 'The black men? Where do they come from?'

The Red Cat looked up. 'You ask that? They are you. Murderers and filth, men without honour. They take our families and because of you all have died. They are you.'

Segovax spat through the bars and hit Ferox in the face. 'Bastard! With my last breath I will curse you and all your seed and all that you love.'

'Who took your families? Why did you come for the boy, Genialis?'

Segovax spat again, and this time Ferox dodged out of the

way, but that brought him closer to the cage and for a moment the warrior's hand grabbed his shoulder.

'Trouble?' A thickset slave appeared carrying a cudgel, raising it ready to slam it down on Segovax's wrist.

'No. No trouble.' Ferox stared at the warrior. Segovax released him and pulled his hand back in. 'These ones all for tomorrow?'

'Yes. Some for the beasts and some for the gladiators,' the slave said. A voice called for him and he went off.

'I shall see if they will let you die in a fight,' Ferox said quietly.

'With you?'

'Not with me.'

Segovax sat down, his back to the bars, and the Red Cat dropped his head down again. Ferox left, and because he had time and was not hungry he strolled along the main street of Luguvallium, past the fort and out onto the long timber bridge. A dozen ox carts rumbled over the planking, ungreased axles screaming. The drovers said that the noise kept away evil spirits, and Ferox wondered idly whether it might help to lift a curse. He stared down at the sluggish water and after a while the last cart went by and the piercing squeals grew fainter. People and animals passed and he paid them no heed. The Romans believed in curses. You could go to the market place and a pay someone to write out the whole thing for you, if you did not feel like coming up with the details on your own. The Silures knew that luck was fragile, that the power of a man's spirit could shrink as well as grow. He was not sure what he believed, but part of him wished that he had not bothered to visit the brothers at all. 'They are you.' There seemed no sense to it, and yet it must mean something. The sound of horses was coming closer, until it stopped just behind him.

130

'If you want to jump, it's deeper in the middle,' Vindex suggested. He was leading a dozen of his scouts.

Ferox turned back to look down at the river. 'With my luck, I'd land in a boat.'

'Aye.'

'Did not expect to see you here.'

'Didn't you send for us? The orders came for me yesterday to come quickly with as many men as I had.'

'Not from me.' Ferox sighed. 'Must be someone's bright idea.'

'Huh. Does that mean we're about to get humped again?'

'Probably.'

'Shall we all just jump and get it over with?'

Ferox went back across the bridge, walking alongside Vindex who did not bother to dismount. Before they reached the end of the bridge nearest the town a cavalryman clattered onto it.

'Flavius Ferox?'

'Yes.'

'You are to report to the legate at once. He is at the principia.'

'Then give me your horse, lad.'

The trooper was reluctant, but faced with the authority of a centurion he gave way. 'Get some rest and something to eat,' Ferox said to Vindex.

The fort was twice the size of Vindolanda, but many of the buildings were older and showing their age. As Ferox rode towards the central range of buildings he went past a work-party raising a new barrack block. They had already driven the square corner posts into the ground and the row of smaller round poles along the sides. Stacks of hazel branches were waiting alongside and men were starting to fix them in place to create the panels they would daub with clay. A pair of them held each branch straight so that another with a hammer could drive it into the ground. It looked odd, and then he remembered that the men at Vindolanda always laid the branches horizontally. Ferox wondered which method was better, but guessed that it was just the old army way of doing things differently for the sake of it. Most of the standing barracks were left plain wattle and daub, so that the rows of buildings were drab. It made the rendered and whitewashed principia and praetorium dominate the place even more than they would have done through their sheer size.

Ferox had seen too many army bases to pay much heed to the grand buildings. Instead he looked at the two horses being walked in circles outside the headquarters. As he came close he saw the white sweat on their neck and sides and the blood drying on the side of one of the animals.

There was more than the usual bustle inside the courtyard as another of the governor's singulares led him across to one of the main rooms beside the shrine to the standards.

Neratius Marcellus was pacing up and down on the far side of a long table. Crispinus and three more officers sat at the table, as did a little man in a crumpled toga, who smiled with genuine enthusiasm when he saw the centurion. Quintus Ovidius was a poet, philosopher and friend of the governor. He was also one of the least military men Ferox had ever met, and yet insisted on going with his friend on campaign and to the wilder parts of his province, determined to see a little of the world and not simply read about it.

The legate saw this mark of welcome and glared. 'Where the hell have you been?' He barked at Ferox.

'Standing on the bridge, my lord,' Ferox said.

Neratius Marcellus stopped pacing and frowned, trying to

decide whether this was insolence. He was a small man, almost a foot shorter than the centurion, but he had the confident assurance of a former consul who deferred to very few others apart from the emperor. There was a restless energy about him, which sometimes spilled over to upset the calm of the experienced politician and orator.

'Well,' he said after a long silence, broken only by the sound of stylus pens scratching away as clerks copied orders. 'At last you are here. Tell me, what is your opinion of Claudius Super?' The question was abrupt and was not what he had expected.

'He is a brave man, my lord.'

'Of course he is, he is an *eques* and an officer.' There was just enough hint of irony to show that he was not serious, although no one smiled apart from Ovidius. 'What about his judgement? Is he a scaremonger?'

'It is not my place to comment on a senior officer, my lord.' Ferox saw Crispinus roll his eyes.

There was a flash of anger and that surprised him, because in the past the legate had seemed very much in control of his emotions. 'It is your place if I say it is!' Neratius Marcellus turned, took three paces away from him and then spun around again. 'Hercules' balls, man, this is no time for playing dumb. I know you, and you are not short of ideas or disposed to doubt your own views. You think Super is a fool?'

'Yes, my lord.'

'At last.' The governor went back to the table and drummed his fingers on the wood. 'My impression was that you felt your superior officer to be a drooling imbecile who despised the Britons and had all the subtlety of a kick to the stomach.'

'A kick in the gut can be effective, my lord,' Ferox said, but he was wondering about the tense, for the legate was a man of precise speech. 'In the right circumstances, that is.'

The legate reached for a wooden tablet and opened the folded sheets. 'Yesterday I received a message from Claudius Super saying that there were worrying signs among the Selgovae and that he feared trouble. He asked that you be sent to join him along with those scouts of yours. Presumably he thought that it would be advantageous to have someone who plays dumb and avoids answering questions.' Ovidius chuckled again, ignoring the disapproving glances of the officer beside him.

'This morning I receive a new message to say that he fears that druids and priests are abroad, stirring up rebellion. He worries that that rogue Acco is at large.' The big room with its high ceiling suddenly seemed cold. 'Ah, perhaps I have your attention at last. Have you heard anything about that fiend lately?'

'No, my lord. Nothing at all.'

'Hmmm. It is probably too much to hope that he has gone away for good. But does that mean you would be surprised if he turned up now, among the Selgovae?'

Ferox tried to think. Acco was clever and good at concealing his presence. Had there been signs that he had missed? 'I have not heard anything, my lord.'

'It seems Claudius Super had, or at least thought that he had. Rumours of magic and dreadful sacrifices of men and women. Because of this I was intending to summon you anyway, and was simply waiting for your Brigantians to arrive. Orders summoning them were sent yesterday.'

'They are here, my lord.'

'Really. No one tells me anything. I'm just the legatus augusti, of course, no one important.' A soldier marched into the room, handing a note to one of the clerks. The man took the wooden sheet, nodded for the man to leave, and then looked up.

'The scouts have arrived, my lord.'

'Ah, the slow turning wheels of bureaucracy get there in the end.' Neratius Marcellus gave a thin smile. 'I should not joke, not at a time like this.'

'Surely laughter is most needed at a time like this.' Ovidius' voice was thin, but clear.

'Philosophy. Well, we shall need more than that – and more than bad jokes as well.' The legate stretched his arms as if yawning. He stayed in the pose, staring up at the ceiling. Ferox wondered why Roman aristocrats had to turn everything into a performance.

'Half an hour ago a pair of troopers arrived. One was wounded badly, and I fear the poor fellow will not make it. The other one is babbling of ghosts and demons.'

'Has the regionarius sent another message, my lord?' Ferox asked, although he did not doubt the answer.

'Not as such.' The comment came from Crispinus, who seemed to have been encouraged by Ovidius' efforts at levity.

Neratius Marcellus brought his arms back down to his sides. 'Not as such,' he repeated. 'The poor bastard.'

'They killed him?' Ferox wanted them all to get on with the matter, but he sensed that the legate was delaying and perhaps the man was trying to make up his own mind about what to do before he sought advice.

'If the soldier is to be believed,' Ovidius said, since the rest had fallen silent, 'somebody burned him alive.'

XI

FEROX FELT NOTHING. He thought of his last encounter with Claudius Super, of the man's desperate efforts to be fair and honest after years of open scorn. It was odd how people often believed that they could change the past with a few words or a gesture. Yet perhaps it had worked, for he had long considered Claudius Super as his enemy, a dangerous man who needlessly stirred situations into violence. Now the man was gone, but there was no satisfaction at the death of an enemy, or guilt because in the past he had so often wished the man ill. No doubt they would appoint an even bigger fool to replace him.

'For the moment, assuming that the man is telling the truth, you will assume the duties of senior regionarius.' The legate had stepped towards him. Few men could intimidate when they were forced to look up at someone, but the provincial governor came close.

'Huh,' said the bigger fool.

'I beg your pardon, centurion?'

'A cough, sir. Sorry, sir. I meant to say that I shall be delighted to serve the legate in whatever way he wishes.'

'It was not so long ago that druids wanted to seize the Prefect Cerialis and his esteemed wife to burn in the fire. Do you think this is an attempt at some similar sacrifice?'

Ferox was not sure what to think. 'Hard to say, my lord. Then they wanted the blood of a king and queen. A centurion is not so important. Until I take a look we shall not know whether or not it was a sacrifice. The Selgovae can be cruel. It may just have struck them as the right thing to do to an enemy in their hands.'

The legate sighed. 'Barbarians.'

'If I am not mistaken, at this very moment prisoners are being thrown to the wild beasts.' Ovidius was staring down at the table.

'As an object lesson,' Neratius Marcellus intoned, fully aware of the irony. 'Not for religion or mere cruelty.'

He ignored the muttered 'That makes all the difference, of course,' from his friend.

'Gentlemen, morality is not our main concern at present. It seems that at least some of the Selgovae are restive. As the noble Crispinus has said, the start of the census in their lands always risked provoking trouble.' Ferox had half forgotten warning the tribune about this all those weeks ago. 'They have ambushed a detachment of our soldiers, murdered a centurion in an extremely savage way.'

'This is surely the start of bigger trouble. Yet Fortuna smiles upon us pious Romans, for we happen to have plenty of troops concentrated not far from here for the summer's manoeuvres. This means that in just a few days I can assemble an expedition big enough to march through the valleys of the Selgovae and smash anyone who dares oppose us. We must prepare the orders to make this happen should it become necessary. Ferox?'

'My lord.'

'I shall want you to stay with us as we begin to plan, but in two hours' time you are to ride out with the scouts and an escort from my singulares to find out as much as you can about what has happened and what will happen. How many men will you need for your escort?'

'A dozen will do, my lord.' He would have preferred to take no more than a couple of men to use as couriers, but he doubted that they would agree to that.

'So few? Claudius Super had twice as many.'

'I shall have Vindex and his men, my lord. They make a big difference.'

'As do you, no doubt.' Neratius Marcellus turned to a clerk. 'I want eleven of the best men led by a *duplicarius*. Ensure all are well mounted and have food for three days. Fresh mounts to be provided for the scouts and the centurion. That should do it.' He gestured at another of the headquarters men. 'Longus, here, will show you the messages from Claudius Super and the survivor of the ambush.'

'Thank you, my lord. I should like to speak to the trooper.'

'Certainly, although I doubt you'll get much from him. Go with Longus, but be back here as soon as you can for we will need your knowledge.'

'Yes, my lord. My lord?'

'I take it centurion, that you are wondering about the whole business. From all you have said about Acco he is shrewd and cunning. So you are wondering whether what he seems to intend and what he actually intends are two very different things. That perhaps he wants to draw me into a hasty attack on the Selgovae, either because more tribes will join them and we may be overwhelmed by sheer numbers? Or perhaps he has mischief planned elsewhere and simply wants us distracted? Were you thinking something like that, and that your governor had no more wit that a newborn child and would not see the possible traps?' Neratius Marcellus grinned.

'I was wondering something like that, my lord.'

'I am glad to hear it, centurion. Now hurry off and be back as soon as you can.'

There was little in the messages. Claudius Super had sensed an unease among the tribe. That was something of a surprise, because in the past the centurion had appeared unlikely to have sensed when it was raining. Perhaps the fight at Aballava had made him wary or just plain nervous. The people struck him as hostile, and warriors shadowed his escort, without coming close. His second message told of a farm near the coast that had been burned to the ground, the families living there all killed, their corpses ripped open and mutilated. Super's mood was reflected in the deep, almost brutal strokes his pen had made, stabbing into the wax and wood behind it.

The report of the survivor was of little use, so Ferox went to the small cubicle where the man was being kept. They had brought him bread, salted meat and wine, but the trooper had touched none of it. He sat on a stool beside the little table, bent over, his hands grasping his face. When Ferox spoke to him, the habit of discipline took over and he sprang to his feet. His eyes stared past the centurion into a distance no one could measure.

'Report, Trooper Candidus.' Ferox did not shout, but made it a command, hoping that training would force the man to speak quicker than a show of sympathy. 'What happened to the rest of you?'

'Dead, sir. All dead.'

'You were escort to the centurion?'

'Yes, sir.'

'Helping out with the census. Then a messenger comes from a chieftain asking for help and the centurion takes you towards Uxellum and people there complain of cattle being stolen and blame some of the Novantae. They're on the border there, so it happens often enough.' Ferox was piecing together Claudius Super's reports with some guesses and trying to convince the man that he already knew the answers. 'You pushed along the coast and just before sunset yesterday find the farm and everyone killed and cut about. All of them, men, women and children.'

Candidus's eyelids flickered, but he showed no other emotion.

'You were all angry, and pushed on. Didn't fancy camping there, did you?'

'No, sir. Horrible it was.' For the first time the trooper looked at him.

'So you found another spot to camp, and you and Dannicus were sent ahead to check on another farm nearer the beach. It was empty?'

'Yes, sir.'

'And as you rode back to the camp you heard the noise?'

'They were screaming. Shapes darker than the night. Not human, sir, not really, but arms and legs distorted, eyes bulging.' Candidus was breathing hard, gulping the words out. 'Blacker than pitch and taller than any man, but flying across the ground faster than bats and shrieking, and our boys screaming as they were cut up. They were dying in front of us, the tents burning, fire everywhere, but the light didn't show them, they were still just black. Dead men risen up or ghosts or monsters from the deep.' His eyes were wild, his breath coming in pants and for a while he could not sleep.

Ferox did not see any point in asking how many of them there were. 'They came for you, then, didn't they?'

Candidus nodded. 'Just appeared out of the night. Dannicus threw his spear, which was more than I could do. Hit one square on and it just bounced back. Didn't slow it, didn't hurt it, but they screamed at us and there was a whistling sound like the hiss of dragons, and then they stabbed at Dannicus and he cried out and my horse reared and then shot off like the bolt from an engine and Dannicus' horse must have done the same. We didn't go through the camp, but close enough to see the centurion being carried in the air. Others were throwing wood onto the fires and something that flared up into the sky. We kept going, riding as hard as we could and we didn't look back, but we heard him screaming. Some of the others too, and that whistling followed us. And so we rode here.'

Ferox patted the trooper on the shoulder, making the man flinch like a nervous colt. 'You did well to get away. Try to get some rest.

'Find somewhere where he can sleep,' Ferox told Longus.

'Sir.' As they left the clerk cleared his throat. 'Sir? Do you believe all that about demons or ghosts?'

'Men did the killing,' Ferox said, and hoped that he was right.

At the governor's consilium they asked him a few questions about places and the local people, but in the main they got on with the planning while he sat and waited. Ovidius had gone, so that there was no one else not doing anything, and he waited in silence.

'We had better not keep you any longer,' Neratius Marcellus said at long last. 'Get something to eat and then get moving. The sooner you return with news the sooner we get to the bottom of all this.'

Crispinus walked with him as he left.

'I wanted to wish you good luck.'

'Thank you, my lord. I am guessing someone else will look

141

after the Hibernians while I am away. Oh well, it looks like your expedition over there is unlikely to happen.'

'We shall see. That all depends on what you find out.' They were in the courtyard, and for once it was empty. 'You know that the legate is my uncle?'

'Yes, my lord, I seem to recall that he mentioned it.'

'The legate is worried. That campaign against the Stallion was a narrow scrape and might have gone horribly wrong. The emperor still cannot afford a bad defeat anywhere on the frontiers.'

'He's ruled for two years now, surely there's no more talk of challengers?'

Crispinus shook his head. 'Don't be naive. There will always be men wanting the throne when they think they have the slightest chance of getting it. Trajan is still not liked, and has not proven himself. And – as you have said so many times – the garrison in Britannia is weaker in numbers than it has ever been, and unlikely to grow anytime soon. We have a good force already gathered, but we cannot afford to "go fishing with a golden hook", as I believe a certain centurion once said.'

'I was quoting Caesar Augustus.'

'I know. Look, I shall not ask you once more to trust me, since that seems to offend you so deeply. But help the legate to make the right choices, and you help Rome. If it is Acco behind all this, then he must be stopped before he commits worse slaughter.'

They went out through the big arch. Vindex was waiting with the scouts, as well as a dozen singulares with their deep blue cloaks. There was a tall black horse saddled and waiting for Ferox.

Crispinus was impressed. 'One of my uncle's own,' he said, nuzzling the animal until it tried to bite him. 'Shame about

Claudius Super. Do you know that he recommended that I be awarded the corona civica? Yes, of course you do. He told me. Not sure it's much of a rescue if the poor devil gets killed so soon afterwards.'

'It happens, my lord.' Ferox grabbed a horn on the saddle and leaped, just managing to swing up. He guessed that the diminutive legate must need a mounting block or someone to lift his leg to climb onto the back of this huge animal. 'Do not worry, my lord. The recommendation has gone in and it doesn't matter whether the man who sent it is still alive. I dare say you'll get the crown.'

'Oh yes, I will.' It was not a boast, merely a statement of fact.

'Then you had better stay alive to receive it.' A thought struck him, and he wondered why he had not thought of it before. 'My lord, are the games to continue tomorrow?'

'To be quite honest, I have not the slightest idea. They might be delayed, I suppose.'

'There are a couple of prisoners awaiting execution – two northerners Vindex and I brought in earlier in the year. I'd be glad if they could be kept alive until we return.'

'I shall see what I can do. Good fortune, Flavius Ferox. You too, you old rogue.' The tribune waved to Vindex.

'Cheerful little sod, isn't he,' the scout said, as soon as they were out of earshot. 'So just how badly are we humped this time?'

XII

VINDEX SUCKED THE breath in through his teeth, seemed to be about to say something and then decided against it. All of the men, Brigantes and cavalrymen alike, were just as stunned, so that they said little as they worked. It was the smell that was the worst, seeping into them until nothing else, not even the traces of smoke, the heady blossom or the faint hint of salt was left. There was just the half sweet and half sickly smell of cooked meat starting to rot.

The centurion had not died quickly. Many of the soldiers had been hacked or stabbed as the wave of attackers flooded over the little camp. There had been a lot of attackers. Ferox reckoned fifty or more men had come against Claudius Super and his escort, and they had got very close. The two Roman sentries had died without giving the alarm, so the attackers had crept up on them like men who knew how to use the night. Ferox no longer doubted that they were men, for he could see the prints of their boots, softer and smooth in outline, unlike the hobnailed footwear of the soldiers. Most of the prints were big, but no bigger than his own, and if these were large men, then they were not giants.

With the two sentries gone, there was no warning as the attackers came out of the night and caught the soldiers cleaning equipment, grooming horses and starting to cook. There was a cruel irony there, he supposed, for after they had killed or captured everyone in the camp, the men in the soft boots had taken three of the soldiers and butchered them as if they were pigs, cooking the meat in the great fire they had built. He was not quite sure whether all three men were dead when this was done. There were some innards still on the ground that had been chewed while raw, but that might have been by a dog or other scavenger. Claudius Super was certainly alive when they began to cut him. They did not want food, not at that stage, and the wounds to his arms and legs suggested someone with a good knowledge of how to inflict pain – even some of the Emperor Domitian torturers would have had little to learn. Candidus and the other cavalrymen may well have heard the centurion screaming, along with the other men, even though he was not yet being put on the fire. They burned him later on, and unless they just relished his agony, Ferox could only think that they wanted to ask him questions.

Ferox stood up. Claudius Super spoke no more than a few words in the language of the tribes, relying instead on interpreters. That suggested the attackers had someone able to speak Latin, unless they tortured a man without realising that he did not understand what they were asking. They had taken a long time about it, and for all his stubbornness by the end he would have told them anything to stop the pain. After that they had killed him, cutting out his heart and other organs and cooking them. Like the other human meat they had taken, they had only eaten some of it and left the rest for the carrion beasts and birds. It was almost as if they needed to taste something of their enemies, because they were not so desperate for food and had ignored the tethered horses. All but one of the animals had broken free, galloping away from the fire and the stench of blood and cooking flesh. The last one still stood just outside the camp, cropping the grass.

'Poor bastard,' Vindex said, coming over to look at the remains of the centurion. 'Didn't like him, but this... Never seen anything like this.' His words sounded loud after the long silence. 'Come on, the trail leads towards the sea, as you expected.'

The weapons were gone from the camp, as were the helmets, shields, and armour. Almost all the dead had been stripped naked, except when their clothes were so torn or thick with blood that they were not worth taking. Yet that was all, apart from a few trinkets. They had not taken cooking pots, food, let alone the horses, saddles and the blankets. Neither had they taken anyone with them, slitting the throats of all the prisoners they had not decided to eat.

They left most of the men to finish laying the bodies out as tidily as they could and covering them with blankets or the unburned panels from the leather tents. There were no tools to dig proper graves, so that would have to wait for a burial party to arrive. Ferox took Vindex and two of the scouts, just in case he missed something, and left the duplicarius in charge.

'I do not think that we will be long. Then we can all leave this benighted place.' The relief on the senior soldier's face was obvious and no one could blame him. Men had done this, not monsters or ghosts, but that did not make it any less evil.

The trail was easy to follow, going almost straight and with no attempt to conceal their passing. For men so obviously skilled at moving stealthily in the dark, that seemed odd and made him nervous. Ferox led them carefully, riding ahead of the other three, searching for any sign of ambush. There was none. After ten minutes he came onto the sand dunes behind the beach. This time his mood was too dark to be lifted by the old smells and sounds of the sea. The gulls seemed sinister, and he wondered how many of the ones circling over them had pecked at the corpses.

'That's it, then,' Vindex said. 'Bastards did come from the sea. Got clean away too.'

'Not all of them,' Ferox said and sped towards what looked like a pile of dark boulders with a gull perched on the largest. Up close, it was not a rock, but the corpse of a man, his body covered in a dark cloak. Ferox jumped down, and pulled the cloak away. One of the scouts hissed an oath as they looked at the body. The man was dressed wholly in black, his face daubed in black apart from a few streaks where it had washed off. He was tall, his dark hair streaked with grey, although it was hard to tell his age with his face painted. He wore a loose tunic, but it was slashed over his stomach, so that they could see that he was wearing an iron mail shirt, the rings split where a sword had punched through. It was a bad wound, and someone had stabbed him through the back of the neck to end his suffering.

'At least they got one,' Vindex said. 'Wonder why they carried him all this way, only to leave him here?'

For the moment, Ferox was more interested in the man's belt, of heavy leather decorated with plates of much tarnished brass, with a few traces of silver decoration on some of them. There was a sword on his right hip, a gladius like hundreds or thousands of others made for the army.

'Deserter?' Vindex asked.

'Perhaps.' A good Roman sword was a prize worth trading or killing for far outside the empire, but the belt was a soldier's belt, and one of the panels was even shaped to read COH I. It was odd that they had left something so valuable with the dead man, unless he was their leader and this was a mark of respect.

'We had better take him back. Wrap him up in the cloak and tie it fast around him.'

There was nothing left to detain them. The tide had come in and was well on its way out, so that there were no traces left by boats dragged onto the sand. They went back to the site of the slaughter and then all were glad to turn for home. It was the second day out from Luguvallium, and if they were lucky they might make it back soon after nightfall. On the return trip they saw more sign of the locals. On the way there, Ferox had seen a few men watching from the hills, and some riding ponies coming a little closer. All had fled if anyone had gone off towards them. Now they came closer, if warily, and he managed to speak to a few. The Selgovae were frightened, not sure where the attackers had come from or what they wanted.

'We did not kill them,' he was told several times. The last man he met said more. 'They came from a great ship.'

'A black ship?' Ferox asked. If the attackers had come in a merchantman than they may have come from far afield.

'No. One like the soldiers use. A grey ship.'

Did the man mean a warship? 'A ship with oars.'

'Yes, and a square sail.'

Ferox wondered why he did not feel more surprise, but when he went back to join the others his mind was reeling. A dead man who looked more than half like a soldier or former soldier, and now a whole trireme full of raiders, who did not act like any Selgovae or Novantae, or even Northerners or Hibernians. Truth was they did not act like anything he had ever seen or heard of whether in Britannia or further afield. Was it all another plot against the emperor, with someone powerful enough to control a force of men and stir up war, hoping that there would be a disaster big enough to discredit the princeps?

Ferox rode on, and suddenly a long-forgotten story rose up

in his memory. A tale from before his posting to Britannia, and one that men only whispered because of its horror.

'Did you ever hear of the Usipi?' he asked Vindex.

'No.'

'I think we might be about to hear a lot about them,' Ferox said, and something about his tone made the scout shudder. 'Bring the rest of them along, I'm riding ahead as fast as I can.' He gave no more explanation and set the big horse running, its hoofs heavy on the grass.

A little later, Vindex caught up with him, leading a pair of the horses they had rounded up from Claudius Super's escort.

'You might need me,' the scout said, coming alongside, 'and we might need these to keep the pace up.'

Ferox nodded, but it was a while before he said anything. When he started, the story poured out, the details coming to his mind as he told them.

'All happened seventeen, maybe eighteen years ago. A new cohort was raised from a Germanic tribe called the Usipi. They'd been causing trouble, so after they had been shown the error of their ways, they conscripted five hundred of the young men into the army and sent them to Britannia to keep them out of further mischief.

'It's something the Romans do often enough, and usually it works. They get pay, weapons, a chance to win glory fighting the enemies of the emperor and everyone is happy.'

'Except the enemies.'

'That's their problem.'

'I'm guessing this time it did not go to plan.'

'No, not quite. There was trouble. Some savage punishments, which only spread the resentment. Then there was mutiny. They slaughtered their officers, instructors and just about anyone else they caught. Then they went to the coast and found part of the classis. They took three triremes, killing anyone they couldn't frighten into joining them. This was down south, not far from Deva. After that they put to sea and followed the coast north, coming ashore to take by force anything they wanted. They killed a lot of people, took women and food wherever they could find them. Some of the locals fought, and killed a few of them in turn, but it was hard to face hundreds of well-armed men who landed without warning. The army was too busy to chase them properly. This was near the end of Agricola's time as legate.'

'I remember Agricola,' Vindex said softly. Agricola was the man who had led the legions far into Caledonia, conquering new lands that were then quickly given up as troops were withdrawn.

'The Usipi kept going. At some point they started to turn against each other. Food was short and perhaps that was why they took to cooking men as food. Two of the ships vanished, the other kept going right the way across the north of Britannia and then turned south. Some of them ended up east of the Rhine, where the Frisians caught them and either killed them or sold them as slaves. It was from men bought in the markets in Germania that the rest of the story was learned, but even then it left a lot unaccounted for. Perhaps they drowned.'

'Or perhaps not.' Vindex scratched the stubble on his chin. 'I'm guessing you are wondering whether some survived, living far in the north or on some island, and now they are back. And maybe now they forced the Red Cat and the other lads to come south and take Genialis for them, and had a fellow who could pass as a Roman to tell them where to find him. Why?'

'That I do not know, but it makes me think they might try again. Perhaps killing Claudius Super wasn't a decoy and they wanted information. Or perhaps they are going to Alauna.'

'Oh bugger,' Vindex said. 'Still, they should all be in the fort, shouldn't they? Her and the boy. Not in the villa.'

Ferox did not say any more, and just slapped the rump of his horse to urge it on.

The sun set blood red over the western sea.

XIII

THE BLACKENED SHELL of the villa still smouldered as the shadow of the building lengthened in the late afternoon sun. The outbuildings had been flimsier and burned faster, leaving smaller carcases. Behind them, towards the sea, the fort showed few scars from the night attack. Several parties of attackers had got inside, blackened faces and bodies hard to see as they slipped over parapets of walls too long for the small number of soldiers to patrol.

No one had expected such a direct attack. Aelius Brocchus was with two turmae off north along the coast, responding to a report from one of his patrols who had discovered the corpses of some of Probus' herdsmen. Another turma swept south in case raiders came from that direction. They had not, but late in the day a warship had arrived at the little harbour. The centurion in charge of the ship and twenty marines had marched to the fort, reported that they were patrolling the shore, but had had an accident and had three men needing medical attention. It all seemed in order, the duty decurion directing them to the hospital and calling for the sole medicus in the garrison. The naval troops were allocated accommodation in an empty barrack block, with space for the rest who would come once they had finished repairing damage to the ship.

Night fell, and in the second watch the centurion and marines came quietly out of their barracks and marched to the gate, just as some thirty sailors came to join them. The guards were quickly cut down, and at the same time three groups each of a dozen or so swarmed over the walls and into the fort. Two bigger groups went straight to the villa. Nowhere was there much resistance at first. Most of the Hibernian warriors were still with the kings at Luguvallium. The few who had stayed at the villa fought and died to protect their queen. One of Probus' slaves swore that he had seen Brigita clad in her yellow dress and sword in hand, fighting alongside them. He did not see her fall, but there was no trace of her amid the bodies of her warriors. He also talked about the constant sound of whistles blowing throughout the fighting.

The Usipi, or whoever they were, had taken the queen. They had also snatched Genialis, but apart from a couple of slave girls they had killed everyone else they found at the villa or in the outbuildings. The only survivors were those who had managed to slip off into the darkness and find a hiding place.

The soldiers at the fort had responded more quickly, but it was hard to organise to meet a threat they did not understand. Cerialis gathered seven or eight Batavians and a few men from the alae and formed them up outside the praetorium, while the women, children and staff escaped through one of the side doors. It was a hard fight, outnumbered two to one, but they had stood shoulder to shoulder like towers and kept the enemy back. The man dressed as a centurion died on their spears, as did half a dozen of the marines and several of the black-painted warriors. Numbers would have told in the end, but then a horn blew and the attackers gave way. The prefect took the two remaining unwounded men and went to look for his family. He never reached them, for he must have run into another group of warriors. Ferox traced the signs of a struggle in the mud. One of the Batavians was found dead. The other and the prefect had simply gone. So had Sulpicia Lepidina.

'She saved us,' Claudia Severa explained. 'It was all her idea taking everyone to the cells.' There was a building used as prison alongside the workshops behind the praetorium. It was smaller than the one at Vindolanda, and rarely used, but it was in a quiet spot and had the stoutest windows and doors of anywhere in the fort. Sulpicia Lepidina led them straight to it. 'She had a much clearer memory than I can boast. But just before we got there, we heard some men coming and saw the glint of their weapons. We hid in an alleyway between some buildings, but they were coming closer. She whispered that I was to lead the others, and then she just ran out from the alley into the main path. They saw her, of course, but then she screamed and ran in the opposite direction, leading them off. They followed like hounds, and when they were gone I took everyone inside and we locked the door, and then locked ourselves into the cells. Then we just kept very quiet and prayed.'

Aelius Brocchus held his wife close, the relief in both their faces obvious. He and his men had galloped back as soon as they saw the flames of the burning villa, but arrived to find the enemy gone.

'They must want hostages,' the prefect said. 'The queen, and Cerialis and his noble wife, are rich prizes for ransom.'

It made sense, and Ferox hoped that he was right for that might offer them some protection. Yet with such strange and brutal captors it was hard to know. They had acted to deliberate purpose, but it was hard to guess just what that purpose could be.

Little Marcus began to cry, and Claudia Severa insisted on taking him from the maid and soothing the baby herself. Ferox looked at the boy, his heart torn between love and terror at the thought of what might be happening to the child's mother.

'We shall care for the children until their parents are restored to them,' Aelius Brocchus announced, and his wife stroked his cheek with great fondness.

On the next day Neratius Marcellus arrived with his singulares and a glimmer of hope for that restoration.

'A man brought this to the fort.' He showed them a papyrus roll. 'He was a mute, unable to speak – or be persuaded to speak for that matter – but the guard commander had the wit to realise that it might be important. It is a letter, addressed to me, damn their impudence, and says that they will return the hostages to us if we hand over one hundred good swords, fifty helmets, and ten thousand denarii.'

'That is not all that much,' Brocchus said.

'Perhaps, but since it is clear this was written before their raid they may not have known who they would get. There is one more thing. They want Probus as well.'

'With more money?' Crispinus asked.

'They do not say. It is possible that they will then seek to extort money or something else from him for his own release and that of his son. Yet I rather wonder whether they just want the man, and suspect they have nothing too pleasant planned for him.'

Brocchus grimaced. 'Is he willing?'

'I am sure he will be,' the governor said smoothly. 'I have had him placed under close guard.' He smiled. 'For his own protection, of course.'

Crispinus shrugged. 'It will upset some important people.'

'Then let them be offended.' Neratius Marcellus' voice was

unusually harsh. 'I'll not stand idly by while an equestrian officer and a senator's daughter are in the hands of pirates or whatever these people are.'

'Where and when will the exchange take place?' Ferox asked.

'Ah, centurion, to the point of the matter as usual. Well, they say that we are to take everything to the place of the kings in Hibernia, for the raising of the high king in two weeks' time. It seems they knew about the embassy, as well as too many other things.

'Which means that the tribune will get his wish and lead a delegation across the sea. A warship and two transports, one hundred soldiers, including a few of your scouts, Ferox, and the kings and their remaining followers. All to be ready by the day after tomorrow to sail from here.'

'My lord, I request permission to accompany the expedition,' Aelius Brocchus' tone was formal, but his eyes were imploring.

Neratius Marcellus shook his head. 'I understand your feelings, but I need you for another purpose. It is possible that we can get the hostages back merely by giving them what they want. On the other hand, they may see our agreement as a sign of weakness, and make further demands. Or they may plan treachery from the start.' He stared at each face in turn. 'I hope that my fears are unjustified, I sincerely do, but hope is not a sound basis for a commander to make up his mind.

'We need to be prepared for the worst. There is a chance that they will kill their captives whatever we do. In that case I will not rest until we are avenged. That is my job as legate of the emperor, since I cannot permit the majesty of Rome to be damaged lest others are inspired to commit worse depredations. These men must be punished. If they are indeed some of the Usipi, then they must also pay for their past crimes.' The practised orator was in full swing, the words flowing, each slight gesture of the hand and each rapid glance full into a man's eyes was fluid and forceful. Yet Ferox sensed that the sincerity was not feigned. This was more than simply a good performance.

'Yet I will cherish my hope for as long as I can. If there is the slightest chance of getting back Cerialis and his wife then I will seize it. I need not remind you that the Lady Sulpicia Lepidina is a relation of my wife and very dear to me as well. So if there is any chance at all, I will take it with both hands. Thus, we must consider a rescue, in case these scum do not do as they promise. We do not know where they live, or where they are likely to hold the hostages, but we may be able to find out. The thought occurs to me that they may lurk on some island, either off the coast of Hibernia or further north off Caledonia or even distant Thule.

'We will find them, wherever they are, but we must have sufficient force to strike a certain and deadly blow. I wish you to command this force, my dear Brocchus. It will consist of two triremes, perhaps another if it arrives in time, along with transports and several hundred picked soldiers. Will you do this for me?'

'Of course, my lord. It will be an honour.'

'Good, then I know that I am relying on a man who can temper prudence with boldness. You will wait here until word comes from Crispinus that it is time to act. It is the task of his expedition to find out everything he can. If there is the slightest chance we must seize it.' The legate clapped his hands to emphasise the point.

There was much to sort out and very little time, but before he hurried off to arrange his side of things, Ferox had one request to make.

'If you are absolutely sure.' Neratius Marcellus' doubt was

obvious. 'Might it not be prudent to keep one as surety to the other's behaviour?'

'They may not agree,' Ferox explained. 'They will only accept if I show some trust.'

'It is a risk.'

'Yes, my lord.'

Ferox rode back to Luguvallium with Vindex. Thankfully the games had been suspended, so they were able to collect the corpse of the warrior they had found on the beach and go to where the prisoners were held. Together they lifted the dead man off the horse, and rolled the black painted warrior onto the ground in front of the cage.

It was the first time Segovax and his brother had shown much interest in anything.

'Was this one of the men who took your kin?' he asked.

The Red Cat spat through the bars at the body.

'He says yes,' Vindex interpreted.

'We are going after these men,' Ferox said, and tried to think how best to explain it so that the northerners would understand. 'They have taken a Roman chief and his wife prisoner. I am bound by solemn oath to them. I will get them back, if I can. Whether or not I can do that I shall have vengeance and kill every last one of these bastards. Will you come with me?'

Segovax lifted his arms so that the manacles rattled.

'If you give me your oath you may come and fight beside us. When it is over you may go free, wherever you will, with weapons in your hands. Up until then you will not try to escape.'

'What oath?'

'To follow me and help me in any way you can to find these men. Then you will aid us to get back the captives and wipe the land free of these murderers and eaters of men.'

158

The brothers looked at each other. No word was spoken, but it was a while before the Red Cat gave a slight nod.

The man with the red face turned to them and spoke slowly. 'We will swear to serve you and hunt them down, to kill them and free your chieftain and his woman. But that is all. Once it is done we are free. We do not give up our promise to kill you and this one. Those are our terms. Do you take them? If not then we will die here for that is our fate.'

'I accept them,' Ferox said. Vindex gave him a sidelong glance, but said nothing.

'Then we swear by the gods of our people, by the sun, moon and stars, by the four winds and green earth, by rock and by breath to serve you faithfully, to fight and die at your side, until the men of the night are killed and your captives safe or dead. Then it is over.'

XIV

QUINTUS OVIDIUS WAS the most surprising addition to the expedition, attracting even more puzzled glances than the two northerners, clean now, and with their long hair braided back and issue spatha swords at their sides.

'It is the urge of a man of letters to see the world rather than simply read of it,' the little man said whenever he was asked. He spent most of the voyage peering out over the side of the ship. 'My dearest wish is to see a whale, or some other monster of the deep.'

No whales or monsters appeared, but the voyage was smooth and fast and brought them to a little trading port on the Hibernian coast. There were two other ships already there, both quite small, their crews busily unloading amphorae of wine and heavy wooden boxes.

Waiting on shore was a band of sixty warriors, thirty for each of the kings. All were mounted, and they had brought ponies and supplies. The kings, as befitted their rank, had chariots to carry them inland. Crispinus' escort consisted mainly of cavalrymen, a mixture of Batavians and men from the ala Petriana. There had only been space in the transports for thirty-five horses, but with the ones provided by the warriors they were able to mount fifty troopers as well as the officers, Vindex and a few of his scouts. The rest were to stay with the ships. As they were preparing to depart, one of the troopers nodded amicably to Ferox.

'Longinus,' he said in acknowledgement. He had seen the man on board, but they had not spoken. The cavalryman was old, by the far the oldest man in cohors VIIII Batavorum equitata and had lost one eye many years ago.

'Flora sends her greetings,' the man said quietly. 'Asked me as a favour to try to stop you from getting killed.'

'Kind of her,' Ferox said. The brothel mistress and the old soldier were friends from long ago and a different life. Once the man now called Longinus had been an equestrian officer called Julius Civilis. Like Cerialis he was a Batavian, and like Cerialis he was of the tribe's royal line. A promising career went badly wrong in the civil war after Nero's suicide, and a rising in favour of Vespasian had turned into a rebellion to establish an Empire of the Gauls. Most of the Batavian auxiliaries had followed him, and they had won quite a few victories before Vespasian – by this time victor in the civil war – sent a big army to settle matters. Civilis and his allies were defeated, but the man had vanished and escaped punishment by finding anonymity in the ranks of the Ninth Cohort. Ferox had learned who he really was during the trouble with the Stallion, but otherwise it was a secret shared only by the rest of the cohort. Longinus was a good soldier, and even the officers of the cohort craved his good opinion. Even so, Ferox was a little surprised to find him serving with the expedition.

'I owe the lady's family, you know that,' the trooper said. 'And himself' – he meant Cerialis – 'is one of us, and king by rights, so it is my duty to help him.'

They left the harbour in bright sunshine, and were soon riding over fields rich with the greens of early summer.

'Doesn't look that different,' Vindex said on the third day of their journey and the second day of unbroken drizzle. 'Wetter, though.'

Ferox said nothing. It all reminded him of home, the rain as much as anything else, but that was what he had expected and other things occupied his thoughts. The night before, Ovidius had asked to speak to him and to Crispinus in the tribune's tent. The guards were ordered to keep their distance, and make sure no one overheard anything.

'It is a rare thing for a poet to boast more knowledge of the world than men of action such as yourselves, so please forgive me if I have been jealous in guarding it for as long as possible. I assume that you have long since concluded that I was not sent by the legate for my prowess as a warrior or experience of diplomacy.'

Crispinus smiled. 'Or to see whales?'

'Or that sadly. Before we came to Britannia, the legate and I went to the Lord Trajan on the Rhine and I bought a slave in the market. I did not particularly need one, and it was simply chance that took me past the auction, but the cries of the auctioneer pricked my interest.' He paused, watching them for the moment.

'Please go on,' Crispinus said. 'I presume there is a point to this homely anecdote.'

'There is indeed, and at least you have not merely assumed that this was no more than the ramblings of an aged mind. The slave was called Felix, as so many are, though with heavy irony in his case. He was one of the Usipi, not that the name meant anything to me, but when the auctioneer called out that he was a cannibal and did his best to make the flesh of his audience creep, I became interested.'

'Where is this Felix now?' Ferox cut in.

'Dead. But I shall come to that, my young friends, and you must be patient. They were trying to sell him as a brute who could be set to any unpleasant labour, or even trained to guard property, so were a little surprised to find a poet bidding. I was curious, as what poet or philosopher would not be? Here was a man said to have committed one of the greatest impieties, a sin so great that few save illicit love between parent and child could be worse, or consign a man to more terrible punishment in the Underworld – or to exactly the same nothingness as all the rest of us, depending on your viewpoint.

'I bought him because I wanted to know his story and try to understand the evil he had done. He was one of the men conscripted by us to form the new cohort. As you know, the Usipi live beyond the Rhine and are not under our direct rule. They had raided our friends and murdered some traders and so were punished. However, it seems that their chieftains did not wish to provide us with their best warriors or most loyal men, and instead they picked on the poorest, the thieves, the lazy. On those they least wanted to keep, as it were. Felix claimed that he was chosen because one of a chieftain's warriors wanted his wife. He had taken no part in the raids or other attacks and resented being chosen. There were others, he claimed, snatched from their families and sent away as prisoners. Still more were slaves and captives bought or snatched from other tribes. Including fifty or so from the Harii. You have not heard the name before?' Ovidius looked pleased. 'It is significant, I assure you.

'They were all rounded up, treated as prisoners rather than

honourable recruits, and eventually shipped over to Britannia to train. I am no historian, but it has always struck me how often the worst possible men are given an important task, and that was certainly true in this case. A centurion from Legio XX was put in charge of organising and training the new cohort. I am guessing he was also chosen because the legion did not want him around, but perhaps he had friends. He made few new ones. While I understand that *disciplina* is important as a great martial and Roman virtue, from what Felix told me this was not good discipline but blatant tyranny. The centurion flogged, starved, and executed men for slight infractions. He withheld pay from all of them, cut the rations to something barely short of starvation. Worse yet, he had many of the recruits stripped naked and brought to him at night, so that he could satisfy his lusts and his appetite for violence. More than one hanged himself after the experience.'

'The official report was less detailed,' Crispinus said, 'but could not hide the gross abuse of power. If the outbreak had been less violent, most of the men might well have been pardoned.'

'To Felix and the others it seemed that they were trapped, without any hope. Yet the rising started for another reason. The Harii kept to themselves most of the time, under three leaders whose word was law to them. No one in the cohort had been allowed to bring their families with them. That is the regulation, I understand.' Ferox nodded. 'But I also see women and children in most forts, especially with the *auxilia*, so I assume it is a regulation rarely enforced. Yes, I thought so. Well, it was imposed on the Usipi, and then suddenly, months later, seven women turn up at the fort where they were training. All of them were Harii, and the leaders were twin sisters. Felix never liked to talk about them. Even after all these years his fear was obvious. It took a while – and I fear some compulsion – to get him to say that their blood was special, that they came from a line of priests and priestesses, or perhaps witches would be a better word because he said they had power to heal and to hurt, power to see into the minds of others and know the future.

'The twins were the lovers of the leaders of the Harii, all three of them, for it seems the customs of these folk are strange. Twice they were evicted from the fort along with the other five women, but within a week they reappeared. The centurion ordered that they be beaten this time if they had not left by the next dawn, and one of the witches cursed him and cursed any man who obeyed him.

'That night the cohort turned on every Roman and every outsider they could find. Felix could not quite understand it, but afterwards he was told that the witches had put a potion into the men's food. He just said that he found himself sword in hand, chasing after one of the legionaries who was training them. He said that he knew the man well, and liked him, for he was fair and taught them dodges as well as the regulations, but still he ran him down and hacked him to pieces, cutting down again and again long after the legionary was dead. It was the same for all of them, their rage was red and raw and they had no mercy, murdering even the young slaves who looked after the pack animals.

'The Harii caught the centurion and killed him slowly. Then they ripped out his bowels and the witches bit into steaming entrails. Some of the warriors did the same and swore a horrible oath binding themselves together. It was the Harii who took the lead in all that happened later. The other men began to feel their rage subsiding. Felix thought it was the magic wearing off, but who can say. Instead they were overwhelmed by fear, for they knew that the army would have no mercy after what they had done, whatever the provocation. The Harii led them to the coast, where there was a station of the classis Britannica. On the way, they stumbled on a convoy carrying supplies and pay to the legion's base at Deva. The escort was not large, or expecting an attack from hundreds of desperate mutineers, for word had not yet spread of the outbreak. They were caught by surprise and slaughtered to the last man. The witches performed the same rite on a badly wounded tribune who happened to be travelling with them, ripping out his guts while the poor fellow was still alive. The rest of the Harii ate of his flesh and took the oath.

'They pushed on to the coast, found three warships and I believe that this part of the story is well known. One of the ship's masters refused to cooperate and was killed, along with any of the rowers who were unwilling to join the mutineers. What you probably do not know is that there was discord among the leaders of the Harii. One was stabbed to death, and another vanished, taking with him one of the witches, who was with child. No one was sure whether she went willingly or as a captive, but the sight of approaching cavalry stopped any thought of pursuit. Everyone boarded the ships and they rowed out to sea. That was the start of their marauding. They killed, abducted and raped women, and took whatever supplies they needed. The Harii were the leaders and enjoyed the pick of everything. Anyone who opposed them was slaughtered, but they mainly ruled by the fear of the witch's power and their dreadful oath. One by one, some of the others ate the entrails of the dead and took the same oath.

'As they went ever further north the pickings became less, while the ferocity of the inhabitants and the sea itself became greater. Food ran short, and it was then that they started to devour human flesh simply to stay alive. Sometimes they took captives, sometimes the witch cast lots or just pointed at the ones to die. It was never any of the men who had taken the oath. Eventually there was a fight, with heavy losses, but no clear decision and in the night one of the galleys vanished. On board were all the remaining Harii and others who had taken the oath, along with the witch and quite a few women. The other two ships kept going and rounded the north of Britannia. One ship sank in a storm, the other pressed on, raiding whenever there was the chance. Felix said that by now eating men had become natural. If you would like to know, he said that it is all in the cooking. One would have thought some men are tastier or more tender than others, but he said that they were not fussy.'

Crispinus grimaced.

'The trireme ran aground, and they would have been stranded had not a merchantman stopped in a nearby bay. They overran the ship, crammed themselves on board and sailed through storms and savage seas until weeks later they were wrecked on the coast well east of the Rhine. The Frisians snapped up the survivors, selling them as slaves, and thus the story of their fate came to us.'

'Was Felix a good slave?' Crispinus asked. 'I take it you did not let him anywhere near the kitchens.'

'He was willing enough in his way. Not a bright soul, even by the standards of those without education or any trace of civilisation. He was good at carrying things, good at sweeping up and cleaning, and he would fight to protect my property. The other slaves did not care for him, of course, saying that he was cursed and would bring evil on them. He was not very happy, but then how could anyone who had lived through all that be happy.'

Crispinus appeared to be about to make another joke until he thought better of it.

'What happened to him?' Ferox asked.

'He was murdered, his throat cut from ear to ear. It was very messy, and of course he was the one who normally did the cleaning.'

'Inconsiderate,' Crispinus said, but Ferox was more interested in when this had happened.

'In Londinium,' Ovidius explained. 'Barely a few days after we arrived in the province. There was a break-in to the mansio where we were staying. Yet nothing was taken and he was the only one hurt. Everyone else swore that they saw nothing.

'Now perhaps you will tell me that I am a poet and that I am letting my imagination run away with me, but in the last week I have been thinking. When the mutiny occurred the pay chest of the cohort was full, because the centurion had been withholding their pay. Apart from their salaries there was most of the *viaticum* each man had been given on enlistment, and that should be in gold, should it not?'

'Yes,' Ferox said. When a soldier joined the army he was given road money, three gold *aurei*, the equivalent of seventy-five silver denarii, as a bounty and to help pay the expenses he would incur. Even conscripts were given this gift in the name of the emperor.

'On top of that there was the convoy bringing the pay to the legion. All in all, there must have been hundreds of thousands of denarii, mostly in silver, and none of it has ever been seen again.'

'Probus,' Crispinus said, snapping his fingers just as Ferox came to the same conclusion. 'He was the leader who abandoned the others.'

Ovidius smiled. 'Perhaps we are all poets. But it did occur to me that all that money would have been a wonderful start for a man going into business. My guess is that he hid it, went for a while to where he was not known, took a new name, and did not come to reclaim it for years.'

Crispinus sat up straight. 'The boy,' he said.

'Young Genialis is of an age to be the son of that priestess. Probus does say his wife died giving birth to his son, so maybe that is what happened. It would make the lad part of that sacred bloodline, so that might explain why they want him.'

'It may also be chance, and I thought no more of it until these last days, but Probus was among the town councillors, merchants and other good folk welcoming the legate when we reached Londinium. I wonder if he saw Felix and recognised him. There is no proof, of course, none at all, but it does fit together very neatly.'

'It does,' Crispinus agreed, nodding his head several times. 'It truly does. We should inform the legate.' He caught Ovidius' expression and smiled. 'I am sorry. May I presume he already knows? Good. It would have been nice to have to have been told about all this.'

'That is why I am here.'

'And to see whales.'

'And to see whales and monsters and the wonders of Hibernia. The legate felt that it is better not to broadcast the story – wheat always flies further than the sower intends, as they say – so I have waited until there was a chance for some privacy. We still have little more than suspicion.'

'It all sounds right,' Crispinus said.

'Assuming that the trireme carrying the Harii was not lost, and left the others deliberately,' Ferox said, trying the idea out as he spoke, 'then they must have settled somewhere.'

'My guess would be an island of their own,' Ovidius says. 'I read that there are many of them off the coast of Caledonia.'

'Yes, that seems likely. So at first there were a couple of

hundred at most. Some were women, so they may have had boy children and a few of them would be old enough to fight by now. The rest would be older, like that corpse we discovered on the beach.'

'Why reappear now?' Crispinus asked the question without looking at either of the others, and Ferox was not sure that he was expecting an answer. No one spoke for a few minutes. 'Who can say,' the tribune said at last. 'Perhaps they did not learn of Probus and Genialis until recently?'

'That is assuming that our guesses are right,' Ovidius said, sounding even more like a schoolmaster than usual. 'We may be quite wrong and it is all just chance. Oh yes, there is one thing I forgot to say. Felix said that the Harii prefer to fight at night. They wear dark clothes, carry black shields and paint their skin black. Curiously enough, only the other day I read the same thing in Cornelius Tacitus' book on the people of Germania.' Ovidius chuckled. 'The mutinous cannibal and the famous orator in agreement.' His laugh became deeper and his thin body shook with mirth.

'It really does all fit,' Crispinus said. 'Although at the moment I am not sure how it helps us.'

'Do not trust Probus,' Ferox said.

'I never have,' the tribune replied.

'Yes, but if we are right, he is an even more dangerous man than we thought.'

XV

THE PLACE OF the kings was vast, stretching for miles between great monuments raised long ago. Several tracks led towards the sacred hill at the heart of it all, and as they came closer the land filled with people. Most were warriors, following their chieftains, who in turn followed petty and greater kings. They wore bright tunics, tartan cloaks, helmets of polished bronze with high nodding plumes and here and there shirts of mail or scale. Many rode in chariots, first dozens, then scores and finally hundreds thundering across rolling fields awash in a sea of wildflowers. Ferox had never seen so many, or such fine teams of ponies, even though his own tribe had dearly loved such things.

'It is like the *Iliad* sprung to life before our eyes,' Ovidius said in genuine wonder. Philo was close enough to overhear the comment and showed obvious delight. Ferox was often surprised at how well read the young slave was. All the more because they had spent little time in cities or towns, let alone near libraries. Bran was simply wide-eyed, for the Novantae were not a numerous people and never gathered in such numbers.

'It must have been like this in the old days at home,' Vindex said softly. 'Before the Romans came and brought us peace, of course.' He had spoken in Latin, but did not bother to hide his wistfulness. This was a world of proud kings and folk who seemed much like his own kin. No doubt his father, or certainly his grandfather, had seen great gatherings of all the Brigantes, which must have looked much the same.

'Were the old days always so noisy?' Crispinus asked and grinned. Alongside the chariots and the warriors walking on foot there were trumpeters everywhere, carrying the same tall bronze trumpets they had seen at Aballava. The long curving tube came apart, so that it could be screwed up as one great curve or as an S-shape. Either way the musicians played long, throbbing notes, each taking turns to lead the group so that the sound never ceased.

It was like seeing an army gathering, save that none of the warriors carried spears or standards. A lot of men had scabbarded swords at their belts, and all carried brightly painted shields, but there was a truce for three times seven days and for the same number of miles in all directions for this festival and the raising of a new high king. Much of the time Epotsorovidus and Brennus rode in their chariots on either side of Crispinus, and bands of warriors had come to swell their following so that the Romans were part of a much bigger procession, thousands strong.

Epotsorovidus said little, his already meek spirit shattered by his wife's abduction. If word had come asking for something in ransom, then he had not shared it with his new Roman allies. From what Brennus said and he overheard from others, Ferox suspected that without Brigita by his side, Epotsorovidus was now unlikely to be named as high king. That in itself might explain her abduction, and perhaps the Harii or Usipi, or whatever the men of the night now called themselves, were in league with a rival.

The different approach roads merged together close to where a great mound rose out of the plain, surrounded with a grassy rampart and ditch. It was a lot like many he had seen all over Britannia, although bigger than most. Men said that they were tombs of great kings of long ago or of giants, and were filled with silver and gold, but bound by terrible curses. He did not know if this was true or when they were built, but he had never seen so many close together, for others lay across the plains ahead of them, leading to the biggest of all, unless it was a real hill, even though it seemed very round and was surrounded with a similar rampart.

Even Crispinus seemed to sense something of the awe of this place, which did not stop him cursing at how long everything took. At the spot where the main paths met, lines of men dressed as animals danced to the beat of wooden drums and the blasts of the great horns. After two hours of this, a black bull and a white calf were led round and round in a circle for some time, before they were sacrificed by priests.

'Druids?' Crispinus whispered to Ferox.

'Like druids,' was the best answer he could give. He did not know why, but it had been many generations since men from Hibernia had travelled to Mona to learn the lore of the druids.

It was a little after noon, but they went no further that day and camped near the place of sacrifice. Ferox guessed that there were more than twenty thousand people in tents or lying under the stars, with the scent of the burned sacrificial animals mingling with that of many meals being prepared. He saw Vindex sniff in distaste.

'I know,' Ferox said, his mind dragged back to the place where Claudius Super and his men had died, 'I know. But you have to eat.'

Probus was already known to quite a number of the chieftains and kings. He explained that he had twice sailed to Hibernia on trading ventures. 'Horses,' he replied when Crispinus asked what it was he wanted from the tribes. 'You only have to look around you to see how fine their horses and ponies are. I sell mounts to the army, and this looked to be a good place to pick up plenty of fine animals at a very good price. They don't really use money much over here, but the kings will give you a lot for wine, spices and silks.'

Half a dozen leaders came to visit Probus that evening. He rose to greet each one, led them back to sit with him around a campfire and eat roasted meat. Each chieftain was accompanied by a warrior, while Falx, the gladiator, stood silent and motionless behind the merchant, a gladius on his hip. He was taller than Ferox and a good deal broader, with the massive arms and legs that came from years of weight training of the sort only done by wrestlers and gladiators. His nose had been broken more than once, one of his ears was a mangled remnant, and there were scars on all his visible skin. The man almost never spoke, and rarely let any noise escape his surprisingly small and thin lips. When Probus gave an order it was instantly obeyed. With anyone else he was slow to the point of surliness. The falx was a two-handed sword favoured by the Dacians, curving forward like a sickle and ending in a heavy point. A skilled warrior could lop off a man's arm, head, or even both legs with a single blow, and the name was an apt one. Falx's eyes were small, with all the emotion of well-wrought iron. He was a weapon, and nothing else, and he was in the hands of Probus.

Ferox had been surprised when he learned that the gladiator was to accompany them, and even more surprised that once they were on the ship there was no sign of Probus being held against his will – or being closely protected for his own good, as Neratius Marcellus might have said.

'He wants his son back,' Crispinus assured him when Ferox raised the matter. 'As I said weeks ago, the gods alone know why, but that's a father's love for you. He will do anything to bring the boy home.'

'Anything?'

'Be surprised if he is keen on sacrificing himself, especially given all that Ovidius has said. Doubt these pirates have anything too pleasant planned for him. He'll try to free Genialis and get away, and I doubt that he will care too much about the prefect and his wife if it comes down to a choice. With his sort of money, he can always disappear somewhere in the empire, or even beyond it.'

'What is to stop him slipping away from us, my lord?'

'Too soon for that. Reckon he will want our protection for a while yet, so I should not think that he will wander off until word arrives about the exchange. Even then, he might decide that he is better off sticking with us and trying to plan his way out at the last minute. I'd be much obliged if you kept a close eye on him. At least that great lump of a fighter shouldn't be able to vanish too easily.'

Ferox told the Red Cat and his brother to watch the trader. The order did not seem to surprise them and they simply nodded, not asking for an explanation.

'Do we kill him if he runs?' Segovax asked. He was sitting down, rubbing his leg. The break had healed well given the time, although he limped a little.

'Not unless I tell you to. Just make sure you know where he has gone.'

The great gathering did not go far on the next day, simply advancing to a grove of oak trees. There were more dances, and a sacrifice of a stallion and a mare. The trumpets rarely stopped, and the different leaders set up another camp and cooked another meal. As the day wore on they drank beer from barrels and wine from amphorae.

People were always moving around the camps and after a while Ferox began to see a pattern. Individual warriors went to other encampments, greeting men they knew with simple verses of praise, for everyone seemed to know everyone else. Later some of the chieftains did the same thing, but they went to men of similar rank and the compliments were fuller and took far longer.

On the third day they processed along a path lined with holly bushes, which led past another mound. The priests appeared again, although this time there were no dances. Three ewes and three sows were sacrificed by an ancient woman dressed wholly in black. Crispinus glanced at Ferox when he saw her, but the centurion shook his head because he was sure that her dark garb was coincidence and not anything to do with the Harii.

That afternoon and evening the senior chiefs started to visit each other, each one accompanied by a bard to sing praises of his master and the men he visited. A little after sunset a few of the kings rose from their own campfires and went out. Brennus was one of the first to do this, avoiding everyone's gaze as he strode through the camp, followed by a young bard. A priest was waiting for him and led him away. Epotsorovidus sat by a fire, staring into the flames and said nothing, but he seemed to shrink in on himself.

'Ah, this is politics,' Crispinus said softly to Ferox. 'That is something I understand.'

An hour later a king came to them. Epotsorovidus looked up, hunger in his eyes, but the ruler, his bard and one of the priests ignored him and went to where Crispinus sat on a folding camp chair. The praises took a while, and Ferox did his best to translate the flowery language. He was surprised at how well they had prepared verses about the young tribune, praising his birth, courage, prowess in battle, and his hair, which marked wisdom exceptional in one so young. A second king arrived after the first had left, and this one's bard even knew the name of Crispinus' father and praised him as a great warrior and leader of warriors.

'They do not ask for anything,' Crispinus said afterwards. 'So I presume that it is the visit that is important. Like a candidate being seen with influential men in the Forum. It is a mark of support.'

Ferox had spoken to some of the chieftains and felt that he understood. 'It takes a long time. Those who choose to call on another show their willingness to support him. The more visitors a leader has, then the greater his influence and importance. Everyone is watching what is going on. Usually they predict whose opinion matters, but sometimes there are surprises and it shifts. As one leader's prestige rises, then the rest must decide whether they will adhere to him or try to build up another to counter him.'

'As I said, politics.' Crispinus smiled. 'It is not so very different. Brennus has gone to call on someone else, so that means he does not expect our friend over there to become high king. And so far no one has come to visit Epotsorovidus. Is he finished?'

'My lord, he was finished the moment he lost his wife.'

'She was the steel in the partnership, there is no doubt of that,' Crispinus said.

'That is true, my lord. But how can a man who cannot keep his own woman keep a kingdom? Let alone rule over other kings and tribes?'

'Poor devil, no wonder he looks so down.' The tribune's sympathy did not extend beyond words. 'So if he is no use to us, how do I judge where our support will be best placed? Is the matter already decided?'

Ferox shook his head. 'No, not yet. As far as I can tell there are three or four being considered. There is still a lot of time. Tomorrow night more of the kings will call on each other. They are paying you a compliment by treating you as a monarch.'

'I'm the son of a senator, how else should they treat me?' Crispinus said, but his pleasure was obvious. 'We shall have to find out as much as we can about the rivals, so that we can best judge what is to our advantage.'

Ferox said nothing.

'I have not forgotten our main purpose,' the tribune assured him. 'But until we hear from these pirates there is little we can do. Do you not agree?'

'Sir.'

'Go away, Flavius Ferox.'

'Yes, sir.'

Bran was waiting for him outside his tent. Ferox had asked the boy to keep his eyes and ears open for any sign of the men of the night, for no one was likely to pay much heed to a servant boy looking after the horses.

'It is an island, further north, off the coast of Caledonia. Not big, but near a larger one and very close to a smaller one. The small one is ringed by cliffs and hard to reach, but someone special lives there. Warriors go there to learn.'

That was an old legend, known even among the Silures. It was said that far to the north an old woman lived who knew more about weapons and killing than anyone else. Whenever she died she was succeeded by another chosen woman. Only the best were accepted as pupils, and only the very best lived through the ordeals she set them. Quite a few heroes of the old tales were said to have honed their craft on that distant island, but Ferox had never heard of a man who had been there.

'And the bigger island?'

'It has more people. The chieftains are scared of the men of the night and pay them tribute. So do some on other islands. That is how they live.'

'Who spoke these things?'

'A young lad who sails with a merchant. He saw the island once, and heard the master of the ship and the sailors talking. They were scared because they had come closer than they intended during the night. There were stories that the pirates were preying on those who strayed too near, something they had not done for many years.'

Ferox wondered whether the Harii had managed to repair their old trireme. He doubted that they could have built one from scratch and it had been a long while since any of the classis Britannica's ships had gone missing.

'Could the lad find this island?'

Bran frowned in scorn at such a suggestion. 'He's just a lad. None too bright either.' Ferox suspected the 'lad' was a fair bit older than his servant.

'Do you know who the merchant is? No. Well, find out.'

The next morning was grey, and before long rain started to fall on them as the great gathering walked on, the main hill now coming close and looming over them. This was the first break in the weather after days of warm sunshine, and perhaps this was why the trumpets went silent. Neither were there drums when the dancers reappeared, and the lines of men in their animal skins and head-dresses whirled and stamped, and circled in an eerie silence. For hours the dance went on, and the dancers paid no heed when two priests led a young man into the middle of the circle. He had a halter around his neck and a thin circlet of gold on his head. For a while the two priests circled him, not dancing but pacing slowly. They were joined by two more and the old woman in black. No one held on to the lead of the halter, and the man wearing it stood and stared up, arms raised so that the rain spattered onto his face and left his long brown hair dark and wet. He wore a bright white cloak that reached to the ground.

'Is he a slave or a priest?' Crispinus asked, his own cloak drawn tightly around him and water dripping from the rim of his plumed helmet.

'He is both,' Ferox said, 'and he is king of the feast.' He had heard of such things among the Dobuni, the neighbours of the Silures, but never seen the ritual.

'Oh,' Ovidius said in surprise. 'Like at Massilia?' His tone was one of curiosity more than anything else.

Ferox nodded, while the younger tribune looked puzzled as well as damp and weary. 'Is there a sacrifice today?' Once the sacrifice was done they crowd dispersed and there was the prospect of shelter and warm food.

Two of the priests went to the man and took the cloak from him. He was naked underneath, his skin pale, but shiny with oil. As well as being tall he was slim and well muscled. The man knelt.

'Hercules' balls,' the tribune gasped as he realised, and then was embarrassed by his own lack of composure.

As he kneeled the man swayed his body from side to side, arms still up and face staring at the heavens. A priest carrying a club carved from wood so dark that it was almost black came up behind him. The old woman drew a bronze knife from its sheath.

The dancers stopped. There was silence apart from the pattering of the rain. Crispinus went rigid, mouth hanging open.

'Say nothing. Do nothing,' Ferox whispered to the tribune.

The priest swung the club and struck a glancing blow against the side of the man's head, who was pitched over onto the grass. He rose, shaking his head, and the woman slashed the knife across his throat. Blood spurted out, splashing onto the man's white skin where the rain washed it away. He staggered forward, spluttering and choking. Another priest followed him, matching his steps.

'Say nothing, my lord,' Ferox whispered softly.

The victim fell to his knees, and the priest grabbed the rope of the halter and tightened it, bracing himself by placing one foot on the man's back.

Crispinus looked as pale as the dead man's flesh.

The dancers started to gyrate once more, and the drums began, softly at first, but gradually growing louder and louder.

That night five kings came to see Crispinus, who received them in his tent, its front flaps held open so that the visits could be witnessed. The tribune was happy to be dry, and his horror of the sacrifice of the young man had had time to fade. Ovidius had found it amusing. 'The noble Crispinus is a devotee of the arena, and yet finds this shocking,' the philosopher and poet had said.

'And you do not?' Ferox asked him.

'Horrible. Truly horrible. But I am an old man and have seen too many foul things in my time. And as a man of letters I have read of acts of appalling cruelty – I would call it inhuman cruelty if that made sense, but it cannot because it was done by men and not monsters.'

Ovidius sat in on the meetings, as did Probus, who was known to most of the visitors. Brennus had returned, and pitched his tent close to the tribune. Epotsorovidus sat alone, for most of his chieftains had left him. His warriors stayed, but had a hopeless air about them.

By the end of the evening it was clear that most men now expected Togirix of the Woluntioi to be named by the priests as high king.

'He is the stallion,' more than one of the visitors declared. Ferox wondered whether another old ritual would be performed, with the king joining his earth as a stallion mounted a mare, but decided against trying to explain it to the tribune. If it happened, there would be time enough to tell him. After all were gone the tribune held a council.

'My impression is that Tigorex—'

'Togirix, my lord,' Ferox said.

'Thank you, centurion. My impression is that this Togirix is likely to win because no one hates or fears him as much as the others.'

'Now where have we heard that before,' Ovidius said happily. Ferox presumed that he was thinking about the elderly Nerva, chosen as emperor by the Senate after the murder of Domitian four years ago. Nerva had then adopted Trajan and died before two years was out. 'I am guessing they hope to avoid war.' They both looked at Ferox.

'They probably want to avoid a really big war between all the tribes. A weak high king will let them raid and murder each other on a smaller scale, but stop any one leader becoming too strong. Epotsorovidus might have been more forceful, at least with Brigita telling him what to do. They might either have kept the peace or started an even bigger war.'

'Given the consequence,' Ovidius mused, 'are we sure that

some or more of the leaders here did not help the pirates snatch the queen? Or at least promise reward for their deed?'

'It does seem likely,' Ferox said. 'Which one is harder to say.'

'In my extensive experience...' Crispinus beamed at them '... it is always worth considering those apparently closest to a leader. They see his frailties close up, and are very aware that he is just a man and yet has such power. Tempting to consider that you are also a man, no different in most respects from the ruler. Could you not have what they have?' He glanced out of the still-open tent as Brennus passed, returning from a visit, his bedraggled bard trudging along behind him.

'He will not get the power.' Ovidius spoke quietly, and before the others could say anything he explored the thought. 'But he might get more power than he had.'

'And the woman,' Ferox said.

'She'd eat him alive,' Crispinus snapped. 'Sorry, poor taste.'

'It is one of their greatest crimes for a wife to kill a husband or husband to kill wife. If she were compelled to marry him, he might be safe.'

'All true, although does that not also mean that the wife is closest than anyone else to the leader? Perhaps she did not want him to succeed? After all, Ferox, you were the one who said that she was up to something.'

Ferox was not listening, for a figure was moving through the camp towards them. The man was tall, with a gladius hung from a red leather belt over his shoulder. That was the only splash of colour on him, for boots, long trousers, long-sleeved tunic and cloak were all black or so dark that they seemed black.

'They're here,' he said.

XVI

THE PIRATE WAS young, no more than sixteen, with thick black hair and olive-coloured skin. He did not look like any German Ferox had ever seen, and he guessed that this was the son of one of the sailors or marines who had joined the mutineers. The navy was the only branch of the army open to men who were not freeborn, so perhaps the father was a former slave from Syria or Egypt. His son spoke Latin peppered with a few Germanic words, and it was easy to follow the sense if not every detail. He hissed something that sounded like a curse when Probus was brought over, so must have been given a good description of the merchant because he was too young ever to have met him.

Probus did not react, and the meeting was short and without incident. They were to meet on the next night, an hour after sunset. Ferox thought how odd it was for a man who came from a remote Caledonian island to speak of so Roman an idea as an hour. They would bring all that they had promised to the mound where the first sacrifice had occurred. By the time they met, the high king would have been named, the celebrations under way. The peace reigning over this place during the festival would last for another day and a night, so they had better not think about trying to seize back the captives by force.

'Would the crowd turn against us on behalf of these folk?' Crispinus did not hide his scorn or lower his voice.

'Yes,' Ferox said. 'This time and this place is sacred and cannot be polluted.'

'The punishment?'

'I believe being torn apart by wild horses.'

'We shall honour our pledges,' the tribune proclaimed. 'And expect you to do the same.'

'We will bring the captives,' the young warrior said. 'None of your high folk have been harmed in any way. They will only be hurt if you do not give us what we want.'

'Do you trust them?' Crispinus asked after the man had gone.

'They're bandits, pirates, kidnappers and cannibals,' Ovidius said, 'and you wonder whether they are honest!'

Ferox ignored them and strode away, pretending not to hear the tribune when he called.

Vindex was waiting with a pair of horses. 'The Red Cat has gone ahead to keep an eye on the lad. His brother is keeping an eye on Probus.' Segovax was a lesser tracker than the famous thief, but still better than almost anyone else they had with them.

They led their horses until they were beyond the cluster of camps. Vindex had watched the northerner head to the north west, and after they had circled around two more big groups of tents and figures hunched under damp blankets they came into the open and found his trail. The only people out here were those defecating, none of whom were bothered by riders unless they came too close. They pressed on, catching up before long.

'He is not worried about being followed,' the Red Cat told them, and Ferox could see that the youth was riding straight across the fields, his horse leaving obvious prints. They followed for a while, and the path still led towards a line of low hills beyond yet another old mound.

Ferox reined in beside a copse. 'Wait for me in there. Keep a good watch, because these are men who know how to move at night. If you have to kill anyone, make sure no sees you do it.'

The centurion dismounted and walked off into the darkness, heading at an angle to the trail left by the young warrior. Ferox guessed that they were camped somewhere among the hills, relying for safety on the rules of the festival. At first he walked, for the rain made it hard to see or hear any distance. Every now and again he would stop and crouch, watching and listening. By the time he could see the mound a long bowshot away to his right, he was still more than he moved. The rain came on even harder, making it difficult to see because his eyes and eyelids were filled with water. Gambling on this as cover, he jogged ahead, slipping on the wet grass more than once.

At the last fall something told him to keep still. Like any Silurian boy he had spent hours learning to move with stealth at night and he knew that a man's fears could conjure up all sorts of dangers. He also knew that a man's instincts kept him alive. Ferox lay flat on the sodden ground.

The rain slackened and he saw movement less than ten paces away. A man walked into view, moving slowly and stiffly. He was little more than a shape, darker than the sky, and as he walked there was a soft bump with every second step. Ferox guessed that it was a scabbarded sword patting his thigh whenever he moved that leg. It was a sloppy mistake, but he forced himself not to relax or do anything foolish. This wanderer might be nothing to do with the pirates, although he doubted that. More likely he was young and inexperienced.

He wondered how many of the true Harii were left, and whether they had taught the rest all their tricks.

Ferox waited for the man to wander off, waited a little longer, and then began to crawl through the grass. Above him the clouds parted and a bright moon shone down, turning the landscape silver. He froze again, lifting his head as little as possible to look round. The man he had seen was a good hundred paces away, and there was another sentry a similar distance away in the other direction. Both men paced up and down. If they were clever they would have posted a few men a little back, lying on the ground and watching. Ferox went slowly forward for a dozen paces, stopped, waited, and did the same again. He was making for the lip of a low rise, up ahead. As he came closer he started to hear voices in muffled conversation. There was a dim light, which grew, and someone had got a fire going because there was a glow beyond the rise. It seemed that they were not clever.

It took a long time, perhaps an hour or a little more, to reach the crest. The camp was just below him, so close that he could see individual faces around the fire and smell the bacon or pork they were cooking. At least he hoped that it was bacon or pork, and could not help feeling hungry.

Ferox watched them for some time, making a careful count. There were forty-seven men with anywhere up to another dozen or so out on guard. There were no women. He scanned the scene again to make sure that he was right, but no one was asleep and all were clearly visible. He could see Cerialis, his hands bound, so that one of the Harii was leaning over and helping him to eat. Genialis was not there, and there was no sign of any other captive apart from the prefect of the Batavians.

Edging back on his elbows, Ferox went down the slope. He had seen all that he could and needed to get back. Turning around, he stared out across the slope and could only see one of the sentries. Staying on his belly he crawled and slithered on. The second time he stopped he saw the other warrior, squatting on the ground. It was an odd posture for watching and then he heard the man groaning and straining. Ferox crawled forward, taking almost as much time as he had during his approach, until he decided that he was far enough out to get up and walk.

A wind came from the west, sighing and hissing over the grass. Ferox was wet and weary, and shivered when the first cold blast bit into him. It no longer felt like summer. He tried to tell himself that the Harii had brought the prefect because they wanted to extort more for the rest of the hostages. They would make new demands for the release of Sulpicia Lepidina, thinking that handing over the prefect showed the Romans that it was worth paying in the hope that they would be given the lady next time. Ferox did not honestly care much about Genialis, and from what Ovidius had said they may anyway want the lad to join them, assuming he was the child of one of their priestesses. Brigita's own kin may be ransoming her, or not, given the fall of Epotsorovidus, and that was not his main concern. Ferox tried to make himself think of the slaves and others they had abducted, but the vision of Sulpicia Lepidina filled his mind and his fears pictured her in torment or dead. She was not here, which meant that he must go to where they kept her. He hoped that Bran had found out more.

The man sprang up from the grass and came at him, hurling himself at Ferox's waist. There was not time to curse himself for letting his mind wander, and all he could do was brace his feet and then twist as the man slammed into him. They both fell. Ferox was struggling for breath, but managed to strike with his knee and was rewarded with a grunt of pain.

The man's fingers reached for his throat. They rolled, Ferox on top for the moment, and he jabbed down with his elbows, breaking the lock the warrior had on him and staring into the black-painted face. Then they rolled again, and the warrior was on top. A shout came from somewhere else, and someone was running over to them.

Ferox punched. He had no real room to swing, but the blow caught the man under the chin and that made them turn over again. Ferox butted with his forehead, felt the savage impact and dull pain as bone met bone. The man groaned, and the Roman hit him again, full in the face, and his elbow pressed onto the warrior's windpipe. Someone ran up, then gasped as the breath was knocked from him and he fell on top of them. Blood was wet on Ferox's face, but the man who had fallen was dead weight, sliding rather than attacking, so he hit the man beneath again and again until he lay still.

The corpse was dragged off him. Beside him the Red Cat nodded, and the gesture somehow conveyed his bafflement at the centurion for letting himself be surprised. The man on the ground moaned softly, and the northerner readied his sword.

'No. We take him back. This one too.' He gestured at the dead man. 'We'll hide him in the trees.'

The Red Cat hooted like an owl. Vindex rode up a few moments later, leading the other horses. They went back to the little patch of wood, their captive still unconscious. Ferox told the others where they were to join him, and by the time he reached the camp he had the rest of the plan in his mind. The tribune was asleep, and he toyed with the idea of going ahead without his permission, before deciding that it would take longer to persuade anyone without his orders. Crispinus would have to know, but first he went to see Bran, who had the 'lad' and his master in tow.

'Five thousand denarii,' the man demanded. He was of average height, broad and thick limbed with the weather-beaten skin of a man who had lived through many a gale.

'You will have it,' Ferox promised.

His next visit was to Probus. The merchant was angry at being disturbed, but listened to what he had to say.

'Very well. We'll be ready.'

Crispinus was harder to persuade. 'You want to leave us?'

'They only have Cerialis, so they will want more from us. Get him back, my lord, and in the meantime I will go and see if I can rescue the others. We know where their island is, I have arranged for a merchant ship to carry us, and I have one of their men who will tell me what I need to know. You free the prefect and then come after us. We will leave a sailor who can guide you, so send him to the legate and Aelius Brocchus's force. You can all come and rescue us in case we cannot get away and before the rest of the Harii return.'

Crispinus was dubious. 'What makes you sure they have not brought the other captives, but simply are keeping them in another camp?'

'Why should they?'

'That's not a real answer. And why do you assume their warship is at a harbour here in Hibernia with most of their fighters. You may find their island and be faced with hundreds of warriors.'

'They need to take the ransom home. Better not to trust that to a hired merchant ship. My reckoning is that the galley came here after the raid, dropped off Cerialis and this band, and then took the others north to their lair. Why should they fear us chasing them or coming to find them, when we have no idea where to go?' He tried to explain his reasoning, knowing that there were a lot of guesses.

'What if you are wrong, centurion?'

'My lord, what difference will it make to what happens here if we are wrong? Show your open support for Togirix and he will help you. If they try to cheat you at the exchange, it will be hard for them to get away if the high king turns against them.'

There were more questions, but in the end the tribune gave his assent. 'How many men will you take?'

'Not many, as we must not diminish your escort too much. I'll take Vindex and all but one of his scouts. You can keep the one who speaks decent Latin. Then Probus and his gladiator, Segovax and his brother, and I should like half a dozen Batavians if you are willing. Volunteers for choice.'

'I make that fifteen, including you.'

'Sixteen, my lord. I am taking my servant boy as well, although I should be grateful if you kept Philo here. I'm not including the sailors and crew, because I am not expecting them to fight.'

'Sixteen, one of them a boy.' Crispinus fought to stop himself from yawning. 'Are you sure this is wise? Why not ask Epotsorovidus for some of his warriors? They look handy enough, and would surely fight for their queen.'

'He is unlucky, and I'd rather not be buried with him.'

'Fortuna,' Crispinus said softly. 'She's a fickle enough goddess at the best of times. I just hope that you are lucky, centurion.'

Ferox shrugged, then wondered whether he ought to say something to invoke the Roman goddess or any other power who might favour them. The moment had passed and it was too late.

'I had better get everything organised, my lord. Best if we leave before dawn.'

'Very good, centurion.'

XVII

THE SMALL SHIP rose on the wave, lifting high until it pitched forward into the next great trough, cold water bursting over the deck. Ferox braced himself and pulled his cloak tight, for soon they were rising again. An hour ago a shower of hail had left the deck white, until the spray washed it back to the dark wooden planking. Apart from a couple of tiny cabins at the stern there was hardly any shelter. Some men went to the hold, but most came back up fairly soon. Down there every movement of the ship was magnified, with no warning of the next lurch until it began. Even men with strong stomachs were soon vomiting, and the reek made others do the same. It took either great courage or a mind as empty as their bellies for men to stay there, crammed in between barrels and sacks and hoping the lashing keeping them in place would hold, not knowing whether the ship was about to go down. At least on deck you could see disaster coming, even if you could do nothing about it.

This was the third day at sea. The first had been perfect, a wind more southerly than westerly filling the ship's sail and driving them along across a smooth, blue-grey sea. Everyone felt the elation, and spirits were high. The Batavians leaned over the rail, laughing and joking, saying that this was no more than the rivers of their homeland. Some, like the one-eyed

Longinus, knew how quickly the sea's mood could change, but it did not dampen their mood. They were doing something, going to fight men who deserved to be killed and save a lady they all loved, who was one of their own. Bran was even more excited, helping the sailors whenever he could, hanging around them the rest of the time and watching what they did, for he had never been on such a large boat. Vindex and the scouts were suspicious, for they did not care much for the sea, but after a while admitted that this was not too bad, less crowded than the trireme and without its lingering smell of stale sweat. Quintus Ovidius beamed at everyone, asking them to call out if they saw a whale or anything else of interest. The philosopher was a surprising addition to their party, added on the insistence of Crispinus. Ferox was still unsure why.

The second day started well, until the wind died away to nothing. Now and then a brief flurry would stir the sail and carry them a short distance before fading away.

'Glad we are not further north,' the master said. 'Not and be this close to the shore.' On a calm day like this it would be easy for the Novantae or other raiders to row out in their little boats and catch becalmed ships. Fortunately they were still near the Roman province. Ferox thought that he could see Alauna, but was not sure in the hazy sunshine. He wondered whether the message they had sent in one of the transport ships had reached Brocchus. It seemed doubtful, since surely the same weather would have brought that ship to a halt as well. There were two sails on the horizon, but neither was close enough to recognise.

In the afternoon they sighted something else, a low grey shape coming from the north. It moved steadily across the water, its mast bare of a sail, but never came close enough for them to see the foam stirred up by the three banks of oars.

'Odd,' the master said, watching the distant galley warily.

'You don't often see any of the classis up here.' Ferox could see that the man knew what this meant. For over an hour they watched as the trireme edged past. The deck was silent apart from the low creaks of wood and rope of a vessel at sea. They waited, fearing to see the pirates turn towards them. There was no reason why the Harii should know who they were, no reason at all, neither was there cause for them to attack and plunder their ship rather than any of the other sails in sight. None of that meant that the pirates would not decide to come their way.

'Would we have any chance at all?' Ovidius asked, his tone one of curiosity rather than anxiety.

'None at all, my lord. That is if the wind does not pick up soon. Even then, they can sail as well as row, and probably outnumber us ten to one.'

'At least they are going in the direction we expect, returning to Hibernia for their comrades. We must hope that by now Cerialis is free, and the tribune heading back to the ships, while the Harii will be carrying off the ransom to meet with their ship.'

'That is what we must hope.' They had agreed to tell the pirates that Probus had fled the camp, fearing for his life, and that Ferox had gone in pursuit. The tribune would promise to hand the merchant or his corpse over to the Harii when they met to give up Sulpicia Lepidina and the other captives.

'I'm no mariner,' Ovidius said a little later, 'but it seems to me that they are well past us now.' The fringe of white hair around his bald head rippled. Above them the sail started to fill, and the master began shouting at his crew to get to work. The whole feel of the deck beneath them changed as the ship surged forward. 'Ah, now that the danger has passed we have what we needed to save ourselves,' the old man said. 'It has always struck me that one of the main proofs that the gods take an interest in mankind is the sense of humour that is so embedded in the affairs of the world. Often cruel, though it may be, it is surely there.'

'My lord, why are you here?' Ferox asked him.

Ovidius smiled. 'My boy, we shall make a philosopher of you yet! But the answer is simple. I'm am here for the adventure.'

The storm came that evening and lasted throughout most of the next day. Ferox had sent Ovidius into the cabin, and wondered whether the old man was still so keen on adventure. One look at the stocky master of the ship was enough to show how worried the man was, and perhaps it was better not to know more about the sea and its moods. Even Bran, who had revelled in the life on board, was pale and terrified as he huddled next to Ferox, Vindex and the Brigantes. They kept together because somehow it made them feel a little less terrified. Ferox thought about Sulpicia Lepidina, imagining her imprisoned in a dirty cell, perhaps alone, struggling to hold on to any hope. At least they were all free, albeit at the moment free to drown or be dashed onto the rocks.

If they survived, Ferox felt that they had a chance of saving her and the others. The captive warrior had told them a lot, his initial reluctance to speak changing after Vindex and Segovax spent some time alone with him. His name was Duco, and once he began to talk the words spilled out in a great flow as they sailed north.

'He's broken his oath,' Vindex explained, 'the oath sealed with flesh and blood. There's no going back for him, not now, because he knows what his mates will do to him.'

Duco was one of the original Usipi, and claimed to have been swept up in the mutiny against his will. He told them about the terror of that first night, then the horror of what had followed, culminating in the eating of dead men, binding them all in a ghastly brotherhood of damned souls. He had stayed on the ship when they raided Alauna, and said that the captives were not harmed, only kept in chains so that none could escape. It was cramped down among the ballast of the ship, filthy, dark and stinking, but they were fed. The trireme had then sailed to Hibernia, and he and the party who would receive the ransom had taken the Roman prefect ashore. Then the ship went north to their island with the other prisoners, and would return to collect the others once they had been paid.

'The prisoners will be kept in the tower,' Duco assured Ferox. It was the safest place, built out on its own tiny island in a lake and approached by a narrow causeway. 'It was there when we arrived. Home to a chieftain, and we had a hard fight to cut our way in, but his men were few, not well armed or experienced. They were mostly fishermen and we killed them and took their women.'

'How many warriors will be in the tower? Especially at night?'

'Five or six. There is no danger and Cniva is in Hibernia.' Cniva was their lord, the last of the brothers who had led the mutiny. 'He does not stay in the tower since his woman died last year. She had the sight, and the power, and he misses her.' Duco shuddered. It seemed the witch commanded more fear than love from the rest of the band. 'That is why he wants the boy, for the power will be in his blood.'

'And you are sure that they will all be in the tower?'

'Yes.' Most of the others lived in a sprawling walled settlement by the bay on the far side of the island. A few had huts out on their own. 'They are there, with some of Cniva's oldest men to guard them. All are Harii, and he trusts them, but they are no longer fit enough to raid. They will fight, though.' Duco spoke of the narrow winding corridor that was the sole way into the tower, and of the little rooms and chambers on either side where men would wait in ambush.

'Dogs?' Ferox had seen similar towers from a distance and visited a couple. Both had had big guard dogs chained up in the entrance. He could still remember how loud their barks echoed in the gloomy corridor.

Duco shook his head. 'She hated dogs and had them all killed.'

That was something at least, and as he sat and did his best to weather the storm Ferox worked on a plan, picking away at it, trying to spot any problem, any risk, and find answers. It began to seem possible.

Late in the afternoon the wind slackened. The ship's master asked everyone to throw something of value to them over the side as thanks to Neptune, for they were much closer to the shore than he would have liked. Slowly and painfully they began to beat back out to sea. The ship could not sail very close into the wind, so they crawled forward at a snail's pace, travelling what seemed like miles to gain a hundred paces. The next day was only a little better, but it did not get worse and they crept westwards for that day and the next. After that it became easier, the wind shifted and became steady. If not as glorious as the start of their voyage, it took them at a good speed where they wanted to go. Soon they were passing islands, and parts of the Caledonian coast that looked like islands. The master named them, although Bran often had a different name, and much of the time Ferox knew little or nothing about any of them.

'That's it,' the master said gruffly late on the following day. 'Not that I ever wanted to see the cursed place again. Beyond it is the isle of the hag warrior.' He made a sign to avert the evil eye. 'They are not welcoming either.' Ferox could see high cliffs all around the visible part of the little island. It looked a harsher, bleaker place than the gently rolling fields of the pirates' stronghold.

Duco told them more. He pointed, and through squinting eyes Ferox thought that he could see a tiny spike that must be the tower. The harbour and main settlement were on the north-western side. 'It is the best place for ships to anchor, and the arms of the bay give shelter from the wind.'

Ferox asked about the warrior woman on the other island.

'We do not trouble them. At least we did not. Years ago, ten of our men boasted that they would go and have her head. They were drunk,' he added in explanation. 'None of them came back, but a week later we found their heads lying in a circle on one of our beaches. The witch told Cniva to stay away, but now that she is dead he has said that the old hag has power and that we should take it. That is why he wanted the queen.'

'Brigita?' Ferox was surprised. 'You said that Brennus promised you fifty young women and girls every year for the next five years to snatch her and stop her husband becoming high king.'

'That is true, but he also wanted her because she is a daughter of the warrior queen. She wears the mark of that kin.' Ferox wondered whether that was the neat scar between her breasts. 'He will threaten her to make the warrior queen do what he wants.'

'How many live on her island?' Ferox wondered whether they might find an ally, although it was hard to think of any way to reach her.

'We do not know. Perhaps fifty, perhaps fewer. Boats come and leave fish and food on the beach, but no one stays unless they go there to learn.'

'Go and get something to eat,' Ferox said, and then raised his voice. 'Eat as much as you can. It's going to be a long day.'

He leaned on the side of the ship, staring at the islands, wondering whether he needed to change his plan.

'This looks like the end of the world,' Ovidius said, coming up beside them. He was very pale and seemed even thinner. The same was true of most of those on board.

'The end of this journey.' Ferox pointed to the south of the island. There were grey shapes skimming above the waves.

'Dolphins. Wonderful creatures, to be sure, but I have seen plenty of them before,' the poet said, and then his gaze went further and he spotted the dark hump beyond them. It spouted, then dived and a moment later a great black tail rose above the sea. Ferox watched the sheer excitement in the old man's face. 'That is truly a delight for the eyes.'

It came closer for a while, the shiny black back of the whale surfacing just twenty paces from them, and they heard the great exhalation of breath. When it sank again, there was an oily film on the water where it had been. For a while they watched, waiting for it to reappear, and just when they were about to give up were rewarded when the whale surfaced again, much further away. The sky was turning grey, with low clouds and mist coming towards them.

'This is it, then,' Ovidius said quietly.

'You should stay on the ship, my lord. It will be rough.'

Ovidius chuckled. 'What a strange way with words you military fellows have. I imagine Odysseus, back after twenty years, corpses of suitors piled in mounds around him, and when Penelope asks how it was, he just says, "Rough. Really, really tough."'

'Well, it was. Apart from all the nymphs and goddesses.'

Ovidius looked up at him. 'Let us go and save a goddess of our own.'

'You are sure?'

'I am. Quite sure.'

'Very well, my lord. Now, if you will excuse me, there is much to prepare.'

'Of course, I never said it was sensible,' the old man said softly after the centurion had gone aft, calling for Longinus and his men.

XVIII

THE ROUND TOWER loomed up against the night sky, shaped almost like a vase, its walls curving inwards. The point of a conical roof must have been at least thirty-five feet up in the air. It was too dark for Ferox to see either the thatch or the huge dry-stone walls, plain and without any windows or other openings. At its foot were three round-houses, also of stone, although the roof of one had long since collapsed. None had doors on the outside, and the only way in was through the main entrance, which snaked between the buildings before it led into the tower.

The only way in was through that main door, unless the Red Cat and the others were right and they could climb up and break their way through the roof. Ferox could not rely on them and, at best, it would give him an extra edge. He still wished that Bran had not wanted to go, but the boy assured him that he was an excellent climber, used to scaling cliffs in search of birds' eggs, and in the end he had given permission.

They had landed as the grey day came to an end, shielded from hostile eyes by the thick mist on the sea. Only nine could cram into the ship's boat at a time, including the two rowers and a helmsman, so it took three trips to bring all the men ashore and another for the sacks of supplies. Then the boat rowed back to the ship and they were alone. It was not safe for them to stay on the beach. If all went well, they would signal with torches and the sailors would row back in to pick them up. It was the weakest part of the plan, because Ferox knew that it would mean several trips to carry them all, the numbers of those left behind to hold off any enemies growing smaller and smaller all the time. He could not think of any alternative. They would just have to hope that with most of the pirates away, the others would be slow to respond.

Ferox, Duco and the two northerners set off inland, leaving Vindex to guide the others and follow at a distance. There was no sign of anyone. A few damp sheep stared forlornly at them as they passed. Ferox had asked the prisoner whether they ought to paint their faces and hands black.

'We only do that to frighten others,' Duco said dismissively. Ferox still thought of him as the prisoner even though he was helping them. He did not think treachery was likely, but had quietly told the brothers to kill the man at the first sign of falsehood. The centurion found it hard not to grin at the irony of asking two men who had sworn to kill him to keep a watch on another forced companion. Their oath would hold for the moment, and he needed them and their hardness.

They came in sight of the tower after no more than twenty minutes, and he spent some time circling it, taking a good look. A chink of red light showed the entrance at the end of the causeway. In the dark he could not make out whether this path was natural or made from piled stones, but it went straight out from the shore to the entrance. No one was visible, whether at the tower, on the causeway or on the shores around the lake. This part of the island seemed empty.

By the time they had circled again and gone back to the low rise on the far side of the lake, Vindex and the others were there. Ferox smelt fresh blood, and noticed that Falx the gladiator had the carcase of a sheep over his shoulder. One of the Batavians was carrying another dead animal.

'Best to have as much food as we can,' Longinus told him, and Ferox wondered why he had not thought of it.

He patted the one-eyed veteran on the shoulder. 'You know what to do?'

'Yes, sir. Stay back out of sight. If fighting starts we pile straight in. If not, I count to one hundred and then pile in.' Longinus would command the main force. The Red Cat, Bran, and one of the younger scouts were to wade or float using some pieces of timber, crossing the lake behind the tower. The old thief swore that he could climb the wall and break in through the roof and the other pair had volunteered to go with him. Ferox, Duco, Falx and one of the Batavians were to walk across the causeway and try to bluff their way in.

Ferox saw the huge gladiator lifting the dead sheep.

'Wait,' he said. 'Keep it.'

Falx stopped in the middle of the movement.

'Do as he says,' Probus commanded, and the man hefted it back onto his shoulder, where it looked no bigger than a puppy. The merchant was to stay with Longinus and the others, waiting back in the shadows.

The causeway was solid and flatter than Ferox had expected. He and the three others walked across, not hurrying and doing their best to look natural. There was still no sign of life from the tower, apart from the glimpse of firelight.

Ferox walked towards the tower. They were more than half-way across, the lake water a deep black pit on either side. Each man had his sword, and Ferox had his dagger as well, but they carried no shields and their armour was covered by their cloaks.

'Halt!' The challenge could have come from the sentry at an

army base. Even after all these years some of their training still clung to the mutineers. 'Who goes there?'

'Is that you, Flavus?' Duco called out before Ferox could say anything. 'It's me.' He started to walk forward again. Ferox and the others followed.

'Duco? That you?' The door opened, spilling red light and silhouetting a tall, thin man who stepped out to meet them. 'What's happening, brother? What do you want? I didn't think you were back.'

'I'm not. This is all a dream.' They were getting closer. Ferox could see the sentry's lean face. He had an army-pattern belt, the plates glinting faintly and a gladius on his right side.

Flavus laughed. 'Whose dream? If it's mine then it must be a nightmare. Why'd I want to dream of you?'

'Because I'm beautiful and I've brought you food, you miserable old scragg.'

'Who are your friends?' Flavus asked, and his hand went down to his sword. 'Didn't know you had any.'

'Don't you recognise me?' Ferox said, trying to sound offended. They were only a few paces away. Flavus started to draw his sword.

'Ignore him, he's an idiot,' Duco said. 'Cniva sent us. He wants the queen.'

The name of their leader made the sentry pause. 'Don't blame him. Although that bitch would kill you as soon as look at you. The chief got plans?'

'He's always got plans, always. But we've got mutton.'

Falx tossed the sheep onto the stones. Flavus looked down, and as he did so Duco drew his gladius and stabbed his old comrade in the stomach, putting his left hand across the man's mouth to stifle his groans. Ferox drew his sword and dagger and ran through the open door. A man was in an alcove, sitting on a stool and holding a bowl of stew. Ferox kicked the stool, knocking the man over and ran past him, leaving him to one of the others.

A third sentry appeared around a bend in the corridor. He was holding a small round shield and with his sword down low, but although he had his weapons ready he was sluggish with surprise. Ferox hooked his dagger over the rim of the shield, jerked it to the side and lunged with his gladius, the long point driving into the pirate's throat. There were shouts from further along the tunnel. A man appeared from another side room, wearing only trousers but carrying a sword. Someone else was shouting. Ferox dashed at the man, and the tunnel wound again so that he could see another warrior with a spear at the end of the corridor. A pair of torches burned in brackets on the wall.

A great bellow thundered along the tunnel. Falx pushed past him, crouching because the roof was so low, and charged. His left hand clasped his right wrist and even in the narrow space he swung the sword so that its wickedly honed blade opened the chest of the man in trousers. The gladiator lifted the dying man by the throat, holding him one-handed, took three paces forward and flung him at the spearman. Both pirates were down, the spearman trying to get up when Falx reached him and jabbed down. A woman screamed as the gladiator went through the doorway at the end of the tunnel. There was a grunt from behind him as the Batavian finished off the man who had been sitting on the stool.

Ferox ran after the gladiator, coming out into a wider room, its wooden ceiling about seven feet high. There were four doors around its roughly circular wall, and another open alcove filled with sacks. A grey-haired woman cowered down inside, screaming again and again. A ladder was ahead of him, Falx just starting to climb, his sword ready to thrust up.

'Wait!' Ferox yelled, feeling that he ought to take the risk and go first. The gladiator stopped, jumped down to the floor, so that a thrust spear narrowly missed his head. Falx grasped the shaft with one hand and jerked hard. A man appeared through the opening, coming head first and arms still clutching the spear. He let go, as the big man shook the shaft again. Ferox raised his dagger, aimed and threw, but it missed, bouncing off the ceiling next to the man. He ran past the gladiator and bounded up the steps, as the pirate vanished. By the time he came through the opening into the main living space, the man had picked up a sword and pulled it free from the scabbard. Ferox glanced around. There was a fire in the middle of the floor, raised on a stone base. A naked girl was pressed up against the wall, clutching a blanket to her, but there was no one else in the wide room, although a couple of sections were fenced off by wattle panels and hanging blankets. He could not see if there was anyone else on the raised floor that was mounted higher up on the wall to provide more space.

The man came at him as he pushed himself up onto the floor. The first jab was at his face, and Ferox rolled sideways to dodge it. He gave a wild slash with his gladius, hoping to catch his opponent on the leg or ankle, but missed. The man stabbed a second time, and Ferox rolled over again. The tip of the gladius missed his face by a few inches and drove into the timber floor. The man cursed, pulled it free, but then gave way because Falx appeared at the top of the ladder. Ferox pushed up, lunged and caught the warrior on the thigh. The pirate staggered back, hissing, and the centurion followed, slashing up and then back to cross the warrior's stomach. He dropped his sword, hands clutching at the gaping wound and Ferox thrust the blade hard, driving the slim point through the pirate's left eye.

There was noise from above them, and something landed on

207

the raised floor so that it quivered. The Red Cat looked down over the edge, took in the scene, and grinned.

'Check through there,' Ferox told the gladiator, pointing at one of the fenced-off sections. This time there was no hesitation, only the prudent caution of the fighter.

The girl started to sob loudly, her body shaking, although whether from fear or relief it was hard to say. 'My lord,' she gasped, and the thin voice was familiar. It was Aphrodite, Brocchus' slave.

'It's all right, girl,' was all that he could think to say. 'You're safe.'

Falx held his sword low and wrenched back the blanket hanging across the opening. He stepped in, moving slowly, then flicked his massive arm up to block a blow and sent someone flying back into the side room. He raised his sword and then stopped.

'You!' The petulance in the voice was familiar. Ferox went up behind the gladiator and saw Genialis rubbing blood off his lip.

The Red Cat came down the ladder onto the main floor, with Bran and the scout close behind.

'Search the rest of the rooms up here,' Ferox said. He turned to the youth. 'Where are the others?'

'Don't know. They kept me up here all the time.'

There was shouting from down below but no sounds of fighting and Ferox guessed that Longinus and the rest of his force had arrived. 'Your father is here, boy,' he said, and went down the ladder onto the ground floor, just as Probus appeared, following a couple of Batavians into the tower. 'He's fine. Up there.' He gestured towards the opening in the ceiling.

Simple wooden bars held shut each of the doors on the ground floor. Ferox beckoned to one of the Batavians to be ready, lifted the first one and eased the door open. A cow with soft brown eyes and a calf suckling on her stared at him. The second room held two barrels, some amphorae marked as containing oil and sauce, and a few sacks. There was a sound as he opened the third door and his heart leaped, only to see a big sow and a row of piglets lying on the straw. He began to worry that they had got it all horribly wrong. Someone was shouting for him from higher up in the tower, but he ignored them and wrenched the bar up on the final door, flinging it back.

Sulpicia Lepidina let out a long breath when she saw him. She sat on the rush-covered floor, her feet and arms shackled. Her pale blue dress was ragged around the edges and dirty, her hair wild and around her shoulders. She still wore a necklace and pearl earrings, and there was no mark of injury on her. To Ferox she glowed, and he felt relief flood over him. Brigita was beside her, chained in the same way, her yellow dress drab with dirt and badly torn, but he barely noticed her.

'You are safe, my lady,' he said, adopting the same soothing tone he had taken with the slave girl upstairs. 'It is over,' he added, not believing it but wanting to reassure. He repeated the same phrases in the language of the tribes, so that queen would understand. 'We'll soon have you free of those.' He went forward, crouching down to look at the irons. They were fastened with pins and he managed to knock the first one off, freeing one ankle. 'Come on, man, lend a hand,' he called to the Batavian, who went over to assist the queen.

The other pin was harder, but he hit it with the pommel on his gladius and eventually it came free. The lady wriggled her legs, smiling with joy to be relieved of the weight and grip of the shackles. 'We're here, and you are safe,' he said softly.

'I knew you would come,' she whispered.

Sulpicia Lepidina began to cry.

'My lady, it is a joy to see you.' Ovidius was at the door. 'Centurion, you are needed up above,' he added, and for once the poet sounded like a man giving an order.

Ferox had released one of her wrists and waited to finish the other.

'We can do that, centurion,' Ovidius insisted. It came free and the lady rubbed her ankles with her hands.

'I must go,' Ferox said.

Longinus was looking down through the hole in the ceiling. 'Up top. It's bad news,' he said.

Ferox climbed up to the first floor, then onto the raised platform. They had lowered a rope through the hole they had made in the roof and the Red Cat was sitting up there, waving his arm. Ferox scrambled up, wishing that he had that agility with ropes that seemed to come so naturally to others. The northerner helped haul him up and they both lay against the thatch, looking out over the rim of the wall. It was cold up here after the fug and dust of the tower. The sky was clearer, stars appearing.

Out to sea, their ship burned in the night.

XIX

THE TOWER WAS not a fortress. Centuries ago a chieftain had got his people to raise it on the tiny island so that his household could live there. It was difficult to approach, and its height reinforced the sense that here was the home of a man of importance. The walls were high and strong, but not designed for defence. There was no parapet or walkway on top, although now that they had knocked a hole in the roof someone could move around up there as long as they were careful. While there, they might just throw spears or rocks down at any attackers, for it was little more than a dozen feet from the closest part of the top wall to the mouth of the winding entrance tunnel. Without windows or slits of any sort, there was no way to do that from anywhere else. The narrow tunnel at least made it hard for anyone to force their way in.

'Hard, but not impossible, given last night,' Ovidius said.

'They have the numbers. If they don't mind losing plenty of men, they can keep attacking and in the end we will be worn down. A man can only fight for so long, even if he isn't wounded. If they keep on coming and take the pain, they'll win in the end.'

The poet looked older and smaller than ever.

'But if they are smart, they won't bother,' Ferox went on. Ovidius had not needed to come, but now he was here he ought to know the truth. 'What they should do is gather brushwood and anything else that will burn and pile it up at the entrance.'

Ovidius' big forehead creased into a frown. 'The stone won't burn.'

'No, but the smoke will come down this tunnel. This whole building is like a big chimney, especially now that there is a hole in the roof. It will suck the smoke in and we shall all choke.'

'Oh,' the old man sighed, and then shrugged. 'I am sorry, but I cannot think of anything clever or brave to say at this point. Should we leave and try to hide somewhere else?'

'It's their island. They've been here for years, so ought to know every nook and cranny. From what Duco says, there is nowhere better than this.'

The former pirate had also said that his comrades had no archers. 'The Harii fight at night, and they are the ones who lead us. They kill up close, terrifying a man so that he does not fight back. In the old days, a few of us made simple bows to go hunting,' he conceded. 'But there is nothing left to hunt.'

That offered them a chance. 'We need to make it hard for them to get to the entrance,' Ferox explained to the old man. 'That means fighting out on the causeway.' He had sent most of the men out to start work as soon as he had come down from the top of the tower.

The causeway was a little short of forty paces long. In the middle, he had them start to prise up stones. They would not be able to break it altogether, but the water was a good four foot deep at this point, which would make it hard for a man to wade around the side and still fight. One of the barrels in the storeroom was empty, the other half full of beer. Ferox ordered the drink poured out in buckets or bowls or anything else they could find, and in the end they put half of it into a trough meant for the animals. Then they rolled the barrels out so that they were behind the break in the causeway and they filled them with stones. That formed a solid base for a barricade. There were some empty sacks in another of the inner rooms, and they filled these with earth and laid them on top of the barrels. The stones ripped up from the causeway and any big bits of timber they could find were added until they had a wall at chest height. In front, they had taken a foot or so out of the causeway. It was not much of a ditch, but made the barricade even higher for anyone attacking it. They took any smaller branches, cutting them down and driving them as hard as they could into the earth and rubble of the ditch. Once they were in firmly, men worked to sharpen the tops into points. Ferox wished that he had thought to bring caltrops.

Sulpicia Lepidina stood at the entrance, watching the work and sucking in the night air with all the hunger of someone held prisoner for days. Ferox tried not to look at her, so busied himself with the work. They said that Roman soldiers liked a commander who mucked in with the men, sharing their rations and the hardships of campaign. For a mere centurion, with such a small force, there was no real choice, and sometimes it was simply easier to do a thing himself than explain it to others. Every few minutes he glanced up to the top of the tower, where Bran sat, legs dangling over the outer wall. Each time the boy waved to show that there was no sign of anyone coming.

The Harii may have spotted their ship and rowed out in boats to attack. Duco said that they had plenty of the little native craft, captured when they took the island or taken from fishermen. Yet if small boats had gone to the ship, surely they would have sailed it back to their harbour rather than burning it. It made more sense that the trireme was already here, back from the trip to Hibernia. They were fast ships and the pirates might have followed a different course and missed the worst of the storm that had struck them so hard. Cniva and his men had then seen their ship. Once again Ferox had to wonder why they had not captured it. The obvious answer was that they had burned it because they had learned about the party on shore. It was a message that there was no escape and no hope. That meant that the enemy was coming, and so they must work fast and keep a good lookout.

After a while the lady called to one of the Batavians and took him to a store of baskets in the tower, explaining that the grey-haired woman had told her about them. Once she learned that the attackers meant her no harm, the woman seemed glad to be free of her old masters and was making herself useful. Ferox had the baskets filled with stone and began another barricade just a pace or two in front of the entrance. This one was smaller, and would not cut across the entire causeway, because at some point the defenders of the first line would have to give way and they would need to retreat. They had plundered stone from the walls of the house without a roof and from the animal pens around the base of the main tower to help with the main barricade and now more was stripped away for the second. Ferox kept a couple of the baskets aside and had men selecting good round pieces suitable for throwing to take up to the top of the tower.

Ovidius appeared, greeting the lady warmly with a chaste kiss on each cheek. Ferox felt a flash of envy at even this slight contact.

'I have assured the Lady Sulpicia that her family are all safe,' he said, as Ferox walked over to them so that he could inspect the work from that side.

'At least Marcus is too young to know what is happening,' she said. 'And it is some comfort that dear Claudia is there. She will be as kind to them as if they were her own.'

Ferox wondered whether the poet had told her about her husband.

'I must pray that the prefect is safe,' she went on, smiling as they murmured sympathy. 'As pirates go, these have not been so cruel as captors as you might expect. I think they will have released him. There is purpose in all they do. This Cniva has a shrewd look about him, apart from when he flew into a rage. Then he was a monster. I can only hope the shrewd man prevailed and he has released my husband.'

'We all hope that, lady,' Ferox said, and meant it.

'They were cruel only to the slaves.' Sulpicia Lepidina gave a brittle smile. 'A fault that is not confined to pirates and bandits. They used the girls hard – so hard that one died of the treatment and poor Aphrodite has suffered much. I have told her to eat and get some sleep. I hope that she can.' Once again they both murmured their sympathy. Sulpicia Lepidina watched them expectantly, waiting for more. 'I fear that you are hiding things from me,' she said. 'I am not a fool, and know that this rescue may prove temporary. How much hope do we have?'

Ovidius glanced sidelong at Ferox. 'This is your field, not mine.'

'We are alive and they no longer hold you,' Ferox began. Her eyes studied him, daring him to insult her by hiding the truth. 'It really depends on how soon Aelius Brocchus and the others arrive.'

Her head tilted slightly, her eyes showing approval of his candour. 'And how long will that be?'

'A day or two, perhaps.' He shrugged. 'In truth, it is hard to say. It depends on how soon the message reached them, and then on the vagaries of wind and sea. Their journey might take days or even weeks if everything goes wrong. We have to hold out for as long as we can.'

'And if they do not come?' There was just the slightest tremor in her voice.

'We take as many of these mongrels with us as we can.'

Sulpicia Lepidina laughed, throwing her head back so that her hair shook. Men stopped their work and looked up in surprise. Then they all grinned, even the hulking and silent Falx.

'Spoken like a true Roman,' the lady said. 'Thank you for your honesty. There may be one cause for encouragement, though. Throughout this ordeal they have treated young Genialis with something akin to reverence. I do not believe that they would willingly harm him.' Ferox hoped that she was right. 'Now, I shall see if there is anything I can do to help inside.'

'My lady, I should be most grateful if you would take charge of our provisions.'

'Hmm,' she sniffed. 'Even in battle a man expects a woman to run the household.' She laughed again. 'Of course, centurion, it will be my pleasure.'

After she had gone, Ovidius shook his head. 'There are some rare people who make you feel as if you are so crude and vacuous, and yet make you love and admire them all the more at the same time.'

Ferox nodded. 'I had better get back to work. Before long I'll get half of them to eat and rest. We had better keep the rest awake for a while. Don't want them to surprise us by turning up early.'

Longinus insisted on being one of the men who kept the first watch, and Ferox was glad because he knew that he could trust the former rebel. He had a couple of Batavians, along with Probus and Falx. Ferox wondered whether the merchant might try to take his son and slip away into the night, but decided that they had nowhere to go.

'If you will take my advice, sir, you go and get some food and sleep,' Longinus spoke in that tone ordinary soldiers reserved for giving orders to their superiors.

Ferox smiled. 'I will,' he said. 'But first I want to look in all the odd corners of this place.' He went inside, wondering why the tunnel now seemed a lot shorter than when they had charged into it. On the ground floor, Brigita was practising cuts and thrusts with a sword taken from one of the dead guards. Ferox realised that he had not given any orders about their corpses, but could see no sign of them, so hoped they had been taken out and dumped on the shore.

'You use that blade well, noble lady,' he said. 'I am glad that you are safe.'

'It could do with being heavier at the point.' Her voice was matter-of-fact. 'And the grip is clumsy, but otherwise it will serve.' She sliced down as if slashing at an opponent's chest and stomach. 'I hear my husband is not high king.'

'No, he is not.'

'He would not have been a great king,' she said in the same flat tone. 'But I would have been a great queen.'

'You are still young.'

Brigita spun around, jabbing with the blade and stopping it an inch from Ferox's face. He did not react, and stared at her with mild interest.

'I will fight with you when they come,' she told him, and it was a moment before he realised that the words were in Latin. All the time she had understood what they were saying and hidden her knowledge, for her speech was clear and choice of words fairly good, apart from the small ambiguity, for it could be taken to mean that she would fight against him.

'As you wish.' Ferox did not relish the prospect of trying to stop her. 'But I am leader here, and I must command.'

217

She withdrew the sword. 'So be it.'

Ferox went past her to an alcove at the far end. It was covered by a blanket, so he pulled it aside and found what he was expecting. Stone stairs curved upwards inside a hollow in the great outer wall. It was dark, but not so dark that he could not see his way and the soft light was that of the night sky. He caught a hint of salt in the air, and realised that somewhere up ahead was an opening to the air. He followed the stairs, his feet echoing softly, the passageway curling around with the shape of the tower as it climbed. He came to where he thought he must be level with the first floor, wondering whether there was an entrance, but found only solid wall. It amazed him that anyone could make so huge a building without mortar, let alone the concrete that allowed the Romans to build so many miracles. For a few paces, the stairs became a level corridor, and he wondered whether the workmen had needed this while they were raising the tower. Once before, he had climbed a similar stair in another tower far away, and that had become smaller and smaller as it climbed higher, until a man could only go along it if he crawled. He pressed on, and there were more steps, but like that other tunnel the roof was getting lower. Ducking his head, Ferox climbed around another great curve. Up ahead the stair turned sharply and then stopped. A couple of paces ahead there was a solid wall apart from a narrow tube down which came faint starlight. He could go no further.

A footstep sounded faintly behind him. The sound was soft, on the edge of hearing, and if he had not stopped he probably would have missed it. Ferox turned, as slowly and gently as he could. There should not be any danger, for he could not believe that any of the defenders had survived, and he had certainly not passed anywhere where a man could hide. The steps came closer. They were slow, tentative, like someone who was nervous or trying to be silent. He waited, hand on the pugio in its scabbard, for in this confined space it would be hard to use a sword.

Whoever it was halted, breathing softly, waiting before taking another step. A dark shape came around the corner and he let go of the dagger's hilt and grabbed it with both hands, pulling it to him. The person was short, soft hair against his chin.

Sulpicia Lepidina gasped and looked up. 'Barbarian,' she whispered, and then touched her finger to his lips. Her other arm curved around his waist. Ferox held her tightly, even though this meant pressing her against his mail cuirass. He leaned down and they kissed, her lips soft and yielding. 'We are at the end of the world,' she whispered. 'Who can judge us here?'

Ferox kissed her again, and they spoke no more.

XX

A HORSEMAN CAME just after dawn and stared at the tower for some time, before riding away. The corpses of the defenders were laid out in a line beyond the causeway, and when he had found out they were there Ferox had wondered about telling his men to hide them. There was not really any point, since the barricades were there for all to see.

It did not matter, and when morning came he had other things to worry about. Encouraged by Sulpicia Lepidina, the slave girl Aphrodite had eaten some stew and then gone up onto the raised floor to sleep. When the lady had gone to rouse her this morning, she found her dead, stabbed through the heart, dried blood all over her bedding.

'Who would do such a thing?' Sulpicia Lepidina asked him when he arrived, summoned by the commotion. She looked pale, although not as white as the bloodless girl. There was a cruel echo of the other time they had made love, for the day after that they had found another murdered slave. Ferox thought of Ovidius' comments about gods with a black sense of humour.

Nobody had been seen climbing the ladder to the raised platform, but then most of the night people had been asleep or outside on guard.

'Was she violated?' Ovidius asked. Ferox could see no sign

of it, although the poor girl had been forced so many times by her captors that it was hard to tell, and at least it offered a motive. He did not really know any of the Batavians apart from Longinus, but the latter had vouched for them all when they were chosen and that was good enough for him. He could not believe it of Vindex and his men, or of the northerners, for all their grimness. Ovidius seemed unlikely, Bran too young, and he could not think of any reason for either of the women to kill the slave.

That left Probus and Falx, and it was easy enough to believe the gladiator capable of any cruelty, but hard to believe that he had sneaked up without being noticed. People tended to be very aware of the huge man wherever he was. Probus also seemed unlikely, for what would he gain? The man was rich enough to take pleasure with as many slaves as he wanted. The same was true of his son, but Ferox remembered Genialis trying to rape the girl all those months ago. He thought of the delight the youth had shown when he stabbed the Red Cat's son to death. There was also the archer who had ambushed him. From what Duco said such a skilled horse archer was unlikely to have been one of the pirates. On the other hand, there were surely plenty of former cavalrymen among the employees of the merchant and his son. The boy might easily have promised one of them a rich reward to revenge himself on the centurion for not giving in to his every whim.

Sulpicia Lepidina said that the lad had been well treated by their captors. Ferox wondered whether that had extended to letting him rape the girl. That might explain why Genialis was on the first floor when they stormed the tower, and not chained up with the other captives. The boy had been more nervous than sullen since they had arrived, and Ferox had assumed that this was because of the hard glances shot at him by Segovax and his brother. Most of the time he kept close to his father. Ferox wondered about saying something, but he had no proof and for the moment he needed Probus and especially his bodyguard. Now that the horseman had seen them, it would surely not be long before Cniva and his men arrived.

Ferox put the Red Cat and Bran on top of the tower. They were there to keep watch in case the pirates did what they had done and sent men to scale the wall and get in through the top. Ovidius insisted on joining them. 'I'm not much use with a sword, but I believe that I can throw a stone and sometimes hit what I want.' Ferox agreed, and added Genialis because it got the youth out of the way, and perhaps the sight of him would deter the attackers from anything too bold.

The others were split into three groups. Ferox led the first, with Duco, Segovax and two Batavians. They would make the first stand at the barricade. Longinus led the second group, with the other three Batavians and Falx, who would wait by the entrance and the smaller wall there. Vindex, his scouts, Probus and the queen waited in the tunnel as reserve. Brigita had donned a mail shirt, one of those captured from the defenders, and under it had a man's tunic, which left her legs bare from the knees down. Her long hair was platted into a pigtail, like the ones the northerners wore, but she had coiled some of it up so that the bronze army helmet, also taken from the dead sentries, was not quite so loose.

'Well, she certainly frightens me,' Vindex said. 'That and other things.' He sucked, baring his big teeth, making his face even more horse-like than usual.

'Thought you were a married man,' Ferox replied.

His friend shrugged. He was sitting in the tunnel and running a stone along the edge of his sword. 'Still a man,' he said. 'And you know a funny thing about that? Well, about you.'

'What?'

'You don't know, do you? You really don't. Although I must say you look happy this morning.' The Brigantian seemed to leer knowingly, but his face was made to leer and in the shadows of the tunnel it might be no more than his imagination.

'I am happy,' Ferox said. 'It's morning, and we are still alive. I can't promise that will be true by the end of the day, but we may as well make the most of it.'

'All right, don't tell me, and don't ask?'

'Ask what?'

'My wife's name.'

'Haven't I asked you that?'

'No.'

A call came from out on the causeway. 'No time now,' Ferox said, and ran out, dodging past the smaller wall and heading for the main one.

Half a dozen horsemen were on the shore. Their ponies were various shades of brown, and they wore silver and bronze scale or iron mail armour, but everything else about them was black.

'That's Cniva,' Duco said as the centurion reached the men on the barricade. He was pointing at a rider who was a little ahead of the others. The man was small, narrow shouldered, and his black beard and hair were streaked with grey. He did not look much, but looks were so often deceptive, and Ferox did not doubt that he was a killer. The question now was whether he was also a talker, and would try to persuade them to give in.

Behind the horsemen a file of soldiers appeared over the crest of the low ridge. They came four abreast, marching in step and in silence like a regular unit. Bronze helmets gleamed dully in the morning light, their mail shirts looked grey, and both were bright against the black tunics, trousers, and oval shields painted black. Even the shafts of their spears were painted in dark colours. At the head of the column a man carried a *vexillum*, its ornate and highly polished spearhead glittering above a plain black flag.

One of the Batavians, a tall man with dark brown eyes and a broken nose, spat over the barricade. 'Cheeky buggers,' he said.

Ferox grinned, and adjusted the cheek pieces of his iron helmet with its tall, transverse feather crest. He counted some two hundred men including the riders, which meant that there were likely other pirates to come. A glance back at the tower showed Ovidius and the others on top, looking all round as they were supposed to and giving no warnings of other threats.

The column wheeled to the right, processed along the ground a little back from the shore, and then turned into a line four deep.

The tall Batavian applauded mockingly. The other auxiliary trooper laughed nervously. Segovax rubbed the mail shirt he had been given after they took the tower, but his face was impassive. Duco was breathing deeply, sucking his lips back over her teeth. All of them had helmets, mail, a shield – three of them the plain black of the pirates – a sword and a good spear. They waited.

Cniva kicked his horse and walked the beast on to the start of the causeway. Here it comes, Ferox thought and waited for the boasts, threats and offers of mercy. The horse did not like the look of the stones and the water lapping softly against it as the wind blew across the island. It tried to shy away, and the pirate leader held the reins ruthlessly to keep it there. He began to whistle, softly at first, but growing louder and stronger, and he raised his arm to point at them, ending with a snap of his fingers and a wave. He went silent, glaring at them, and even at this distance his eyes burned with a dangerous hatred that reminded Ferox of the Emperor Domitian in one of his most murderous moods. Then Cniva turned away, and trotted back up the gentle slope to join his foot soldiers.

'Can we go home now?' the Batavian asked.

Duco was gripping the top of the barricade tightly, staring at the departing leader. 'That was a curse.'

'From a man who eats people?' the Batavian with the broken nose said. 'Piss on him, what does he know.'

'That he's got two hundred and we haven't got twenty,' the other auxiliary said.

'They won't have so many soon.' The man with the broken nose reached up and tugged at the horse hair glued to the top of his helmet. It was coming loose and he fiddled with it.

'You'll make it worse,' his comrade said. 'Then think of the trouble you'll be in.'

Twenty of the pirates jogged out of the line and came forward. Ferox had not noticed anyone give an order, but then he heard a whistle and at that the men ran onto the causeway. Another dozen peeled away from the main force and headed for the shore, javelins raised. The first group stopped and raising their oval shields began to bang their spears rhythmically against them. One of the ones on the shore threw a javelin, which whistled through the air and splashed into the water. Another missile hit the front of the barricade.

The main group came on again, the neat row of shields breaking up even though they were walking. Ferox wondered how often these men had fought against enemies who were not surprised and terrified. A javelin clattered onto the causeway behind him, sliding across the stones. Ferox stood in the centre, with Segovax on his right and Duco on his left. The two Batavians were a pace back, their shields ready to block any missiles coming from the sides. This was the formation he had planned, and they all took their positions without him having to give the order.

Four abreast, the pirates came on. One broke into a run and leaped across the shallow ditch at the barricade, impaling himself so hard onto Segovax's spear that the weapon went through his mail, his body, and burst out the other side. The northerner let go of the shaft and the screaming man fell back, knocking over two of his comrades who had jumped into the ditch.

'Spear!' Segovax's open right hand reached behind him.

The Batavian did not know the word, but guessed at its meaning and gave his spear to the northerner.

Ferox jabbed down into the upturned face of one of the attackers, driving the spearhead into his eye. Duco thrust and struck a shield, sending up splinters. The pirates were struggling to reach them with any force or aim. A spearhead thudded against Ferox's shield, but the impact was slight. He stabbed down again, glancing off the cheek piece of a helmet and piercing the man's neck. Someone threw a javelin at him from down in the ditch, but it went high.

No one spoke. There were no war cries, no oaths. The living grunted with effort and the maimed and dying gasped or screamed. Duco ran his spear into a man's body, piercing his mail, and another of the pirates hacked at the spear shaft until it broke. Segovax killed another, and then the pirates were going back, dragging their wounded and leaving two dead men in the ditch and another who had fallen into the lake, blood spreading in the water around his corpse.

'Three dead, a few more wounded and out of it. Another hundred and ninety odd and we really can go home,' his comrade said to the broken-nosed Batavian. 'They're providing us with the weapons as well,' he added, gathering up a pair of javelins from the causeway behind them.

The second time it was harder. Seven pirates ran across the causeway and into the ditch, while eight more came behind ready to hurl javelins over their heads. Other men still hovered around the shoreline, but as Ferox had hoped, the range and angle were poor for them to aim well and reach the men at the barricade. He was relieved that so far Duco had been proved right and there were no archers.

They had to hold their shields up to defend against the javelins lobbed over the top of the men in the ditch. One punched a hole in Ferox's shield, but fell away when he shook it, and by chance the movement revealed the face of an enemy peering over the barricade. He thrust with his spear straight into the pirate's mouth. Segovax killed the next man to appear, and Ferox had rarely seen a spear used with such speed and efficiency, for almost as soon as he had withdrawn the weapon, it darted forward once more, breaking through the cheek piece of a helmet and going through teeth and jaw. The pirate slumped back.

'Spear.' Segovax's empty hand reached back again.

'None left,' the Batavian replied, having just used his second and last javelin to wound a man trying to wade closer to them. Segovax drew his sword.

Duco staggered as a heavy spear smashed into his shield. He stabbed forward, but a hand grabbed the shaft of his spear and jerked it down. Another javelin spun through the air and took him in the chest, knocking him back. The broken-nosed Batavian dragged him away. One of the warriors was pushed up by his comrades and came over the top of the barricade. Ferox turned, showing his right side to the enemy, and drove his spear into the man's side, tipping him back, but losing the spear in process. A javelin came at him, and the centurion ducked just in time, feeling it brush against his high plumes. He came up again, turning so that his shield faced front once more, and realised that he had let go of his spear. His hand grasped the gladius and it slid from the scabbard. The Batavian was beside him in Duco's place, but once again the enemy gave way.

Ferox panted for breath. No one said anything this time. There were more bodies in the ditch and a couple more bobbing just under the surface of the lake, dragged down by their armour. Duco was groaning. He might live or he might not, but there was no doubt that he was out of the fight.

Longinus led his men forward, before Ferox could signal to him. They came with care, all along one side of the causeway, so that the men at the barricade could retreat without leaving it undefended for more than an instant. They went back, Ferox helping one of the Batavians drag Duco away, the spear still in him. They needed to get him back inside before they could do anything to help.

The next attack was much like the others, although Ferox heard more of it than he saw. He and his men were back in the tunnel, resting, while Vindex and his group stood ready at the second wall. Cniva must have seen that new men were at the main barricade, but perhaps he thought that Ferox had already used his best fighters and that these would be easier to overcome. The sight of the towering Falx ought to make anyone think again, but the enemy did not. The pirates came on, supported by men throwing javelins, and the boldest died. The gladiator was a big target, and javelins grazed his right arm and hit him in the head, twisting his helmet around, so that he could not see for a moment. The pirates cheered, almost the first noise they had made, and tried to scramble up the slope of the barricade, only to die on the spears of the Batavians. One of the auxiliaries took a slash on the wrist, but it was not bad and he could still fight.

Yet they came again, the wall less of an obstacle because they were now standing on the corpses of their comrades. They grabbed a spear and hauled one of the Batavians over the edge. Ferox heard the screams as the soldier was slashed again and again. His comrades threw their own spears down into the mass, wounding two, but leaving them with a shorter reach. Behind the leaders, the pirates who had been throwing javelins ran forward, leaping into the packed ditch. Men were lifted or jumped onto the rampart, and another of the soldiers reeled away, slashed across the face. Longinus jumped back to avoid a spear and the first of the pirates was across. The one-eyed veteran killed him, but in that time two more were up and the rest swarming behind them. Ferox had run to the entrance and saw the crisis.

'Go!' He shouted to Vindex.

Falx saved them. He bellowed in rage, punching with his shield and knocking one of the enemy off the causeway and into the water. He slashed with his gladius and beheaded a second pirate, the blood jetting up like a fountain from the severed neck. Then he dropped sword and shield and ran at the barricade, grabbing one of the enemy, lifting him high and hurling him back into the mass. Longinus killed another, the remaining Batavian pushed a pirate into the water and then slashed down with his sword, cutting through helmet and into his skull. It was over before Vindex and his men arrived.

'I read somewhere that Spartacus used corpses to fill in a ditch and let his army cross,' Ovidius said, appearing behind Ferox. 'Do not worry,' he added, seeing the centurion's expression. 'I have nothing to report from our high eyrie, and I needed to stretch my legs. Glad to get away from Genialis as well. The boy treats all this like something from the arena.'

'Why are you here, my lord?' Ferox could not help asking the question.

Ovidius smiled. 'Back to philosophy. Well, centurion and prince of the Silures, I am here because I have spent most of my life reading about the world. My wife died decades ago bearing our daughter who outlived her by barely a day, and I have never had the inclination to take another and risk the same pain. I am rich enough, comfortable enough, and if I chose could live on in this wealth and luxury for my remaining years, and I would do all that, never having seen the world. This is the wide world.'

'Not the safest place.'

'What does it matter? Apart from that I have confidence in you. And in the gods' and goddesses' sense of humour.'

'Anything in your books that would tell us how to make some special weapon to save us, my lord?'

'Sorry, centurion, I dozed off on that page.' Ferox was about to go back out when the poet plucked at his arm. He was obviously struggling to raise something. 'I was wondering,' he said at last, 'what you think will happen to the hostages if we are overrun? It seems unlikely that they would spare anyone. Except young Genialis. Should we let the others – and indeed ourselves – be captured if the worst comes to the worst? I do not like to think of the Lady Sulpicia in their hands.'

'No,' Ferox agreed. 'It's best not to think about it.'

Longinus and the others limped back, and Ferox went over to Falx to take a look at his head wound. The gladiator said nothing, but that was not unusual, and sat on the stool while Ferox cleaned and bound up the wound. Professional fighters were used to being fussed over by others.

'Do you have your freedom?' Ferox asked after he had finished.

The small eyes looked at him suspiciously for a while. 'The promise,' he grunted after a while, and jerked his head out of the entrance towards the barricade where his master now stood.

Perhaps it was the sight of Probus, but a howl of rage came from the pirates and a new attack surged forward sooner than Ferox had expected. This time there was little organisation, but a couple of dozen warriors ran across the causeway and started scampering up the mound of corpses.

'Come up if we look like breaking,' Ferox shouted to Longinus, who nodded wearily. 'You three stay here,' he added, turning to Segovax and the Batavians. Then he ran towards the barricade.

The spears held them for a moment. Vindex put a man down with a thrust to the throat, Probus drove his spear through an upraised shield and into the arm of the man carrying it. He could not free the spearhead so let it go. One of the scouts stabbed forward, gouging along a pirate's sword arm, but another of them grabbed the shaft and the Brigantian let it go rather than be pulled over. Another of the black-clad warriors bounded up the backs of his comrades and leaped onto the barricade. He had no shield, but cut with his sword and struck the scout in the neck, just above his armour. The man staggered back, clutching at the wound to staunch the flow of blood, and the pirate jumped down in his place. Brigita threw her spear at a warrior following him, hitting him in the groin, so that he shrieked and fell backwards. The man over the barrier hacked at the wounded scout, cutting off his arm below the elbow, and then barged him aside so that he fell into the lake. Another of the scouts took a spear in the face as he tried to close the gap. Vindex and Probus were fencing with opponents over the barricade, while the other scout tried to keep back two men who had waded through the water on the right-hand side.

The black-clad warrior was a big man, tall and rangy, and he went for the queen, who stood in his path. She brought her shield forward, but he was stronger and his left hand yanked it aside as his sword went up ready to cut down with a ferocious power that no helmet or armour would stop. Then he froze, gasping and coughing because Brigita's right arm had shot forward and the tip of her gladius punched through his windpipe and throat so that it came out the other side. Ferox had hardly seen her move. Blood from the dying man sprayed across her face and armour.

Probus had lost his helmet and one of his cheeks was slashed, but he had put down his opponent. The scout had wounded one of the men in the water with a javelin, and his comrade helped him wade back to the shore. Vindex still had his spear and finished another of them, and they were going back. Both sides were struggling for breath.

'That was a good stroke, lady,' Ferox said.

The queen sheathed her sword, and then wiped her hand through the blood spattered across her face. 'He had no skill,' she said, as if it were nothing, and walked up to join them at the barricade.

Sometimes a man knew how a fight was going not by anything he could see but simply how he felt. The last repulse had taken the first heart out of the Harii and the rest, and Ferox knew that it would be a while before they came back. Cniva and the others had ridden away. There were a dozen or so men dotted around as sentries, none of them closer than fifty paces to the shore.

'Aye,' Vindex agreed. 'They'll give us a break for a while. Probably don't realise how much they have hurt us.' That was just as well. Five men were dead or badly wounded, and a few of the rest had wounds even if they could carry on. Nearly all the spears were broken or gone, and it would be harder to hold the barricade with swords. There were a few javelins, thrown by the enemy and still in good enough shape to use, but they had slim shafts and were not designed to be thrust.

'Come on,' Ferox said to the lean Brigantian. 'Give me a hand and clear them away.' He vaulted over the barricade, landing unsteadily on the enemy dead. Vindex followed and they began to lift the corpses and tip them into the lake. Ferox would have preferred to put them on the shore, but he doubted the pirates would let them. He just had to hope that the water nearer the tower would not be poisoned by the dead bodies.

One of the corpses stirred, moaning. Vindex drew his sword and stabbed down. He caught his friend's glance. 'They eat people. I'm not going to let him recover and do it again.'

'So, what is it?'

The scout frowned. 'What is what?'

'Your new wife's name.'

'After all this time, I'm not sure I want to tell you. You're supposed to be a friend.'

'We're not friends.' Ferox began the old joke, one he had not made for more than a year. 'I just haven't got around to killing you yet.'

'Well, don't hang around,' Vindex told him. 'Or someone will beat you to it.'

XXI

T HEY DID NOT come again during the rest of the long day, and Ferox wondered why. His best answer was that they were planning to attack at night. After all, that was what the Harii did. He leaned on the barricade with Probus, while the two Batavians sat on the causeway behind them. Segovax was on duty at the main entrance, and after all the losses he had reorganised everyone into two groups. Longinus had everyone else, and apart from one sentry to support the northerner they were to rest until they took over at the barricade halfway through the night. It was a long time for anyone to watch, but there were too few of them left for him to grant them shorter spells on sentry duty. Hopefully, everyone should get at least a few hours of peace, perhaps even of sleep if they were lucky. The sky was clear, a rising moon dimming some of the brighter stars but casting a pale light over the world. Ferox could see a few of the pirates standing or squatting on the shore, watching them.

'I know that one,' Probus said, nodding at a corpse they had left on the causeway ahead of the ditch. 'I just can't seem to come to his name. He was Usipi. Thick as pig shit and about as good company. Didn't know left from right, but a bastard in a brawl.'

'Does it all seem a long time ago?'

The merchant paused, realising that he had just admitted who he really was. The soldiers were watching them, and even a duller man than Probus would have sensed their hostility. A man who submits to the army's discipline has no love for someone who breaks away.

'A lifetime,' he said eventually. 'Another man's lifetime at that. I was born the son of a great man among the Harii, but he took a wound at the moment of his great victory and his blood turned bad. He screamed a lot before he died.

'I was twelve, and Cniva a couple of years older. Did you know he was, or is I suppose, my brother? There were three of us, all boys, and the two girls, children of our father's sister, who was a priestess of the white goddess. He was a great man, and it's the same out there among the tribes as it is in the empire, or up here – great men make lots of enemies. Men came at night.' He laughed grimly. 'Of course it was at night. Burned our farm, killed his remaining men, and took us as slaves. Those were bad years and they seemed to go on forever and ever. Yet hard work makes you strong and we grew into men. A slave cannot be bold, so you have to hide your spirit, burying it deep within you and letting no one see.

'We kept together, and that was something, although we lost sight of the girls often enough. Somehow, they always came back. Three times the farms where we toiled were raided and burned, and so we found new masters. Burgundians, Goths, Lemovii, each came in turn and we went to lands far from Rome and our homeland. We survived. Good, hard-working slaves have a value, but as we grew into manhood we were strong and people saw it. The last chieftain to hold us got a good price selling us to a man from Gaul out buying slaves. He sold us to the Usipi because they were raising the cohort for Rome and so we became soldiers of the emperor. Might have been good ones, too, if they'd put decent officers in charge of us instead of the vicious and the weak. That camp near Deva became a nightmare.'

Something splashed on the lake over to their left. They froze, watching and listening. There was more splashing and flapping and then a bird rose into the air. They kept watching for a long while, but there was no more movement or noise.

'Easy, lads,' Ferox said at last. He leaned his arms on the barricade again. 'That's the problem with authority. Too often ends up with the wrong people.'

'Yes.' Probus agreed. 'But who are the wrong people?' He drew his sword and felt the edge. 'Needs a bit of work.' The merchant reached for a whetstone before he continued.

'It probably would have happened anyway. There is something inside Cniva. He has hates that are not quite human, but seem to have a force of their own. All three of us hated. How could we not? But he seemed to enjoy it. Over the years he always had plans for escape and revenge. Sometimes it was just revenge, telling how he would die over the mutilated corpses of our tormentors. Then the girls came and found us again. The gods only know how they managed that. It all must have been worse for them. It always is for women. And they were women now, beautiful in spite of it all, and filled with their own power. They dreamed and saw the future, looked into the souls of men. They made things happen. Men would do things and not know quite why.

'Cniva wanted them both, and had them too, in the same tent we shared with five *contubernales*, all of them Harii. His seed took in them and they soon told us that they were with child. When a woman like that tells you something, you know it is true. They had us afterwards as well, but the optio found them and had them thrown out of the camp. They kept coming

236

back, and each time they were thrown out, the beatings they were given became more brutal. The last time the centurion said he would have them flogged, but first he had them bound and brought to his tent.

'That was the night we killed them all. The whole cohort rose as one man. I have said how those women could make men do things. Once it started all the resentment at our treatment spilled over. There was a lot of killing. The sisters had us drive stakes through the centurion's limbs, pinning him to the ground. Then one of us held open his mouth and they took turns pissing down it. I guess he drowned or choked. I've heard people say that they ate his bowels, but that isn't true. All that came later.

'You probably know the rest. The convoy, and seizing the warships. Cniva wanted revenge on the whole world. He didn't care about living, not then, for he was so filled with hate. My brother and I saw a chance for freedom and a good life somewhere, but all he wanted was to kill and burn. The money in the pay chests was nothing to him. While we got some men to bury and hide it, he was tearing the captured tribune apart. I do not know whether it was madness or a plan to bind us all to him, but that was when he ripped out the man's entrails and ate them, urging others to join him. Even the women were shocked, at least at first. Our brother yelled at him when he found out about it, and Cniva killed him without blinking an eye. He did not hesitate, did not seem to think, he just stabbed him in the belly. I thought for a moment that he was going to feast on him as well, but after the killing he had some sort of fit. The older sister declared that he was blessed by the gods to lead us to vengeance.

'That night I ran, taking the younger woman with me. She was always the milder of the two, so had suffered more in the years of slavery. It was a hard life at first, hiding from the soldiers out looking for the mutineers, but we managed to go south and finally bought passage on a ship to Germania Inferior. I got work as a butcher. I'd learned how to do that over the years. Genialis was born in a tiny room behind the shop, and my cousin died in the act. I was sure you could see her power passing into the baby, and when it was gone she was just an empty husk. I worked hard and my master took to me. He adopted me and then died a few years later. It was nothing to do with me, although I know people say otherwise. He caught a fever and died. Genialis was only four, slow at talking, but you could see he was special. When I had him with me life seemed to fall into place. It was like luck, but stronger and less fickle. The hidden money was still there when I went back for it. From being quite well off, we became rich, and that let us grow richer.'

'The noble Ovidius had a slave,' Ferox said.

'I was sorry about that. I remember the shock of seeing him in Londinium. Knew his face at once, even though he was cruelly scarred and withered by what he been through. Genialis knew who he was too, and that puzzled me because he cannot ever have seen the man. As he grows, more of his mother's power comes to him.

'But I could not take the risk. There was the money of course, and the fact that I was a mutineer. Rome does not forget that sort of thing. I guess even being a slave who enlisted in the army would be enough to get me executed.'

'I think in your case the blame would be on the man who gave you to the army claiming that you were freeborn.'

'Well, that's a relief.' Probus gave a grim laugh. 'It was a risk for me, but it was the boy I did it for. Genialis is innocent and I did not want him to suffer.'

'And now?'

The merchant stared out at one of the enemy sentries. 'Can't see his face from so far away, but wonder if I know him.' He peered at the man, as he went on. 'And now? Could you prove any of this in court?'

'Perhaps,' Ferox said. 'Perhaps not.'

'I'm not going back. The lands, all the rest, none of it matters. If we live through this I'll go to Hibernia and stay there. I have some friends. Genialis can come with me, unless he wants to stay in Britannia. Be nice if he could keep at least some of the estates. Still, I know that that is not for you to say.'

'No. All I know is that you have fought with us and for that you have my thanks. I know you came for your son, but you have helped us as well.'

'He isn't my son, though, is he? That bastard out there – my brother – is his father. Genialis has brought me good fortune and I have loved him as if he was my own, but he isn't, much as I loved his mother.

'I know what he is like,' he added in a softer tone. 'There's a vicious streak in him. Maybe I was too kind. When you've been a slave you are desperate to give something better to a child. I have indulged him too much, or botched it all when I tried to be firm. It isn't just that. He's different to everyone else, just like his mother and aunt – and even his brute of a father. From early on he sensed it. He has dreams and sees things. And there is the luck. That's why Cniva wants him, more than anything else. I'm guessing he wants more than this island, and whatever he wants will come through fire and slaughter.'

'That's why we need to stop him,' Ferox said. 'Stop him now and wipe them all from the earth.' He had an uneasy sense that he sounded like Acco when he talked of Rome.

Probus sniffed. 'Just us?'

'Help will come.'

The merchant lifted his sword. 'Will it? We won't last another day like this one.' He stiffened, but Ferox had already seen the movement on the lake. There were two, maybe three dark shapes out on the lake to their right. He scanned the shore, then the water on the other side of the causeway and saw nothing. Some instinct made him look ahead again and he saw creeping shapes heading for them.

Ferox tapped one of the Batavians on the shoulder and pointed out across the water. 'You watch them,' he whispered. Then he picked up one of the javelins propped beside the barricade. The shapes on the causeway were still indistinct, but it was clear that men were crawling towards them.

'I wouldn't worry about it all.' The centurion spoke to the merchant, resuming their conversation. 'They'll be here soon enough. I dare say the tribune and the legate will speak up for you and your boy with the emperor.' The shapes were coming closer. He thought that there were three or four of them. 'The Lord Trajan is a good man, they say, ready to understand. After all, it's not as if you ate anyone...'

One of the shapes sprang up and rushed at them. Ferox threw, the javelin hit the man in the midriff and he grunted as he fell. Probus threw another, which dug into a second warrior's thigh. He yelped, and then screamed as his comrades helped him back. The Batavian threw their third and last javelin, but cursed as it splashed into the water. The dark shapes retreated.

It went quiet and they waited.

'That looks like it for the moment,' Ferox said. 'But they might come on again.'

'Why should they?' Probus asked. 'We cannot go anywhere. All they have to do is wait.'

'Help is on its way.'

'Is it? And do they know that? Cniva won't want to lose too many men because they are hard to replace. Why not let hunger do his work for him?'

'They will come for us,' Ferox assured him, believing it was true, but wondering whether they would come in time. 'Cheer up. You have just said that your son brings good fortune.'

Probus chuckled. 'Yes. But he might bring it for Cniva.'

Ferox laughed, and once he started he could not stop and had to lean against the wall. Sometimes this Roman habit of chattering away could lift spirits.

Nothing happened in the rest of their watch. He told Longinus and Vindex about the brief attack. There was no need to warn them to be on their guard. In the entrance, Falx and Brigita sat honing their weapons. Their task was to guard the doorway and act as reserve to the others. The queen had her armour on, but was bareheaded, her dark hair once again neatly coiled up on top of her head. Bran sat on the floor beside her, polishing the bronze helmet with dedicated reverence. Ferox thought of the boy's ardent wish for a wife with long dark hair and he could not help smiling. Probus patted the gladiator on the shoulder as he went past, as a man might pat a favourite hound. The big Dacian did not react or say anything, but that was nothing unusual.

Ovidius was waiting at the end of the tunnel. 'All well, centurion?'

'We're still alive,' he said, and thought at once that that was cruel to the fallen. 'You look as if you have been in a battle, my lord.'

The poet's hands were bloody. 'Sulpicia Lepidina, *femina clarissima* and daughter of an ex-consul, has been showing me how to cut up and joint piglets.' Ovidius was smiling in self-mockery, and yet there was a trace of pride in his words.

'Who is up top?'

'That silent northerner with the red mark on his face. Your son, my dear Probus, is due to relieve him in a moment.'

'Then I had better see him before he goes on duty.' The merchant was walking stiffly from fatigue, but went to the ladder and began to climb.

'You should get some sleep, my lord,' Ferox said to Ovidius when the man had gone. 'Butchery is hard work.'

'I am tired. It's quite a novelty. I mean, everyone feels like sleep at times, but I cannot remember when I last felt so truly weary. The Greeks must have a word for this sort of revelation, when your senses become more alive.'

'I need to sleep, my lord,' Ferox interrupted, because he sensed that this might be a long digression.

'Of course, of course, my dear fellow. Here am I wittering on. Oh yes, I nearly forgot. The lady would like to have a word with you about provisions.'

'She is awake?'

'Still at work with the bacon. Goodnight, centurion. And thank you for what you are doing.' The little man clambered up the ladder.

Ferox saw the light from the room that had been her prison. The door was ajar, and he knocked before he entered. Sulpicia Lepidina wore a tartan dress, sleeveless and gathered in at the waist by a rope belt. It was something they had found in the tower, simple and rough woven, and Ferox wondered whether it had belonged to Cniva's woman. He doubted that she had filled it half as well, for the lady had the curves of a draped statue. The prefect's wife must have found some pins from somewhere, because her hair was tied back in a bun, and that made her more formal, except for the fact that she was working with bloodied hands to rub salt into cuts of meat.

'Centurion.' She nodded, her tone formal.

Ferox closed the door shut behind him, and hoped the gesture did not appear presumptive.

She gave him a thin smile. 'You must be exhausted.'

'It has been a long day,' he conceded. 'But I see and hear that you have been pretty busy.'

'No doubt from Ovidius. He is a fussy little man, but I do like him. He means well and tries so hard. However, it is just as well that that poor animal was dead before he did what he did to it.'

'Butchery is a difficult skill, they say. Yet it appears not beyond the capacity of a senator's daughter.'

She made a face. 'I told you long ago that noblemen raise their daughters to run a household. After all, that's easier than running it themselves. So we have to know about everything or we will be cheated by our own slaves.' The lady went back to her work and started to hum a song as old as the hills, sung by the tribes of Britannia and Gaul alike. It was a tune and verses that told of the meeting of a hero and the woman who would become his bride. Vindex loved it, and had kept whistling and humming it when Ferox had first met Sulpicia Lepidina and the Brigantian had sensed his attraction. 'I see a sweet country, I'll rest my weapon there.' Ferox thought of their first encounters, and the sudden passion of last night.

'How well off are we for food?'

'Ah, all business, I see.' She put down the slice of meat and straightened up, mimicking a soldier at attention. 'Yes, sir, certainly sir. We have a good store. This bacon will last, and we have enough fresh to feed us tomorrow without having to slaughter any more of the animals. There were three round loaves when we got here, and grain to bake more or make gruel. It's barley—' she grimaced at the mention of food for slaves

243

and the poor '—and will have to do for the animals as well, as long as we keep them. There is milk from the cow, beer and good water. No wine, I am sorry to say.' She raised her arm in salute. 'Is that to the centurion's satisfaction?'

'How long will it last, soldier?'

'Yes, sir, certainly, sir, beg to report sir.' She lowered her arm. 'If you had asked this morning I would have said ten days at best. After today, the mouths that are left can eat well for at least that long, and survive for another four or five days after.'

'Yes,' he said. 'After today.'

'He looks a lot like you,' she said, and her smile was gentle now, without any mockery. 'Little Marcus. It's not just the mop of dark hair, but his expression. He can be very serious.' She gave an exaggerated frown and stuck out her lower lip.

Ferox did not know much about babies, and had always assumed that one looked much like another.

'I thought he looked like you,' he said, sensing that it was the right thing to say.

'He has my laugh, poor thing.'

They smiled at each other awkwardly.

'You must be exhausted, my lady. You should get some rest.'

'I am not so very tired.' Sulpicia Lepidina washed her hands in a bowl of water and wiped them dry. She glanced down at the floor, where she had been chained for days. Now there was fresh straw, a sack for a pillow, and some blankets. 'A little bit more comfortable than bare stone,' she said, and reached up to the pins in her hair.

'Let me,' he said, stepping over to her. He fumbled with his fingers, but eventually the long golden hair fell loose around her shoulders. It was as if she changed, standing differently, no longer the formal aristocrat and just the woman. The same treacherous thoughts came into his mind, telling him that there was no reason why she should bother with him unless she wanted him for some dark purpose, and he pushed them away as he pulled her close. Her hair was soft, her skin softer still and her lips were sweeter than any sweet country. His fingers came to life and unclipped the simple brooch from one shoulder, letting the dress flap open on that side. He kissed her shoulder and her neck.

'I love you,' he murmured, because he could not stop himself from speaking, and his hand undid the brooch on her other shoulder.

Sulpicia Lepidina pushed him away, and he feared that he had said too much, but she smiled as the top of the dress fell down to her waist. She wore a breast band of cloth that must once have been a brilliant white, although it was now stained by the rigours of the last weeks. Her hands went to the rope belt, undoing it, so that with a slight twitch the dress dropped to the floor. Apart from a triangle of white cloth in front and behind she was bare down to her sandals.

'We are at the end of the world,' she said, and he wondered whether she had decided that there was no hope of rescue and it did not matter what they did for no one would ever know. The lady bent her arms back to reach the knot on her band. Then she stopped. 'No. Your turn.' She always made him feel like a centaur or satyr, ungainly, lustful and crude in the presence of a nymph or goddess. He obeyed.

Later they lay beside each other and sleep did not come to him. He knew that he was weary, but wanted to save every moment of this in his memory so that it might stay fresh for the rest of his life, however long that proved to be. They did not speak, but she rested her head on his chest, and although he could not see her face he knew that she was awake.

Then the shouting started.

XXII

BY THE TIME Ferox had dragged on his trousers and drawn his sword, others were calling out and stumbling awake. Probus appeared at the top of the ladder, naked and paunchy, and asking what was going on. Ovidius appeared behind him. Ferox ignored them and ran to the tunnel. At the far end, Falx was on his knees, gasping for breath, and a pirate with a blackened face was standing over him. The man lifted his sword, but it struck the stone ceiling, giving off bright sparks. There was a scream of pain from outside, and then Brigita bounded in and sliced into the pirate's arm. He squealed, dropping his sword, and the queen hacked at his neck, half severing it. The pirate slumped forward against the big gladiator, their blood mingling.

When Ferox reached them the warrior woman was breathing hard. She looked at him, then kicked the dying pirate over. Vindex appeared at the door, asking what was going on. There were five dead or dying pirates around the little wall outside the entrance.

'He got three,' the queen said, 'even after they stabbed him.' She was trying to staunch a big wound to Falx's stomach. Longinus called to Vindex to come back to the barricade, and Ferox went with him, but it seemed that the attack was over. Five pirates with their bodies painted black had floated across the lake on logs, paddling from behind the tower, so that they could come at the entrance from either side. No warning had come from the top of the tower, but by chance the gladiator had gone outside. 'He was pissing,' the queen explained, 'and saw two of them, but then they were on him. He knocked one down, got the other around the neck and snapped it, and was drawing his sword when the other three came from behind.' The queen stopped, her eyes empty like so many men after a fight, and Ferox knew that she could not remember all the details of what had happened.

It was easy enough to guess. Falx took a cut to the shoulder that did not break through his armour, then turned and got the thrust into his belly, which punched through the iron rings and padded jerkin underneath. The man who did it died a moment later, his throat opened to the bone. One of his companions sliced into the gladiator's left hand, cutting between the fingers, but the big man held the sword tight and stabbed the man in the face. Brigita killed the one he had knocked down, and came back just in time to save the big man as he slumped down.

'I fell asleep,' Genialis explained when he was summoned. 'I am sorry.' His eyes flickered in the torchlight and he did not sound repentant. He seemed fascinated by the great bulk of the gladiator. They had taken him to lie out in one of the little rooms off the entrance tunnel. It took six of them to lift him and they did not want to take him any further. They cleaned him up, Sulpicia Lepidina supervising as they bound up his wounds.

'I would like to make a poultice, but I do not have what I need,' she said. 'Pack this over the wound.' She handed them some padded cloth. 'We shall have to change it every few hours.'

Falx said nothing, but now and again he gave a gentle sigh. Probus came in and knelt beside his man. 'You are free,' he said, reaching for his hand and then realising that it was the injured one. 'Do you hear me, you are a free man. When we get home, I'll give you a farm or money to go wherever you will. You don't have to fight anymore.'

Falx said nothing, his little eyes staring up at the bare stone roof. Ferox wondered whether it would be any comfort to be promised freedom and doubted it. Still, Probus had been a slave, so maybe he understood better.

'Keep him warm,' the lady commanded.

'You heard, boy.' Ferox had to stop himself from snarling the words at Genialis. 'Get some blankets and do your best to make him comfortable. That is your job from now on.'

'I am not your slave. Get the boy to do it.'

His father stood up. 'Go on,' Probus said. 'He's earned our thanks and more. If he hadn't held them up then we'd all be dead.'

Genialis left, avoiding their gaze.

'It's my fault,' Probus said after he had gone. Ferox was not sure whether he meant the gladiator's terrible wounds or his son's sullenness or both. 'I wonder if he knows who he really is,' he added, and then realised that the lady was still with them.

'I had better go,' she said, not seeking an explanation. 'I could do with more rest, although I am sure you men need it far more. Thank you for what you are doing. All of you.' She smiled at Probus and then crouched down beside the gladiator. Gently she ran a hand through his close-cropped hair. 'You are a brave man,' she said to him, and kissed his forehead for an instant.

Falx pushed himself up on his elbow, staring at her. His lips moved, as if he was trying to speak, and then he simply smiled and lay back down.

'Be dawn soon,' Ferox said. 'You should get some rest, my lady.'

She left, just as Genialis returned, with a couple of blankets flecked with straw. The lady ignored the youth as he looked her up and down. Then he threw the blankets onto the floor.

'Give me a hand, son,' Probus said, and Ferox went out to check on the causeway. Longinus waved from the barricade to show that all was well.

A grey dawn came, windless and with a mist so thick that even from the barricade the shore was only just visible. Ferox, Segovax and the two Batavians resumed duty on the causeway. Even the northerner was tense, because it was so easy to imagine invisible enemies massing for an attack. Once or twice they saw a lone warrior walk to the edge of the water and stare at them.

No attack came, and after four hours Longinus and Vindex came out to relieve them. Around noon the mist was thinner and they could see sentries dotted around the shore. Cniva and a few other horsemen rode around the lake and then vanished. The wind picked up, blowing from the south west, which was a good direction to speed rescue. It stripped away the last of the grey mist, but then it turned northerly and that was not so good. Ferox and the others returned to the barricade and the day wore on. Bran and the Red Cat were both up on the tower, and the boy waved if he saw anyone glance up.

Part way through his watch Vindex strolled out to join them. A knot of a dozen or so pirates stood twenty paces back from the causeway, and a few more were over on their left. Each group held their shields up in a wall, but made no attempt to come closer.

'Volunteering for extra work?' Ferox said, watching the enemy to see whether they planned to do any more.

'Just stretching my legs,' the Brigantian replied. 'You know how I hate crowds. That place is like a city.'

'We're getting less and less of a crowd all the time.'

'I know. Donnotaurus just died.' He was the scout wounded in the neck the day before.

'I'm sorry,' Ferox said. He had not known the man at all well, and struggled now to picture his face, but he meant what he said.

'Aye, well, so was he. Bit surprised he lasted this long.'

'The Carvetii are tough.'

'Aye. Near the end he asked me for a promise. I gave it to him, but I won't be able to do it without you.' The scout rubbed his lean, skull-like face. 'Aye, you'll do it because you know it's right. He made me promise that we kill every last one of these bastards.'

'We will.' It was always a surprise when Segovax broke his habitual silence. 'Every last one.'

The only time Ferox could remember the Brigantian hating as strongly as this was when the Stallion's men had buried a boy while he was still alive. He knew how both men felt. There was an evil in this place and in these enemies that cried out for vengeance. Neither of the northerners had any doubt that their families were dead, and he was sure they suspected that they suffered a lot before the end came. Even if they hurt Cniva and his men so badly that they never tried to raid the province again that would not be enough. To let them lurk up here and trouble villages and farms far away from the empire was an impiety. These were men who should not be allowed to live after what they had done and were still doing.

'I vow it to all the gods and spirits who are listening,' he said, hoping that they would all be spared long enough to fulfil the pledge.

Vindex nodded. 'Good.'

An arrow struck the barricade, sticking into the top of the

barrel inches from Ferox's finger. Another came from the other side, whipping through the air just over Vindex's head.

'Bugger,' he hissed. 'Well, we're humped.'

Two more shafts came a moment later, one sticking into the causeway behind them and the other bouncing off the barricade. Ferox could see an archer behind each cluster of shields. The group closest to the causeway started to walk forward, keeping in rank, the archer shooting over their shoulders.

Ferox ducked as another arrow whipped past. Neither of the archers were very good, and their bows were not strong, but that did not matter because they had no way of replying.

'Time to go, boys,' he said. Vindex had not brought a shield. 'You keep behind us.' He stood up, shield braced. Segovax joined him on the right and one of the Batavians on the left. 'Keep it steady. Back a pace at a time.'

An arrow struck his shield and stuck there, but only the very tip of the point came through.

'Back,' he said. Vindex dashed away at a crouch, and the other Batavian saw the danger and caught an arrow aimed at the scout on his shield. The pirates charged along the causeway, while the archer ran out to the flank.

'Keep together,' Ferox called. 'Back, lads, back.' The tone mattered more than the words. The black-clad warriors were in the ditch, and for the moment they were in the way and stopped the archers from shooting. The second group were rushing to join them, and twenty more pirates ran over the little hill and down towards the causeway as well.

An arrow skittered across the stones next to Ferox's feet. They took another step back, and another and he was trying to remember how many paces there were to the second wall and the shelter of the entrance.

A tall man clambered onto the top of the barricade. Bareheaded, his long blond hair and thick beard were a stark contrast to his drab clothes and black shield. He brandished a black-shafted spear and his mouth was open, teeth bared, but he made no sound.

'Bastard!' Segovax screamed.

'Stay with us,' Ferox yelled at him, sensing the man's hatred. Two pirates scrambled over the barricade and jumped onto the causeway. 'Back!' Ferox called again. He knew that they were close now.

'Come on!' That was Longinus, and Ferox risked a quick glance over his shoulder. The Batavian covering their rear was past the wall and back in the entrance. Longinus and Vindex were at the wall, swords and shields ready.

'Nearly there, boy,' the centurion told the others.

The enemy charged, three swordsmen in front, a pair behind with spears, and the blond-haired warrior urging them on from behind. A stone smashed into the causeway at their feet. One of the pirates looked up and a second rock struck him full in the face, snapping his helmeted head back. The others faltered, raising their shields and two more stones flung from the top of the tower thumped onto the wooden boards. Back on the shore, the bowmen started to shoot up. A last stone came, hitting a man on the toe of his boot and making him yelp, but then there were no more.

More pirates came over the barricade, forming behind their comrades and raising their shields over their heads. The formation was rough, not the well-practised testudo making a roof of shields of well-trained legionaries or auxiliaries, but it would do. Ferox and his men reached cover, and he pushed the others behind him so that he stood in the gap next to the wall. Longinus nodded to him. Segovax stayed close behind his shoulder.

The Harii shuffled forward, keeping together. Arrows whipped through the air, seeking out the men on the top of the tower. A stone came back and bounced harmlessly off the roof of shields, prompting two more shafts. Ferox could see the faces of the three men in the front rank, their teeth bared and eyes wild. No doubt he and his men looked much the same. The one facing him had a spear, so must have replaced the one hit on the head with a stone. The weapon was long and awkward in such a close formation, and after a few tentative thrusts, he lowered it so that it was underarm. It would have been better to drop it and draw his sword, but Ferox never minded the enemy making a mistake.

They were close now, and after another step the arm lunged with the spear, aiming below his shield at his unprotected calves. Ferox cut across with his sword, saw splinters come from the wooden shaft, but knew that he had not done much damage.

'Huh!' the three pirates grunted as they came forward together, close enough that Ferox could see that the spearman had stained teeth and a scar across the bridge of his nose. The man feinted low, and then turned it into an upwards thrust, trying to get past the side of his shield. He blocked it, the spearhead biting through the calfskin outer layer and the board of his shield. Ferox stabbed forward, elbow back and sword at eye level, and the pirate tried to dodge back, but the next rank was too close and the long point of the gladius speared into his left eye. It was not a fatal wound, for he had pulled away enough to stop that, but the black-clad man dropped his spear and staggered back. The roof of shields wavered. A stone dropped from up above, through the opening and fell harmlessly onto the ground, somehow missing everyone in the crowd. The testudo closed again and the next missile banged off the overlapping shields.

Longinus and Vindex were watching their opponents, waiting for a chance, and the enemy were just as cautious. After a moment of confusion, the wounded pirate was hustled to the back of the formation and a new opponent came at Ferox. This one had dyed his beard black, but the dye was washing out and there was plenty of pale grey in it. He had his sword up, matching Ferox's stance. The pirate feinted, but held back when the centurion twitched his shield up and was about to jab forward.

'You're going to die, Roman.' The man hissed in a thick Rhineland accent. It was a shock, because these warriors so rarely made any sound. Ferox did not have the breath to spare for an answer. Next to him, Longinus took a cut to the shoulder, but it was not a strong blow and his mail was not broken. Vindex slashed and was rewarded with a yelp as he grazed the face between the cheek pieces of a helmet.

Ferox's opponent punched at him with his shield, a savage blow that rocked him back and he only just had time to sway to the side as the point of the man's gladius stabbed where his head had just been.

'You're going to die.' The man was laughing, but the sound was nervous and Ferox had already recovered. A bold warrior would have followed up the advantage and tried to push him back, but men in a testudo liked to huddle together because it made them feel safer. Ferox was tired, his legs and arms feeling as heavy as lead and just as soft, but he stamped his left foot forward and punched with the boss of his own shield, wishing he had a solid legionary *scutum* rather than this light shield taken from the pirates. The man gave way only a little and laughed at him again.

A large block of stone hit the roof of the entrance way just behind him, flinging pebbles and shards of rock against his back. A Batavian swore vilely in a mixture of his own language and camp Latin. Ferox's opponent attacked, sword low and trying to slip past the side of his shield, but failing.

The grey stone was almost a foot long and half as big on each side and hit the top of the shield above the pirate's head, brushing it aside and slamming on to his helmet. Ferox glimpsed the bronze being crushed by the weight and the man fell. Another missile followed, almost as big and far larger that the hand-sized missiles they had gathered in preparation. It shattered one of the black oval shields and the formation scattered as another warrior dropped, his shoulder broken. Men were screaming, panicking, and then a splash of steaming liquid spattered down. There was not much, but one man was screaming as his face burned, and others cursed or yelled in pain. Ferox smelt the rancid tang of burning olive oil and heard a woman's excited shout.

The archers stopped shooting. Behind the ruined testudo stood the blond-haired warrior, staring in shock at the carnage.

'Bastard!' Segovax pushed at Ferox so that he had to drop his sword and grab onto the wall to stop himself being shoved off the causeway. The northerner ran at the warrior, vaulting over the dead and injured. There was no trace of his limp as he sped along. A pirate, his helmet wrenched off and one side of his face red and blistered from the oil, blocked his path. Segovax ducked a wild stroke and slashed at the man, his blade striking just under the knee and cutting clean through the man's leg. The pirate fell, stump up in the air and spouting blood.

The tall warrior recognised him. He waited, then threw his heavy spear. Segovax raised his shield in time, but the iron head burst through the wood and kept going, striking him on the chest, so that he staggered back. The blond drew his gladius and rushed forward. Segovax threw down his useless shield, but his boot was in a slick patch of blood and he slipped, falling forward. The blond yelled in triumph, shouting something Ferox did not understand and brought his sword up ready, and ran at him.

Segovax dived, rolling as he hit the ground and thrusting up. It was instinct more than anything else, and if he missed he was surely dead, but the stubby point of his army issue sword took the blond in the groin. The shout of victory turned into an unearthly shriek of pain. The northerner twisted the blade and then pushed it in harder with both hands. Scream turning into a sob, the pirate toppled over. Segovax stood, and grabbed the man by the hair, lifting him half up. He hacked with his sword at the pirate's neck. The third cut finished the job.

The victor stood, face expressionless, and he lifted the severed head in his left hand, holding his sword up in his right. He glanced down at the rest of the body and spat. A shout of joy came from the top of the tower, and Ferox guessed that it was the Red Cat.

'Come on, man!' he shouted.

Segovax turned his back on the enemy and walked slowly along the causeway. One of the pirates was pushing himself up, moaning, and the northerner almost absent-mindedly jabbed down into his neck. Blood jetted across his leg. An arrow whisked through the air, missing him by feet, and he turned and spat his contempt at the enemy.

The second arrow hit him on the calf of his good leg, spitting it so that the iron head and an inch or two of shaft came out the other side. He staggered, and another arrow struck his left hand, making him drop the head. Ferox ran out, shield ready, and Vindex came with him. Segovax shook him off when he offered to help, so the two men used their shields to cover him as he made his way back. Arrows banged into their shields, but the bowmen no longer seemed quite so accurate and they all made it back without injury. Ferox turned and looked at the wreckage on the causeway, the dead and dying pirates, the big stones and the broken shields and dropped weapons.

'We're still alive, then,' Vindex said.

'Who threw the oil?'

'The queen,' Longinus said. 'She climbed up on top of the tunnel. 'The lady heated it up for her, and one of my lads lifted it up. There wasn't much. Helped, though, didn't it.' The one-eyed warrior grinned. 'Just as well most women don't fight. Reckon they'd be too good at it for the rest of us. She's gone inside,' he added, 'so you'll have to thank her later. She was complaining that it was the only oil we had.'

Neither of Segovax's wounds were too serious, but he would struggle to walk quickly or do much with his left hand. 'Was he the one who took your family?' Ferox asked the Red Cat when the thief came down to see his brother.

'One of them. We will find the others as well.' Segovax said nothing, but the fierce determination in his eyes spoke as loudly as his brother's words. The Red Cat had cuts on his fingers, while his hands and face were heavy with a grey-brown dust.

'They want you on the top,' the thief added. 'The boy thinks he has seen something. I have not, but he swears that he has.'

'Thank you for your help,' Ferox said, and once he was sure that everything was in place in case the enemy attacked again, he made his way up to the roof. Probus was there, along with Bran and an ebullient Ovidius. All three were covered in dust. Ferox pulled himself up onto the thatch. A large section of the surrounding wall was gone, and he realised that they had pulled it apart to use as missiles. He looked over the edge. It was a good ten feet or so to the mouth of the entrance below, and some of the shaped stones had gone further than that.

'I did worry that we might touch a capstone or something

like that,' the old poet said. His eyes were bright, and he was struggling to stop from grinning. 'Thought we might pull out a single piece and have the whole tower fall down around our ears.'

'That would have been unfortunate, my lord,' Ferox agreed.

'I rather fear I was not strong enough to do more than give orders, which the others were courteous enough to follow. I threw one and it struck the roof.'

'It nearly hit me.'

'Sorry. I almost hit that fiery Hibernian queen as well, as she hauled herself up onto the roof.' Ovidius pointed down to one of the half-ruined houses alongside the winding entrance tunnel. 'Oh dear, that's a long way up,' he said, looking nauseous. 'I really do not care for heights. When something is happening it is fine, but now...' He trailed off.

'It is like that. Sometimes you are too busy to be afraid.'

'That must be so.' Ovidius was puzzled and intrigued, and Ferox sensed an approaching discussion. He turned to Probus.

'You did the throwing? That's a hell of a long way.'

'I was a slave once, and a soldier,' the merchant said. 'These days I'm rich, but a man should still do some of his own work. The other lad is smaller than me and lobbed them just as far.' He meant the Red Cat. 'The boy reckons he's seen something.'

'I kept a lookout while they were fighting.' Bran's face showed resentment at not being able to hurl big rocks as far as an adult. 'And I saw them. Three sails, maybe four.'

Ferox went to the other side of the tower and looked out to sea. The weather was closing in again, clouds sweeping over the waves so that he could not see much more than half a mile out across the water.

'Anyone else see anything?' There was silence. 'What about the Red Cat?'

'He was busy,' Bran insisted. 'And by the time the fight was over, it was harder to see. He reckoned he saw something, but was not sure and he said that he would go and get you.'

Ferox peered out, shading his eyes as if somehow that would let him penetrate the grey veil. 'What makes you sure?'

'The shape. Only your army ships have sails like that.'

'Good lad.' He leaned on one arm as he made his way around the conical thatched roof. There was not much high ground on the island, apart from to the north east and that was furthest away from the ships – if that was what the boy had really seen. An idea was forming in his mind, a wild, foolish idea, and he was not sure whether he should say something to Ovidius. For all his vagueness, the old man was a noble and had the ear of the legate.

An arrow struck the wall in front of him and bounced off the stone.

'Keep down, everyone. No sense in getting killed now that help is on the way.'

'You really reckon they're coming?' Probus asked the question that he sensed Ovidius was also itching to raise.

'They're coming,' he said, and saw Bran swell up with pride. 'What we have to do now is work out how we can help them.'

XXIII

'I T'S USUALLY better to attack if you can.' Longinus spoke
the words cautiously, as if weighing up each one. 'Defence
is all very well, but if the bastards won't go away then
you'll lose in the end. I did.'

Ferox had taken Vindex and the veteran to the room with
the cow and its calf, and once he had got there said that he
needed the advice of Julius Civilis. His mind was made up, but
he wanted to see if the men he trusted the most could make
him change it or would prove that he was right.

'There are ten of us left who can fight,' Vindex said. 'Eleven
if you count Segovax.' The northerner was insisting that he
was not slowed down by his wounds enough to matter. 'He
probably can fight on if we stay here, and he doesn't need to
move about much.'

'There are three wounded who cannot go anywhere,'
Longinus, or Civilis, equestrian, prefect of a cohort and leader
of the Batavian rebels, pointed out. 'And you cannot expect the
old man to survive long out in the open. Or the lady, spirited
and tough though she is. And that boy of yours is raw.

'Much depends on whether the child really did see warships
on their way. If he did and the weather holds, then they may
be here tomorrow, or even tonight. They will not know where
we are or even whether we are still alive.'

'We could signal,' Vindex suggested. 'If we lit the thatch the fire ought to go up and the stone cannot burn. We may have to come down from the upper floor, but we should be safe enough.'

'It's raining hard,' Ferox said, 'even if it was safe.'

Longinus nuzzled the cow, which started to lick his fingers. 'Assuming that help is on its way, what will Cniva do?'

Ferox sighed. 'If he knows? Either make a last effort to kill us and then hole up in his stronghold on the far side of the island, or take to his heels. He has a ship. We might follow him for a while, but he can probably guess that we won't hunt him forever. Even after his losses he has a lot of well-armed warriors. They could easily take another island.'

'Or wait until we have gone and come back here,' Vindex suggested. 'Doesn't it depend on how much he wants Genialis? If the boy has value to him then he might have another go. It's quiet out there now, but if they get in it won't last long.'

'What if he could not leave?' Ferox looked at them in turn.

'You are thinking of his ship?' Vindex said. 'Burn it, like we did those boats at Aballava?'

'I was thinking something like that.'

'Big thing to burn.'

'It is.'

'If you trap him here then he must fight.' The one-eyed veteran was still fussing the cow. 'So maybe he will go back behind the walls of his settlement and prepare. If he has seen the ships coming he will guess at how many are coming for him. So he will know that he is outnumbered two or three to one. Can he hope to beat those odds?'

'Will he have a choice?' Ferox asked. 'He cannot leave, so as you say he must fight. This is not the country to face bigger numbers in the open, and there is nowhere to hide. Behind a stout wall he has a chance. We have held them off so far and he might do the same.'

Longinus nodded. 'Our boys won't have the equipment for a full siege or the time for it. So Cniva might be wondering how much food Brocchus and his men have brought with them. There is not a lot to take up here, not to feed hundreds, and if Brocchus sends men to sail off to the coast or another island that takes time and weakens his force. Hold out for long enough and the Romans might leave.'

'Might be weeks or months, or maybe never, before they come back,' Vindex conceded. 'This is a long way from the province. If he can hold them off Cniva would tell everyone that he was a great leader, a man whose spirit is strong. But he's failed so far here. What's to say that some of the rest don't kill him and find someone else to take charge?'

'Does it matter?' Ferox said. 'The choices are the same. They know that they'll not get terms. Not after what they have done. And Cniva's lasted a long time. You don't get rid of a man like that easily.'

Longinus stopped petting the animal's head and walked around behind it, running a hand along its back. 'How are ten fighters, one of them a woman, or eleven if you include a tough old bastard who can limp quickly, to fight their way past a couple of hundred warriors, who may object to having their trireme set on fire? Leave the tower and you abandon those who cannot move, and almost certainly lead the others who cannot fight to their deaths. Probably all will die.

'If we stay here then all or most may survive. That is if rescue is close and if we hold off any attacks that come before it gets here.'

'A lot of ifs,' Vindex said. 'And at best we survive.'

'We cannot leave the tower,' Longinus said, watching Ferox's face closely. 'But I do not think that is what you have in mind, is it? Most of us must stay.'

Ferox nodded. 'There is little point in all of us going. Eleven against two hundred or more, the odds are absurd. But they are not much more absurd for one or two against a couple of hundred, and one or two might slip past unnoticed and be able to reach the ship.'

Vindex gave a grim laugh. 'Is this one of those times when you presume on our friendship?'

'Perhaps.'

'Bugger,' the scout said.

Longinus did not smile. 'You should stay. If anyone is to go with the centurion it should be that old thief. He's used to creeping about in the dark. And maybe the boy?'

Ferox was surprised, even though the same thought had occurred to him. Longinus' one eye glittered in the torchlight, and he felt as if the old man was looking inside him.

'It stands to reason,' the veteran said. 'You want to get out to a ship. And maybe if you are thinking straight and reckon you have luck on your side, you want to get off that boat and escape afterwards. They won't have the ship on the beach. It's from the classis Britannica and they tend to build in oak for these northern waters, so it'll be too heavy to drag ashore unless you are planning to be there for a while. So, you'll need to find a small boat to get out to it, because I don't think they'll have a jetty and it will be too far to swim. Bran is the best waterman we have, young though he is. And if I'm to hold on here with what's left, I'll need this Brigantian rogue. The boy you can take if you want to play the hero, and you can have the thief because his brother is the true fighter, but I'm keeping him.' He flicked Vindex around the head.

'You think it would be better if all of us stay?' Ferox asked the old man.

'Give us all a better chance of living. Still might not be enough, but there's nothing we can do about that. I came here to get the lady back safe, because I owe her family and she is one of our own by marriage – and I happen to like her a lot. That job is not yet finished, and it matters to me more than anything else. So, if I was in charge, we'd all stay here and live or die to protect her. The most I'd let you do is creep out at night and see how many of their throats you can slit. No harm in keeping them nervous, but I wouldn't take a risk with her life. But I'm not in charge.'

'Lost the war when you were, didn't you, father?' Vindex said.

'Yes, I did.' He smiled. 'Not sure I could ever have won, but then if that's true maybe I shouldn't have fought it in the first place. Didn't have the choice, though, after what they did to me. Your lot didn't do any better, did they?'

'Us? We never fought the Romans. The Carvetii have always been friends to Rome – leastways while anyone's looking.' He jerked a thumb at Ferox. 'He's the one whose folk thought it was a good idea to take a crack at the Romans.'

'In case you hadn't heard, we lost,' the centurion conceded.

'I know,' Longinus told him. 'I was there under Frontinus.' For some reason Ferox had never thought of this old man fighting against the Silures. He wondered if Longinus had been there when his own father had been cut down by the Romans, or when others of his family had died or been enslaved. 'It isn't nice to lose, is it?'

Ferox said nothing, and the veteran turned his attention back to Vindex. 'Thought you Carvetii call yourselves the brave ones?'

'Aye, but not stupid. When you see a huge bastard with an evil temper coming to visit, covered in mail and with a sharp sword and looking angry, it's time to make friends rather than get in his way. Don't your folk understand that?'

Longinus laughed. 'We're Batavians. We are the big bastards with evil tempers. But sometimes the odds are too big.'

'Not wise fighting when the odds are stacked against you,' the Brigantian agreed. 'Wouldn't catch sensible men like us doing that, would you?'

Longinus ignored him and came around from behind the cow to face Ferox. The animal's gaze followed him until its head could not turn far enough. After that, it leaned down and began to eat some hay. All the while the calf drank milk and ignored them all. 'Well then,' the veteran said. 'I'm not in charge. You are and you want to do this damned fool thing. I'm guessing you hope to slip out during the night. Maybe see if you can get some black clothes from their dead and wear those. Their sentries will have to be blind not to spot you, whether you try to swim through the water or crawl across the causeway. Odds are you are dead or captured before you get a hundred paces from where you start. But the rain may help, and if they're blind and daft there is a slim chance that you'll get through. Next you have to cross the island for a couple of miles to reach the harbour. Lots more of them out there and plenty of chance for them to catch you. What if you bump into a patrol?'

Ferox shrugged because he did not have an answer.

Longinus continued. 'So, let's say you get out to their boat. I don't think you'll get within bowshot of it, because if you know how valuable it is to them, then you can bet Cniva does. How are you going to start a fire big enough to do some damage? Will you tell me that, centurion? Because if you can't then I'll kill you before you leave this tower and put us all at risk.' The one eye glared at Ferox.

'Thought you promised Flora that you would look after me?' he said.

'I'd be giving you a quicker, cleaner death than you'll get out there. Be a consolation for the old girl. In fact, I can do it now, unless you can convince me to change my mind.' The veteran tapped the hilt of his sword.

'I have an idea,' the centurion began, and explained his plan.

Longinus listened and then sniffed. 'Might work, might not,' he said grudgingly. 'And you might be a rare genius or the biggest fool ever to swear an oath to the emperor.'

'What's the difference?' Vindex said.

'Luck,' Longinus told him. 'That's what it comes down to more often than not.'

'Well, I'll be all right then,' the scout declared. 'Don't know about you two.'

'If we are really lucky the first of Brocchus' men will be here soon and then he will be in charge and he can make the decisions,' Ferox said.

'And if the lad was imagining things?' Longinus' voice was harsh. 'What if he just saw some merchant ships sailing along, oblivious? Or he was right, but a storm picks up and drives them away from the island?'

'Then we're humped,' Vindex said. 'But worrying won't change it.'

The veteran sighed. 'Still, maybe you are lucky, and maybe if they realise some of us are abroad and up to no good they will be worried. Cniva might just pull away from here to protect his stronghold and his ship. But my money is on you not being able to get out of this tower in the first place. So you'll get nowhere, or be dead, or they'll have you and we can watch while Cniva slices you up and promises to finish the job unless we surrender.'

'In that case spit in his eye, whatever he does to me.'

'That was my plan,' Longinus said without a trace of humour. 'You agree, lad?' he added, glancing at Vindex.

'Oh aye. I'm comfortable here. No sense in going out.'

Ferox went to check on the men guarding the entrance. Probus was there, along with one of the Batavians and the last of the scouts, and they had nothing to report apart from the driving rain. Another Batavian lay on the floor in one of the rooms off the winding corridor, dozing in his armour. Brigita sat on a stool beside him, honing the edge of her sword. She stared at Ferox when he looked in, but said nothing. He went back inside, heading for the store room. He found a sack, and then the rags soaked in oil from the broken amphora. Adding handfuls of dried straw, he stuffed it all into the sack. What he wanted was something that would catch fire and burn well, so that it was hot enough to spread. It was not much, but if he could get on board and have the time to gather ropes and anything else that would catch alight, and if he could jam it all somewhere out of the wind and rain, and if he could set it on fire, and if no one came to put the fire out before it took hold... Ferox did not follow the train of thought to the end. As Vindex had said, it was a lot of ifs.

'I hear that you are leaving us, centurion.' Sulpicia Lepidina was in the doorway.

'Longinus told you?'

'He did, and then Vindex told me. Although I rather think that I might have guessed.'

'I always thought I was inscrutable.' He tried to smile and could not.

'To some perhaps.' She came in and closed the door behind

her. It was a small room, and with one step he was beside her. He dropped the sack and put both arms around her waist. They kissed once, and then she pulled away. ' Longinus thinks that you will die.'

'What about Vindex?'

She grinned. 'He says that you want to be the hero in a tale, but that the gods love fools and might just let you get away with it.'

'What do you think?'

'That I do not have the right to tell you what to do.' Sulpicia Lepidina ran her fingers lightly over his hand. 'But that I do not want to lose you. You mean too much to me.'

Ferox pulled her close again, and this time she let him. He wondered about her words. His heart thrilled with love, especially now, when she was in his arms and he could pretend that it would always be like this. She had longed for mother-hood, but given up real hope, and now he was the father of her only child, even if no one could ever know. Her marriage was one of convenience, a business arrangement made by her indebted father, passion wholly absent on each side. It was not unpleasant, for Cerialis was kind and decent, but it was a life of duty and he knew that she felt trapped and always forced to play a part rather than live as she would wish. She might truly love him, or at least love him enough that their rare encounters lifted her spirits and gave her memories to treasure, a glimpse of another life.

Yet he still wondered whether there was more. She was a *femina clarissima*, daughter of a man who had once been important and still was a senator and friend of many of the greatest men in the empire. Her brother was an exile, and that was another reason for the marriage to Cerialis, only an equestrian, but favoured by Trajan as well as being a wealthy man. Politics was the lifeblood of senators and their kin and he sometimes wondered whether she saw him as useful, a tool to save for some future struggle for power. He was a killer and she knew it, and politics sometimes required the keen edge of a sword.

'Don't die,' she whispered, as he ran one hand through her hair and the other traced the outline of her hips. 'Please don't die.' They kissed again, and he longed to peel off her dress, but knew that there was not the time. Both of them were breathing quickly, gasping as they held each other.

The door opened, and they started like children who were not quite children anymore surprised by a suspicious parent. It was Brigita and her face was solemn. She was not wearing a mail shirt, just a dark blue tunic.

'Lady,' she said in Latin. 'I must speak with the centurion. It is important.'

Sulpicia Lepidina stood away from him, straightening her hair. 'I should check on the stew.' She nodded to Brigita as she left, shutting the door behind her.

'You do not seem surprised,' Ferox said to the queen.

'No.' At first he thought that this was all that she had to say, but after a moment she rubbed her hand over her chin, an oddly manly gesture in spite of the sword at her belt. 'We spent days chained up in a tiny room. She spoke about her husband one way. When she spoke of you...' The tall woman trailed off. 'A high-born woman rarely can choose a husband for love.' Ferox thought of her vague, elderly consort. 'When I met her, I thought that she was beautiful, but soft. I was wrong. She said that you would come for her – for us even – and you did.'

'I did not come alone.'

'No, you did not. Nor can you do what you wish alone.'

'And what do I wish to do?'

The queen ignored the question. 'How well can you swim, Roman – or should I call you Silurian?'

'I can swim,' he acknowledged.

'There is enough wood to make a raft for the weapons and the clothes,' she said. 'I have found some reeds and if we cut one or two of them then I can swim under the water. Perhaps you can do it too?' He nodded. 'We leave from the rear of the tower and go in the direction of the sea. I have looked and they rarely have more than one or two men watching from the shore on that side. We kill the men, the others come behind us with the raft. Then we leave.'

'If the weapons are on the raft how do we kill the guards?'

She sniffed scornfully. 'Daggers, but you know that blades are not really necessary, are they?'

'It is too dangerous.'

'You have seen me fight.' The words were matter-of-fact, neither angry nor a boast. 'Here, in the narrow entrance or inside the tower, strength and size matter more than anything else. In the open skill counts. And I have been on this island once before, many years ago. I know where we are going.'

'You are a queen,' he said. 'It is too great a risk.'

'I was a queen.' Once again there was no emotion, no regret, just the clipped speech the Hibernians practised. 'My husband is dead by now, or a nothing who might as well be dead. There is no reason to go back.' She pulled at the top of her tunic, revealing much of her breasts and the scar between them. 'This is the mark of the sisterhood. I spent three years on the island over yonder, learning to be a warrior. The mistress is as a mother to me, the women and girls there are my sisters, the lads my brothers. Cniva wanted to use me to make her submit to his rule. He and his men must all die.' For the first time there was anger in her voice.

'Revenge?'

'He threatens my family, the only real family I have now. What would you do?'

Ferox stared at her and the queen met his gaze and held it. It would leave Longinus with one less sword, but she was right. Now that they were shut in, her speed and skill would count for a lot less. The veteran would probably not mind if she left.

'We will go at midnight,' he said.

XXIV

T HE RAFT WAS prepared in one of the ruined round-houses beside the tower. They entered through a door off the main corridor, while one wall was low enough for them to lift everything out and make their way round the edge of the little island, but for the moment they prepared in the slight shelter provided by the stone walls and few remnants of the roof. Ferox wrapped the sack in rags and straw and then wound their clothes around it and placed the weapons on top in the hope of keeping it dry. With great reluctance, he decided against taking a mail shirt or two as well. Bran was wide-eyed as the queen lifted her tunic over her head and added it to the bundle of clothes. She stood there, completely naked like the rest of them, and started to rub soot onto her skin. Ferox smiled, thinking that with her long black hair she must fit the lad's wildest dreams. Once they were in the water the soot would start to come off, but it might help them to sneak round to the back of the tower without being spotted.

'You all ready?' Vindex said. He had come to assist, or so he claimed, but made no effort to hide his scrutiny of the queen.

'You're a married man,' Ferox told him.

'Aye.'

A scream of sheer horror split the night air, rising over the

272

drumming of the rain. Ferox pushed Vindex out of the way and ran. The door into the corridor was ajar and he burst through, knocking into one of the Batavians and slamming him against the wall. Ferox ran on, sprinting around the sharp bend, feet echoing on the stone. A man was yelling in surprise and anger, and then Sulpicia Lepidina was in front of him, screaming again and with blood on her dress. Fear and raw anger surged inside him. She pointed into the side room, and as he came closer he realised that the blood was not hers. In the little room Falx lay out in the floor. His throat was cut, the top of his tunic stained dark where it had flowed. Worse was the great gash across his belly, a new wound, and someone had dragged his entrails out of the hole and then bitten into them.

Sulpicia Lepidina stopped screaming and leaned back against the wall, panting as she struggled to breathe. Ferox ran past, turning again to reach the entrance. Probus was sitting with his back against the low wall, clutching at his thigh, which was pumping blood. Longinus knelt beside him, trying a strip of cloth tight above the wound. A Batavian was standing at the rampart, shouting angrily. 'Little bastard's got away!' A shriller voice was calling something over and over again, but he could not catch the words.

Ferox came up beside the auxiliary, but could see nothing in the darkness. 'Little shit Genialis has stabbed his own father,' the auxiliary said. It was the man with the broken nose and for the first time he seemed genuinely shocked. 'His own dad. Then ran off into the dark. It was so quick I let him go.'

'He'll be all right,' Longinus said. 'Leastways if you stop waving that in his face.'

Ferox had forgotten that he was naked. He crouched down to see the merchant better. In the dim light from the torch back in the corridor, Probus looked stunned.

'He murdered Falx,' Ferox said. 'Then I think he ate some of his guts. I know what he's done, but I don't know why.'

'Don't reckon he thought we could win,' Longinus suggested.

'Cniva will give him power.' Probus' voice was barely more than a whisper.

'He's got wealth,' the veteran said. 'That brings a fair bit of power.'

Probus shook his head and then winced at a spasm of pain from his leg. Longinus finished adjusting the bandage. 'I told him about going to Hibernia,' The merchant explained. 'Said he could come or that I'd try and make sure he kept some of the land if he wanted to stay in Britannia. I don't think he listened.'

'So he's joining them.'

'Maybe I told him too much about them.' Probus' voice was only just audible above the driving rain. 'Cniva will let him kill, let him do what he likes. That's more than I can offer.'

Longinus placed his hands on Ferox's shoulders. 'Listen. The boy will be over there telling them everything. If they didn't know already, then he'll tell them that Brocchus could be here any moment now. He probably will say that you are planning something as well, even if he does not know the details. You cannot keep secrets in a place as small as this. So either you go this minute or forget the whole thing and we wait here.'

'We go.'

'Then let's hope the gods love a great fool.' Longinus stood up, and stared out into the night. 'You might make through in this, especially if he distracts them. Good luck.' He offered his hand, and Ferox rose and took it.

He passed Vindex in the corridor. 'You've got something on your face,' the Brigantian said.

Ferox reached up and soot came away on his fingers. Sulpicia Lepidina laughed nervously, until she glanced down and took in his lack of clothing. She started to giggle and could not stop, fright turning into hysterical laughter. She tried to speak, but could not say anything and simply waved at him.

When he reached the others, he gave a quick explanation and chivvied them on. He and Brigita crept along behind the tower and lowered themselves into the water gently. It was cold, and deep in this spot, and as he pushed out he soon stopped feeling ground under his feet. With the reed in his mouth he ducked under the dark water and swam, the surface shimmering above only a little lighter than the gloom of the water.

It took longer than he expected, and then suddenly the ground was shelving and when his feet kicked out they brushed against pebbles. He surfaced, spitting out the reed, and as the water cleared from his eyes he could see the bank only a few paces away. There was no sign of a sentry. He waded slowly towards the shore, all the while scanning the darkness. A leather belt, tightened to make it short, was over one shoulder, and he looped it free, drawing the pugio from its sheath. A vague white-ish shape slithered onto the bank beside him and he realised that the queen was already there. She tapped him on the shoulder and pointed to the right. He nodded. The rain was hard, stinging his skin until he felt almost numb, and making him blink all the time so that he could see.

Ferox kept low, a hunched shape that might just confuse any watching eyes. Whenever he had looked in the daytime, the sentries here were some way back from the shore. No challenge came from the darkness and he saw no sign of movement apart from the long grass swaying in the wind. Still crouching, he went on, knife held down. The ground was boggy, so that his feet squelched into the mud.

He did not see the warrior until it was too late, and he tripped against him, toes hurting from stubbing against a man wearing mail. The pirate lay, face down in the grass, and a quick exploration showed a wound at the back of his neck. It was a neat job, from someone who knew just where to strike, and that was not true of most soldiers or warriors.

A shape appeared, white and naked, with her long hair plastered down over her back and some on her chest. 'There is another over there,' Brigita hissed. 'Like that one. I think they are the only ones.'

Ferox whistled, and then they both kneeled down to wait. 'Your brothers and sisters?' he asked, for it was hard to know who else might have killed these men, unless Cniva was facing a challenge from within his own band.

'Perhaps.'

Bran and the Red Cat appeared, carrying the equipment. They dressed, although Ferox was so drenched that he did not feel much warmer. It was good to have boots on again, to feel a sword on his left hip and pull a dark cloak around him. At the very least the dull clothes made them less visible.

They headed for the beach, taking them almost in the opposite direction from where they wanted to go, but the hope was that this should also take them away from any sentries or patrols. The Red Cat went first, and Ferox and the others followed, just keeping him within sight. All the while the rain hammered against them and showed no sign of relenting.

Like the swim, the walk towards the beach seemed to take far longer than it should. That was the way of things at night, especially in weather like this. Apart from a few animals scurrying across their path they saw no sign of life. Neither was there any sign of boats on the beach. Still, there was no particular reason for Brocchus to land on this beach, just because they had done so.

Swinging to the left, they followed the coastline. Ferox planned to reach the midway point on the island before heading inland towards the anchorage on the far side. After an hour the rain stopped, so abruptly that his battered face took a few moments to register the change.

The Red Cat halted and dropped to one knee. Ferox had felt the same thing at almost the same moment, that instinct that they were not alone. He gestured for the other two to stay, and went forward, squatting beside the northerner. Nothing was said and they both peered into the gloom, listening for any harsh note as the wind hissed through the grass and stunted bushes. They were on a low bluff, above a stony beach, the whitecaps of the incoming tide very bright in the darkness.

Something moved ahead of them, a shape briefly silhouetted against the sky, before it went down behind a fold in the ground. Ferox stared after it and then thought he heard a moaning that was not from the gale. He drew his sword, worried that it might betray them with a glint but not wanting to be unprepared. The Red Cat did the same. He pointed for the northerner to go around to the left, while he looped to the right, onto the edge of the beach. The other two would have to catch up, and he hoped that they would be careful. The wind howled, plucking at his cloak even though it was soaking wet and heavy. It slackened and once again he heard moaning. There was a grunt and the moaning stopped. A man laughed.

The beach opened out behind the low rise. Ferox touched the hide frame of a small rowing boat as he walked past it, stepping as lightly as he could to avoid making noise as he crossed the shale. There was a little rocky headland, and he kept close to it, using its shadow. Then a yellow light that seemed brilliant sprang to life on the beach. It was a lantern, suddenly unveiled, and he saw a cluster of dark figures around it, looking down at something on the small patch of sand at the edge of the pebbles.

There was more laughter, and one of the figures got down on his knees in front of the others, and he glimpsed someone lying down. The sound of ripping was loud until it was lost in more laughter.

Ferox started to run, no longer caring as his boots crunched on the stone. All of the last days, the worry, the horror, the sight of Sulpicia Lepidina screaming and covered in blood, and seeing good men cut down at his side erupted in an all-consuming rage. One of the men turned and saw him, shouting a warning, but by then Ferox was close enough to stamp forward and lunge, and the superbly balanced gladius took the pirate in the throat. Twisting it free as a second man came at him, Ferox cut first, a furious blow that chopped through the warrior's right arm, so that his hand was still clutching his sword as it fell onto the beach.

There were three of them left, one still on the ground, bottom bare where he had lowered his trousers, another holding the lantern up, sword still in his scabbard, and a third who took one look at Ferox and ran. He went to follow, but saw a shape coming out of the night and the fugitive ran onto a glinting blade that ripped into his stomach.

The pirate dropped the lantern. 'We were going to share,' he said. 'Honest. Just having fun before we took her back.' Ferox guessed that he thought they were Harii, and then remembered their black clothes. Yet it was surprising that he seemed to accept the slaughter of his comrades so readily, but perhaps failing to share plunder or captives was one of the band's greatest crimes. Ferox kicked the kneeling man hard in the back, pitching him over. A woman lay in the sand, shaking her head as if in a daze, her tunic torn open to reveal pale skin. She was not tall and had a delicate figure.

'Drop the sword,' Ferox commanded the other man. Brigita

came over to them, wiping her sword on her cloak. She said nothing, walking past the woman on the ground. The man who had been about to rape the girl was struggling with his trousers, pulling at them as he lay on his side. The queen looked at him for a moment, and then darted her sword forward, aiming carefully so that the point speared into the man's crotch. He squealed, an awful, high-pitched cry of agony, more like an animal than anything human.

'Fight,' she said to the last pirate.

He licked his lips. 'Who are you?' He started to draw his sword, for he had made no move to drop it. Brigita bounded forward and slashed across his face before jumping back. It was not a deep wound, and the man licked his lips again and spat blood. His finished drawing his sword, but before he had it ready she came in again, the sword carving a gouge across his right arm. He dropped his gladius, clutching at the wound with his left hand.

'Pick it up,' she told him.

Ferox took a step and swung, the gladius almost singing through the air as it sank into the pirate's neck. He fell, hands now clasping his throat as the blood sprayed from it. 'We haven't got time to play games,' Ferox said harshly. Brigita stared at him, her face filled with the same sort of rage he had felt a few moments ago, and then she nodded. She went over to the screaming man, waited for the right moment, and killed him with a neat thrust.

The woman was stirring, pushing up, so that the remnants of her tunic fell away and she was bare. Although on its side, the lantern gave enough light for Ferox to see the little scar between her small breasts. A young man lay dead a few yards away, several bad wounds to his chest and stomach. Ferox guessed that he was the one they had heard moaning until it was cut short.

Brigita went to the woman and held out her hand. She spoke words he did not understand, but they seemed to reassure her and she grasped hold and let herself be pulled up. The queen unclipped the brooch on her cloak and handed it over. Ferox guessed that the woman was young, perhaps sixteen or seventeen.

Bran appeared, wide-eyed again, but it was hard to tell whether this was from the sight of another naked woman or the carnage around them. The released captive put the cloak around her shoulders, then searched in the grass until she found a long sword, blunt tipped, of the sort many tribesmen used for cutting. A little further on she found a belt and scabbard and she fastened these on.

'Time to go,' Ferox said, although there was no sign of the Red Cat. He would have to rely on the thief finding them. 'She can come with us if she wants, or go and find her own folk.' Although the boat on the beach was small, Ferox guessed that it had brought at least three or four others to the island.

'No need,' the woman said.

Warriors came out of the night, the light from the lantern glinting on the keen points of their spears. There were a lot more than three or four. Ferox counted ten and thought that others were behind them. All were men, but it was clear that the woman they had saved knew them and trusted them.

'You come with us,' she said. 'Give me your swords.' There were two warriors behind him, and another in front. Any resistance would be brief and would probably doom Bran as well. He held out his sword, pommel first. Brigita brought her blade up when one of the men went to take it. The woman gently pushed him aside and came up to her. After a moment, the queen nodded and let her take the weapon. Ferox's arms were pulled behind his back and tied there. The same was done to Bran, but not the queen.

'Come on,' the woman said, and led them up the beach. Soon they were climbing a gentle headland dotted with bushes and heather. It was higher than the fields around, and Ferox could see right across the island. There was a distant red light, which grew suddenly bright and strong.

'That's a ship,' Bran said in a tone of wonder. 'Their ship.'

Ferox had great faith in the boy's eyesight and hoped that he was right. The warriors kept going, and crossed two more rises before they came down into a cove with another beach. Several boats were drawn up on the pebbles, and dozens of warriors were squatting on the rocks at the edge of the beach.

A woman's voice greeted them, but it was hard to see the speaker in the gloom cast by the low cliffs. Then a tall, spare figure stepped out of the shadows.

'Ferox,' said a voice he had not heard for some time. 'It is true then, you are here.' A man held up a torch as Acco came towards him, his long beard and hair blowing in the wind as the light flickered. 'I rather think I would be wise to have you killed.'

XXV

THE LITTLE DOG was lame, flea-ridden, and had lost most of one ear and several patches of fur. A stale smell of decay grew stronger as the druid tickled the animal under the chin and fussed it. The dog did not seem to mind, but it was panting for breath and did not respond apart from a few wags of the stubby remnant of its tail.

Ferox always struggled to remember Acco's features. Even now, with the old man only a few feet away, there was something indistinct about what little of his face was visible behind the beard and long hair. Both were filthy, as was the man himself, and his smell was only a little less pungent than the dog's. Ferox found it much easier to picture the dog than its owner.

When Ferox was young, the druid had sometimes visited his grandfather and spoken to the boys who were being trained with him. In his mind's eye, he could recall the silence that greeted Acco's appearance, the fear that swept over all of the boys, who the rest of the time tried to parade their fearlessness. The druid must have been younger then, but already seemed old. He never shouted, or even raised his voice, and yet it was filled with power and menace. Ferox remembered the soft words that somehow were always clear, but in his memory the druid himself was a vague shape in a grey robe. It was almost as if the man walked on the green earth and at the same time saw into the Shadow world. Some of the boys swore that this was so.

Ferox looked at the druid and wondered whether they had been right. The sky had cleared, but dawn was coming and the stars beginning to fade. Most of the warriors were preparing to leave in their long boats, their wooden frames covered in stretched hide. A few were still on shore, watching in case the pirates came, but it was clear that they did not really expect this. Acco sat on a folded cloak laid out on the beach and played with his dog. A warrior stood on either side of him, each holding a spear, its butt resting on the pebbles. Ferox's arms were still tied behind him as he sat cross-legged in front of the druid. Bran was a short way away, gnawing the last meat off a sheep's rib. No one had offered Ferox any food. Brigita sat with a cluster of young men and a few women, who kept themselves apart from the others.

'The Romans are here,' Acco told Ferox. 'Two galleys and three other ships carrying men. They will be landing by now, in the bay on the far side of the island. That will take a while, and then they will attack the dun held by Cniva and his men. I would guess that they will begin the assault in three or four hours, although it is possible that they will surprise me. Brocchus is a prudent man, but he will be angry, and that young fellow Crispinus is impetuous.'

Ferox said nothing, and hoped that his face was impassive. Acco always seemed to know all – or almost all – of what the Romans had done and were about to do, so he was not really surprised to hear him speak in this way. The druid watched him. 'Do you have nothing to say?' he asked after a while.

'I am glad they are here. Glad they burned Cniva's ship so that he cannot escape.'

'They did not.' There was another pause. Acco sighed. 'I had almost forgotten how mean the Silures are when it comes to spending words. Your grandfather would be proud of that about you, at least.

'The Romans did not destroy the ship. These men did. Some of them, anyway, and two were killed in the act. These folk are from the other islands and the mainland. They are poor, their life hard, and the Harii steal or extort more than they can afford so that their life becomes even harder.' There was a slight pause, as if he hoped that Ferox would be impressed by this new detail.

Acco sighed. 'Stubborn, just like all your kin. When I learned of the Roman expedition, I hurried here. In the past, they lacked the strength to resist. The Harii and Usipi are many and well armed. It has taken them years to repair their trireme and make it seaworthy again, but in that time they have raided in captured merchant ships or simple wooden boats. These men could not hope to burn all their boats and strand them forever in this place, and they feared to stir them up to greater anger. Cniva is a bad man.'

Ferox thought about the plot to take Cerialis and his wife and burn them as a sacrifice. Acco had helped the Stallion, and then slowly killed the man as an atoning sacrifice when he failed and was beaten. A lot of people had died because of the druid's plans and more would die. Ferox flexed his wrists. The rope had worked a little loose. Trying not to be too obvious, he twisted his fingers back, feeling for the knot. If he could only get free he might just grab one of the spears and drive it through the old man.

Acco smiled, his beard parting to show his broken and blackened teeth, as if he read the centurion's thoughts. 'I really should have you killed,' he said. 'I had hoped that you might have come to your senses, but I can see that you have not. You will keep your oath to an emperor who cares nothing for you or your kin, and to an empire that is smothering the world. So be it. I tried once to persuade you to join me and you refused. I shall not waste more breath on that.' The druid stood up. The little dog started to rub against his leg and he gave it a gentle kick. It scampered away, breath loud with effort.

'Sometimes a cur is too used to the leash ever to be free,' Acco said.

Ferox felt the rope rubbing his skin raw as he struggled.

'I shall not kill you today,' the druid said. 'Others may, but I shall not, because it is possible that you can be useful and do a good deed for a change. Have you seen Cniva's stronghold?'

'No.'

'He did not build it, of course, and just stole it from the folk who lived there, but he has made it stronger. It lies on a headland, and the two encircling walls do not go all the way around because there are cliffs too sheer for anyone to climb. Your leaders will throw their men at the walls because they have no other choice and because they hate the enemy so much. Cerialis will wish to avenge his wife, even once he knows that she is safe.'

Acco smiled, and Ferox guessed that he had betrayed his surprise and relief at the news. 'A woman?' the druid said, as if musing. 'And a fine woman at that.' He stared down at the centurion. 'That would explain much.'

'The Romans are good at storming cities,' Ferox said, trying to change the subject. 'You must know that.'

'Yes, but they will not have all of their equipment to help them. If they have any sense they have brought ladders, or perhaps they can make some. It will not be easy.'

'More men would help.'

'Perhaps,' the druid said, 'but I doubt it, and these warriors have already risked much. They will not join your men, so you Romans must fight your own battle and pay the blood price. You may win and you may not.'

'It is better if we win.'

Acco flung his arms wide and raised his voice just a little. For someone so softly spoken it was akin to screaming. The dog started to howl. 'It would have been better if Romans had never unleashed this evil on us in the first place. They are here because of you. They have killed and raped, stolen food that could not be spared and when they first came they brought a plague that killed whole families.

'Rome is evil and she spreads evil across the lands. Even here, no one can escape her.' Acco dropped his arms and seemed to calm. He kicked the dog into silence. 'These men have risked their lives to trap the Harii and Usipi on this island. Now it is up to the Romans to wipe this stain from the earth. All must die, for such evil must be punished. They made the sickness, so they must cure it.

'Others feel differently.' The druid waved a hand towards Brigita and the cluster of young warriors. 'It is their fight, for their reasons, and it is up to them to tell you if they choose. They will fight it in their way, not yours, but my heart tells me that you should go with them. You have a task to perform on this day, and so I shall not kill you. Do not presume that I will be so indulgent the next time we meet. You have chosen your path and must follow it to the end.'

'Don't we all do that?'

The druid ignored him. 'I foretell that it will be a bitter end, that you will suffer much and lose all that is most precious to you. And for what? Oaths sworn to Rome and its emperor?'

'An oath is an oath,' Ferox said, quoting his grandfather, 'and a faithless man is nothing.'

Acco must have recognised the words. 'The Lord of the Hills was a greater man than you will ever be, and yet he failed, and gave in to Rome at the end. He should have fought until his last breath.' The druid drew a short bronze knife from a sheath on his belt. He ran the blade across his palm, and tipped his hand on its side so that the blood ran down. 'He was the greatest of the Silures.' Acco rubbed his hand across Ferox's forehead. 'You are a Roman, and one day soon you will die with all the others.'

Ferox blinked because some of the blood had got into his left eye. Once it was clear he stared up at the druid.

'Death is the middle of a long life,' he said in Latin, for he knew that the druid spoke the language.

Acco licked the cut on his palm and then spat onto the pebbles. 'What would a poet and a Roman know of such things?' He said no more and simply strode away towards the boats. The spearmen went with him. 'Dog,' the druid called, without looking back, and the little mongrel scampered awkwardly after him. The smell of the old man and his pet lingered after they had gone. Ferox wondered about his last words, for it seemed that he had known the saying came from Lucan's *Pharsalia*, although the poet claimed that this was what the druids believed.

The warriors pushed the long slim boats out into the water and then jumped in. Acco sat in the stern of one, his back to the beach and he did not glance back. The great red ball of the sun rose above the horizon ahead of them, while overhead the gulls burst into a frenzy of harsh cries, one calling out and others answering. A single long canoe remained on the shale.

Bran untied him, and they sat there, waiting. After a while Brigita came over to them. 'Come,' she said.

Nine young men sat in a circle at the edge of the beach, a few in trousers and the rest in the tunics of the kind favoured by Hibernians. Six of them had smooth chins, not yet requiring the touch of razor, and the other three were not much older. One had cultivated a thin moustache, and he might have been seventeen, but no more. He was the only one wearing a mail shirt, although several others had bronze or iron helmets, all of them simple bowls with stubby neck guards and cheek pieces. All had stout shafted spears lying on the ground beside them, several with large, jagged edged blades, and a couple of slim javelins. All of them had swords, mostly the long slim blades of the tribes, some pointed and some blunt.

The three women were a little older, although none were much more than twenty. One had blonde hair and wore a scale cuirass, alternate scales gilded and polished bright. Another was a redhead, in a short cuirass of horn and hide of a type Ferox had seen now and then among the Sarmatians on the Danube. He wondered how it had travelled to this faraway place, because the wearer had the look of the Creones about her. The third woman was the one they had saved from the pirates. Her tunic was badly torn, and her repairs had left it as little more than a skirt. It left her breasts exposed, and it was odd that no one, with the exception of Bran, paid any attention, for she was a handsome woman, if stern, her brown hair plaited and made into three coils.

All three women wore short tunics, and had bare legs apart from the soft calfskin boots that covered their shins. The redhead and the blonde had helmets resting beside them, and both were wrapping their long plaits into a tight ball so that they could put them on. All three women wore swords at their belts, similar in fashion to those of the young lads, and like them had a spear and a pair of javelins. Shields were a mixture of shapes and sizes, from the little square and round ones favoured by many northerners to big oval and hexagonal ones.

If Ovidius had been here he would no doubt have spouted

Herodotus and spoken of amazons. In truth, the boots and tunics did give them something of the look of those mythical female warriors. Their skin was fair, almost the white of so many paintings, since they were all Britons or Hibernians. Ferox had seen Brigita fight and knew her skill, and in this place there seemed nothing at all unnatural about a band of warriors including both women and men. All of them, even the ones who were no more than boys, moved with the care of long hours of training, never wasting effort and doing what they wanted to do and no more. They were not soldiers, and in some ways reminded Ferox more of gladiators or even athletes.

Sitting in the middle of the circle was a silent figure covered in a long, hooded cloak. Brigita led him between a couple of the sitting warriors. 'These are my sisters and brothers,' she said, and then stopped suddenly. He looked at her, then at the hooded and cloaked figure, but no one said or did anything. The gulls were still shouting.

The queen placed her hands on either side of his face and stood on the balls of her feet to kiss him. It was sudden and more than a little aggressive, as well as pleasant. It was a long kiss, and then it was over and she stepped back. 'I was curious,' she said. 'I am not curious anymore.' The warriors, male and female alike, laughed, sounding much like a group of children.

'Enough games.' The voice was husky without being manly. Throwing back her hood, a woman stood up. She was not especially tall, and her arms were big enough to suggest strength without seeming out of proportion. Her hair was a dark blonde, long and unbraided, her eyes a deep brown, and her skin darker than was common among the tribes. Ferox wondered whether there was some Roman or Mediterranean blood in her family, for it was more than the shade that came from long exposure to sun and wind. He guessed that she was less than forty, perhaps a good deal less, although it was hard to tell. She wore a simple tunic in a drab blue-grey, had a sword at her belt and the same boots as the other women, but had neither armour nor helmet.

'This is my mother,' the queen said, bowing her head.

Ferox guessed that it was a kinship of oaths, like her brothers and sisters.

'My name is not for you,' she said gruffly. 'Some call me a witch or hag.' The lines of her face were strong, not pretty or soft in any way, and yet striking. 'These are my children, bound to me by oaths and come to learn from me if they prove worthy, as others have come in the past to learn from my mother and all the mothers back until the start of all things.'

'I had often thought that you were a fable,' Ferox said. 'And feel now as if I was walking in a song.'

'Then the song must carry us with it,' she said. 'It is time for a reckoning. Your people attack the dun from the land?'

Ferox nodded. In the past he had found Acco to be well informed.

'They will have a hard fight. We will see whether we can help them, but we must come by another path.'

'There is a place where the cliffs can be climbed,' Brigita explained. 'I climbed it once when I was training. It was hard, but I reached the very top of their stronghold, where it reaches a peak.

'Cniva and all his kind must die,' the 'mother' said. 'Brigita tells me that you are a warrior of renown. She says that you fight well, if a little crudely.' Thank you kindly, Ferox thought, and wondered whether that was the mark of a good soldier. 'My children are the best of many tribes. A few have fought and killed. Most have not. I teach them to fight alone. Today, you must lead them. Will you do that?'

Ferox looked around him at the young faces, most of all

Bran, who had for the moment given up trying to sneak glances at the brown-haired girl in the hope that her cloak had slipped open to reveal her bare torso. He wondered what Acco and Brigita had said about him. It seemed mere chance that had brought him and the others here, and yet the druid had spoken of a purpose and a task ahead of him. There would be fourteen of them, for he could not count Bran and somehow sensed that the mother, for all her skill, would not fight.

Fourteen was not many, even if they managed to climb this cliff and get inside the stronghold. They might be able to help the main assault, or they might be surrounded and slaughtered if the attack bogged down or failed.

'Give me my sword,' he said.

XXVI

T HE STRONGHOLD LAY on a narrow headland on the
north side of the bay. Its two stone ramparts crossed
from shore to shore. The first was about fifteen feet
high, including a simple four-foot-high stone parapet. A ditch
ran in front of it, filled with a dribble of water, which would
make it slippery if nothing else. The first wall had an open
entrance near the sea on the left, which the pirates had blocked
with a small wagon piled up with sacks and barrels. Behind the
first line the land climbed, and added to the height of the second
rampart, where the stone was reinforced with timber and
topped by a wooden parapet, much like the one at Vindolanda
or any other army base. A man on the second wall could easily
throw missiles down onto the first or into the ditch in between
them, but it would be much harder to shoot back at them. The
main gate was on the right, protected by a tower. Inside were
houses, arranged without much sense of order, and the ground
rose as it narrowed. A single house stood inside a wicker fence
at the end of the promontory, looking down over the bluffs.

Around the anchorage there were a dozen or more houses,
a mix of the round native type and low rectangular huts were
dotted around the open country, but all were empty by the time
the Romans landed. The pirates left behind a small merchant
ship drawn up on the sand, a few scant possessions in the

buildings, and the smoking hulk of a trireme, burned almost down to the waterline. The glow of its fiery end had guided the convoy to the harbour. It seemed a strange gesture, and Crispinus wondered whether it was meant to show that the pirates would fight to the end because they had chosen not to escape. He saw no sign of unexpected allies eager to help.

'You reckon at least one hundred and fifty fighters?' Crispinus had already asked the question several times.

'At least that, my lord, and probably a good few more.' Vindex gave the same answer. 'We may not have seen their whole strength. A good few are dead or won't be fighting anyone for a while.' The Brigantian had arrived as they were landing, accompanied by a Batavian, both of them shouting that they were friends to avoid being mistaken for Usipi. He had told them about the fight at the tower, and of Ferox's plan to burn Cniva's warship.

'But he didn't get near it. The Red Cat says they met a band of warriors who took the centurion and the others away. The ship was already burning. He reckoned that the warriors may have done it, but could not say for sure. They all left by boat after that.'

Crispinus was not inclined to count on help from mysterious allies, and preferred to believe that the pirates had made a grand gesture of their own. They certainly looked determined enough. He was three hundred paces from the outer rampart and he could see it lined with dark figures carrying black shields.

'Say two hundred or so,' Aelius Brocchus concluded, 'along with women and others who can throw or drop rocks if they cannot swing a sword.' If the cavalry prefect resented the presence of the military tribune, he did not show it. Crispinus had travelled back quickly from Hibernia, and by luck as much as the shipmaster's judgement had sighted Brocchus and his ships already at sea and joined them. In spite of his youth he was senior, so assumed command of the expedition. A victory here would do much to round off his first spell with the army, adding to his earlier achievements and the promised corona civica.

Cerialis had gone with thirty Batavians to secure the tower and his lady. They had found a small cart by the houses, and the men dragged this along to help carry the wounded. That was more than an hour ago, and they ought to return before too long.

'No archers, you say?' Brocchus said.

'A couple,' Vindex said. 'But not that good.'

'Slings?'

'None we saw.'

'Good,' the prefect said. 'So javelins will be the big danger, and stones thrown by hand. He turned to one of the centurions commanding a trireme. 'Are the ladders long enough?'

'Should be, my lord. I cannot see how deep the ditch is behind the first wall, though. If it drops a lot, then they may not reach.' They had brought four ladders with them, each a little over twenty feet long, for Brocchus had guessed that the pirates' lair was likely to have some sort of stronghold. He wished now that he had brought more. Men had been sent to scour the buildings, but there were no timbers long enough to be made into ladders. The sailors had produced ropes with grapnels on the end, but he doubted that anyone other than the ships' crews would have the skill to climb them.

Over half their force was from the classis Britannica, which was good in many ways because their life made them strong. Forty were marines, each man with a helmet, mail, sword, long hexagonal shield and a javelin. There were also two hundred and fifty rowers, apart from the men who remained on board the ships, but these sailors lacked body armour, and only about half had a helmet and a shield. The rest were set to entrenching a position around the beach. It might be useful, especially if they failed to break into the fort on the first day. Yet the sailors were nervous, saying that they feared a fresh storm coming in. It would be better if they could win quickly.

Brocchus had brought a hundred legionaries from II Augusta. They were picked men, all from the first cohort, with many six feet or more, tall and all experienced. Two centurions commanded them, both sound men, and Crispinus knew that these were the heart of his force, although he also had a good deal of confidence in the Batavians. Brocchus had brought fifty infantrymen under a centurion from cohors VIIII and there were also thirty of the troopers who had accompanied him to Hibernia. Cavalrymen were never keen on fighting dismounted, but anyone could sense the hatred all of them felt towards this enemy. One advantage was the detachment of twenty archers, reinforced by sailors with half a dozen of the smallest engines used by the army, little bolt-shooters. If pressed they were light enough to be carried and operated by one man, but the sailors worked in teams of two, which was more efficient, and had a third and a fourth man carrying baskets of bolts.

Crispinus summoned the officers to a consilium. He was relieved that the pirates were not choosing to make a stand outside the ramparts. Although they would be driven back in time, it would cause delay, wear his men out, and he doubted that this Cniva would be foolish enough to be lured forward and destroyed in the open.

Cerialis rode up as they were gathering. They had brought only a single horse, and the tribune had given it to the prefect to speed him as he went to find his wife.

'I trust the Lady Sulpicia is safe, my dear Cerialis,' the tribune said, doing his best to make it sound like no more than a polite question about someone's health.

'Indeed she is, my lord,' the prefect replied, 'but now that I have seen her, I would not wish to miss the kill. I have a good deal to pay back.'

'Of course, of course. Well, your Batavians will form in the centre, and be the first to attack,' Crispinus informed them. The infantry would lead, supported by the archers, and with the dismounted troopers in reserve. A second column would form on their right, led by the marines, supported by one hundred sailors as well as the bolt-shooters. Each of these columns would be given two of the precious ladders. The legionaries were placed on the left, closest to the gate in the outer wall. Half, under the junior of their centurions, would be ready to advance, with the remainder following as reserve under the command of the *hastatus* of the legion, Julius Tertullianus.

'You are to wait for my signal, my dear Tertullianus.' Crispinus was more than usually courteous, for the centurions of the first cohort were men whose opinion mattered. Tertullianus was in his early thirties, a thickset man with a bull neck, the iron shoulder bands of his segmented cuirass making him look almost square. Crispinus found himself thinking of coins of Mark Antony, for there was the same flat nose and face, giving off a sense of brooding anger. Tertullianus was young for a man of his rank, suggesting at friends in high places as well as considerable talent, and he was the choice of the legate. All of this made a display of trust in him prudent.

'I intend to hold the legionaries back a little,' the tribune went on. 'We may take the first wall without their assistance.' The senior centurion's face was rigid. He looked angry, and that was his natural expression, but Crispinus also sensed doubt. 'The second wall will be far harder, because it is difficult for us to approach it. I suspect that your men will lead that assault, but I am not yet sure whether to send you against the gate or part of the wall itself.' He tried to read the impassive face, wondering whether the centurion thought this all too vague. The tribune turned to Brocchus. 'Any luck finding material to burn the gates?'

'Not much. It's too early for the heather to be any use. We have stripped some thatch from the houses, and filled all the sacks we have. Tied up a few bundles of branches as well, but it is not a lot.'

'Well, it may serve, and we shall have torches ready to light it if the chance occurs. Otherwise, it will be down to your axemen, Festus.' This was to the centurion in command of his ship. Half a dozen burly sailors would carry axes and picks ready to hack through the gates.

'We shall cover you like a roof,' Tertullianus said. Even though he ought to be prepared for it by now, Crispinus still struggled not to smile at the high, squeaking voice coming from the mouth of so formidable a man. 'The Capricorns will protect them.' Formed by the Divine Augustus, the legion had his capricorn symbol on their shields.

'Yes, you can rely on us,' Crispinus added, for he was tribune of II Augusta and it never did any harm to flatter the pride of a unit.

The plan was a fairly simple one, and yet once again Crispinus was surprised at how long it took for the various parts of his tiny army to form up in position. Brocchus was busy, guiding the leaders to the right places, urging the men on and joking with them. Crispinus admired the courage of the troops, for he had seen men much like these fight and win against heavy odds, but they remained strangers to him. He would have liked to make them laugh and show how much he trusted them in the way the prefect seemed to find so easy. Yet he did not know how, and in the past when he had tried it had sounded stilted and been met with silence.

Crispinus stared at the fort instead. Now that Cerialis was back, the tribune had mounted their lone horse. He told the trumpeter and the man carrying the red vexillum with the golden embroidered figure of a Victory to stay there, while he rode a little closer to the fort. There were black-clad warriors along the first rampart. He counted fifty or so and wondered whether more were hidden. More of the enemy were visible on the second, higher rampart. At first they were silent, but when he came within one hundred paces a few started to yell.

'Boy-lover!'

Vindex had spoken of a couple of archers, and the tribune hoped that they were as unskilled as he claimed or saving their arrows for the real assault. He rode on, gripping his sword tight in case he dropped it in his nervousness.

'Come here, sonny, and I'll give it to you up the arse!'

The tribune rode closer, back straight and head erect. A muscle in his thigh gave a spasm of cramping pain, and he tried to ignore it. He was seventy-five paces from the wall, and the faces along the rampart were distinct. He saw plenty of older men, most with beards, and a few younger ones. At the moment they were all bare-headed, no doubt waiting until just before the fight to don heavy and uncomfortable helmets.

'Hey, I think he's in love with me!' one of them shouted, and there was a roar of laughter.

Crispinus kept going, knowing that at this range even a bad archer would struggle to miss. He was still not quite sure why he was doing this, and he imagined Ferox's scorn at the gesture. That made him wonder where the centurion was, for the man was surely out there somewhere, and unlikely to sit out a fight unless he was held captive. Crispinus did not know, but wished the grim centurion was here, because he so often came up with a clever idea. The tribune could not think of one, so he must attack straight into the face of the defences and trust to his men to win.

At fifty paces he reined in.

'Looks like you've upset the pansy!'

'Probably smelt you and changed his mind!'

'Oh love, come to me.'

Crispinus ignored the taunts and the laughter, and the man who thrust his bare bottom over the top of the parapet. He waited, his thigh twitching and sweat on the palm of his hand where he gripped the bone handle. At last there was silence.

'In the name of the Lord Trajan, three times consul and master of the world,' he began.

'Reckon they're surrendering,' someone shouted.

'Well, tell them to piss off!' another yelled.

'You have broken your sacramentum.' Crispinus knew that he still had much to learn to reach the highest levels of oratory, but his was a trained voice and he made it carry without seeming to shout. 'That oath is to the emperor and to Rome. You have broken it and committed horrible crimes.'

'We have, sonny.' No one on the wall laughed this time.

'By order of the emperor, every man in this place is condemned to death. That sentence will be carried out today.'

There was silence, apart from the heavy breathing of the horse. Then Crispinus felt the animal's spine twitch. Its tail went up and he heard the heavy smacks as the steaming droppings fell to the ground. There was nothing he could do, so he tried to make the best of it. Keeping the back legs where they were and holding the reins tight, he kicked the horse on the side to make it turn on the spot. Once it was round he pointed the tip of his sword at the dark brown pile.

'Your lives are worth no more than that!' This time he did shout, and the sound echoed back at him. He spat, hoping that the whole vulgar display might work for his audience. A javelin was flung from the wall, but the range was absurdly long and it fell short.

'Coward!' a voice yelled. 'Come back and fight me man to man.'

Crispinus ignored him and rode back to his men. A canter would have looked like nervousness, but he let the animal trot because he could imagine the archers coming to the wall and sighting along the line of their shafts. He waited, feeling his back tense underneath the armour as he imagined a hissing arrow flying straight at him. None came. As he got close the sailors and marines started to cheer. The Batavians took up the shout, banging the shafts of their spears against the rims of their shields. The legionaries were silent, but they were further away and kept under tighter discipline.

Aelius Brocchus nodded to him as he returned to the vexillum that marked the position of the commander. No other standards were carried by the force. Crispinus decided to take the gesture as one of approval, although it was hard to tell for he could be a stern man. Lucius Ovidius showed no such restraint, and the tribune was surprised to see him there, along with others from the tower.

'Very bold,' the old man said cheerfully. 'But a word of warning, though, as a man of letters – if you ever put all this to verse, I'd skip the part about the horse shit.' Ovidius noticed that Sulpicia Lepidina was walking over, and immediately reddened, nervous that she had heard his vulgarity.

'My lady, it is a joy to see you safe and well,' Crispinus said, and meant it. The prefect's wife cut an uncommonly fine figure in her simple peasant dress. Crispinus suspected that on his return to Rome in a year or so his father would insist that he marry, and at the moment he felt he could not wish for more than a younger version of this lady – or at least one from a family less heavily in debt. He was surprised that this prudent thought made him feel a pang of guilt, and decided to avoid a conversation. 'Now, if you will forgive me, we must set to our duty. Perhaps the noble Ovidius will escort you to a place of safety?'

'Of course,' he said, while the lady gave a slight incline of her head.

'My dear Brocchus, would you be kind enough to tell Cerialis that he may advance when ready.' The prefect jogged the twenty yards to give the order, and Crispinus wondered whether he ought to have sent a simple soldier as messenger. Yet he had not thought to keep more than the trumpeter and vexillarius with him. He noticed the one-eyed Batavian and a couple of other troopers with the lady. 'You and you.' He pointed to the veteran and one other. 'Come here. You will serve as runners.'

'Sir.' The one-eyed soldier had a hard gaze and the tribune was not sure whether the man resented being given the order. After all, they had fought and barely lived through a very tough fight in the last days, so could well feel that they had played their part. Crispinus looked around for Vindex, wanting to add him to his followers as well, but he could not see the scout so gave up the idea.

A low rumbling shout began, making the horse spin around to see what had caused it. The Batavians had begun the *barritus*, shields raised high in front of their mouths so that the sound reverberated. There were only eighty voices, and they began quietly, letting the sound rise like waves washing against the shore. The horse's ears twitched, and the sound took the tribune back to the campaign against the Stallion. There was something unearthly about the noise, as it grew stronger and stronger. The Harii and Usipi were Germans as well, but no answering challenge came from the fort.

'It's all right, girl.' Crispinus spoke softly to the horse as the shout reached its crescendo and ended with a bellow of sheer fury.

'Silence!' Flavius Crescens, the centurion leading the Batavians shouted the command in a clear voice. 'Listen for the orders. Keep in formation. Forward march!' Six soldiers carried each ladder, and the remaining thirty-six followed them in a column four abreast, the centurion at the head and the optio bringing up the rear. The archers scattered and jogged ahead of them. Cerialis waited for a short time, and then led his troopers in support.

There was silence apart from the rhythmical rattles and thump of armoured men marching in step. The field was flat, the thin grass short, and the men kept in their formation without difficulty. Crispinus was behind and to their right, so he could not see the red symbols on their green oval shields, but the dark hair-like moss stuck to the tops of their helmets gave the infantrymen an oddly drab look. At this distance, the bear and other animal fur glued to the helmets of the troopers looked little better.

When they were a hundred and fifty paces away, a great cheer went up from the fort. Cow horns blew and there was the shrill sound of dozens of whistles. One of the archers stopped and loosed, the arrow striking the stone parapet and bouncing back. The duplicarius in charge of the auxiliary bowmen cursed the man and told him to wait until they were closer.

Crispinus turned to Longinus. 'Tell the fleet to attack,' he said, and the lean veteran loped off towards the marines and sailors. They sent up a great whoop when the order came, and banged weapons against shields as they advanced. All of the marines were in a block, ten broad and four deep, and the lines were soon a little ragged in spite of the pounding of shafts against the rims of their hexagonal shields. These were painted blue, with white tridents pointing from the top and bottom edge towards the central boss. Their mail cuirasses were covered with blue-grey over-tunics, so that only their bronze helmets glinted in the sun. Sailors carried the ladders, and the teams of men with each of the hand-held bolt-shooters spread out on either side. Other men ran forward, clutching javelins.

The legionaries had not moved and stood in silence as if on parade, formed in two rectangles, the rear one echeloned back to the right. Crispinus glanced over to them, but felt no worry that they would surge into the attack before he gave the order. Tertullianus stood at the head of the leading formation, and that made the tribune wonder whether he intended to lead from the front and not stay with the reserves. After a while he decided that it was better to let the man do what he wished rather than send a fussy order to check that he understood his instructions. The burly man with the high-pitched voice had been decorated for service on the frontier in Egypt, as well as during Domitian's wars against the Germans, so he knew what to do.

'Hah!' Aelius Brocchus slapped his thigh with delight, and Crispinus realised that the archers were starting to shoot. 'Got the swine right in the face,' the prefect explained. His relish was surprising, for he had always struck Crispinus as a calm, even mild man. Then he remembered the raid on Alauna, that these men had threatened the prefect's family and abducted his friends. Crispinus could sense that same hatred in all ranks. It would spur them on, but he must be careful not to lose control.

'Come on,' he said, 'let's take a closer look.' The tribune walked the horse towards the fort. It was a shame that there was no mount for Brocchus, but he could not help that and might need to move quickly from one place to another. For the moment, the ambling walk of this animal made it easy for the men on foot to keep up.

The Batavians were fifty paces from the wall. One of the men carrying the ladders dropped, an arrow in his thigh, and the five remaining men staggered as they passed him, but kept going. The auxiliary archers were shooting, and this time Crispinus was looking at the right spot when a pirate was pitched back, a shaft sprouting from his throat. The enemy had their helmets on now, and with the protection of the wall and their oval shields, nearly all of the arrows struck harmlessly.

Javelins and stones were coming from the defenders, and the men with the ladders were especially vulnerable, for it was hard to run with their burden and still keep a shield steady in the other hand. The team a man short lost another to a javelin that pinned his foot to the ground, and then a third man's shield swayed at just the wrong moment so that a stone smashed his nose. An arrow hit the thrower at almost the same time, driving through his eye. The three men left dropped the heavy ladder, and men ran from the main group to aid them. The other team ran on unscathed, jumping down into the ditch. They waded through, ankle deep in mud. There was a dull clang as a stone hit one man on the helmet and he let go, falling to his knees in the brown water, but the others kept going and planted the ladder at the foot of the wall and began to raise it up. A pirate leaned over the parapet, javelin in hand, and then gasped as an arrow pierced his mail. He dropped rather than threw the javelin and it fell harmlessly.

With a cheer, the Batavians surged forward into the ditch. The second ladder was there as well, and men began to climb the other one.

'They're breaking,' Brocchus said, his tone almost one of disappointment with a timid enemy. Crispinus had been watching the marines and sailors, who were also close to the wall, and when he looked back saw that the prefect was right. The pirates were running from the rampart in front of the Batavians. Before they went, they hoisted heavy baskets onto the parapet. One Usipi was killed by an arrow as he worked, but the rest kept on and Crispinus could imagine them grunting with effort as they tipped the baskets over and the big rocks showered down on the packed ditch. There was confusion, but the enemy were still fleeing and the first Batavian climbed over the parapet onto the wall. More followed.

Crispinus glanced back at the waiting legionaries, but decided this was too soon to add them to the attack. The marines were at the wall. A few men had fallen to missiles, but the bolt-shooters were more accurate than bows at a longer range and had driven the defenders down behind the parapet. Once the ladders were in place the defenders fled. If they had baskets of stones they did not use them, and the marines rushed up the ladders and leaped onto the wall.

'You bring up the legionaries,' Crispinus said to Brocchus. 'Bring Tertullianus and get him to clear the entrance to the first wall and then be ready to assault the gate in the second.' Without waiting for an answer, he spurred the horse into a canter straight at the marines and sailors. He wanted to be up on the wall, seeing what was going on so that he could judge what orders to give. In moments he was at the ditch, and jumped off, closer than he wanted, so that his boot slipped and he skidded down the side into the mud. His legs and the pristine white pteruges of his armour were stained dark. Sailors grinned at him and he grinned back, getting up and wading through to the nearest ladder. He patted a man on the shoulder just as he was about to climb, receiving a curse and then a hasty apology from the marine. Crispinus smiled again and pushed the man aside so that he could climb.

The ladder was steep, and the mud on his boots made him slip off one of the rungs, but he clung on somehow, round shield in one hand and sword in the other. More than a dozen men were up on the rampart above each ladder, and there were shouts of triumph and confusion. Crispinus reached the top, and one of the grey-uniformed marines reached out to help him up. The tribune was almost over, one leg on each side of the rough stone parapet, and he could see the last of the defenders running through the open gate.

'There you go, sir,' the marine said cheerfully, and then the man's eyes widened and his mouth moved, but only gasps came from it. He slumped down onto the parapet, and Crispinus saw the shaft of the javelin that had struck him in the back. More missiles came, and he managed to raise his shield and block one before it hit him in the face.

The Romans were spread along a walkway about four feet wide, and above a sheer drop almost as high as the outside wall, for in the past someone had laboured to dig a ditch on the inside of the wall. Crispinus glanced down and saw several ropes down there and guessed that this was how the defenders had escaped. A stone clanged against the helmet of a marine next to him. The man turned, and the tribune saw his eyes flicker before he started to sway forward.

'Grab him!' the tribune yelled, and one marine dropped his spear to hold onto his comrade and stop him from falling off the wall.

The defenders were above them, no more than twenty feet away and they had javelins and stones and even a few clubs and axes piled ready and waiting. A stone struck a marine on the foot, breaking bone, and the man staggered so that a javelin came past his shield and drove through the mail shirt into his belly. The centurion of one of the triremes was yelling at his men to keep their shields up, but even when crouching it still left some of the head and legs exposed. Some marines hurled javelins up at the enemy, but the wooden parapet gave them much better cover, and so far no one had scored a hit. In return the missiles kept coming, wounding men, making it harder for them to protect themselves.

'Come on!' the centurion yelled, and leaped down from the wall, but he screamed as he landed badly, twisting his ankle, and then a heavy spear came from the inner rampart and its sheer weight let the narrow point punch through the left cheek piece of his helmet and drive deep into his head. The centurion was flung against the wall and collapsed in a heap back into the ditch.

Two of his men went after him, and although one hit the ground awkwardly, both were up, raising their shields protectively over the centurion.

Crispinus wondered whether he should follow, for the gate was still closing, and hoped it was not simply fear that stopped him. One of the marines in the ditch took a spear in the side a moment later, and when he fell he was pounded with rocks until he lay still. The other scrambled up the bank and ran at the gateway. A big stone slammed into his helmet when he was just yards away and the wooden gate closed as if to reinforce the hopelessness of his bravery.

The Romans screamed defiance at the defenders, but there was nothing they could do to stop this torment. The javelins and other missiles kept coming and now and then found a gap. A stunned marine tumbled down into the ditch. Another yelped when a stone clipped the toe of his boot, but the others were too distracted to laugh.

'Back!' Crispinus yelled, making up his mind. 'Back down the ladders.'

They did not want to go. Partly it was because they feared the time it would take for them to climb down, and having to get over the parapet and be vulnerable to missiles, but mainly it was anger and pride. They had taken the wall from a hated enemy and they did not want to give it up.

'You.' Crispinus grabbed the closest marine by the arm. 'Over the wall and back down the ladder. Now!' The man nodded, then his head jerked to the side as a rock hit his helmet. He sank down.

'You, lad.' The tribune pointed at the next man. 'Over you go.' A javelin struck the wall near him, but the marine got over and then dropped his shield to make it easier to descend.

'Go on, all of you.' Crispinus' shield rocked in his grip as a javelin struck the wooden boards before falling back. He had decided that he must be the last one down. The marines were moving now, but they seemed slow, so slow. He crouched, sheltering as much of his body behind his shield as he could. He glanced to the side, and now that men were going back he glimpsed the Batavians further along and realised that their attack had stalled in the same way.

Crispinus hoped that Cerialis would have the sense to order a retreat. A stone banged against his shield, and the tribune hoped even more that his life was not about to end here, on an old rampart on an island that seemed to have no name – or at least no name a civilised man would recognise. Up on the higher wall a great chorus of whistles blew and there were mocking shouts.

XXVII

T HE BOAT ROSE over a wave, a spray of cold water
drenching the rowers and passengers alike, and Ferox
sat in the stern, trying to remember what it was like
to be young. As he stared at the taut faces of the warriors, it
was their lack of years that he saw more than anything else.
They had something of Brigita's confident assurance, and he
could remember that it was so much easier to believe yourself
invulnerable and invincible before the world had knocked such
nonsense out of you.

They were not soldiers. You could take twenty *tirones*,
looking nervous and lost as they paraded in ill-fitting uniforms
and uncomfortable armour, and over time you could teach
them their trade. One or two would never be any good, and
it was better for all concerned if they deserted or were found
some job in the camp that would keep them out of the way.
Most would shape up well enough, looking and acting like
soldiers and more or less reliable. A few turned into the real
fighters, the men who would go first, who had the knack not
simply of staying alive but of killing. Anyone who had served
in the army for a while and trained recruits would know this,
just as they would know that it was not always obvious which
of the raw lads would fall into each category. He had heard
that it was much the same with gladiators. Even when they had

no choice about fighting, some of the most promising looking ones were never any good.

Ferox looked at the mother's warriors, some toiling at the oars, while the others sat between them. She trained them hard, of that there was no doubt, and they were fit and strong and knew how to handle the weapons they carried. As she said, she also taught them to fight on their own, for among the tribes a nobleman needed to beat opponents in single combat if he was to make a reputation. A little to his surprise he was less worried by the women, who were all that bit older, but apart from Brigita he was not really sure how they would fight. The queen had explained that the mother was bound by sacred oaths to teach those who were worthy enough to reach the island and survive the tests she imposed without favour to anyone's family or tribe. She could not fight, for she was also bound never again to kill or be with a man.

'It is a hard climb,' Brigita told him as they came around the headland. She pointed at the next promontory, but they were so close that he could not see what was on top, apart from a tall thatched building above the highest cliffs. 'I did it once and brought back an egg from the birds who nest in the crannies.'

'Is there a beach?'

'At this time of day there should some ground at the foot of the cliffs.'

The queen's memory was true, although the little landing place was even smaller than Ferox expected. The cliffs towered overheard around the little inlet. Gulls cried out from their nests above them, but when Ferox looked up it seemed a long way.

'I can do this.' Bran's confidence surprised him.

'Then you come with me,' he said.

'No, I go first.' The boy gave one of his rare smiles. 'I do not want you falling on top of me.'

Ferox had climbed a lot when he was young, for that was expected in his tribe, but it had been many years since he had attempted anything even half as difficult as this. Still, he wanted to be the first – or now the second – up, because he was not sure what they would meet and trusted himself more than any of the others to cope. He had a rope coiled over one shoulder and had pulled his gladius around so that it hung on his back.

The first stretch was easy, sloping in rather than fully vertical. Bran bounded up it, and Ferox followed the boy as he got onto a ledge, worked along it, and then started to climb. The rock was dark, with a rough, pitted surface, but there were plenty of little outcrops, so that for a while it was not hard to choose the next step.

Yet Ferox had forgotten how hard work this was, and soon his fingers were bruised. He had little cuts from gripping onto jagged holds, while his knees were battered and scratched. He glanced down and noticed that one leg of his trousers had a big tear. Faces stared up at him eagerly, still nearer than he had expected, and he felt a flash of anger because they struck him as impatient.

Bran was a fair way ahead. Ferox forced himself on, but when he grabbed at the next crack, some of the stone came away in his hand and his raised foot slipped back to a ledge a few inches down. His heart was pounding. He took things slowly for a while, trying to remember how the lad had done it. His arms and legs were aching with the effort, he felt hot and he had a strange urge to relax and drop backwards, imagining himself splashing into the cool water. He shook his head, and was cheered when the next few feet were straightforward.

There was still a long way to go, but Bran was no more than fifteen feet from the top. Perhaps he should have given the rope to the boy in the first place. It was too late for that, and Ferox made himself keep climbing. The cliff was sheer now, and his foot crushed a nest as he stepped on a ledge. The birds were circling, calling out in alarm. He could feel the beat of their wings as some swooped close behind him. Something hot, wet and stinking spattered against his cheek. With white-ish stains of bird excrement all over the rocks it did not take imagination to work out what it was.

Ferox worried about the noise. It must be nearly noon, and he had no idea when the Roman attack would be launched. If the defenders were not distracted, then there seemed no reason at all why someone might not wonder what had upset the seabirds and take a look over the edge of the cliff. Bran was almost at the top, and the boy had stopped. Ferox hoped that it was simply to let him catch up and not because he had heard or sensed danger. He imagined black-clad warriors with spears, peeking from cover, watching him toil up the rock face and waiting to kill him because it was funnier to let him suffer first.

The last twenty feet seemed to take an age. Aches were now a stark pain in his arms and legs, every movement an effort. Bran smiled at him, the indulgent smile reserved for infants or the elderly and infirm doing the simplest thing. Ferox struggled on. The whole right leg of his trousers had split and hung open, his skin grazed and cut by sharp edges.

Bran moved, climbing the last couple of feet and peering over the lip. Then he scampered up and over and was lost from view. Ferox followed, muttering curses under his breath, blaming Trajan, Crispinus, damned women, and all the gods and goddesses for bringing him here. The stern silence of the Silures no longer mattered so much to him compared to venting his rage and frustration. He climbed on, the top seeming no closer, and suddenly the boy appeared, staring down and smiling.

At last Ferox scrambled over the edge. He was breathing like a hound after a long chase, and moving like an old man. Bran was crouched behind a wattle fence that crossed the grass in front of them. Beyond was the building, long and broad, but a lot lower than he had expected. There was no sound apart from the angry gulls, the wash of the sea and his own panting. He pushed up on all fours and crawled over to some boulders, where he sat, resting his back. The boy was puzzled and came over.

'Shall I tie the rope?' he whispered. There were some low rocks, but none were big enough to hold the weight. 'You will have to move.' Ferox realised that the only place was where he was resting. He smiled and forced himself up. Once he was standing it was easier. He drew his sword and went over to the fence. Peering over the top, he saw a patch of cultivated ground around the house and a couple of pigs rooting around for food. There was no door in the building on this side, and no sign of anyone, but the house blocked his view. He moved along to the end and could see more buildings dotted around the slopes below, and he ducked because a couple of women came out of one. They did not seem to have noticed him.

While the others started to climb he rested. Brigita was first, then the boy with the thin moustache, and next the brown-haired woman. With the aid of the rope, none of them seemed to have picked up as many cuts and scars on the way as the Roman.

The others frowned when they heard the shouting getting louder, but Ferox knew the barritus. 'They are just starting,' he whispered, but it was frustrating because from up here they could not see what was going on. At least it should keep the defenders busy, but as the rest of them came up the cliff the noise grew indistinct and certainly drew no closer. Between them they brought a helmet, cuirass and shield, which the mother had provided for him. It was a scale shirt, clumsy and a little tight, but better than nothing. The helmet was an iron legionary one, with studs on the cheek pieces, a deep and broad neck guard, and embossed shapes meant to look like eyebrows in front. He tied it in place, wishing he had the woolly hat as padding. The shield was small and square, and had a black eagle painted on it.

When it came, the scream blotted out all other noise and seemed to go on forever. One of the lads looked back and went pale. Ferox peeked over the fence, saw no one, and then ran to the edge.

'It was a bird,' Brigita said. 'It flew straight into his face and he slipped.' The twisted shape of one of the young warriors lay on the little beach.

Ferox was tempted to go on and let the rest catch up, but with so few of them it was foolish to split up for no reason. Still, it would do no harm to look in the house. He whispered to Brigita and the lad with the moustache to follow and then pulled himself over the fence. One of the pigs squealed because he landed beside it. He went to the back wall of the building and waited for the others. He guessed that the entrance would face south, and they came around the corner and saw it ahead of them. Ferox gestured at the youth to go to the other side. Looking downhill, he could not see much apart from other buildings and thatched roofs, and the top of a tower. Pirates were on the top, and he saw one throwing something down. The wind had veered, blowing from behind them, and it was hard to hear anything. Then trumpets blared and he heard a great shout. The Romans must have resumed their assault.

He hefted his shield and walked towards the entrance. At least it was not a roundhouse, where he would have to duck to get through the low door, and his reason told him that no one should be waiting to kill him as he burst in. He still wondered, and took a deep breath before he kicked the door hard and it flew back. There was firelight in the house, which was like a long hall with a fire in the middle. He ran in, the air thick with the smell of damp rushes and wood smoke. A girl of no more than ten stared at him wide-eyed. An old woman, her long, thin hair white under the layers of dirt, turned around.

'Who are you?' Ferox was wearing the black cloak and trousers taken from dead pirates, and he guessed the woman assumed he was one of the band. 'Come closer where I can see you.'

Brigita came into the hall and no one would mistake her for one of Harii. The little girl gasped and ran to cling to the older woman. A male voice shouted out in anger, and Ferox knew it at once and felt his rage coming back. He went to one of the bowers fenced off from the main hall, and as he reached it the drapes were wrenched aside. Genialis appeared, his young face more than usually cruel in its anger.

'You!' he said in surprise as much as horror.

Ferox punched Genialis with the boss of his shield, sending him back, and then punched him again to knock him down. A woman screamed, then another, and Ferox saw that there were two naked girls in the little room. One had a black eye and both scrambled away and crouched by the wall, whimpering. Genialis was on the floor, bare apart from a blanket half-draped around him, and trying to wriggle away. Ferox jabbed with his sword, stopping the point inches from his face. The youth froze.

'I'd be doing your father a favour if I killed you,' Ferox said.

'Cniva is my father.'

'Then I won't do him a favour.' Ferox pulled his sword away, and stamped hard on the youth's leg. Genialis screamed, so he kicked him in the crotch. 'Quiet,' he yelled. The lad sobbed, but said nothing.

There was no one else in the house. They found rope and tied the boy up, and Ferox set the warrior with the moustache to watch their prisoners. 'If he speaks or moves, just kill him,' he said, and repeated it in Latin to make sure that Genialis understood. Brigita whispered something to the young warrior that made him grin.

'He will do it,' she said.

'Good.'

There was a yelp and Ferox saw that the old woman had kicked Genialis as he sat with his back to the wall. She kicked him again and spat in his face. Then she went in to the naked girls and spoke softly to them. It was clear that these people had no love for Cniva's son, and he wondered if they were captives kept as slaves.

'We will leave one of the younger lads here as well,' Ferox decided. That left him with half a dozen boys, the three warrior women, Brigita and Bran, although he would try to keep the boy away from the fighting if he could. 'Will your mother stay with them?'

'She goes where she wishes,' the queen replied, and it was clear that she wished to stay with the main group.

Ferox had them go through the stacks of firewood and find a few branches to make into torches. By the time they began to walk downhill towards the rest of the houses, a swirling wind whipped at the flames. He could hear shouting and horns blowing. There was no sign of anyone abroad in the settlement, so they walked towards the houses. Ferox led, with Brigita beside him. The others came as a single rank after them, with the mother and Bran at the rear. A tethered goat bleated at them from outside the nearest building.

The nearest building was a smaller version of the main hall, and again lacked any windows. Half a dozen more houses clustered behind it, narrow and muddy alleys threading their way through the jumble of buildings and fenced gardens. Ferox led them into the nearest. There was still no sign of anyone, giving the place an eerie, abandoned air. A woman appeared in a doorway, and she had the same dull and fearful gaze of the ones in the house with Genialis. He nodded amicably to her and she vanished.

They turned sharply, following the path around the next thatched house, this one built from timber framing, with big patches of the whitewashed mud daub missing. The place reminded Ferox of villages he had seen on the Rhine and Danube, and he had never discerned much sense of order in those either.

A woman almost bumped into them, going the other way, so that she dropped the bundle of firewood she was carrying. She was young, little more than a girl, and had the slim face and limbs of a Hibernian.

'I'm sorry, lord,' she gasped, flinching back from the expected blow. Then she saw Brigita, and the red-headed warrior woman and her mouth opened. She ran, leaving the wood where it lay. The redhead raised a javelin, but Ferox beat it down.

'No. We'll do more good if we make Cniva nervous. She'll tell of enemies within their walls, and he will not know how many. Come on.' He led them back the way they had come and they took another of the narrow paths, running between two houses whose eaves almost touched. It led them to another barn-like building next to an open space and beyond that another cluster of houses. Ferox could see the top of the gate-tower behind them, so they must be getting close.

Three men appeared at the far side of the narrow clearing.

One's bare head hung low, and the others had their arms around his shoulders to help him along. All three were clad in the black and drab colours of the pirates, with the wounded man in scale armour and the others wearing mail and bronze helmets of the simple patterns often issued to auxiliaries.

Ferox ran at them, shield up and sword raised. A javelin thrummed in the air beside him. As the men looked up the missile struck one of the carriers in the chest. The man gasped, pulling free, and the wounded man slumped down. The third reached for his sword, but Ferox was on him before he was ready. The pirate crouched away, tipping his head so that he could not see his attacker. The centurion slashed, avoiding the top of the helmet and cutting into the pirate's neck above his mail cuirass. Blood sprayed as he wrenched the gladius back up, but the man was already falling and there was no need for a second blow. Brigita drove her javelin into the eye of the injured man and had to put a foot on his chest to yank it free. The redhead was kneeling beside the one she had hit with her throw, dragging his helmet off. Her sword was on the ground beside her.

'No time for that now!' Ferox said, guessing that she wanted his head. With an expression of mild disappointment, the young woman picked up her sword and sliced through the man's throat.

A shout came from behind, and they turned to see that two pirates had opened the big door of the barn. The young warriors swarmed around them, jabbing and cutting with more frenzy than skill. They went inside, leaping over the dying pirates, and there were more screams.

'Keep an eye open,' Ferox told Brigita, pointing at the mouth of the alley from which the three men had come. By the time he reached the barn the warriors had finished. There must have been a dozen injured Harii and Usipi on the straw of the barn with a man and some women tending to them. The last of the men died as he came into the building. A lad with the face of Eros was still twisting his spearhead in the pirate's belly. Poets often spoke of the beauty and innocence of youth, but rarely rejoiced in the viciousness that lived in many. Still, that was something for Ovidius to debate when it was all over, and none of these men deserved mercy.

Another of the lads dropped his shield and javelins and grabbed a girl, who looked barely a year or so older. With a quick motion, he ripped the top of her dress down. She did not scream and that was odd, and no doubt told a story of the lives these slaves had with their masters.

Ferox ran over and smacked the boy on the side of the head, using a fist still clutching his sword. He must have hit harder than intended, for the boy fell. One of the others laughed, and the lad glared up at him, looking more than ever like a child. A voice cut over the laughter. The mother said just one word, and it gave the youth a harder blow than Ferox's punch. He stood, picked up his weapons, and then, oddest of all, he gave a little bow to the girl and scampered off with the others. The mother was already outside. Brigita and the redhead came back to join them as five pirates appeared, led by an older man with a long, brown beard that spilled out of the cheek pieces of his helmet and fell almost to his waist.

'Form with me.' Ferox pushed himself through the rest and stood, shield braced. Brigita and the redhead came up on his left and the other two women on his right. A glance to see they were there showed him the bare breasts of the one with brown hair, and it added to the unreal quality of this day. The boys split and joined them on either side. 'Come on!' he shouted, and charged. Javelins were thrown, and one of the pirates reeled, spitted through the thigh, while another had two missiles strike his shield and burst through the board. Ferox was screaming in anger and the others joined in, a strangely high-pitched battle cry. He headed for the bearded man.

The enemy stood their ground, and most of the chargers stopped, apart from one boy who flung himself bodily at the pirate on the far left of the line, sending them both sprawling. The black-clad man next to him reversed his spear and rammed it down, pinning the boy to the ground. A moment later one of the other lads stabbed under the pirate's guard, striking the fringe of his long cuirass. The armour held, but the blow was hard and forced the man back.

Ferox's shield banged hard against his opponent's. The bearded man had his sword at eye level, elbow bent and waiting for the chance to jab. Ferox had taken the same guard, and they eyed each other warily, feinting without committing to a blow. The pirates were outnumbered from the start, and scattered so that sometimes two came against one. The redhead almost managed to slip her spear past a man's shield, and when he moved to block it, Brigita thrust her sword into his belly. Rings snapped as the point struck, but they took enough force from the blow to stop it being fatal. The man grunted with pain and slashed at the queen, and then the redhead's broad spear point took him in the leg and he sank down. Brigita cut again, the sword making a dull clang and leaving a dent where it struck the helmet. The other woman drove her spear through the pirate's boot and foot, and when he shrieked in agony his head went back and the queen stabbed him through the throat.

The bearded leader realised that his men were losing, so attacked, jabbing at Ferox's eyes. He swayed out of the way, jerking his shield up so that the rim struck the man's arm. His own jab was stopped, the point catching on the edge of the helmet's cheek piece, but the two blows unbalanced the man. Ferox followed up, using the round wooden pommel of his gladius to beat the pirate in the face. He felt teeth and bone snapping, struck again and the man sank to his knees. Ferox kicked him over and a moment later one of the boys appeared and hacked again and again at the pirate's bloodied head. The blows struck the bronze helmet, which must have been a good one because after three or four the blade of the boy's sword had bent out of shape. The pirate moaned, and Ferox killed him with a stab to the throat. Blood spurted higher than he expected, most of it spraying over the boy, who was laughing hysterically.

All of the pirates were dead. The fair-haired woman had a small cut above one eye, and one of the boys a longer graze along his right arm, but no one was badly hurt and only the one boy had died. The mother remained behind, watching, and if he had had more time Ferox might have resented her scrutiny. She was the only one still carrying a torch, and he guessed that the lads had dropped the others in their excitement. Bran stood beside her like a faithful hound.

'See if you can set fire to the big barn,' he told them, 'and then wait for me behind it.'

Ferox walked over to the alleyway. It ran straight, one of the few paths in this stronghold that did, and he could see the back of the rampart and part of the gate. Pirates still held them, but he could see that they were fighting hard, and as he watched one was flung back off the wall. There were shouts and the odd blast of a trumpet, but the whistles were silent now.

Ferox went to the far end. Most of the black-clad warriors were on the wall, in the tower or behind the gate. Those on the wall clustered around a few spots and he guessed that this was where the Romans were attacking. He saw men and women working at fires to heat a couple of cauldrons, and that meant boiling water or oil was being prepared. No one liked to face that, and he wondered whether he should lead his little band to stop it being used. About thirty men sat or crouched on the grass nearby led by a man on horseback and even if they managed to get to the cauldrons and tip it away he doubted that any of them would survive. Instead he would act on the plan that had been forming in his mind since they had captured Genialis.

The centurion strode out into the open.

'Cniva!' he bellowed at the horsemen waiting with the warriors. 'Cniva!' They were no more than fifty paces away, the small rider's face clear. 'I have your son, Cniva! Come and get him or I will put him to the knife. You hear me, Cniva!'

The leader of the Harii gaped at him. Ferox expected rage and even a lone charge, but he could not catch the words as the pirate chief shouted something to his men. The men sprang to their feet, began to move and only then did the horseman come for him.

Ferox ran.

XXVIII

THE TESTUDO LED the second attack and did it slowly. Five abreast and ten deep the legionaries went through the cleared entrance in the first rampart and then turned right, heading for the main gate. A spear came down and stuck into one the shields, standing up straight and wobbling slightly each time the soldiers took a pace forward. The next javelin struck the dome-like boss of another shield and bounced back.

'Keep in step, boys,' Tertullianus called out. He was in the third rank, his own curved rectangular scutum held up over his head and interlocked with those of his men. 'Steady now.'

The legionaries had practised the drill many a time, although few had done it with a real enemy up above. A stone banged hard at the point where one scutum overlapped the next, sending a quiver across the whole roof of shields. Men flinched at the noise, looking up nervously.

'Steady, boys. Keep going,' the centurion called. His voice was firm and carried well for all its high pitch. He knew that the tone mattered more than anything he actually said.

Archers came behind them, but it was hard for them to dodge missiles in the narrow space between the inner ditch and main rampart, and harder still for them to shoot up at men on the wall. One of the auxiliary bowmen fell, struck on the helmet by a stone. Then another had his left arm broken and staggered away. Arrows stuck into the wooden parapet or sailed harmlessly overheard.

With a rumble, a basket of stones cascaded onto the testudo, scraping the calfskin cover of one of the shields so that its wooden boards were exposed. The soldier underneath went pale. Next to him a man started to mutter a prayer.

'Liber Pater, be with me now.'

At the front, men could glimpse what lay ahead over the tops of their shields and knew that there was a long way to go. The men on the flanks saw the ramparts on either side of them inching past. Those at the back saw nothing, apart from the helmets and shoulders of their comrades, arms held up to keep the shields in place.

'We're doing well, boys,' Tertullianus told them. 'One step at a time, that's all we need.'

Behind the archers came the Batavians, infantry and cavalry mingled together and with Cerialis at their head, a bandage around his right shin. With them went Vindex, a limping Segovax and his brother, and the other survivors of the tower, including Probus, whose bandaged side made him wince each time he moved, and Longinus, who had slipped away from the tribune. The auxiliaries carried two ladders salvaged from the first assault, and they went to the left. A few of the Harii followed them, and a trooper was pitched over with a javelin in his back, for it was hard to shelter behind shields when going in this direction. The centurion had a line of men walking backwards, shields together, but sometimes they slipped or wavered and, even when they did not, plenty of missiles sailed over their heads to strike the main group behind them. A team of sailors with a bolt-shooter stood in the open entrance way and the first heavy dart struck a pirate in the face with such force that the pyramid-shaped tip burst out of the back of his head. The second shot killed another of the defenders, and then the marines forced their way through the entrance and the men had to stop shooting. The marines had one ladder – the other had been broken in the earlier fighting – as well as a couple of ropes, and they followed the legionaries and the archers.

The testudo continued its slow, jerking progress. Up on the rampart, one of the pirates climbed onto the lip of the parapet and stood up straight, a big rock held above his head in both hands. He flung it down, his comrades grabbing his legs because he nearly unbalanced with the motion. The impact was dreadful, and the noise far worse, as the boulder cracked the boss of a man's scutum, forcing him down to his knees. For a moment, there was a gap in the shields. Someone threw a burning torch from the rampart, but it missed the hole and simply lay on the top of the testudo, smouldering for a while before it went out.

'Liber Pater, be with me now.' The prayer was almost a whimper.

'Bastards,' hissed another legionary. 'I'm going to kill every bastard bastard of the bastards, and that bastard god if he gets in my way. Let him stick to wine and wild women.'

'Wish I could,' said another, and there was laughter – tense and nervous, but laughter nevertheless.

'Steady lads, keep together,' the centurion called. 'Not far now.'

The soldier stood up, knuckles hurting, and his shield rose to meet the others again. An arrow struck the man standing on the parapet, the point forcing its way through where four scales of his cuirass joined together. He twisted away from the blow, and his friends lost their grip so that he fell off, limbs waving, and smacked into the roof of shields.

'Shit!' yelled the soldier who had been praying. The noise was appalling, and half a dozen men staggered as they felt the blow, but the weight was spread and they soon recovered.

'Come on, boys,' Tertullianus said. 'Not far, not far.'

The testudo jerked along, the spread-eagled body of the pirate lying on top, moaning.

Behind the legionaries, Batavians and marines were falling, and men tripped over the wounded and dead, but already Cerialis' men had raised the ladders. A pirate tried to push one over, but ducked back when a javelin struck the parapet beside him, throwing up splinters.

'Follow me!' the prefect yelled, pushing one of his troopers aside and scrambling up the wooden rungs. He did not use his hands, and had sword in one hand and his raised shield in the other, so that he could not see the top of the ladder or the wall. Something slammed into the shield, but he kept going. Close by, one of his men was climbing the other ladder, but then slumped back, his helmet dented from the strike of a stone, and the man stuck there, legs caught so that he hung down and blocked the way.

Cerialis saw the wood of the parapet, the drab shield of one of the defenders in his path, and a spearhead came past his own shield and only just missed his face. Then the pirate vanished, falling back with the bolt from one of the engines in the throat. The prefect took another step, then another, and punched a warrior in the face with the boss of his shield, knocking the man back. With a shout, a soldier had pulled the stunned trooper off the other ladder and was climbing. Cerialis stabbed with his sword through the opening in the parapet, striking against a shield, but once again his opponent went back a step. Vindex watched from the ditch, saw a man coming from the side, knew the prefect could not see him, saw the slicing blow of his sword break through the boards of Cerialis' shield, but then the pirate fell with a bolt in his shoulder.

The testudo was almost at the gate, the wounded pirate slipping with each movement and sobbing with pain. Up on the rampart men were lifting something heavy. An archer saw the bronze cauldron and yelled a warning, even as he loosed an arrow. One of the pirates carrying it let go, clutching at the shaft in his arm. More archers shot, and it was enough to panic the men so that the cauldron tipped too early. One of the pirates screamed as the scalding oil splashed onto his legs. Wood on the parapet smouldered, but most of the contents went in a wave down the stone side of the rampart. A legionary yelped as little spots of hot oil flicked onto his breeches. More struck the pirate lying on top of the testudo, and he writhed, making the shields bob underneath him. Then the cauldron thumped onto his chest, breaking ribs, and the men underneath staggered.

'Hold together, lads. Nearly there,' the centurion called. 'Another pace, another. Now!'

The front rank had held their rectangular shields ahead of them. Now they raised them, adding to the roof of shields so that it reached the timbers of the gate. The second rank was tightly packed against them, for it consisted of sailors with axes and the dolabra pick-axe that was the army's universal tool, and these men squeezed past to get to the front. There was not much room, but they swung the blades and started to bite into the timber. Stones smacked onto the shields above them, and then a pirate who had leaned over to throw at them screamed because an arrow hit him in the face.

The marines were raising their ladder, men starting to climb, when a second cauldron appeared on the wall. It was too heavy for the pirates to carry up to the gate and use on the testudo, so they raised it here and strained as they tipped the mouth over. Warning shouts came too late, and the stream of yellow liquid hissed as it fell. Men screamed as their flesh was scorched and blistered. One fell from the ladder, arms flailing. Another man was desperately struggling with the shoulder buckles on his mail because the liquid had seeped inside and was burning him. A shout of triumph came from the rampart.

Over to the left, near the sea, Cerialis was on the wall and could not remember how he had vaulted across. Two infantrymen and a trooper were beside him, the closest pirates dead, wounded or holding back, and the prefect bellowed because they had done it and were up.

'Come on,' he shouted to his men, and led them along the walkway to clear it of enemies. More and more Batavians clambered up behind them. There was a smooth ramp behind the wall, and the prefect kept an eye open in case some of the Harii gathered to attack him in the flank, but there was no sign of this. Men on the wall saw him coming and turned to face him, and he stabbed and hacked at them, smelling their rank breath as he killed them.

Vindex grunted with effort as he pulled himself up over the parapet. To his right the prefect and a dozen Batavians were making good progress along the wall, as the centurion led another twenty down across the ramp to cover their advance. There seemed fewer of the Harii and Usipi than he expected, and no sign of a reserve waiting to beat back any breaks in the line. Dark smoke rose from the cluster of roofs inside the stronghold. The Brigantian waited for Segovax, the Red Cat, and the others to join him. Probus needed help to get in and his pain was obvious.

'You should stay here and rest,' Longinus told him.

'No,' was the only answer the merchant would give. Behind them, Crispinus led the fifty legionaries kept in reserve and a force of sailors in through the entrance. Cerialis had passed the spot where the smoking ladder raised by the marines still stood, and the blue-grey clad men threw a couple of grapnel lines onto the parapet and were starting to climb. The rampart curved so that he could not see the gate, only the tower above it, and pirates were still there, hurling anything they could find down into the ditch. Vindex doubted that the legionaries would break through before the gates were opened from inside. The stronghold was falling, there was no doubt of that.

'Which way?' Longinus asked.

Vindex pointed at the smoke from the burning building, suspecting that his friend was behind such mischief. He circled his arm to point that they would work their way round to the left. No one spoke as they headed down the grassy ramp behind the wall.

The barn burned faster than Ferox expected, part of its thatched roof collapsing in a great gout of flame and smoke as he ran past it, feeling the wave of heat. There must have been something stored there to make the fire rage so quickly. He saw Brigita, waiting where the alley wound sharply round a house. Women were screaming, but he could not see them and guessed that the cries were prompted by the fire. He coughed because the smoke was blowing around him, little pieces of burning thatch wafting on the wind.

Ferox came around the corner, and was glad to see that someone had had enough sense to take them all back past the next bend. Around that corner the path opened out, and he found his little force waiting for him. He stood in the middle, Brigita beside him, with the redhead next to her and two of the lads to make up the rest of the front rank. The others waited behind them. The house to their left gave them some shelter from the smoke, but he could hear their pursuers spluttering before they reached the corner.

A hope that Cniva might lead so that they could kill him proved vain when half a dozen pirates spilled into the lane ahead of them, their shields on the wrong side because of the bend.

'Now!' Ferox yelled and the second rank threw javelins. One of the enemy was hit in the leg, another on the hand, making him let go of his sword.

'Charge!' Ferox screamed the command in Latin, but the others understood and followed as he ran at the pirates. Men turned, wanting to flee, but there were others behind them and in the tight alleyway there was no room to escape. He punched with his shield, making the man with the wounded hand stagger, and then rammed the gladius into his belly, feeling the long triangular point snap through the mail cuirass. Brigita cut down another before he could turn and use his shield for protection. A lad drove his leaf-headed spear right through the thigh of a pirate, so that the head burst out the other side, but the weapon stuck there, and the wounded man turned his scream of agony into one of anger as he hacked at the boy's neck. The young warrior fell, blood jetting high, and the bare-breasted girl stepped over him and finished the pirate with a thrust through his mouth. A man came at Ferox, his shield up too high so that he could not see, and he swept underneath with his sword, cutting almost through the pirate's leg.

Suddenly the Harii were gone, apart from those left dead or moaning in the mud of the alley. Ferox glimpsed the rest running, then a waft of black smoke made him blink.

'Back!' he yelled, 'Back!' because he knew that the relief would be short. He led them out past the buildings onto the open slope leading up to the lone hall where they held Genialis.

They were only just in time, for a couple of men in black had appeared from another lane through the houses and could have got behind them.

'In a line,' Ferox shouted. 'Here we make our stand.' These youngsters were trained to fight as individuals, and with their small shields and inexperience he was not sure how long they would last in close slogging fights among the buildings. Here in the open they could fight as they had practised and prove themselves. Or they might just run away if the enemy came at them in a rush. Ferox was not sure, but reckoned that this was their best chance.

Three pirates came from the other lane, and they charged as soon as they saw the young warriors. One of the boys shouted something Ferox did not catch as he ran for the leader, and he wondered whether the lad was calling out his name or a taunt, but it did not matter when he ducked a wild hack and stabbed the pirate underneath his armour. Another boy, a little older than the first, slipped on the grass, and then gasped as the point of a gladius went through his armour and into his chest. He fell back, sobbing, the sword still in his body and pulled from the pirate's grip. The redhead threw her last javelin, the point breaking through a pirate's shield and sticking fast in his belt. She drew her sword and hacked the empty hand of the man who had lost his sword, then followed up, slicing into his leg just above the knee. He fell, and she strode past, going for the last man, who was struggling to drop his shield but could not because the spear would not move. The young woman's face was contorted with hate as she spat at him and then hacked hard at his neck.

More pirates appeared, but these came with more caution. A whistle blew and Cniva rode out behind them, and they shook themselves into a formation two ranks deep.

'Back!' Ferox called, and the lad and the red-headed woman came back to form a line facing the enemy. Someone pushed Brigita aside to stand next to him and he was surprised to see that it was the mother. Her face showed no emotion.

Cniva blew his whistle, a shrill note, and then drew his own sword. He did not join his men as they began to walk up the slope, going slowly to keep in line. All of the second rank and most of the first had spears, ready to thrust overarm.

'Cniva, you bastard!' Ferox yelled, taking a pace forward. 'Do you dare to fight me as a man?'

The leader of the Harii said nothing. His men took another pace forward and the distance now was no more than a dozen steps.

'Kill them all!' Ferox yelled. This was not the fight that he had wanted, but it was too late for that. 'Come on!' He turned the last word into a scream of rage and ran at the black shields of the enemy. There was a strange ululating screech in his ear and he realised that the mother was making it as she came with him, and then the other women took up the unearthly cry. The boys shouted, one of their voices beginning as a deep bellow and cracking into a squeak and that might have been funny if their deaths were not in front of them.

Ferox could see the faces of the men over their shields, and most were fair haired, but their skin was lined and he guessed that these men were Harii and Usipi from the days of the mutiny. There were none of the young boys who had grown up or been captured and raised by these pirates.

The former auxiliaries and mutineers did not flinch. One of his young lads threw himself at the enemy and was impaled through the head on a spear, but the others sensed their determination and stopped a little short. A spear point jabbed at Ferox and he caught it on his little shield, then gave way as the man punched at him with his own, bigger shield. Beside him, the mother had found a shield from somewhere, presumably from one of the boys who had fallen, and she twisted it, so that the edge half spun as she flicked it over the top of her adversary's shield and smashed his nose. The pirate reeled and her sword darted upwards, taking him in the chin just where his cheek pieces tied together. The man's eyes rolled up, so that only the whites were visible, and when she drew the blade out with a sucking sound he slumped forward. The woman jumped back, then came forward again before the warrior in the second rank could take the dead man's place. She ducked, going under his spear, and he panicked, dropping it and reaching for his sword, a movement that opened him to a thrust into his side. The mail was strong enough to stop it being fatal, but he yelped and let go of his shield. The next attack was a thrust to the face and the man stepped back to avoid it.

Ferox's opponent's eyes flicked to the side when the man next to him died. The Roman jabbed at the pirate's face, stopping the blow as the black shield came up to block it, and instead whipped the beautifully balanced sword down to strike the man's thigh. It was a light blow, but the spear thrust that came back at him was weak and ill aimed. Ferox had his sword up again, point ready to lance forward.

The mother spun around as she slashed the man in the leg and he fell. She was through the formation, heading for Cniva, and some of the men in the second rank were turning around to reach her, breaking the line apart. There was an appalling scream as a spear drove deep into the redhead's upper thigh. As the pirate wrenched it free a fountain of blood pumped all over him from the ruptured artery and drenched his legs and shield. He stepped over her, coming up on the unprotected side of the blonde, who went backwards, feinting against each of her opponents in turn. The neat lines had gone, but numbers were starting to tell. One of the boys, bleeding from a graze on his leg, desperately blocked cuts from a sword, and each time less of his shield was left. He slashed back at the pirate, but the man was bigger and had a longer reach.

Ferox looped his own shield over the top of his opponent's bigger, oval shield, yanking it down so that he could stab the man in the face. An instant before the point speared through the man's eye, the pirate's spearhead struck him on the right side and drove through one of the plates. The pirate fell, and Ferox was gasping for breath, feeling the pain but not yet weakened.

A pirate came from behind the mother, and she somehow sensed and spun almost like a dancer, going towards him and slashing her blade across his throat. Cniva drove his horse at her, and the animal's shoulder knocked the woman over. She rolled away and was up in a moment, but a spear took her in the side. Cniva slashed down, cutting into her shoulder so that she dropped her shield.

Brigita saw her plight and screamed as she hacked lumps out of her opponent's shield, her sheer fury forcing him back. The rest of her warriors were too hard pressed to see what was happening, but the queen shattered the man's shield and then sliced into his arm. The pirate's sword grazed her leg, but she ignored it, stamping forward, right arm out and most of her body unprotected by her shield as she drove the blade through the man's armour and into his heart.

Ferox was sure that the mother looked at him for an instant, then she dived under Cniva's horse, stabbing its belly with her sword. The animal screamed, rearing, and its hind feet trampled on her before it threw its rider and fell. A pirate had his spear in both hands as he ran it into the woman's body.

Cniva was up, helmet gone but sword still in his hands. His horse sank down on its front knees, steaming entrails spilling onto the grass.

'Bastard!' Ferox yelled, his voice croaking because his mouth was so dry, and his side aching. He lifted his shield, saw the pirate meet it by raising his own, and instead twisted his wrist to thrust down, missing the man's face but digging into his neck. Cniva was not paying any attention to him but was looking over to the right and suddenly there was a shout and men were coming at the pirates from behind. He saw Vindex, and one-eyed Longinus, but out in front was Probus, his face very pale.

The merchant's brother said nothing, but waited, and at the last minute dodged the attack, and cut at Probus as his momentum carried him past. Blood pulsed from where the shoulder of his mail split. The merchant turned, thrusting with his sword. Cniva was too fast, ducked down and then grabbed the other man's arm, pulling him into the stab of his own sword.

Ferox tried to push through. A pirate appeared, his beard more grey than brown and speckled blood on his face. The man had a spear down low and although Ferox pushed at the shaft with his shield it gouged a line across his calf. He punched the man with his fist, then hammered his face with the pommel of his sword. A horn sounded from the buildings ahead of them, the distinctive brazen challenge of the army's cornu.

The pirates were breaking. They ran, hoping to escape, and a few threw down weapons and begged for mercy. There was none. Vindex killed two men as they turned and ran, and Longinus beheaded another pirate who kneeled in supplication. The Brigantian stared for a moment as the bare-chested young woman hacked again and again at a body lying on the ground, and Ferox could not tell whether it was the savagery or her nakedness that drew his interest.

Cniva stood in a circle of enemies. Segovax was there, and the Red Cat, and Brigita and two of the Batavians who had held the tower. Already the pirate chief was bleeding from cuts to the legs and arms, not knowing which way to turn as the spears and swords came at him.

Ferox was about to force his way through when he felt a hand on his shoulder. Vindex grinned. 'Leave 'em. They've earned it.'

Segovax drove a spear into Cniva's thigh and twisted it free. Then he swung the shaft, making his brother duck and one of the Batavians swear in alarm, and the wooden pole hit the leader on the side of the head. The northerner dropped his shield from his bandaged hand. He swung the spear again, two-handed this time, battering the pirate chief on the head. Cniva fell. Brigita and the Red Cat leaped at the same moment and their blades punched through the man's armour and through his ribs. Cniva gasped, blood bubbling at his mouth, and if he was trying to speak no words could be made out. The Red Cat stared at him for a moment, and then began hacking at his neck to take the head as a trophy.

Probus had managed to sit up. Blood pooled around him, so fast was the flow from the great gash in his body that it could not seep into the ground fast enough. Pale before, he was now white as the bleached toga of a political candidate. His face twitched when the northerners raised the severed head of his brother. Then he began to laugh, a bitter, haunting sound racked with sorrow as well as pain. It turned into a cough, and blood spewed from his lips before he fell back.

Brigita kneeled by the mother. Her eyes were glassy, but she did not cry, unlike the other survivors who held the dead to them and wept. Vindex stood by the corpse of the redhead and shook his head. Ferox was too tired to know what he felt, although he suspected that the vision of a pretty young woman lying dead in a pool of her own drying blood would return to haunt him in dreams, worse even than the usual ones that came when he remembered past fights. The Brigantian crouched down and spoke to the girl with brown hair, who was cushioning the dead woman's head in her lap, ignoring the blood that covered her.

'She was called Cabura.' The scout spoke with great sadness, and Ferox felt guilty that he had not learned the names of any of the people who had followed him. 'That's my wife's name,' he added, voice filled with the sadness of old loss and fear of pain to come.

Ferox could not think of anything to say, and was spared by the arrival of Crispinus, Brocchus and Cerialis at the head of a mix of legionaries, marines and Batavians. The Batavian's prefect whistled. 'Seems like you have had a bit of a time of it,' he said. In the background there were screams, as the Romans hunted the last surviving pirates out and killed them. The women and children were to be spared, but some of the cries suggested that some of the women were not to be spared everything.

Crispinus was panting, face black from the smoke apart from a few lines made by beads of sweat. He gathered himself. 'Report, centurion.'

Ferox did his best to explain what he had done. He showed them Cniva's corpse. The northerners had planted the head on a spear stuck into the ground.

'Do you want to take it back?' Crispinus asked the prefect.

Cerialis shook his head. 'No, it's unlucky. Leave it here for the crows.'

Then Ferox told them about Genialis. 'I was going to leave

him to his father to deal with. Well, the man who raised him,' he added, remembering that the tribune knew that he was really Cniva's son. Probus lay under a blanket just a few paces away.

'Instead you lay the decision on me, centurion.'

'Yes, my lord. That's what comes with rank.'

'So it does,' Crispinus said. 'Well, let's have a look at the little cuss.' He left, followed by Cerialis and several legionaries.

Ferox felt the wound at his side. At the moment, the surgeons were too busy with the badly injured for him to trouble them. He really ought to take off the scale cuirass and clean it up, but he knew that it would be painful to do, so delayed, telling himself that it was because he might be needed.

'Centurion,' Crispinus called a moment later, so that at present it was not simply an excuse. The short tribune had come out of the hall. His helmet was under his arm, and he ran a grimy hand through his white hair. 'Would you come here, please.'

Ferox marched over. 'My lord.'

'Ah yes, centurion.' Crispinus peered at him as if he had not just summoned him over. 'Your capture of the former hostage and fugitive Genialis was well done. However, when you told me that you had the lad, I did expect to find him with a head still on his shoulders.'

EPILOGUE

ACCO HAD COME. It took a while to coax the story from the young warrior with the moustache, but it seemed that a boat full of warriors had returned to the island, landing on the little beach down below, where Ferox and the others had begun their ascent. The elderly druid had made the same climb, along with two warriors, and they had come to the hall. Neither of the boys left on guard had seen them as enemies. The great druid was a man of mystery and power, one to be honoured and not a little feared. So they had let him slit Genialis' throat, and had watched as one of the warriors had cut off the corpse's head and carried it away. Acco had also stripped some flesh from the boys' thighs, stomach and off his penis.

'Why?' Crispinus asked. 'I mean I'm not sorry to be rid of the pest, but why do this?'

Ferox was not quite sure. The strips of flesh would go into potions, that was obvious enough, although when he explained the tribune and prefects wrinkled their faces in disgust. The Romans spoke of magic with fear, and that was wise, but it did not do to pretend that such things did not happen. Yet why the druid had come for the boy's head was less clear.

'The boy has the blood of witches in his veins,' Ferox suggested, thinking aloud. 'Or rather had. Any head has power

339

as the chamber of the soul. The power is greater with some, and perhaps that is why Acco wanted it? Men like him feed their own strength by taking such things.' It was the best that he could do, for he did not really understand. Neither power nor strength were the right words, but he did not think Latin had any better ones to describe the mystical essence of a man or woman. They would not understand, not really, but Ferox knew that no chance had brought the druid here. Acco had seemed to know everything and known precisely the moment to arrive. Ferox had thought the capture of Genialis mere chance, and now he wondered whether something darker was at work. The timing was more miraculous than the simple truth that an old man had scrambled up a cliff and then escaped. Even with the rope they had left, Ferox did not relish trying the climb again.

He went out of the door and the first thing he heard was the harsh call of Morrigan's raven, perched on the roof. There were plenty of carrion birds come to the island, but this was not chance either and the bird's dark eyes watched him with a spirit not belonging to any mere creature.

Ferox went to the edge of the cliffs. There, a mile or more out to sea was a little dot on the waves.

'It is a boat,' Bran said, the lad appearing from nowhere beside him. During the last fight he had not glimpsed the boy, but was relieved to find him safe.

Crispinus burst out of the hall, face angry, but realised where they were looking and cupped his hand around his eyes to see better. He shook his head. 'I cannot see anything.'

'He has gone beyond our reach.'

'That cannot be helped.' Crispinus grasped his arm so that he turned to face him. 'It is a shame, but we did not come here for him. We came to free our hostages and we have done that. We came to avenge ourselves on the Usipi and Harii and the rest and we have done that. You have made it happen.' He gripped the arm even tighter. 'It is over, apart from victory, and we will not talk too much of that because then we would have to admit that all this was caused by deserters and mutineers. It would not fit well with the dignity of the new era of Trajan if people knew that an equestrian officer and his even more distinguished wife could be abducted by such scum.

'It is over. Be glad that we have won and not lost, and then do your best to forget all about it because this is a story that shall not be told.'

'And Probus?'

'Is dead, along with his son. No one need ever know that the prosperous merchant was a mutineer and murderer. Think how embarrassing that would be to all those influential men who wrote letters recommending him.'

'Quite shocking,' Cerialis agreed.

'So shocking that it could not possibly be true,' Crispinus went on. 'Forget all of this. People die all the time, and it is surprising how quickly they are forgotten by all except their loved ones or those who hated them. Forget it all.'

'It has not happened in secret, my lords.' Ferox did not care that much what people believed, but he did wonder whether it would all be quite as easy as the tribune suggested.

Crispinus let go of his arm and shrugged. 'There will be rumours, of course. There always are. But nothing anyone can prove. None of this should have happened, so it cannot have happened, can it?'

Ferox stiffened to attention, feeling a sharp stab of pain from his side. 'Sir!' he said.

'Good. Now get that taken care of. Carry on, centurion.' Crispinus smiled. 'And well done. To be honest, I never thought that we would get away with it.'

'And you have my heartiest thanks, once again,' Cerialis added, offering his hand.

Ferox shook it, too tired to feel much guilt or sorrow. He was still on the edge of the world, but knew that once again a great chasm had opened to separate him from Sulpicia Lepidina. At least she was safe, and part of him wanted to gaze upon her, even though he knew that the pain would be crueller than any wound to the body.

Six corpses lay in a row near the top of the cliff. The mother was in the centre, the redhead to her right and then two boys on either side. Several of the other lads and girls were wounded, but the woman with brown hair had at last found a tunic and covered herself more effectively.

'I will see that you are helped to do what is necessary,' Ferox said to Brigita. 'They all fought with courage.'

'It was their fight, as much as ours,' the queen said.

'I am sorry about your mother. She did not deserve to die here, but I am not sure whether we would have won without her.'

'To fight broke her oath, and she knew just what would happen, but did it anyway because it was the right thing. But the mother has not died, for the mother can never die. I am the mother now.'

Ferox said nothing. Her tone was firm, and there was no point stating the obvious. A woman who had been a queen was choosing to spend the rest of her life on a tiny island training young warriors.

'I have a favour to ask,' Brigita said. 'Give the boy to me.' She must have sensed his confusion. 'Release Bran from his oath for the moment. Let him come with us and learn and in time he will return and serve you for three years. He has the makings of a great warrior, and you will always have the need of men who can fight.'

The boy's eager expression made his desire clear.

'So be it,' Ferox said.

'Now we must lament the fallen,' she said. 'It is not something that others may share.'

Ferox left them to it and walked back around the hall. As he left he heard a soft wailing song begin and found tears pricking at his eyes. Most of the troops were further down, clearing all the buildings of anything of value and then putting them to the torch. Segovax and his brother sat on the grass on either side of the spear topped by Cniva's head, and Ferox went to them. Vindex sensed the moment and appeared beside him.

'It is over,' Ferox said. 'You have kept your oath and I thank you.'

Segovax stood up, his hand gripping his sword. His brother stared at them for a moment and then got to his feet. He had been holding his sword across his legs. The blade was notched from the fighting and still stained with blood. A gust of wind whipped smoke over their heads and the raven cried out again.

'They are all dead?' the Red Cat said.

'Every last one. So is Genialis. The druid killed him.'

There was no hint of surprise, so he guessed that word of this had already reached them.

The thief rubbed the blemish on his face. 'There are tears to weep for our families,' he said.

'I know.'

'But at least their spirits will know that they have been avenged.' The Red Cat very carefully uncurled his fingers from the handle of his sword and dropped it on the grass

'We will not kill you today,' Segovax rumbled. 'One day perhaps, but not today.'

'I am glad,' Ferox said. 'There has been enough killing, and there are enough tears to shed.' He felt Vindex relaxing beside him.

'We will take a boat from the harbour and go,' the Red Cat told them.

'Never bring the Romans to our land.' his brother said. 'If you do, we will fight until our last breath. Farewell, Romans.'

'Did he just call me a Roman?' Vindex whispered after they had gone.

'Don't worry, people call me that all the time.'

The journey home took longer than expected, for the weather turned against them and for days they had to ride out a storm, which blew them a long way out to sea. Food was running short in the triremes by the time they sighted Alauna. Ovidius travelled in the same ship as Ferox and Vindex and chattered for all of the voyage, apart from when he was seasick or in his rare hours of sleep. Cerialis and his wife were in another of the transport ships, and once or twice in the lighter winds, Ferox saw her golden hair as she stood on the distant deck. In the meantime, Philo fussed over him, shaving him whenever the sea was calm enough and changing the dressing on his wound even when it was not.

On the journey eastwards, they travelled as one company, and the Lady Sulpicia was lively, her laughter filling the air and lifting the mood of all around her. When they came in sight of Vindolanda, Claudia Severa had come out to meet them with the children and there were tears as well as joy. Both ladies in turn gave Ferox a chaste kiss on the cheek to thank him for all that he had done. He felt – or perhaps he imagined – a faint tremor in Sulpicia as she stood beside him. Then little Marcus began to cry and the mother rushed to hold him and calm him. Cerialis had thanked him several times, but now did so again.

Ferox rode to Syracuse alone. Philo had stayed at Vindolanda to buy supplies that he insisted were essential, and his master did not want to linger. Ferox had been wondering about giving the lad his freedom, but his fussy manner had begun to grate and he decided to leave that for another day. Vindex had gone to see his wife.

'Greet Cabura for me,' Ferox said.

'At least you remembered.' Vindex sighed. 'I'll be back in ten days.'

'Thought she'd get sick of you long before that.'

'Nah, she's not the brightest. Good heart, though.'

Mid-summer had gone and the nights were starting to draw in, so that it was dark by the time Ferox reached the little burgus. The Thracian was in the tower, and his voice was very familiar as they went through the ritual of challenging anyone approaching the outpost.

His quarters were dark and gloomy, and it took a while to find a lamp and get the oil lit. Once it was, he could see that the fatigue parties had given the rooms a rudimentary clean, but nothing close to Philo's exacting standards. He found some posca, wincing as he drained the first bitter cup, and was prepared for Crescens when the curator arrived to report. The man always stamped and shouted more than was strictly necessary, but there was a familiarity about that as well.

'Any news?' Ferox asked after listening to the minor reports.

The curator chewed his lip like a nervous child. 'Hard to say for sure, sir. But there are rumours.' Ferox waited and after a moment Crescens made up his mind. 'I think there is trouble brewing, sir. Big trouble.'

'There usually is,' Ferox said, and poured another cup of

posca. Then he offered one to the curator. Crescens looked surprised, but took it.

'Yes,' Ferox said. 'There usually is.'

HISTORICAL NOTE

During the same summer, a cohort of Usipi conscripted
in the German provinces and sent to Britannia committed
a great and infamous crime. After killing the centurion
and soldiers who were put amongst them to teach
discipline, serve as examples and instruct, they seized
three light warships...

Tacitus, *Agricola* 28.

THE MUTINY OF the Usipi appears in a single source, Tacitus' biography of his father-in-law Cnaeus Julius Agricola, legate of Britannia from AD 78–84. His account consists of a single paragraph, and serves a stylistic purpose as a brief interval before he recounts the final year's campaigning that culminated in Agricola's victory at Mons Graupius. The text is not well preserved, so that his sense is not altogether clear, but in broad outline the mutineers sailed from somewhere on the west coast of Britain, circumnavigated the island. They raided, but turned to cannibalism, allegedly eating the weakest among them and then others chosen by lot. Eventually they ended up on the coast of north Germany east of the Rhine, where they were killed or enslaved, and some of the slaves were sold into Roman hands and told their story. Depending on the precise dating of Agricola's operations, the mutiny occurred in AD 82 or possibly 83.

Little is otherwise known about the Usipi. Some of them were part of a group who came into Gaul in 55 BC and were attacked and defeated by Julius Caesar. Their homeland was east of the Rhine and by the end of the first century AD they were not under direct Roman rule, although like most of the peoples beyond the frontier there was presumably some form of treaty relationship. The incident in Tacitus is the only time a unit of Usipi was raised in their own ethnic unit. We do not know the cause of the mutiny and I have embellished the brief story in Tacitus a good deal. He makes no mention of Harii in the unit, but in his discussion of the German tribes, the *Germania*, he claims that this tribe liked to fight at night, carrying black shields and painting their bodies, relying on the terror caused by their appearance.

Tacitus implies that all the mutineers were killed or enslaved, so it is pure fiction to have one of their stolen ships break away from the others and survive. I have also given them triremes rather than the smaller liburnians in Tacitus' narrative. This is novel, not a history, so I have felt free to add to the meagre information we have about these years, but have always done my best to set it all within the context of what we do know about Roman Britain, the army and the wider world in this period.

Apart from this short passage from the *Agricola*, this novel and the others in the series are inspired by the remarkable collection of texts discovered in the excavated forts at modern Chesterholm, once the Roman army base of Vindolanda. These provide fascinating glimpses of life on the frontier of Roman Britain at the very end of the first century and the start of the second century AD. Most deal with the routine and even mundane. There are daily reports made by junior officers of the garrison, requests for leave made by soldiers, accounts of purchases and sales, of goods stored or delivered. Some of the most striking come from the personal archives of the prefect in command of the army unit stationed at the fort, dealing more with their social life than their formal duties. Thus we have a list of food, especially poultry and eggs, consumed in their household to entertain a long succession of guests. We have letters written to and by other commanders, showing the rich social life of these important men. Even more strikingly, we have letters between the wives of these prefects, who accompanied their husbands, whose tour of duty usually lasted for several years. Just as in the more peaceful provinces of the empire, these women supervised the household and the raising of their children in the manner expected of wealthy and well-born wives.

Vindolanda is one of the most remarkable Roman sites in Britain. The first fort was built there in the seventies AD. The fort from our period was the third constructed on the site. The remains visible today are of the later stone fort and the civilian settlement or *vicus* (a more organised version of the *canabae*) outside it. A level of laziness in demolishing the earlier forts when the new ones were built, combined with the water-logged nature of much of the site, created unusual conditions that have allowed the preservation of wood, leather, textiles and other material usually lost. Over five and half thousand shoes have already been found at Vindolanda, more than from anywhere else in the Roman Empire. For more information about the site and the Vindolanda Trust visit the website at http://www.vindolanda.com/.

Although less impressive as objects, the wooden writing tablets were an even more surprising and exciting find. Many are tiny fragments or illegible, but hundreds have preserved some text. Papyrus was known and used in Roman Britain, but was expensive, and much everyday correspondence and record keeping was written in ink on thin sheets of wood. Some were covered in thin wax, so that this could be smoothed down again and re-used, but these tend to be impossible to decipher since scratches from numerous different texts overlap. The most useful were the plain wood sheets, which had been rubbed with only a thin layer of beeswax to prevent the ink from spreading and were then used only once. Even so, little of the ink survives, and it requires careful analysis of the scratches made by the nibs of the stylus pens to trace the outlines of letters. Deciphering the texts and then reconstructing and understanding them is a painstaking business. More detail and many of the texts themselves can be found online at http://vindolanda.csad.ox.ac.uk/.

One of the most famous letters is the invitation from Claudia Severa, wife of Aelius Brocchus at Coria (modern Corbridge), asking Sulpicia Lepidina, wife of Flavius Cerialis at Vindolanda, to attend her birthday celebration on 11 September. This formed the basis of the plot for the first novel. All of these people are real, but until the discovery of the tablets none were attested anywhere else. It is highly likely that objects excavated in the area of the praetorium of the third fort at Vindolanda belong to Cerialis and his family, for instance a fine decorated head-piece for his horse, fine shoes belonging to children and the broken and discarded slipper that surely belonged to Sulpicia Lepidina – all of which can be seen in the excellent museum at Vindolanda.

I have used the names of these real people in these novels, but in the main their characters are invented. There are snippets of information in the texts, and I have used as much of this as possible, and tried my best never to invent anything that would jar with what we do know, but even so their appearance and characters, let alone the events that befall them, are fiction. There is certainly no hint in the text that Cerialis' and Sulpicia Lepidina's tour at Vindolanda was as eventful as these stories make it. However, there is room for this because we really know very little about them and even less about what was happening in Britain at the time.

Cerialis was the prefect of *cohors VIIII Batavorum milliaria equitata* (the ninth double-strength Batavian regiment of infantry and cavalry), which at full strength ought to have numbered over a thousand men, a quarter of them cavalry. He was a Roman citizen and a member of the equestrian order, the social class ranking below the Senate. To give an idea of scale, there were tens of thousands of equestrians compared to around six hundred senators. We do not know even the names of the majority of senators in this or most other eras, so it is unsurprising that even fewer equestrians have left any clear trace of their lives. The Vindolanda tablets give us a hint of the vast amount of writing and record keeping in the Roman world, but also remind us that it takes exceptional good luck for such material to survive into the modern era.

An equestrian prefect in command of an infantry cohort or cavalry *ala* of auxiliary soldiers was a man of considerable importance locally and in his home community. Substantial property was required for a man to be registered as an equestrian in the census. However, by AD 100 there were at least 350 posts as commander of auxiliary units. We think that the average time spent by these officers with a unit was about three years (although there is a lot of guesswork in this), which shows how many of these officers there were and why we should not be surprised that such a small proportion appear in our sources. Cerialis is one of the best documented, and we really know little about him.

His name suggests that he, like the soldiers he commanded, was a Batavian, a Germanic tribe living in what is now the Netherlands. In AD 70 the Batavians revolted as part of the wider civil war and disturbances following the deposition and suicide of Nero. The Civil War was won by the Emperor Vespasian, whose family name was Flavius. The commander he sent to defeat the Batavian rebels was Petilius Cerialis, a task he completed by AD 71. We do not know what happened to Julius Civilis, the rebel leader, for the sources for the end of the rebellion are poor. The combination of Flavius and Cerialis as names strongly suggest that either the prefect at Vindolanda or his father were granted Roman citizenship during or after the rebellion. Presumably the man who was rewarded in this way either remained loyal to Rome (and specifically Vespasian) throughout the revolt, or changed sides early enough to be treated well by the new emperor. Although it is possible that the prefect at Vindolanda was middle-aged, old enough to have attracted attention during the disturbances of AD 70, it seems much more likely that he was the second generation of the family to be a Roman citizen.

Equestrian status came from property, while a command in the army came from influence with those in high places. An old treaty with the Batavians stipulated that they should not pay tax to Rome, but instead provide soldiers for the *auxilia*, but that these men would serve under their own aristocrats. The appearance of Cerialis at Vindolanda shows that this continued to be the case after AD 70, although there are hints that it ceased during the course of the second century AD. There is a hint that Cerialis came from the royal bloodline of the tribe, like Civilis.

Sulpicia Lepidina is only known through the tablets and it is impossible to say anything definite about her family. The daughter of a senator is attested as the wife of an equestrian prefect on the British frontier later in the second century AD, so such marriages did occur, although they were rare. Neither is anything known about Brocchus, Claudia Severa, Rufinus and other names from the tablets who have become characters in the story. Being a Roman citizen and an equestrian did not require any Italian, let alone Roman, blood and such people came from all over the empire. In language and culture they were primarily, sometimes exclusively 'Roman', and they were Roman in law. That did not mean that, like Cerialis, they might also be part of a different ethnic tradition.

Claudius Super is almost a character from the tablets. There is a man who appears to have equestrian status and also to be a *centurio regionarius*, but he is Clodius Super. When writing the first novel I did not check my notes carefully and it was only after it was finished that I realised I had turned him into a Claudius rather than Clodius. By then it was too late to change, so Claudius he stayed. Some equestrians served as centurions in the legions rather than prefects of auxiliary units, whether because they wanted to spend a longer time in the army, could not afford the lifestyle of a cohort commander, or did not have friends influential enough to secure them the more senior post.

The name Crispinus appears in the tablets and he may be a tribune with a legion, but the character is otherwise an invention. Neratius Marcellus was the governor or legate of Britannia at this time and is also mentioned in the tablets. The poet Martial wrote to his friend Quintus Ovidius when the latter was about to accompany a friend going to govern Britain, and there is a good chance that this was Marcellus. He was a poet and philosopher (possibly a Stoic), and may have been exiled under Vespasian and later recalled.

Ferox and Vindex are wholly invented, although a later tombstone records a Brigantian soldier in the Roman army who was the son of someone named Vindex and in my imagination this is our man. It was common for the Romans to take boys from defeated peoples, educate them and grant them citizenship, sometimes even equestrian status, and make them army officers. This was part of the process of absorbing former enemies. It is not directly attested as happening after the defeat of the Silures (who lived in what is now South Wales) in the seventies AD, but is perfectly plausible.

Legionary centurions are often still depicted as sergeant-major types, tough men who rose through the ranks through sheer talent after long and hard service. The stereotype is a powerful one, but is not based on good evidence. Some centurions were commissioned directly from civilian life without any prior military experience, including a minority of equestrians. A few proudly tell us on monuments, most often their tombstones, that they joined as ordinary soldiers, but these are very few. The vast majority of recorded centurions give no indication of having served in lower ranks. Others served only as junior officers before being elevated to the centurionate. It is important to remember that a centurion had to be well educated, literate and numerate, for the army ran on the written word. These men were professional officers, rather than professional soldiers, and their pay and conditions were substantially higher than those of men in the ranks. It is likely that even junior centurions earned more than ten times the salary of an ordinary soldier, and most were probably drawn from the local gentry and well-off families of Italy and the provinces.

Centurion was not a rank, but a grade of officer, with a considerable range in status and responsibilities. There were some sixty centurions in a legion, and between six and ten in an auxiliary cohort. Many served away from their units on long- or short-term detachment. A cohort at Vindolanda in the nineties AD had only one out of its six centurions at the base. Two more were with the biggest detachment of the cohort at Corbridge, but the others were widely dotted around the province. The post of *centurio regionarius* or regional centurion was one of the ones that took these officers away. It is attested in Britain and elsewhere, particularly in Egypt, and was probably common. These men acted as the representative of Roman authority in an area, their role a mix of civil and political as well as military. In Egypt there is good evidence for them acting as policemen and investigating crimes.

Before Hadrian's Wall

The story occurs at the start of the reign of Trajan, whose successor Hadrian came to Britain and ordered construction of Hadrian's Wall around the year AD 122. Our sources have little to say about major events in Britain under Trajan, although there is talk of major conflict, which may well have prompted the decision to build the Wall. The fort at Vindolanda (modern Chesterholm) lies a few miles south and within sight of the Wall and clearly was incorporated within the network of garrisons serving it.

Although Julius Caesar had landed in Britain in 55 and 54 BC, no permanent Roman presence was maintained, and it was not until AD 43 that the Emperor Claudius sent an invasion force across the Channel. In AD 60 Boudicca's rebellion devastated southern Britain, but after her defeat there is no trace of any serious resistance in the Lowlands. This is not true of northern Britain, which was garrisoned by substantial numbers of troops for the remaining three and a half centuries of Roman occupation.

In AD 100 few would have guessed that the Romans would stay for so long. Their presence in the north was more recent, for it was mainly in the seventies and eighties AD that this area was overrun. During this time Roman armies marched far into the north of what would become Scotland, while a naval squadron for the first time circumnavigated Britain, confirming that it was an island. An entire legion – one of the four then garrisoning the province and one of twenty-eight in existence – built a base at Inchtuthil in Perthshire, the biggest site in a network of garrisons on the edge of the Highlands. Around the same time, a system of observation towers along a military road was constructed along the Gask ridge.

All of this activity, which to a great extent is known only from the archaeological remains, makes clear the Romans' intention to occupy this region more or less permanently, but in the late eighties AD priorities changed. The Emperor Domitian, faced with serious trouble on the Danube, withdrew *Legio II Adiutrix* from Britain and did not replace it. It is probable that substantial numbers of auxiliaries were withdrawn at the same time, so that the provincial garrison was cut by at least a quarter. Inchtuthil and many of the other bases were abandoned, and the same thing happened a little later to the remaining sites and the Gask ridgeline. No Roman base was maintained north of the Forth-Clyde line, and soon the northernmost outpost was at Trimontium or Newstead.

Several forts were maintained or built close to what would one day become the line of Hadrian's Wall. A couple of years after our story, a proper road running between Carlisle and Corbridge was constructed and more forts and smaller outposts added. Today the road is known by its medieval name, the Stanegate or 'stone road', and archaeologists continue to debate its composition and purpose. By about AD 106 Newstead was abandoned in another withdrawal. Our paltry literary sources make no mention of any of this, so it left to us to guess from the archaeology just what was going on.

A novelist has more freedom, and once again I have done my best to reconstruct these years for our purposes in a way that never conflicts with any hard evidence. At the very least I hope that these stories tell of things that could have happened. Something made the Romans station significant numbers of troops in this area at the end of the first century AD, and then made them increase these numbers and develop the deployment along the Stanegate just a few years later. All of the forts mentioned in the story existed and were occupied in AD 98. Syracuse is an invention, but typical of the many small outposts set up by the Roman army as needed. I see it as a predecessor to the excavated sites at Haltwhistle Burn and Throp, which were built alongside the Stanegate, although these were stone structures and larger than the fictional Syracuse. In the late first century AD most of the structures built by the army in Britain were in turf and timber. Some sites were being rebuilt in stone, and in the second century this became ever more common.

One of very many mysteries surrounding Hadrian's Wall are the defences along the Cumbrian coast. These were part of the initial design of the Wall and consisted of towers and fortlets matching closely to those on the line of the Wall itself and at similar intervals. Many perch on the cliffs just above beaches and all are very close to the sea. All that is missing is a linear barrier like the Wall itself. We have no evidence explaining why this line of outposts and forts was felt necessary. Later in the second century AD many parts of the system were abandoned, but forts – and just possibly some towers and fortlets – remained in use throughout the life of the Roman province. The most obvious explanation of all this effort is that there was a threat from the sea. Later, this either diminished or was dealt with by other means, allowing the coast to be secured by fewer troops.

Alauna (modern Maryport) now boasts an excellent museum (www.senhousemuseum.co.uk) with a particularly fine collection of inscriptions. The fort visible today and most of the collection date to after our story. There are hints of Trajanic activity on the site, but little is really known. The alignment of the later fort with the road suggests that an earlier base was built in a slightly different position. At Aballava (Burgh by Sands) there was a Roman watchtower on high ground overlooking the lowest fords on the River Solway. At some point in Trajan's reign, this was demolished and a fort for an entire auxiliary unit built on the site. Around the same time, another Roman base was constructed on lower ground to the west. Little is known about it, but it is claimed that timber structures were discovered, suggesting at least semi-permanent occupation and not simply a marching camp used for a few nights or weeks. In my imagination, this is the base used for the legate's manoeuvres and then kept in occupation for some time afterwards following the raid in our story and the ongoing threat of attacks from the sea.

Hibernia, the Highlands and Islands

Much of the action in this story takes place well outside the province of Britannia, but because of the sources for the history and society of these regions I have been deliberately vague about precise locations. Hibernia/Ireland was never occupied by Rome. Merchants from the Roman Empire were regular visitors there, and there was a fair bit of diplomatic activity.

An exiled Hibernian prince came to Agricola asking that the Romans restore him to power by force, but the governor decided not to intervene. There is no clear evidence for Roman troops ever being sent to Ireland. However, a diplomatic escort of the sort imagined in the book would be most unlikely to leave any trace so we need not worry too much about that. Such things did occur elsewhere beyond Rome's frontiers, so it is not implausible in itself.

In recent decades far more Iron Age sites have been discovered in Ireland, but it is fair to say that we still know a good deal less than we should like about life there during this period. There are echoes of it in later literature, most notably the Ulster Cycle with its chariot-riding heroes, but it is very hard to say how much real history lies in the stories. The 'Place of Kings' in the story is inspired by Tara in County Meath, which, like Navan Fort in Armagh, figures in the later poetry. It is a huge complex of monuments, some very ancient even in the Iron Age, and how it was used and by whom is hard to reconstruct. I have taken tribal names from the Greek Geographer Ptolemy, but it is hard to say how accurate his information was.

The same is true of all our literary sources for the Highlands and islands of Scotland. The tower that Ferox and the others take and hold is one of those remarkable dry-stone buildings often known as brochs, of which some of the most splendid are on Shetland. The name came from Norse and goes back to a time when it was thought that these were forts built by the Vikings. Now it is clear that they were much earlier, and part of a wider style of building that appeared in islands and on the western coast of Scotland and occasionally further afield. In some cases it is hard to tell from the existing remains whether the structure was originally lower, forming what archaeologists would call a complex roundhouse. In either case these were buildings for more than a single family, and were strong statements of power. Yet they do not seem designed primarily for defence, and there is a good deal about them that we simply do not understand.

The island occupied by the pirates is fictional, although there are examples of broch-towers built out on islands in lakes. Similarly the idea of a woman warrior teaching young heroes how to fight comes from the Irish poems, which seems to place it all somewhere off the coast of Scotland. The historian in me considers it unlikely; we might remember Greek heroes supposedly going off to be instructed by a centaur, so such romantic invention is a feature of other heroic myths. The novelist is quite happy to take a good story and use it, at least as long as it cannot be proven to be nonsense.

The Roman Army

This is a vast subject, but it is worth making a few points for those new to the topic. In AD 100 the Roman army consisted of twenty-eight legions – two more would soon be added by Trajan – each with a paper strength of some 5,000 men. Each one was divided into ten cohorts of heavy infantry and had a small contingent of some 120 horsemen. Legionaries were Roman citizens. This was a legal status without any ethnic basis and by this time there were over four million Roman citizens scattered throughout the empire. We may think of St Paul, a Jew from Tarsus in Asia Minor, but a Roman citizen and entitled to all the legal advantages that brought.

Supporting the legions were the auxiliaries who were not citizens, but received citizenship at the end of their military service. These were organised as independent cohorts of infantry and similarly sized cohorts of cavalry. There were also the mixed cohorts (*cohortes equitatae*) like the Batavians, which included both infantry and cavalry in a 4 to 1 ratio. Legionaries and auxiliaries alike served for twenty-five years. Most were volunteers, although conscription did occur and was probably especially common with some auxiliary units.

We know a good deal about the Roman army, about its equipment, organisation, command structure, tactics, ranks and routine, although it must be emphasised that there are also many gaps in our knowledge. As a historian, it is my duty to stress what we do not know, but a novelist cannot do this and must invent in order to fill in these gaps. Some aspects of the depiction of the Roman army in these books may surprise some readers, but often this will be because some of the evidence for it is not well known outside academic circles. I have invented as little as possible, and always done my best to base it on what we do know. As an introduction to the army, I am vain enough to recommend my own *The Complete Roman Army*, published by Thames and Hudson. I would also say that anything by the late Peter Connolly is also well worth a look. Once again for more specific recommendations, I refer readers to my website – adriangoldsworthy.com.

GLOSSARY

aquilifer: the man who carried the eagle standard (or *aquila*)
of a legion.

ala: a regiment of auxiliary cavalry, roughly the same
size as a cohort of infantry. There were two types: *ala
quingenaria* consisting of 512 men divided into sixteen
turmae; and *ala milliaria* consisting of 768 men divided
into twenty-four *turmae*.

aureus (pl. aurei): a gold coin equal to 25 silver denarii.

auxilia/**auxiliaries**: over half of the Roman army was
recruited from non-citizens from all over (and even
outside) the empire. These served as both infantry and
cavalry and gained citizenship at the end of their twenty-
five years of service.

barritus: Germanic battle cry that began as a low rumble
of voices and rose to a crescendo.

Batavians: an offshoot of the Germanic Chatti, who fled
after a period of civil war, the Batavians settled on what
the Romans called the Rhine island in modern Holland.
Famous as warriors, their only obligation to the empire
was to provide soldiers to serve in Batavian units of
the *auxilia*. Writing around the time of our story, the
historian Tacitus described them as 'like armour and
weapons – only used in war'.

Brigantes: a large tribe or group of tribes occupying much of what would become northern England. Several sub-groups are known, including the Textoverdi and Carvetii (whose name may mean 'stag people').

bulla: pendant worn by Roman boys until they formally came of age.

burgus: a small outpost manned by detached troops rather than a formal unit.

canabae: the civilian settlements that rapidly grew up outside almost every Roman fort. The community had no formal status and was probably under military jurisdiction.

centurion: a grade of officer rather than a specific rank, each legion had some sixty centurions, while each auxiliary cohort had between six and ten. They were highly educated men and were often given posts of great responsibility. While a minority were commissioned after service in the ranks, most were directly commissioned or served only as junior officers before reaching the centurionate.

centurio regionarius: a post attested in the Vindolanda tablets, as well as elsewhere in Britain and other provinces. They appear to have been officers on detached service placed in control of an area. A large body of evidence from Egypt shows them dealing with criminal investigations as well as military and administrative tasks.

classis: in general the Roman navy or fleet, but also used for specific sections of it, such as the classis Britannica, which better translates as flotilla or squadron.

cohort: the principal tactical unit of the legions. The first cohort consisted of 800 men in five double-strength centuries, while cohorts two to ten were composed of 480 men in six centuries of eighty. Auxiliaries were either formed in milliary cohorts of 800 or more often quingeniary cohorts of 480. *Cohortes equitatae* or mixed cohorts added 240 and 120 horsemen respectively. These troopers were paid less and given less expensive mounts than the cavalry of the *alae*.

consilium: the council of officers and other senior advisors routinely employed by a Roman governor or senator to guide him in making decisions.

contubernalis (pl. contubernales): originally meaning tent-companion and referring to the eight soldiers who shared a tent on campaign. It became more generally used as 'comrade'.

cornicen (pl. cornicines): trumpeters who played the curved bronze horn or cornu.

cornicularius: military clerk.

cornu: curved bronze trumpet.

corona civica: the civic crown was Rome's highest decoration for personal valour. Traditionally it was awarded for saving the life of a fellow citizen.

curator: (i) title given to soldier placed in charge of an outpost such as a *burgus* who may or may not have held formal rank; (ii) the second in command to a decurion in a cavalry *turma*.

decurion: the cavalry equivalent to a centurion, but considered to be junior to them. He commanded a *turma*.

draco (pl. dracones): literally dragon, the draco was a standard shaped like the head of a snake or dragon. It was cast with an open mouth and a colourful windsock attached so that when the carrier ran or rode quickly, the sock billowed and snapped behind and the standard produced a hissing/whistling sound. The Romans copied this from the peoples beyond the Danube.

duplicarius: a senior auxiliary soldier/NCO who earned double pay.

equestrian: the social class just below the Senate. There were many thousand equestrians (*eques*, pl. *equites*) in the Roman Empire, compared to six hundred senators, and a good proportion of equestrians were descendants of aristocracies within the provinces. Those serving in the army followed a different career path to senators.

gladius: Latin word for sword, which by modern convention specifically refers to the short sword used by all legionaries and most auxiliary infantry. By the end of the first century most blades were less than 2 feet long.

hastatus: title for one of the senior centurions in a legion, who served with its prestigious first cohort.

Hippaka Gymnasia: the cavalry games or spectacle was an opportunity for cavalrymen to display their skills in riding, weapons-handling and keeping formation.

lancea: a type of spear of javelin.

legate (legionary): the commander of a legion was a *legatus legionis* and was a senator at an earlier stage in his career than the provincial governor (see below). He would usually be in his early thirties.

legate (provincial): the governor of a military province like Britain was a *legatus Augusti*, the representative of the emperor. He was a distinguished senator and usually at least in his forties.

legion: originally the levy of the entire Roman people summoned to war, legion or *legio* became the name for the most important unit in the army. In the last decades of the first century BC, legions became permanent with their own numbers and usually names and titles. In AD 98 there were twenty-eight legions, but the total was soon raised to thirty.

medicus: an army medical orderly or junior physician.

omnes ad stercus: a duty roster of the first century AD from a century of a legion stationed in Egypt has some soldiers assigned *ad stercus*, literally to the dung or shit. This probably meant a fatigue party cleaning the latrines – or just possibly mucking out the stables. From this I have invented *omnes ad stercus* as 'everyone to the latrines' or 'we're all in the shit'.

optio: the second in command of a century of eighty men and deputy to a centurion.

phalerae: disc-shaped medals worn on a harness over a man's body armour.

pilum: the heavy javelin carried by Roman legionaries. It was about 6 to 7 feet long. The shaft was wooden, topped by a slim iron shank ending in a pyramid-shaped point (much like the bodkin arrow used by longbowmen). The shank was not meant to bend. Instead the aim was to concentrate all of the weapon's considerable weight behind the head so that it would punch through armour or shield. If it hit a shield, the head would go through, and the long iron shank gave it the reach to continue and strike the man behind. Its effective range was probably some 15 to 16 yards.

posca: cheap wine popular with soldiers and slaves.

praesidium: the term meant garrison, and could be employed for a small outpost or a full-sized fort.

praetorium: the house of the commanding officer in a Roman fort.

prefect: the commander of most auxiliary units was called a prefect (although a few unit COs held the title tribune).

These were equestrians, who first commanded a cohort of auxiliary infantry, then served as equestrian tribune in a legion, before going on to command a cavalry *ala*.

princeps: a Roman emperor was called the princeps or first citizen/first servant of the state.

principia: headquarters building in a Roman fort.

procurator: an imperial official who oversaw the tax and financial administration of a province. Although junior to a legate, a procurator reported directly to the emperor.

pugio: Latin name for the army issue dagger.

raeda: a four-wheeled carriage drawn by mules or horses.

scorpion (*scorpio*): a light torsion catapult or *ballista* with a superficial resemblance to a large crossbow. They shot a heavy bolt with considerable accuracy and tremendous force to a range beyond bowshot. Julius Caesar describes a bolt from one of these engines going through the leg of an enemy cavalryman and pinning him to the saddle.

scutum: Latin word for shield, but most often associated with the large semi-cylindrical body shield carried by legionaries.

seplasiarius (or *seplasiario*): military pharmacist working in a fort's hospital.

signifer: a standard-bearer, specifically one carrying a century's standard or *signum* (pl. *signa*).

Silures: a tribe or people occupying what is now South Wales. They fought a long campaign before being overrun by the Romans. Tacitus described them as having curly hair and darker hair or complexions than other Britons, and suggested that they looked more like Spaniards (although since he misunderstood the geography of Britain he also believed that their homeland was closer to Spain than Gaul).

singulares: the legate of a province had a picked bodyguard formed of auxiliary soldiers seconded from their units.

spatha: another Latin term for sword, which it is now conventional to employ for the longer blades used mainly by horsemen in this period.

stationarii: soldiers detached from their parent units and stationed as garrison elsewhere, often in a small outpost.

tesserarius: the third in command of a century after the *optio* and *signifier*. The title originally came from their responsibility for overseeing sentries. The watchword for each night was written on a *tessera* or tablet.

tiro (pl. tirones): a new recruit to the army.

tribune: each legion had six tribunes. The most senior was the broad-stripe tribune (*tribunus laticlavius*), who was a young aristocrat at an early stage of a senatorial career. Such men were usually in their late teens or very early twenties. There were also five narrow-stripe or junior tribunes (*tribuni angusticlavii*).

tubicen: a straight trumpet.

Tungrians: a tribe from the Rhineland. Many Tungrians were recruited into the army. By AD 98 a unit with the title of Tungrians was likely to include many men from other ethnic backgrounds, including Britons. In most cases, the Roman army drew recruits from the closest and most convenient source. The Batavians at this period may have been an exception to this.

venator (pl. venatores): A type of gladiator who specialised in fighting animals in the arena.

vexillum: a square flag suspended from a cross pole. Detachments were known as vexillations because in theory each was given its own flag as a standard.

via praetoria: one of the two main roads in a Roman fort. It ran from the main gate to join the other road at a right angle. On the far side of the other road, the via principalis, lay the main buildings of the fort, including the praetorium and principia.

viaticum: a new recruit to the Roman army was issued travel money (usually three gold aurei or their equivalent), which was both a bounty and to cover their expenses while they travelled to their unit. Similar in many ways to the King's shilling.